CAITLIN

GODDESS OF PEACE

Debbie Behan

Caitlin - Goddess of Peace Published 2017
by Butterfly Kiss Books
Copyright © 2016 by Debbie Behan

Previously published under the title of
Lord of the Planets - Fire Divine
Published 2014 by Butterfly Kiss Books
Copyright © 2013 by Debbie Behan

Caitlin
Goddess of Peace
by
Debbie Behan

ISBN (pbk): 978-0-9954205-2-6
ISBN (ebook): 978-0-9954205-4-0

Dedication

*To the wonders of the universe and
those who inspired me to follow my dreams.*

Alpha Site Command

Axon took in a deep breath and entered the room. He had just taken on a new position and had nothing to report. He dreaded sitting through this meeting with nothing substantial to give. With heavy steps, he trudged through the door as the beating of a NAVpen on the desk grabbed his attention. His boss, Zoren, seemed irritated that he was late, which made Axon's hackles go up. He felt under attack already and tensed his shoulders as he sat. He didn't want a run-in with his boss today. His eyes averted to the seat on the other side of the table where Kayden sat. Axon's eyebrows clamped together, insulted that Zoren had invited him too. Kayden was a mate, but really, what did he know about planets?

Axon cussed under his breath. *What is the leader of the Cloud Riders doing here?* He was in no mood to have the commander of Home Worlds in the stars dictate to him. He was now the Lord of the Planets and supreme ruler, not anything like the prissy wizards and warlords Kayden battled. *We've got nothing in common.* Axon fidgeted, while he glared at Kayden, humiliated he was forced to discuss his business in front of someone lower in status.

The NAVpen stilled as Axon eyed Zoren. Had the powers of the archangel felt his discomfort? He hoped so, as he needed these proceedings to hurry along. He had to get to Earth as he had his first ever meeting with a mixed gender team. The team leader, Rory, whom he had previously met, was assembling them for his perusal shortly and this meeting sounded as if it would be more time-consuming than he had figured it to be.

Frustrated that no one had spoken yet, Axon grabbed a Moonjuice from the fridge, ambled back to his seat and had a gulp. Bored, he watched Zoren who seemed oblivious to anything else around him, as he flipped through the information at lightning speed. The report Zoren read looked detailed and lengthy. How Axon wished he were an archangel some days to power read as he did! The bonus to Zoren's gift was his ability to shorten it and just give the finer details. While Axon waited, he unconsciously ran his finger around the edge of the can, deep in thought until Zoren spoke. The angelic sound caused him to lift his head as he concentrated on the melodic tone that floated towards him.

When his boss wanted attention, he sure knew how to get it. Axon shook off the magical calm that radiated from the Angel.

'Axon I want you to forget about our little problem with Mars for now. I have another mission more pressing.' Zoren flicked his finger across the document to get to where he wanted to be, so fast his hand blurred. 'As you know, Cronus, ruler of Saturn, and his wife Rhea have three sons; Poseidon, Hades and Zeus. What you may not know is their family has gone through hell, and now there is peace they will sacrifice anything to stay together.'

A NAVsky reader clunked on the desk as Kayden put down the report he held.

Axon's frame straightened. 'Guess you're waiting to hear what I know.'

Zoren gave a nod.

'It was a long time ago but a story like that is hard to forget.' Axon took a sip of drink. 'Apparently when his eldest sons Poseidon and Hades were born, Cronus saw them as a threat to his position, so swallowed them and kept them bound inside of him. His wife, Rhea, was more cunning and when she gave birth to her third son, Zeus, she hid him and substituted a rock wrapped in blankets for the child. Cronus swallowed what he thought was Zeus, not realising he had been deceived.'

When Axon paused, Kayden leant forward to assist with the family's history. 'When Zeus grew up he fought his father, won, and forced him to unbind his two brothers. Once free they led a revolt against their father for their terrible treatment. Subsequently, Zeus claimed the title of God of the Sky and Ruler of Jupiter. He gave Poseidon the title God of the Seas and Ruler of Neptune. To Hades, he gave the title God of the Underworld and Ruler of Pluto.'

Not to be bulldozed in front of Zoren, Axon butted back in. 'However, Zeus, being a merciful God, forgave his father and fought the Congress of the Heavens to allow him to keep his title as a god. He won, and this enabled him to allow Cronus to continue his rule over the planet Saturn. Zeus, whom they favoured for his wise decisions, was later ordained and given the title of King of all Gods.

Zoren enjoyed their rivalry and tried not to grin as he spoke. 'You are both correct, but there is more. Afterwards, Cronus spent much time repairing the relations between all his sons and the men have lived in peace for many centuries. They are now close allies and fierce protectors of their new family values. This is why the entire family is up in arms that Pluto had its status as a planet repealed.' The device he held chimed while receiving an update. As he read, his blond eyebrows came together. Axon knew his friend well, and that expression meant a big problem. 'It has just been confirmed that it was the Rulers of Mercury, Venus and Mars who joined forces with Earth, and it was them as a collective that signed the secret ballot, thus resulting in the expulsion of Pluto as a planet.' He sat back in his chair. 'We are on the cusp of a massive war amongst the gods.'

Axon leant on his elbows, his stare fixed on Zoren. 'So let me guess, the family are pushing for him to take over Mercury to stay as a Planet Ruler.'

Zoren didn't need to speak. The slight movement as he inclined his head was enough.

'I can't believe we weren't informed!' Axon was stunned. 'We should have known about this development.'

'I agree. Nevertheless, we were not consulted. This leaves me to assume that the ones proposing the ballot didn't want it challenged.

That or Cronus and his sons were so cocky they never believed the other Rulers would oppose them.' Zoren moved, and his body language made both men sit quietly. 'Hades wants to be back with his family. The only other planet with the ability to direct the dead through its orbit and into the underworld is Mercury, thus keeping Hades in a similar position.'

'I guessed right then.' Axon sat back his arms folded.

Zoren's pitch rose. 'Yes and to cut a long story short, Hermes won't swap Mercury with Hades, so a War of the Planets is about to break out!'

'So what now?' Axon asked. Zoren sat forward. The natural light-blue texture of his eyes flashed and deepened to indigo. 'Hades mostly blames Earth's ruler, the Goddess Gaea, who motioned this change. He is threatening that once he finally takes over Mercury he plans to destroy all humanity on Earth for their evil part in his termination and send them all to the Underworld for eternity.'

Axon sat back. His heart thumped loudly as his blood rushed around his body with the adrenaline boost the shocking news gave him. 'What the hell have I taken on here Zoren? What have you thrown me into this time? These are gods and warlords of the worst kind.'

Zoren threw the NAVpen down. The writing instrument flew across the boardroom table, causing Axon and Kayden to squirm in their seats.

'That's enough whining. Yes, this is bigger than I first thought. The protocol for such a decision as this should be for us to be notified, thus allowing us the opportunity to vote. But that did not happen! The gods and their arrogance have prevented the chance of a reasonable outcome. And as for you, Axon, it is too late to turn back. Under oath, you swore your allegiance to me!' Zoren's angry tone silenced further comments as he stood. Axon put his head down. He knew he would never let Zoren down.

'You are the man I chose as you are the only person I know who will not stand for the tantrums of spoilt gods.' He leant on the desk, palms down. 'I want this fixed and I don't care how!' His words boomed out and with his fist closed in frustration he thumped the desk. It cracked, and both men jumped out the way as the table shattered and fell into pieces on the floor. He looked surprised but continued. 'Now go out and find a team of peacemakers and get them operational and ready by the end of this month.'

Axon had been moody and irritated since he agreed to take on the new role, but his long-standing friend was relying on him. He had to snap out of it and desperately looked for words to defuse Zoren's anger. Axon could see him turning a little transparent. He knew both he and Kayden stood a good chance of feeling a lot of pain any minute if things didn't calm down. Archangels could be ruthless in getting those around them to commit. 'You're right and I apologised for my behaviour of late. I shouldn't let the worry of spoilt gods waver my judgement. Shortly I will be meeting with an elite team on Earth, and although I have issues with women in the mix, I do like their leader.'

Zoren's features softened slightly. Axon had used his pet hate, knowing this always amused the Angel who was always about love where the ladies were concerned.

'Okay, so that's what's been dragging your chain. Look, I know you prefer to work with men, easier to handle and all those other excuses you have always used, but in their defence, Kayden's team could not be without Cassie.'

Axon sighed. 'My squad will have to be forward thinkers, swift, efficient and be very coordinated. I will not tolerate anything but perfection. Their leader insists they are a package deal.' He lifted his chin, his brows squeezed in tight. 'For you, I will attempt to keep an open mind. But so help me if the girls give me the slightest bit of grief! I swear they'll be back on Earth, without delay.' He was irritated at the thought of taking them on.

Using magic, Zoren lifted his NAVsky reader from the floor and after it was in his hand, he turned to Kayden. 'Once Axon makes a decision on what team he wants, I expect your team to train them. We have no time to waste as your team is required on another mission. If one or more of them is not going to make it, let Axon know so he can replace them immediately. We count on your ability to prepare or expel where necessary.' He lifted his free hand, and the shattered pieces of table repositioned. He snapped his fingers, creating magical lights that joined the fractured wood back together. It stood steady, without a mark, and looked brand new. 'You two have your orders. You know where to find me if you need to.' He left the room in a cloud of silence, and his archangel's swiftness and serenity lingered even after the door closed behind him.

Axon leant back in his chair, listening to Kayden.

'Whenever you're ready, just give me the nod, and we're there for you.'

Axon knew Kayden better. This was chit chat and if he didn't have something to say he would have left when Zoren did. 'Okay! Spit it out. I can see you want to give me some advice, so go for it.' Axon gave him a slight grin.

'Look, this is the way I see it Axon, and this is not a lecture, just an observation. You've spent your entire lifetime dedicated to the cause; you were Zoren's rock, together for a long time before I came into it. I can only imagine how frustrated this makes you feel being on my side of the table. Not only have you left your friend's side, but you now have to form an entirely new relationship with strangers, new individuals that you don't know or trust yet. On top of that, there are women, which open up a whole new world of hurt if they give you trouble. How to deal with them is an art and one I learnt after much pain. Until Cassie came along, the boys and I would never have contemplated a female in our ranks. That would have annoyed the hell out of us. That said, I felt from the start that Cassie was supposed to be with me and if you don't feel that straight away with the women coming into your squadron, then I would advise you to look elsewhere. Although in saying that, you are not one to suffer fools and if you have taken to this leader, I'd be inclined to trust his judgement and give them a go.'

Axon drew on the cigar and started to loosen up. Kayden was always very calming to have around and truthfully, he really did need someone who had been through it to bounce things off.

'I'm eager as hell to sign up the men but the women...' he shook his head. 'Actually, a couple of nights ago I had word where they were and visited Earth to secretly check them out. As usual, I was with Zoren and by the time I got to the night club, they had left. However, it wasn't a wasted trip. I did get to meet a redhead to die for.' He smiled.

'Really! Tell all,' said Kayden.

'Nothing too spicy. But maybe another place another time, who knows.' He butted out the cigar. 'Anyway, since then I have contacted their leader and as I told Zoren, will be meeting with him and his team shortly. If I can't deal with the team makeup, I'll move on and look for another group I've heard are hiding in the depths of the jungle in South Africa.'

'Glad it's not my decision again. Geez, it was hell choosing my team. They were scattered across the nations and hated each other at first.' Kayden sucked in his breath deeply as he re-lived it. 'Yes, even the brothers Jason and Ethan. They were a handful, and if they hadn't become brothers in arms, it would have been brothers in jail.' He gave a slight shake of his head, amused.

Axon grinned, as he too remembered Kayden's unruly band of men when they first started out. 'You had time to choose and were tough on them Kayden, but you had to be. They respect you more for how you dealt with them, so it worked out. Me, well! As you've heard, Zoren has pressured me to pick my team ASAP. I feel rushed and worry that I'll just take this group on out of desperation. I'm so annoyed it has to go down like this.'

'Axon, you can only go with your gut instincts. Make a decision and move on, if they're not right for the job my team will soon tell you.'

'Fair enough!'

'We've got your back, as you have always had ours.' Kayden was sincere.

Axon nodded and stood up, eager to get moving. 'I'll ring as soon as I've met them to give you a heads up.'

He shook Axon's outstretched hand. 'Just let me know what

time you'll be arriving, I'll organise the rest. Damn it! Another group of hillbillies to train! My boys are going to love this when I tell them.'
Kayden followed him out.

Saturn's Warning

Rhea, goddess and mother of the Titans, moved from the Roman style bath where her husband still lay. Servant girls dried and wrapped her in sheer lavender cloth, a robe of silk and lace that slipped delicately over her shoulders, tied neatly at her tiny waist with a bright purple sash.

'Careful how you handle this, husband of mine.' She sat to have her long brown locks of hair brushed and styled into a braided topknot.

The powerful god, Cronus, lifted his massive body suddenly from the water. The droplets sprayed from him as he shook his hairy body. His wife sat admiring her man's naked form. Even after all these years, she longed for the strength of him to hold her in a lustful moment of togetherness. Today they had other commitments and no time for what was on her mind. She grinned with a twinkle in her eye only he understood. It made him smile.

'Tonight, my sweet.' He moved close to her and laid a gentle hand to her cheek.

She had leant into his hand before he removed it. 'Shoo!' She gestured for the servants that had finished with her hair to leave. 'Husband, what will our son do – what will you do?' Her voice was quiet and shaken.

'Our son Hades has always been a planet ruler and if I have anything to do with it, he always will. It's preposterous to think they have kicked Pluto out! A Dwarf planet! Can you believe they are calling his Kingdom a blatzing Dwarf planet? The shame of it,' he huffed, while vigorously drying his legs. 'If Pluto is not reinstated our sons and I will go to war and take over the planet, Mercury. Hades will be the new ruler and the current ruler, Hermes, can rule Pluto. That defiant fool will pay for going against us and voting our son out; he will end up with nothing.'

Rhea's head shook. Her silky-woven hair shimmered in the candle light, the clean sheen of her skin glowed magically, and for a moment, it calmed him, giving him inner compassion as he watched his wife handle what lay ahead. It was the first time they'd had a chance to speak and even though it was a lot for her to take in, they no longer held truths from one another.

'So all our friends voted for this change to Pluto?' Rhea said.

He stood still and listed them for her. She had to know this was serious. He felt strongly. If she didn't stand by him, he would do this alone. 'Hermes of Mercury, Uran of Uranus, Ares of Mars, Gaea of Earth and Aphrodite of Venus were all there.'

'And voted against you and our sons!' exclaimed Rhea.

'Clearly, a legal alliance was formed as they have half the planet Rulers' vote of approval.' He bent to cup his wife's chin. 'My love, I have no choice, I will not lose our son to the Ice Worlds. If Pluto cannot stay with us, then we go to war and take over Mercury.'

'Why Mercury? Hades knows nothing about the working of Mercury or vice versa. Hermes will not surrender or swap. I don't know about this, Cronus. What are our boys saying?' Rhea's tone was high.

Cronus didn't like his wife upset, but this entire new law was unacceptable, and his sons agreed. 'Zeus and Poseidon are with me. They believe as I do that Hades will find his feet. Mercury has similarities as it is the first port of call for the deceased. The departed are escorted by Mercury to the River Styx and shipped across to Hades' Kingdom. Hades will now be on the front line and who better than Hades to advise the new ruler, Hermes of Pluto, on the judgment of their fate before sending them to the underworld?' He had put a lot of thought into it and was positive he had covered all angles as the Ruler of Saturn. The planets would still run smoothly once the transition took place.

'Yes, Hermes will need help.' Her lips curled, which showed she was still worried.

Cronus turned to the mirror and studied the formal attire. 'He is only a conductor of souls through his planet. Hades is aware he will need to assist Hermes for quite some time, but we feel this is the only choice we have. He too will find his feet in time as we all have. Even gods can change.'

The grin that spread across her face and a raised eyebrow, made him smile. 'Well, I'd like to think I have changed a little.'

She stood. 'You have, only slightly,' she said and poked her husband's stomach teasingly. 'I will trust you to share with me every detail this time. No secrets.'

He took her finger and kissed it sensually. 'I will. I promised last time, no more cloak-and-dagger from me and I meant it.'

'There is no talking you out of this course of action? You will have to go up against Ares, God of War, and Zoren.'

'Yes, wife of mine. Zoren's army will be difficult to deal with if he dispatches them, but I hear the Cloud Riders are kept busy these days with the Star Worlds, and it would be a stretch to have them handle the planets too. No, I can safely say we will deal with this in-house, so to speak.' He grinned and teased, 'Zoren's team, really, they aren't exactly equipped to handle us gods.'

A squeaky door stopped their conversation. It was their most faithful of servants. 'Sorry to interrupt. Your sons have arrived. I tried to steer them to your chambers as requested, but they have gone straight to the Shangri-la bar. Zeus instructed I get the hell out of there and let them be.'

'That will be all, we are on our way.' Cronus said with a note of concern as the servant quickly bowed his way out of the room. 'Sounds like our boys are in low spirits. We must go to them.'

He turned back to Rhea. 'I have worked too hard over the years to repair the rift within our families and refuse to have this new law disrupt and separate our Home Worlds!' He folded his arms stubbornly as he watched the door close, waiting for privacy. 'No, I will not let this happen to us again!' His words were sharp and deadly as he kept his notorious temper in check, his worry for the situation apparent. He put out his hand. 'Come my sweet, and let us work through this as a family.'

With a lace cloth, Rhea wiped her tears, threw it aside, and took his outstretched hands. 'Don't let them spoil that which has taken us so long to mend, husband of mine.'

He kissed the softness of her lips. 'Never again.'

CHAPTER ONE

The Encounter

Caitlin stood outside a city nightclub. 'I repeat, my name is Caitlin Warner.' She had snapped a nail and Caitlin's tone reflected her mood while giving the required details to the cab company. A glance at her watch left her worried as it was nearly midnight which meant she had been out of it for a couple of hours and was still in a dazed state. *Where are my friends?* Only minutes ago, she'd woken in the women's cubical. The throbbing of her head, poor vision and dizziness forced her lean body to slump against the wall of the nightclub. Suddenly not able to stay conscious, she fell forward and collapsed.

She felt the warmth of a body near her when she regained consciousness. Gradually, the sight of a stranger with a handsome face came into focus. He smiled with eyes that captivated, the streetlight bright enough for her to distinguish the depth and darkness of colour. A dark curl licked at his forehead as he leant down to see if she was hurt. His soft and kind features made her want to stay just a while, even if only to find out his name.

'Are you okay?' He joined her on the steps where she now sat.

Caitlin held her breath at the touch of his hands while he felt for injuries. His lips broke into a smile as he turned her hand one way and the other. 'You are sitting straighter now and appear a bit better. Nothing is broken. I must have caught you in time.'

Caitlin stretched fully. The sensation of him so close made

her light-headed. Trying to stand up, she quickly sat back down, overcome by dizziness once again.

'Not too fast there, love,' he said calmly. 'You've just fainted. Do you know what happened to bring it on?'

Caitlin groaned. 'I think it was something I drank, although I only had a diet cola.'

She thought him sweet the way worry lines creased his forehead. 'Are you on your own?'

'No, I was with friends, but they seem to have ditched me, the ratbags.' She took the phone he handed her, which was now in pieces from her fall on the pavement.

'And you call them friends! Maybe consider getting new ones if they can't be reliable.'

She got up and pulled out of his grip. 'Thanks for your help but I'm fine now. Hope I didn't inconvenience you too much, but a lecture is a bit more than I am in the mood for right now.' With a huff, she turned to walk away. *I hardly need some well-dressed, probably rich-dude-know-it-all telling me who I should and shouldn't associate with.* She staggered just a little, heading towards the cab that arrived. This wobble had him return to her side, ignoring her rudeness, helping her once more.

'I apologise if I've upset you, but you really do need help. Let's get you into that cab and home first before you fall down yet again.' This time he spoke so amicably that she gave in and leant against him, her legs unsteady. She was grateful for an arm to rest on.

In the cab, Caitlin considered the dangers of this stranger, in fact, any unknown person, finding out her address, but, somehow, she didn't feel this man was a threat to her. She could see he genuinely looked concerned and was merely a kind stranger doing what he must have thought a good deed, lending a hand to a helpless damsel.

In the elevator that headed up to her small apartment, she suddenly felt embarrassed for her modest lifestyle. Caitlin wasn't one for possessions and now wished she had listened to her friends and used her money more wisely instead of blowing it on fun.

She fumbled with her keys, dropping them. The stranger

bent and picked them up for her. Propping her up with one hand, he managed to open the door with the other. He helped her inside and laid her on the couch, placing a pillow under her head. Caitlin couldn't stop smiling at him each time he did something nice.

'Coffee?' he asked, heading to the kitchen.

'You don't have to do that, really, I'm fine now.' She watched him switching on the kettle, ignoring her.

'You already told me you were fine when you walked away from me the first time. I think I am a better judge of whether you are or not. Until I think otherwise you are just going to have to put up with me looking after you. I do promise not to annoy you this time.'

Caitlin lay back and closed her eyes. She must have dozed off again. It wasn't until she felt him touch her forehead that she opened her eyes and realised he had made the coffee.

She sat up, apologising for only having one sofa as furniture. Unconcerned, he squeezed in beside her and handed her the coffee. 'I wasn't sure how you liked it. You didn't answer me so hot and sweet it is. Hope that's okay?'

Caitlin watched his large hands wrap around the cup and for some reason imagined being held by them. She shook it off, trying to concentrate on his conversation. He was telling her he was only in town for the night.

'I was supposed to meet someone at that club bar, but a late conference held me up.' He leant over, placing his cup on the coffee table. 'Talk about a fluke that I was there in time to catch you before you hit the pavement.' He smiled.

'Might have been messy, thanks, Mr…'

With that, he stood up, taking her cup, ducking her lead to find out a little about him.

'I'll just clean up and once you're comfortable, then I must get going.' His movements were quick, but his boots seemed to make no sound on the tiled floor. She chatted while he tidied up the kitchen, and his interest in her mundane life surprised her.

Once he finished, she stood and stretched. Her intention was to walk him to the door.

'Now you look better, I'll head off and let you get some rest.'

His movement towards the door at the same time had their hands touch lightly, the electricity making them grab at each other, both swept away in a moment neither expected.

He stared deep into innocent eyes. *This is wrong,* his mind whispered, but his heart ignored the warning. It pumped rapidly in a wild yearning and with an arm around a tiny perfect waist, he pulled her close. He was unable to stop the magnetic forces that drew his lips to hers, longing to taste those plump pink delicacies that moved to entice him each time she spoke. At that moment he was lost in a magical kiss like no other. He lingered his tongue longer than he should as sexual lust gripped his groin and pulsated through his manhood. He groaned. *Cripes, did I just orgasm?* His eyes opened in shock. This has never happened before. *Is she some kind of witch, putting a spell on me? I must leave immediately.* Yet try as he willed it, his lips did not leave hers until he had lifted the maiden and laid her on the bed. In a dreamlike state, he used a poor excuse to leave. She curled her lip at his lame pretext. Her confused yet disappointed stare had him back pedal and he made an effort to make amends for the need to leave so suddenly.

'Look, I have a prior commitment.' He kissed her forehead. 'I promise to contact you when I'm in town next, that's if you still want to see me again.'

His calm voice told her nothing. *He's lying to get away.* Caitlin's temper shot up as she assumed this was his way of letting her down gently. *Me, my home, the kiss, weren't flash enough for a dude like him.*

'Don't bother lying to me. Just admit I'm not good enough for your kind. Just get the hell out.' She rolled over, turning her back on him.

He started to protest, only she put a pillow over her head. 'Get out!' she growled at him and heard loud footsteps as he stomped out the front door.

* * * *

The next morning Caitlin moaned with the painful throb in her head and remembering the events, added embarrassment to her list of why she wished to stay in bed. There was no reason she could now justify for being so rude to her mystery man. All he did was care for her and give her a kiss. She, in turn, had treated him poorly for his kindness. She had to admit it was a shock to feel like that about him. Caitlin had never been so attracted and kicked herself for not asking his name. *Did I tell him mine?*

Getting ready for work, she agonised over his departure that left him nameless. Usually, it was her who backed off and did the hurting. Sadly, she knew how it felt.

The trip to work made her feel no healthier. Whatever it was, had really bombed her out. The elevator doors opened up to show her best friend, Rory, and his new girlfriend, Bree. Both had that, *where did you get to?* look.

'Don't give me that, what happened to you guys last night? I came out of the ladies' and you were gone,' Caitlin snapped before they could speak, still peeved.

Rory's mouth opened, unsure what to say. She had stumped him at his own game. She knew he would have been rushing to get Bree out as it was the first night she had finally let herself go with him. Man, was she going to make him suffer for doing this to her. They had never been romantic, but this felt wrong, unacceptable!

'We thought you'd left before us. We thought you ditched us.' Bree's tone sounded surprised that this was not the case.

Rory's arm shot off Bree's shoulder. The actions showed his annoyance that his sister had let him down. 'Lisha, you can't trust that girl! She insisted the stalls were all empty and that you weren't in there. Sorry Cait, did you get home all right?'

She sighed. Rory's sister was a bit of an airhead at times. Lisha wouldn't think if a door was closed and no one answered, that hey, the person in there may be passed out.

What was making Caitlin cross was Rory's behaviour. Rory was Caitlin's closest friend. It was only now she realised how her indifference towards his more than friendship advances had forced him to look elsewhere. Bree was a newcomer and he had scored with her. Now, as Rory stood with his arm around her, Caitlin felt a pang of jealousy. His tall frame towered over Bree and he looked radiantly happy. His usually gentle light blue eyes seemed to look frosty, and she knew by his tousled sandy hair that he'd most likely woken with Bree and after one more round of lovemaking had come straight into work. Even the sprinkle of freckles across his nose seemed lighter on his handsome face. This revelation that she had lost him for good now, on top of how she felt, broke her heart. She fumbled in her bag and pulled out a tissue.

'Cait, what's wrong? Did something happen?' Bree asked.

'How did you get home then?' Rory had no empathy, demanding answers.

She sniffed, stuffing the tissue in her pocket. Ignoring Bree, she turned to Rory with the intent to make him jealous too. 'A man helped me. We cabbed it home together and he stayed for a while to make sure I was okay.'

Rory exploded. 'What! You did what?'

'I believe someone spiked my drink. I must have passed out on the loo. When I came out, you were all gone. I went out the front to hail a cab and POW; I'm out to it again.' She rubbed her eyes that were still out of focus.

'You passed out?' Bree slipped her arm through Caitlin's. 'You should go home! Are you all right?'

'I'm still out of it a bit.' She placed her hand on her head, and the movement forced Bree to move away. She was dirty on both of them and didn't want anyone to touch her. However, she hadn't finished stirring up Rory. 'The only reason I'm not in a hospital is that this man caught me just before my head hit the pavement. Otherwise, I would have cracked it open for sure.' She forced a grin. 'The sweetie even stayed and made me a coffee.'

Rory turned red with anger. Caitlin hoped some of it was jealousy.

'I can't believe you let a stranger into your apartment! He could have been dangerous! What were you thinking, Cait?'

Bree tilted her head abruptly up at Rory. 'Don't snap at her, she was out of it and needed her friends and where were we? I should have made sure she wasn't there before I let you drag me off. Geez, Rory! We're supposed to look after each other when we go out like that. You know what it's like in some of those nightclubs. We should have known it was out of character for her just to take off.'

'I'm sorry. It was careless of us. But it doesn't excuse the fact Cait was reckless.' He was still feeling guilty, but calming down.

Bree huffed at him, turning her attention back to Caitlin. 'It's okay, honey. Ignore him; he's just his usual possessive pig-headed self with you. You can tell me, I want all the goss and don't leave anything out about this mysterious man that saved you.'

Up until now, Caitlin and Bree had been friends. This morning, however, Caitlin didn't feel like talking to anyone about the way she felt, never mind a mate that had just stolen her best friend. Caitlin glanced in the mirror at the back of the elevator. Bree was tall and generally tied her long dark hair up, but today it hung glossy and sexily down her back. Caitlin cast an envious eye over her figure. It wasn't hourglass like hers, although the cut of her jeans and the stylish halter-top suited her. Caitlin sighed. Jealousy really changed the way she even saw herself. With no energy to blow-wave her red hair, she'd left it to fall in tight ringlets. Her skin was usually pale, but today it looked as though she'd just seen a ghost. The typical bright sparkle in her green eyes was gone. She turned away from the image, annoyed she was even comparing herself to this friend-stealer.

'Sorry, but it's none of your business. I'm sure you two don't want to tell me about what you got up to last night, although I can guess.'

Rory took in a deep breath. 'Cait, what's up with you this morning? Bree was trying to be nice. Don't take it out on us for what happened to you.'

Caitlin eyed Rory as he put his arm back around Bree again. She knew her tone was from jealousy as she was in no mood to watch them together. The rat! She had spent twelve years with him. They were best mates and up until Bree arrived in the group it was her he had the crush on. Seeing them together wasn't easy. Not this morning and not the way she felt. It made her even more annoyed he didn't get that. She looked at what she had thrown away so easily. Her best friend would not be at her disposal anymore. *So I may as well get used to it.*

The elevator stopped. When the doors opened, it allowed Caitlin to make a quick exit to her workstation. The throb in her head and the ill feeling of wanting to throw up had her in no mood to explain. At her desk, her hand that held a glass of water shook. Caitlin put it down and rested her head in the crook of her arm.

A few minutes later, she heard Rory gruffly organising the staff before sitting on her desk. 'You aren't well, Cait, you haven't any colour in your face and I've never seen you with dark rings around your eyes, ever. I'm sorry I was moody with you. I'll drive you home.'

Rory gently picked up her hand and got her to her feet. She grabbed at him as she almost passed out again but regained control and leant into him, grateful for his help.

'Maybe I should take you to a hospital,' he offered.

'You know we can't trust any of the doctors here, Rory. I'll be okay. I'll just sleep it off.'

'Well, if it gets any worse we'll have to trust someone,' he said as he helped her out into his car.

Caitlin slept on and off for two days solid before she felt better. Rory and Bree came around after work and made her dinner at night. Afterwards, Caitlin went straight back to bed and let them see themselves out. It had really knocked her around. It was a few days later when she finally woke and began to feel much better. After a shower, she heard familiar voices and quickly dressed to go out into the kitchen and join her friends. Rory and Bree had stayed the night and had started breakfast.

'Glad to see you look better Cait,' Rory said as he flipped the eggs.

Bree wrapped arms around her and, Caitlin feeling more sociable today about many things, didn't shrug her off. She was glad Bree made Rory happy but so help her if she didn't.

In the kitchen, Rory was in control, as usual, ordering Bree around and yet there was an expression of guilt when he looked up. Caitlin knew he blamed himself but so he should. This might never have happened if Rory hadn't been trying to get Bree into bed. His own rule was never to leave a team~member behind. He had failed and as the leader and the only man in the world she trusted, he should have left the sizzle until after he had checked she was okay.

Rory went crimson under Caitlin's watchful glare. He figured out what those eyes were saying and knew he had put that faith she had in him on the line. If he didn't want to lose her, he had better not let her down again. *Certainly have no intentions of that…* Her body language told him she was still mad at him and doubted she would believe one word he had to say just yet.

Caitlin's attention darted to the door as Zeke and Nathen arrived. They were both tall and well built. Zeke had dark hair, eyes and complexion. Nate was entirely different in every way. With blond hair, fair skin and eyes of the palest grey, he was also the softer of the men in her life. Neither were short of female company yet they preferred to stay as she did, single and without care. They took it in turns to lift Caitlin up, hugged her and skylarked around until Rory butted in. 'Come on guys, this isn't a free ride, set the table and make the drinks.'

While they were busy, Caitlin brushed at her tangles from across the room, laughing at Rory still going crook at the guys as she opened the door to the last member of their group.

Lisha breezed in the door, hugging Caitlin and turning to the others, all smiles after what looked a good night out. With her cropped blonde hair, hazel eyes and tanned complexion, she oozed sex appeal. However, puffy eyes showed a lack of sleep and the smile spoke volumes.

'You had a win?' Caitlin raised a brow at Rory's sister. They were absolutely nothing alike, but he had her adoration. Like the rest of them, Lisha would do anything for him. He was the only person who she'd jump through hoops for and was one of the hardest workers when they trained together. Lisha was stand-out and knew it, but Caitlin liked this about her. It made her strive harder and she valued the rivalry.

'You bet, sweetie.' Lisha held up a perfectly manicured hand and ran the back of it down her cheek. 'You okay, sugar? Rory tells me you've been sick. Sorry about the other night, won't happen again.' Pulling her hand away, she waltzed off. Laughing in her over-confident way, she went over to hug everyone, openly bragging of her huge win at the pokies and what a great night she had with Zeke and Nate.

Caitlin smiled as she watched her friends, each one so different in personality, and yet it worked between them. Primarily, because of one thing they had in common. It was something that kept them all together and had done for many years. They never aged; not one line, not one wrinkle. It was as if they turned twenty, had a growth spurt overnight and then nothing. Caitlin was the only odd one in the bunch. Her skin had never matured as she grew. It stayed soft as the day she was born. It tore easily and was so delicate that when she shook hands with anyone, they would hold her hand and study it, unsure why it felt as it did, yet not bold enough to mention it. Her knight in shining armour had also done this to her. It made Caitlin smile, thinking of him again. She shook her head as she listened to them all chat. This and other strange powers they possessed made them fear others, choosing to keep out of the public eye, hiding from all those that might turn them into lab rats, or worse. They had been in this city for five years and today was their get-together. It was a planned meeting to decide what city they would live in next. None of them ever wanted to stay anywhere for too long, in case their oddness caused curiosity.

Nate handled the passports and personal papers side of it. His computer skills were remarkable. They quite often called Zeke, *Radar*, due to his skills at picking up sounds from miles away. Rory laid out the plans for them and they listened to him. He was the one who had found them, brought them together and ensured their safety and well-being. As their leader, he also made the final decision on where they went and what they did when they got there. At the moment, to keep them together, Rory had organised that he, Bree and Caitlin worked as buyers. Lisha was employed as an office assistant and Nate and Zeke as the sales reps in a corporation he helped set up from scratch. This was Rory's way of keeping them together and safe.

Caitlin sat on the couch, careful not to wrinkle her dress as she spread the pleats out in her skirt. She wondered how Rory managed to cook in her tiny kitchen compared with the condo he currently lived in, with his large chef's kitchen. Nate, Zeke and Bree were more like her. They lived in apartments not far from each other so they could hang out. They enjoyed parties, clubs and the opposite sex far too much to worry about tomorrow. They all saw Rory's point about saving something for the future, but each time they moved to a new location, with new people, the fun always won over logic, and none of them could keep their promises to him.

This time when they moved, though, Caitlin had already decided she would stop blowing everything she earned and start building a nest egg for the future. A few nights ago they had gone out to celebrate her birthday. It was a wake-up call, not only to be drugged and losing Rory to another, but she had a revelation about having nothing to show for her thirty years. She was going to give up the high-life and settle down in the next city. She'd save money instead of living as if she had all the time in the world to enjoy the finer possessions in life. Rory had been her only possession. She had lost her hold over him, and it hurt.

It wasn't until the meal was over that Rory enlightened them on a new life-changing job offer he'd been given, an offer for all of them.

CHAPTER TWO

An Intriguing Offer

Their group arrived at a restaurant where they were to meet the man who was going to change their lives. Caitlin slammed the car door shut and spun around, her eyes taking in the city below. Up so high on the mountain, the tall buildings and rolling hills that surrounded them disappeared into the clouds. Caitlin took a deep breath. The smell of damp wood and pine combined with the sweetness of lavender that grew wild in these parts revived her senses. It had been days since feeling this well and Caitlin enjoyed just being out with her friends.

As they followed Rory towards the steps of the rather old, rustic building, she noted only one other parked vehicle in the customers' car park. It was a European car that looked far too expensive to belong to the owners of this possibly historical site. It appeared their possibly new employer they had come to meet was either seriously wealthy, or else a salesperson, and they were all going to be selling cars for the next five years.

As expected, the restaurant was empty except for one person. Caitlin assumed his name was Axon Stanton, the contact they were to meet. At the bar, he sat with his back to them drinking from a glass. His attire was neat and casual, yet his awareness and character were questionable as she assumed if this was him, he would get up and greet them. If this was their guy, her concerns for this new adventure would be expressed when her turn came to give an opinion. She was already worried.

The table Rory picked for them was near open shutters, the breeze cooling and welcomed. Leaving the others with the waiter, he went over and sat next to the man at the bar.

Caitlin ignored the longing to go with Rory as she always did and ordered a drink instead. 'I'll have a caramel latte, thanks buddy.'

She was the last to order and after, the little Spanish waiter with a moustache too big for his face scurried off. While waiting for Rory's return, Nate and Zeke entertained them with jokes. Laughing, none of them noticed him come back to the table with company.

A large shadow looming over the table quietened them down, and all eyes were now on the man from the bar, possibly their soon-to-be new boss. Caitlin coughed and spluttered as her drink went down the wrong way when she recognised the stranger from the other night. She felt the colour sting her cheeks as his lips parted slightly in a smile. She excused herself, meaning to escape to the ladies', but he moved in front of her path, leaving no room in between the next table and Rory.

He put out his hand in a gesture to shake hers. 'Hi, I didn't get your name the other night. My name is Axon Stanton.' He smiled politely. 'And you are?'

'Caitlin Warner.' She lifted her chin, the fight in her eyes emerging, knowing he had caught her and there was no way out of this predicament. She figured any minute now he would do the guy thing, blab what happened, and make a joke out of it.

He turned to the others, excusing himself. 'I need a minute with your friend. We have already met, and I'd like a private word.'

She knew Rory would already have guessed by using his sixth sense that this was the man she took home the other night.

Axon had surprised her again, keeping hold of her hand. He guided her out the door and into the garden.

'Are you well now, Caitlin Warner?' he asked once they were out of earshot.

She tried to keep as calm and polite as he was, but her nerves felt on edge with every brush of his thigh, every gentle caress of his hand that he still kept on hers. 'I'm fine now, thanks for asking. I slept for two days, but feel better today.'

'I could see you were ready to run in there and apologise for trapping you, but I hope you'll accept my request for forgiveness. It was unthinkable that I should have taken advantage of you when you were unwell. To steal a kiss the other night was wrong of me. I hope you can keep the personal side of our knowing each other from what I wish to discuss with you.'

'If you can then I can too.' She felt happy he was putting it aside but a little sad he was dismissing it so easily.

A little willy wagtail darted between them and was enough to distract her from how close he stood and the effect it had on her. She looked at him. 'I also would like to apologise for being such a handful and a rude one at that. You were very kind, and I have a habit of saying things before I think.'

'Truce then?' He captivated her with charming good looks.

'Truce!' was all she could get out as she stared into dark, intoxicating eyes.

The outcome of their talk must have been pleasing to him, for the rhythm of their matching stride as they walked back made her feel happy. Strangely, she noticed his steps hardly made a sound as he walked beside her. The deal clincher for liking him was when he pulled out her chair. *Now that's a true gentleman.* Already he was a pleasure to be around, and she grinned as he made her comfortable before moving on to the other side of the table to fill the empty seat next to Rory.

What was to come next left them all wide-eyed and speechless as Axon explained that his boss, Zoren, was an archangel and the guardian of the heavens. He took a breath and gave them time to catch up and once they had quietened down he continued. 'Zoren already has an elite group of super powerful immortals called the Cloud Riders. They are the peacekeepers of the many Home Worlds on the stars. However, they are kept extremely busy. Therefore, due to my new position as Lord of the Planets, I'm in search of my own group of Riders to arbitrate and be the peacekeepers of Home Worlds on the planets. The Rulers are in turmoil and your position will be to mediate with them and solve their arguments peacefully.'

'Universal peacekeepers, how cool,' Nathen responded.

Caitlin didn't think her mouth could open any wider, but it did when he added that the Riders moved from planet to planet via portals and on the backs of mythical horses, *namely the legendary Pegasus winged horses.*

'You have to be kidding me.' Rory sat back with his arms up and hands on the back of his head. By this stage, he looked more relaxed and spoke to Axon confidently, as if they'd been mates forever.

'Seriously,' Axon continued. 'The Cloud Riders use the different cloud formations to jump the horses and riders from one portal to the next, depending on the coordinates of the mission.'

They all laughed, but in their minds knew this was no fairy-tale, believing, with their gifts, they were destined for so much more than their current mundane existence.

Rory leant back in his seat, eyeing Axon. 'So you're Zoren's right-hand man?'

'Yes.'

Rory was uncertain and shared his sudden worry. 'It must be a big job if he has had to put the best of the best in charge. What has me concerned is you're looking at us to help; we haven't got that kind of powers you will need to go up against gods at war. Sorry man, but we're not your warriors, no way.'

'Yes, you are, Rory, and more; you just haven't had any training yet. By the time the Cloud Riders finish with you lot I can guarantee, from the power I feel around this table, you're just what I need. All I'm asking is that you trust me and give it a go. You honestly can't tell me you're happy working in a boring office every day, not with your strengths. How you lasted this long is beyond me. '

'We train at night and use up as much power as we can so we don't take it into our jobs. The younger ones of the team party until all hours to use theirs up. And no, it hasn't been easy to hide, but we do the best we can.'

'Well, I'm offering you a chance of a lifetime. Stop with all this hiding and nonsense, quit mucking around with your lives and come with me now. I will make no promises about the future, but I am sure of one thing, none of you will ever want for anything again.' His eyes roamed over everyone now as he stood up, jokes and fun all gone from his tone. 'I'll give you time to hash it out, but I'm not waiting all day.' He was making them commit now, this minute! And the six of them sat speechless as he strolled back to the bar, parked his butt up on a stool, and switched off from them as he did when they first arrived.

Rory breathed out. 'So that's it, guys. Do we follow the Lord of the Planets to the heavens? Do we agree Axon Stanton will be our new boss or not?'

They leant in and privately discussed the fantastic tale Axon had told them, a wild story that they instinctively knew was true. If it were possible that they were immortal and had powers, then why question his story there were other super humans such as them. They then agreed it was possible for gods to be fighting and a universe of planets in jeopardy.

Rory interrupted the debate. 'If we say yes, we go now, today, leave everything behind, not a single trace of what happened to us.'

Caitlin stretched and huffed. 'So we have to go get training. What's that all about, Rory? Geez, we all know what we can do. Can't you tell him we'll be just fine on our own? I'm not good at other people telling me what to do.'

Zeke gently pulled on her curls. 'It's the red hair, ain't it, little scruffer. Got a temper when you get riled up, don't you girlie.'

'Give you girlie!' She punched his leg under the table.

'Ouch!' He laughed, rubbing his leg.

'Okay guys, give it up. This is serious, and I need each of you to give me an answer. One doesn't go, none of us do, fair enough.'

They agreed and quietened to listen further.

'So, here's the deal with our living arrangements. Axon has organised a home on acreage for us to move into after we finish our training with the Cloud Riders. He insists it will keep us safe from prying eyes and we can live there indefinitely if we like it.'

'Most likely an old ranch but we can do it up, I guess,' Nate put in.

'Yes, we can do what we like so he tells me. What won me was not only that it's secret from the world, but whether we make the cut or not, we can stay as long as we want this time. Except for his equipment to travel to the heavens, everything else is ours for giving it a go. He's trying to help us either way.'

'So, he's just an all-round good bloke then,' Zeke said.

Rory agreed, 'that's the way I see it. I really liked the guy on sight, not sure about the rest of you.'

The group nodded.

'Well, we know Red did.' Bree chuckled, and spoke quietly enough for only Caitlin to hear, forgetting about Lisha's super hearing.

'Is that what all that was about, you've met him already?' Lisha whispered loudly enough for them all to hear.

'Later, guys,' Caitlin said with a smile. 'Continue, Rory, and no more tales out of school, Bree.'

'Come on, no more stuffing around. Axon is waiting.' Rory stopped the chatter. 'Any more questions?'

Lisha frowned. 'Okay, I got one. Between the ranch /homestead, or whatever we call it and the action in the sky, you say Kayden's Cloud Riders presumably don't get much time for anything else.'

Rory nodded. 'That's right.'

'Well, did he say it was close to the other team's farm? I mean if we did have down time it would make sense to hang out and have some fun with others like us. You know, so we don't get bored way out in the middle of Timbuktu.'

'That's if we like them,' Zeke added.

'Of course we will like them, they are super human like us. Imagine the rivalry. And yes sis, Axon said it's nearby, in outback Western Australia. Not close but near enough in case we need assistance.'

Caitlin leant towards Lisha. 'Don't forget Rory told us the property has a lake for fishing and swimming, provisions for camping, four-wheel driving, trail bike riding and at the back somewhere a canyon with chilled water for those stinking hot days. All right up your alley.'

'So I guess we can get ready for a trip to Australia. What do you say?' Lisha was suddenly full of smiles. 'Yes, I think I like the idea of the outback already! Sunsets, swimming and never having to work in an office again.'

'Ditto, me too!' Bree added, 'how exciting not going into the office in the morning.'

'Come on guys. This is not a vote on living the good life. Don't vote yes because you think it's going to be one big party.' Rory sounded frustrated with their concentration on the fun and not the duty.

It was a couple of hours later before they were all in agreement to give it a go. The way they looked at it was if they became Riders it would be dangerous, and they could die protecting the planet. On the other hand, after hearing about the conflicts going on up there, to do nothing meant the Earth would be doomed. In that case, they would all die anyway. In the end, there was only one decision; to go with Axon and see where it took them.

Chapter Three

The Best of the Best

At the shopping centre near the airport, it was a buzz of excitement as they ducked in and out of the speciality shops, each buying a couple of changes of clothing. Axon gave them access to his credit card. Caitlin and the girls may have taken advantage of his kindness and over-indulged just a tad on big name designer clothes. They added a couple of pairs each of chic shoes, luxurious silk lingerie and French Guerlain fragrances and makeup, items they couldn't ordinarily afford. Giggling like schoolgirls, Caitlin, Bree and Lisha ran up the steps ahead of the men and onto the private jet, still energised from their shopping splurge. The men shook their heads, wondering who these women they thought they knew were. Laughing at the mess they had already made as they buckled up, the girls sifted through their items, already swapping, mixing and matching.

Caitlin was her usual bubbly chatty self and joked with everyone the whole trip. It made the time go a bit quicker and only towards the end of the journey did she plonk herself down and decide to watch a movie.

Rory spoke quietly. 'At last, we've worn her out. I thought she'd never give us any peace,' he said, putting his arm around Bree and resting back against the seat.

Caitlin heard him and couldn't resist one more annoying jab. Getting up, she jumped on his lap and gave him a last hug. His patience running out, he growled, sending her into a fit of laughter and back to her seat.

'Little pest.' He chuckled.

She knew he loved every minute of her antics. Getting comfortable and pressing in the earplugs, she turned up the sound, happy that even though Rory had a girlfriend, he was still her mate. Relaxing, she felt one of the guys sit beside her and leant into him. It was Zeke, and even though Caitlin adored him, she so wished it were Axon. Her eyes closed dreamily. If it were Axon, she would want to stay wrapped in his arms forever.

Upon landing, they were bustled into a stretch four-wheel drive. A couple of hours into the trip, Caitlin had never seen such vastness, straight roads, or the red dust that blew up and around the car. It intrigued her.

'How did everything get so red?' She stuck her nose against the window, squinting to see outside the dirty glass. Tumbleweeds rumbled over red dirt before snagging on a black stump that sprouted soft green fern at the top. Tall mounds of dirt piled high in cone shapes had her curious, but it was the trees that sported gaping holes in them, the low lying branches giving refuge from the sun to a furry animal, that made her smile. With his big long tail that supported an upright body, the light brown furry bush dweller used his small paws to clean his face and ears. It looked adorable. *Yes, I'm going to enjoy learning about this new country and this land of mystery.* Rory was about to enlighten her on what she saw when her hand went up.

'No, no! Please, let me experience it like this. When we have time to stop and touch and feel, tell me then. I so love this experience.' She squirmed in her seat, other animals catching her attention.

Rory shrugged. 'Little Miss independent that doesn't need me anymore.'

She ignored him, knowing he understood. In her time with Rory, she had to learn much and quickly. He was aware of her need to experience some things alone and would be her mentor when questions emerged.

* * * *

The sounds of tyres sliding on gravel as they pulled up stopped the chatter as they peered out the window.

'We're here!' Axon switched off the engine and turned to them. 'Time to meet some real-life heroes.' He gestured towards the other group they were about to meet. 'The two arm-in-arm are Kayden and Cassie. To the left, the tall one with the red hair is Woody, Kayden's right-hand man. The two on the right with the blond hair are brothers; Jason is the tall one, and the other is Ethan. The one coming towards us with the shaved head and tattoos is Conor.'

'He is so cute,' Bree whispered, getting a sharp look from Rory.

'He is to die for,' Lisha gushed and actually blushed.

Caitlin slapped them playfully. 'Shush! We have to act tough and mysterious. No gooing and aring like gushy girls or these boys are going to eat us up for breakfast.'

Conor opened the door for them.

After the introductions, the new boss and Rory disappeared into the stables with Kayden. The others remained out in the dusty, scorching midday sun, with a threatening-looking Woody, Jason, Conor, and Ethan looming over them. They didn't look friendly, maybe not happy they had to share their secrets. It was a welcoming gesture when Cassie came from behind and threw her arm around Caitlin.

'How about us four girls head inside and leave the boys to get to know each other. Too much testosterone going on here for my liking.' She sounded pleasant and they happily followed.

Caitlin looked back once on the porch. To break the tension, the men were doing what all men do, testing each other. Conor led them to the horse enclosure. It looked as if Zeke and Nate were going on a ride, bareback, and most likely end up in a race. There had to be a winner, always. *Men!* Her lips parted in a smile as she watched them for a few seconds.

Cassie saw her lag behind, watching the men. 'They'll be just fine.' She grabbed Caitlin's hand, dragging her inside. 'Come! Let me introduce you to Woody and Jason's wives.

'Caitlin, Bree and Lisha, this is Sonia, Jason's wife.' She smiled at a honey-haired woman. 'And, this is Ella, Woody's wife.' She nudged a tall, well-dressed stunner that reminded Cassie immediately of Lisha.

Caitlin was amazed to find that Sonia and Ella were not like them, they were mortal women. The love they shared with their husbands must have been something special to be entrusted with the Cloud Rider secrets. *So mere mortals could be trusted.* Up until now, she was sure they were destined never to find real love because they were abnormal, born freaks of nature, but meeting others like them changed everything. Here in this outback, far from where they once lived, they had found a group just like them who had bent the rules. Caitlin felt she was floating; all the recent events were so surreal. Blinking, she pulled it together to tune into the conversation, still unsure how being married to mortals would work. *They grow old.* She checked out both women. The age lines were already appearing, the grey becoming apparent with the regrowth of Sonia's hair.

'How are you finding the heat?' Ella eyed her curiously, looking as interested in her as she was in them.

Caitlin lifted her hand, and fanned her face, her usually pale complexion flushed. 'I don't know how you survive in this heat. I can hardly breathe.' She flopped down at the table where Cassie had poured out iced tea for them. 'Thanks.' She lifted the cup and gulped down half.

Ella laughed. 'This is only a moderately warm day, sugar.' She sat beside her and placed a gentle hand on hers and pulled it away with surprise. Her gaze focused on Caitlin's hand. 'Okay, this may sound, Little-Red-Riding-Hood here, but, what soft skin you have.' With that, Cassie and Sonia had to feel her skin too.

Bree chuckled at the response she always received. 'I'm sure she uses some strange herb to keep it that way to get attention. Actually searched her apartment once but found nothing. Won't tell me her secret but with luck, you ladies can get her to spill the beans.'

Evoking a response, her companions sat riveted waiting to hear Caitlin's story, but she merely shrugged her shoulders. 'Nothing to tell. Maybe it's because I don't do dishes. I love take-out too much.'

She changed the subject.

* * * *

Some time later, Woody interrupted them. His frame filled the entire doorway and the top of his head just cleared the opening height. 'Kayden wants both teams assembled immediately.' He turned to leave and then reconsidered. 'Oh! And for the newbies, get a wriggle on, trust me when I say, K does not like to be kept waiting.'

A shuffle of chairs had four of the women on their feet. Ella and Sonia stayed seated and glanced at each other with a look of *here-we-go-again*.

'Ladies!' Cassie gestured for Caitlin, Bree and Lisha to follow her.

Out in the barn, Caitlin grabbed at Bree's hand as the platform they stood on began to descend, causing her to lose balance. 'Shyte.' She leant against her friend, and the two of them chuckled, not expecting the movement. 'Cassie!' Caitlin cheekily slapped her lightly for not telling them.

Caitlin noted Lisha showed no emotion, as she had nerves of steel. The movement of the lift wouldn't have worried her. She also saw how well Lisha mingled with Cassie and the other two women inside. It was as if she had been here before and loved it, and fitted in perfectly. Hadn't put a foot wrong. Caitlin had never remembered a time when Lisha had just 'fitted in'! She generally took time to settle into new surroundings before making friends.

The platform stopped with a thud. The girls gave another loud squeal and giggled together before they turned to a seriously cool room of wall to floor screens. The excitement of all this oddness was short-lived as they realised all eyes were on them and they looked into unimpressed, stern faces. They stood quietly taking in the hi-tech paraphernalia and possibilities of what it would show them.

'What the …!' Caitlin's eyes finally rested on the table the men sat around. It was lit up with some kind of sky mapping chart. *Astrologers' dream table.*

'Welcome ladies.' Kayden's hand moved in a circle, his tone very official. 'This is our headquarters – come, join us.'

In awe, Caitlin followed Cassie. They headed to the table where the men sat, and she collapsed into the chair Axon had pulled out for her. Kayden waited for them to be seated before he continued. 'As you are all aware, I am the leader of this elite group and have been given the task, along with my men, to firstly evaluate each of your powers and secondly to decide if you are worthy of becoming Axon's new team. I command respect at all times, as Axon will when he takes you from here. There will be no more girlie behaviour, and nor will I tolerate insubordinate behaviour in the Satellite room. Cassie, I will rely on you to keep your new friends in line and poor behaviour such as that just displayed is to cease. Understood?'

'Bully!' Caitlin coughed the words.

Axon looked up from what he was doing, his urge to discipline her obvious.

Immediately upon seeing Axon's annoyed expression, Rory responded, jumping to her defence and looking after his team member. 'Excuse Caitlin, she has been sick and has a terrible cough.' Rory eyed Caitlin, giving a look that only he could give, which told her she was pushing it. A wink from her made him smile. They never did talk much with words as they both knew each other so well. It was her way of telling him she would behave, for him.

Her attention turned back on Kayden who looked like a hard nut to crack. She was unsure if she liked him as he seemed to have some major command issues. *If Rory acted like him, I'd be putting a stop to that grumpy arse attitude.*

Rory rolled his eyes at her concentration. If Kayden didn't turn from her soon she would surely say something smart and get into more trouble, he could see it clearly. He directed the commander's attention back to him to disrupt the eye contact between the two. 'So what's going on here now, Kayden?'

The commander's eyes swept to the location and he started talking Rory through the sequences to pinpoint the blinking problem. Caitlin suddenly felt suitably impressed with Kayden's teaching skills. Rory was picking up the technical side of it quickly. *Maybe*

Kayden isn't so bad after all.

Once the images of the star systems they needed to view were up on the screens, Kayden focused back on the group.

'Before I start, I must clear something up. For the team that has just arrived, I have linked you to me. This means I can hear all. I have also connected you magically to the members of my team by whom you will be monitored after exchanging powers.' He glared at Caitlin and watched her colour redden as she realised he had heard all her insults.

'Caitlin, I am glad you have decided to tone down your view of me. I don't need you to like me, but if I am to train you, I do need your undivided attention and loyalty to the mission.'

'Kayden, um I mean Commander, aw hell! You got me right and proper. I had no idea you could hear! Hope you can accept my apology, no more mucking up.' She held her hand up in a submissive gesture. 'Promise!'

'I doubt you can keep that promise Caitlin, but thank you for giving me your word to try.'

How does he know me so well? She concentrated on her hands, before looking back up, this time to a different Kayden, his smile amused. The rest of his team cracked up laughing.

'There's always one in every group, boss. Damn if it isn't the redhead. And I put my money on the blonde.' Woody gestured towards Lisha.

The meeting now underway, Kayden toned down the tough guy act. When he did, he noticed, Caitlin became a keen student. Her excitement grew when realising they were going on a real mission with the Cloud Riders.

'You mean we're going up tonight, visiting the Teapot?' She slapped hands with Bree and Lisha. 'Man, you got to be kidding us! Wahoo!' She didn't care if her outburst was disciplined. 'This is one party I'm not missing.'

'Cait!' Rory's tone was firm enough to settle her down. 'We're all excited, but let Kayden finish, or we'll never get there.'

Caitlin gave him the happiest grin as she sat down quietly

again. Kayden saw how well Rory handled Cait and, pleased, gave Axon a nod of approval.

'Now, while I have quiet I'll enlighten you on why we have been sent to this particular part of the sky.' He pointed at two flanking constellations each side of the Teapot. 'Who wants to tell our new members the story of Altar and Lyra?' He eyed his group.

'I love this story,' Cassie put her hand up and when she got the okay, kept her attention on the girls. 'Prince Riatla lives in the Home World, Altair. His bride, Princess Aryl lives on the other side of the Milky Way in the Home World, Lyra.'

'Seriously!' Caitlin had eyes wide. 'Why don't they live together?'

Cassie grinned. 'Here's the thing. Their love was forbidden so without parental permission, they eloped. When the bride's father found out, he was furious and banished them to their own Home Worlds, separated by the Milky Way. After much negotiation, the King gave in but had a stipulation. They were only permitted to meet on the seventh day of the seventh moon and here's the sticking point, he had their transporting powers revoked.'

'So they can never see each other?' Bree looked devastated for them.

'Up until now, their saviours were birds, flocks of magpies have faithfully flown to their rescue and on that day, link together to form a bridge for the pair to walk across so they can unite.'

'Awww, that's so lovely.' Bree grinned and high fived Caitlin who had enjoyed the story too.

Kayden intervened, 'but that has now changed.'

Cassie leant forward. 'Really, what's going on?'

'Over centuries, the feathers have worn off the birds' heads. They have rebelled, refusing to help the lovers in their quest to be together. With a heavy heart, Prince Riatla has persuaded the Ruler of Altair and the Ruler of Lyra to help them be together by making a gap in the Milky Way. The opening will cause an electromagnetic force that will pull them close so they can be together forever.'

Kayden stopped, and changed the settings to show the supernova heading towards the constellations. 'Their weapon of choice, a deployed white dwarf supernova, will explode right in the middle of the Milky Way. The blast will not only clear a path through the Milky Way, but will hit the constellation Sagittarius; in particular, the Home World of the Teapot that resides within this constellation. The damage is unpredictable for any Home Worlds in the vicinity; with the worst case scenario being the total annihilation of one or more stars in these constellations.'

Woody squinted as he studied the schematic. 'The Prince could take out his own Home World as well as his bride's, the fool. Check this out, K.' Woody touched a couple of keys on the board and shook his head. 'That white dwarf looks unpredictable; the flares are shooting from it way too erratically. If the thing goes ballistic and detonates at this angle, K, they're all goners.'

'That scenario has been given to the feuding parties, but the prince and princess are determined to proceed, saying if they can't be together they don't want to live. The prince has since convinced Lyra and Altair that the damage report Zoren's team has given them is incorrect, a scare tactic. That the supernova won't come anywhere near them, and the heads of state are standing by the Royals and their orders.'

Flicking off the satellite feed, Kayden leant up against the table, arms folded, eyes darting, assessing each of them before he spoke. 'My team knows what needs to be done from here. For the trainees, our job is not only to intercept and destroy the supernova before it explodes but to mediate between the Milky Way and the two lovers. We will have to come up with a solution, fast.' He sounded calm.

His team also showed nothing. No excitement or anything really. It was poetry in motion and as if they had done this a hundred times before. For them, it was simply another day on the job. Caitlin eyed her team who were almost bursting with the buzz of something so new and dangerous. She could feel how eager her mates were to head out on a mission and could feel the adrenalin running through them. Their team was ready to go now... Caitlin glared at Rory to give permission to leave, to get moving immediately and let them loose on that sucker supernova. The others could stay on the ranch, she thought with a gloat. *Give us the horses, and we're there!*

Her mouth had only just opened when she was silenced by the next set of instructions.

'Dismissed, get some sleep as it will be a long night.' Kayden said assertively.

Rest! What! Someone feel his head, the guy's sick, that or a nutcase. Caitlin chuckled silently. *Our gang are so frigging excited we're hardly going to rest. What a dill!*

With that, Kayden's team walked out the room towards the exit, not even talking.

Caitlin couldn't believe it when Rory and the rest of her team followed suit. *So like little sheep we all went Ba Ba and followed Mr Lamb Dumbo outside.* Rory elbowed her to behave.

'What!' Caitlin put on a straight face, doing as she was told, when a burst of laughter coming from a few of the Cloud Riders, and a snigger from others reminded her that they were linked now, so best to keep all thoughts to herself. *Na, surely they couldn't hear just a mere speculation.*

She grumbled internally but followed the lead as everyone lay around on beds, floors and couches chatting excitedly. The sound snapped off as Kayden put the lot of them to sleep.

On waking, Caitlin shook her head. *The rotten sod put us to sleep. What a dirty trick. I'm going to slap Rory good and proper if he does that to me before he takes me up on a mission.* There was laughter and snickered comments. It was only now she realised Kayden was relaying her feelings. There was no other explanation. She knew Kayden could speak to his team from a great distance, but didn't know he could read minds; had figured those connected to him needed to verbally speak for him to hear. She decided to test her theory while the guys made the coffee.

So Mr Big Shot isn't only sharing his power of telepathy and magical secrets with my Rory but teaching him how to torture us with it as well. Ratfink!

The room erupted in laughter again. Axon pulled her aside. 'Cait, they're having fun with you and Kayden needs to stop. He has taken a liking to you and is relaying your thoughts about him, but I need you to learn all you can while we train you. This is your first warning to conduct yourself in a more professional manner, so I warn, do try not to think.'

'Sod! I thought he was doing something like that.'

She turned to Kayden, thinking her response to him. *Well played, got me into trouble with my new boss and all. We have all night, sugar; just don't turn your back on me or the redhead wins.* She let her lips screw up in a smirk, her eyes alive. Kayden's laughter rang through the house as he ignored her and went outside to summon the horses.

She glanced up at Axon who was giving her a stare that made her feel uncomfortable. She could see he had meant what he said so she decided to ask questions to take his mind off the fact she had just done what he told her not to. Her eyes rested back at Kayden as the screen door flapped behind him.

'What exactly is he capable of? How powerful is his telepathy?' she finally asked Axon.

'Kayden is capable of sending out orders from great distances. He is Lord of the horses and before forming an alliance with Zoren was known to many in the heavens as Ahearn. Once he accepted the position of Commanding Officer, he was given Kayden Hunter as an Earth name. His first mission was to seek out and form an elite group of individuals that you now know as the Cloud Riders and peacekeepers of the stars.'

'So he talks to the horses as well. Why didn't you tell me! I can just imagine what he'll tell my horse to do if I don't behave.' She nudged him and grinned. 'Thanks for the heads up. My mouth is zipped.' She made a gesture with her hands to zip her lips closed, turning a key and throwing it away.

This was met with a straight-faced Axon.

Rory took control. 'Excuse us, I need to speak with my team member.' He put his arm around Caitlin's shoulder and walked with her outside and away from Axon.

'Cait, behave, or I'll leave you here. You're making me look bad. It looks as if I have no control over you. Drop the attitude and the rude remarks and keep away from Axon. I don't like the way you're flirting with him. He's our boss!'

She shrugged him off, noticing the others in her team could see he was about to have another shot at her and had made themselves scarce. Alone, and away from everyone, her eyes lit up, the anger building in her. 'For a start, I didn't know Kayden could hear me, and anyway, if my point of view is put out there for all to hear, then stiff, it isn't my fault. I bet you've had plenty of observations too; he may get sick of me and change direction. Think yourself lucky he's just picking on the frigging redhead and lastly, don't presume I'm flirting unless you know I am.' Her hands went directly to the hips, indignant at his last comment. 'And lastly…'

'Yes.'

'From now on I will flirt, so get used to it. You dumped me for schoolgirl Breesie, so now I can do what I want.'

'You didn't want me anyway. And, you know this is hardly the place to discuss this. What the hell is wrong with you? This is so unlike you to be so bitchy when I speak to you.'

Tears stung her eyes. 'I miss you!'

'Come here!' He held out his arms and she sobbed into him.

'I was your everything.'

'Cait, I don't believe it's me that's upset you.' He wiped her cheek tenderly. 'I think it's all this magic here amongst the Cloud Riders. I can feel the power humming through you. Please don't make this awkward.'

Caitlin sniffed and stood away from him. 'Just forget it, Rory. Forget everything. You're the boss and that's it from now on.' She had lost him, and it hurt. *He couldn't care less about how rejected I feel!* But it would be the last time she would cry for him. He was brushing her off with a weak excuse, refused to believe her state of mind had anything to do with him. Of course it had been him who upset her. She took a brave stance and decided right then how he now fitted in her life. He was to be the head of their team so she would listen to his orders as she had always done, but make her cry again? *I don't think so!* It was over. Her heart sank for a few minutes as she turned to walk back with him to the others. She had never had analyse their relationship before and it upset her that everything had changed between them.

Rory kicked at a stone on the ground. His sigh let her know he was upset that he had stuffed everything up too.

She shook off the tears. *Traitor with my heart!*

Caitlin could already feel the link between her and Cassie. She was surprised it was her chosen, not Bree or Lisha. She still had trouble controlling her powers at times and hoped Kayden knew what he was doing. With her arms folded, still annoyed with Rory, she watched as he went and stood with Bree, giving her that raised eyebrows like, "I'm having trouble with the redhead, but I've got it in the bag." *Like hell you have!* Holding her pride in check, her nose went up in the air as she turned to look away from Bree's sudden stare.

She listened in to Kayden who had started to explain how all the swapping of their unique gifts had worked and how he was now able to tap into team two. *I guess that means us,* Caitlin surmised. *I really have to stop feeling bitter and start listening.* Rory was right, she had never made a move on him. It was her own fault, not his. The crush she would get over— she eyed off Axon. Boss or not he was cute— *maybe more appealing now I am free to shop around.*

Kayden coughed and caught her attention. The colour flushed to her cheeks. Once again forgot about his gift to read her views. Had to remember at any time he could cut them off or relay a message to an individual. He smiled and winked. Caitlin gave him a bright smile. Yes, she liked Kayden too. He had been having fun with her but at the same time knew when not to.

He turned his attention back to the group. 'As I said, I have assessed the powers of group two and paired you up, matching you with a member of group one. This means the special magic controlled by you, has been transmitted into your equal, and it works visa verse. You will be feeling much stronger and a bit overloaded, but it will settle shortly as your body becomes accustomed to the new imprint. With the same gifts, team two will be capable of doing as we do. That is if you buckle down and learn from us. Once the sharing is complete, you will feel more relaxed and comfortable with these surroundings. A link such as this lasts only for a few seconds. For some, this may continue, depending on the blending. Rory, you being the leader, you're with me, and you may find I send you short bursts from time to time. To overload you right now is crazy. You have much to learn.'

Kayden eyed the teams. 'Okay, so it's Rory and me, Nate's with Woody, Zeke's with Jason, Lisha, it's you and Conor, Bree is with Ethan and, Caitlin's matched with Cassie.'

Caitlin smiled and nodded as Cassie slipped an arm through hers. They had started to become close already and this bond was now cementing their new friendship.

'Me and my bestie here are just fine Kayden, thank you,' said Cassie.

Caitlin felt warmed by Cassie's remark, *her bestie*. She had just lost one and bam! She had a new one. She decided this one was better as they would always share a part of themselves with each other and she'd never lose Cassie the way she had lost Rory.

Chapter Four

Girls! Girls! Girls!

Axon passed Rory six golden bridles for his team members. 'Your group will need these magical bridles to transform the mare or stallion given into a flying horse. The animal will be protected in armour and capable of cloud travel through a portal, taking you to the destination required. These horses are from the Pegasus constellation so if at any time you lose them, that is where they will return unless previously instructed.'

'Wow, how surreal!' Caitlin was in awe.

'This is your new world. Get used to it and fast!' Axon's no-nonsense retort silenced any further comment or discussion. Mindful he was under the watchful eye of his boss, Rory handed them around while they observed Kayden telepathically call to the horses. All he did was go quiet for a couple of seconds and next thing Caitlin saw thirteen horses trot from the stable. In formation, the magnificent parade of muscle and shining coats marched out, and the perfect formation lined up before him, hoofs and heads inclined as if bowing. Caitlin wanted to clap, but everyone stood so quietly, so she did too. Kayden gave Woody and Jason the go ahead to show the trainees what to do. As they slipped the golden bridles on their rides, the horses glowed. Caitlin and the others squinted, not wanting to turn away in case they missed something. As the brightness of the light dimmed, the different coloured horses changed within the glow to white and shook out beautiful white wings. Their bodies were now covered in an armour of what resembled large pearls, yet she knew the protection would not be of this world. Each horse was different from the next, yet easily identifiable by a colourful swirly pattern within the armour. This was created by the same pearl-like element.

Once the transformation had completed, Woody and Jason mounted their horses.

'Bravo!' Caitlin closed in on them as the glare dimmed. 'Ritzy makeover.' She chuckled with amazement, while poking at Jason. 'Damn man, you look like an angel.'

Jason was amused with her reaction and winked as he jumped off the horse to give his charge, Zeke, a hand with his horse. Bree and Lisha gave Jason a whistle, seeing him walk towards them wearing black leather pants tucked into knee-high boots. His white t-shirt, which was slashed across the front a few times and exposed parts of his bare chest, allowed them to see glistening skin beneath.

'Still my heart,' Lisha stirred as both girls leant on each other and fanned their smiling faces.

'Sorry ladies, I'm taken.' He laughed with them and kissed his wife, Sonia, on the way past her.

As he walked away, Caitlin eyed off the sword and dagger that had become part of the outfit. She guessed her team would be training with such weapons when there was more time.

'Awesome!' Caitlin stood back as horse after horse, and their riders, were magically transformed. She was intrigued to see how the magic dressed her two friends, Lisha and Bree; blown away and rendered speechless when both girls matched in outfits that made them look hotter than she had ever seen them. The short tight, seductive frocks were split up each side, with only a gold belt to fasten. As Jason's had, their complexions still illuminated with what she now understood would protect and prevent damage to their skin while in space. Their hair had been swept up at one side and clipped with gold and white flowers.

She was the last to bridle her mare, her mind running wild with how the horse would dress her. Axon stood by her, his nearness just enough to steady her imagination that had her quite worked up. She wondered if he knew what she was thinking. Not wanting his closeness to distract her, she moved a little away and turned to him, hoping to loosen the guy up. He was one hard nut to crack. 'Well, I hope it leaves me with a damned bra on,' was all she could come up with and she smiled. Alas, there was no response in the dubious features.

He took his time answering her. 'It's hard to say. Cassie's outfits change with each horse. It will depend on if yours likes redheads with a temper.'

'In that case, I want old Red over there in the paddock; he won't give a toss.'

'That's why old Red's in the paddock; he doesn't.'

She cracked up laughing and not even getting a smile from Axon she turned to Kayden. 'If this horse de-clothes me I'm telling Zoren.'

Axon answered for him. 'Archangels don't wear clothes, so he won't care. Now get on the flipping horse and quit it.'

She swung her head around to Kayden and whispered, 'Don't they?'

Kayden's smile told her Axon was kidding and turning from her, he put out his hand to Cassie. 'Show them what a real beauty looks like on a horse.' He lifted his wife up and onto the horse, their love evident as he kissed her lightly before letting her go. The connection between them had her glow change to a perfect shade of pink. Cassie transformed into the prettiest woman, a goddess and superior in every way.

'Your turn.' Axon sounded impatient. She flushed, embarrassed both teams were mounted and waiting on her. She kicked herself for not making an attempt to get in the saddle sooner. She felt them all watching, while Axon lifted her up and onto her horse as if she weighed nothing. Caitlin, surprised by the quick mount, relaxed the best she could to let the magic take her over. She was pleased when her outfit resembled Cassie's and smiled at the emeralds, her favourite stone, that decorated the knee-high boots that covered white pants. The top was sleeveless, laced up at the front, corset style.

It was made of a glimmering delicate fabric she had never seen before and luckily, decorated with emeralds where they were most needed. With a deep sigh, she pulled at the top as she made an effort to tuck her breasts into it a bit more before taking the reins from Axon. 'Could I look any more tarted up?' She screwed up her lips as she adjusted the emerald-studded silver arm bracelets around her upper arm, her hands going straight to her hair, feeling clips. She shook her head. 'Emeralds too, right.'

Axon hadn't moved, blinked or spoken. She waved her hand in front of his eyes. 'Hey boss man, you still in there? It's not that awful is it?'

Finally, he blinked, his expression unusual, as if he were miles away in thought. It was the same goofy look Kayden had when he put Cassie on her horse. *What is it with these guys?*

Caitlin bent down close to him and whispered, 'you were away with the birds Axon, better get on your horse or Kayden will be on your case next, boss or not.'

Axon's eyes cleared and his forehead rippled. Without a word, he turned and in one movement, leapt on his horse. Caitlin's heart pounded at the sight of his muscles through the slits of the t-shirt he now wore, the skin taut, tanned and illuminated. Ogling made her miss what Kayden was telling them.

'What did I miss?' She leant over to Rory, who had noticed her checking out Axon and was smiling.

Back to his usual self, he spoke to her the way he usually did, making Caitlin feel better towards him. 'He was saying how the glow that surrounded our bodies prevents us from suffering from the glare the stars give off.'

'I guessed that already.' She grinned.

'Okay, smarty pants, did you also guess that it's like wearing a pair of superhuman strength sunglasses?' His tone was friendly, caring but alive with their typical banter. He wanted her back on side, this she knew, but would make him sweat a little longer. *By his side, I will always be.* She smiled at how much she cared for him too, feeling better and knowing that even Bree would never sever their friendship.

'Well, impatient girlfriend dumper, if you hadn't discarded me for that sexy woman next to you, who is really still my girlfriend, not yours, I wouldn't have been looking elsewhere and missed that bit.'

'She's my girlfriend now, so stop trying to steal her back.' He smiled at Bree.

'You only like her more than me today because she looks hot in that outfit.'

'Hot! I'm telling you now, when we get our own horses she isn't ever going to be allowed to take that bridle off her ride.'

Bree slapped him. 'Go stuff yourself. I look good in anything.'

'You'll do what I say, you both will, because I'm the boss!' Rory stuck his nose in the air and trotted off. The attempt at arrogance made both girls laugh.

'All chatter and jokes aside now guys, Kayden has to concentrate,' Woody called back at team-two, who were ribbing each other for looking like fairies with their glowing skin.

Woody and Kayden made an attempt to stifle laughter as they moved through the cloud mist. It was all fun and they held back orders to quieten down. They remembered how much enjoyment they had with the guys in the earlier years when they transformed.

'Newbies!' Woody remarked.

Kayden rolled his eyes at Caitlin, his guess correct that it would be her having the last word.

'If it gets dark in the clouds, Rory, you have our permission to moon us girls so we can see where we are going.'

Kayden relayed what she had said to both teams for those who may have missed her comment. With the group in fits of laughter, Kayden moved them into the first portal. Usually, he would discipline his team for mucking about, but Caitlin had him drawn into her every word. He wondered if it was a power that she didn't yet know about.

* * * *

As if sound had no place here, all banter ceased as the weirdness of the experience took over the new group. The silence was deafening as they flew quietly into the cloud cover and through the first portal. They had no clue what to expect and all opinions of how funny their appearance was vanished, as did the world they left behind. The awareness and oddity of coming out of a portal and into another dimension were all that was on their minds. Caitlin watched as the clouds began to spin beams of coloured light around them. Bright blue, green, red and purple gathered in front of them, forming the shape of a star. The sharp lights twisted, turned and sped up until the colours blended and a hole appeared in the middle of the star. The sound of a whip cracking snapped at the portal opening, now large enough for their horses to fly through. Caitlin pondered if they would break apart as many movies had portrayed it.

Kayden's orders took her mind off her uncertainties, his tone strange now he used telepathy to communicate. *The next is a cumulonimbus cloud so hold on tight. This one will ascend hundreds of metres. Get ready for the whip upwards, it can give you quite a jolt if you're not prepared.*

Caitlin's first impression was that she would enjoy this. The blend of colours puffed around them like cotton candy, soft and calming. Not for long though as the ascent became sharp, the horses moving so fast the prettiness blurred. Her hands grabbed and tightened the reins as she leant forward to hold on, her fingers twisting around the horse's mane, for fear she would fly off the back of the mare. She was thankful when the fissure appeared, as the crack of the portal opened to allow them an exit from the crazy ride. *What the …?* She looked back, once clear of the cloud. She didn't like that one at all. Rory had better not use that sucker, *cumulonimbus cloud my foot, shyte myself cloud more like it.* She quietly giggled. When there were no other sounds of laughter, and she was glad Kayden had finally switched off. The mission was keeping him busy. *At last, I can be me again.*

With a gasp of awe, all she had been thinking faded as she glanced around. The stars, although slightly out of shape, radiated luminous points where she now knew the Cloud Riders used to position themselves when controlling a star. The planets were different in every way. They were perfectly rounded, the cloud of dust and gases surrounding them defining the colour of the glow. They looked like painted perfection. Her pride that the group she belonged to would soon be visiting them sent a thrilling shiver down her spine. She was here because of Rory and felt sorry that she had believed he had neglected her. He had fought for them to all stay together. He had found her, given her a home and, now showed her where she belonged, where they all belonged, with him!

The real excitement was only just beginning as Kayden pointed to the *Teapot* and headed for the star, Nunki, Home World of the constellation's ruler.

Close to landing, Caitlin put her hand over her mouth to stifle laughter. On the surface, she had spotted a huge big teapot with windows and a door. *You have to be kidding me!* She shook her head with amusement as they landed.

A large woman appeared in the doorway and waved with excitement, her grey hair pulled into a tight bun.

In the woods by the edge of a brook, eccentrically-dressed animals sat at a table. A teapot, cups and saucers complete with a tall cake-stand laden with cupcakes covered the top of a red and white chequered tablecloth that blew in the light breeze. Implausible as it all looked, Caitlin squinted and cracking up laughing when one of the animals with a waistcoat pulled a watch out of his pocket and checked the time.

'You're kidding me! A high-tea party!' She nudged Bree as they trotted together past them and up to the teapot house. Both girls held back a loud shriek of incredulous disbelief. Not even Cassie had warned them of what to expect. They turned at the sound of Cassie having a chuckle at their astonished expressions. Trotting past them, she held her head high, at home with this weirdness.

Their horses came to a halt causing Bree to almost fall off. Both muffled most of their cries of amusement as Caitlin steadied her. Axon saw it as fooling about and gave them a sour look as he and Rory dismounted. Both men were stern, which made the girls refrain from any more skylarking. They got the hint loud and clear, it wasn't polite to poke fun at the locals or carry on so unprofessionally.

While Axon, Kayden and Rory went to speak to the ruler of the constellation, Woody gave the order for them to have a stretch but not to go too far from the horses. Both girls dismounted, and Caitlin's delight in this world skyrocketed as weird dog-like critters appeared and nuzzled up to her and Bree for a pat. Woody pulled out his sword, scaring them.

'They are star critters, called dogitters, but you have to be wary of them as they change shape and the other head that appears will give you a nasty sting if it bites.'

They felt sorry for the little brown fluff-balls that tripped on long floppy ears. They didn't believe Woody until they barked at him. As he said, they grew a distorted second head with a set of vicious, snapping teeth. The yapping critters attempted without success to nip at Woody before they ran off. Strangely enough, Caitlin felt comfortable here amongst it all. The dogitters did not worry her at all, but she refrained from encouraging them further, resolving to listen to Woody's teachings regarding life on these planets. The session was interrupted by the return of the three negotiators

No one mentioned to Kayden that Bree's horse had a limp and yet he knew and bent to check the mare's hoof. He pulled out the offending splinter and brushed off his pants as he stood to address them. 'Mrs Lekett, the Ruler here, is pleased to see so many of us to protect her Home World. The Leketts and their community are peace-loving and keep no weapons for any line of defence. The Centureans, who usually protect the Lekett family, have put up shields to safeguard their own world. Unfortunately, they didn't have the resources to help their neighbouring Teapot Home World. In other words, we have a lot to do so let's get a move on.' With that, Kayden lifted Cassie onto her horse. He glanced around, seeing Rory, and his team had all mounted their horses and sat ready. He stared back at Cassie, frustrated none of his own men had begun to get on their horses. She knew that look and leant over to him, smiling. 'They are waiting for the rest of it, sweetie. You know they love her so-called tea.'

'Blatz you guys. Okay, the Lekett family are having a victory tea party, and yes, we are all invited back here if we manage to save their Home Worlds. Not alone though. She has a couple of the neighbouring Rulers attending, so best behaviours, please.'

'Yahoo!' Woody and his men let out hollers and took only seconds to mount, slapping hands and looking pleased.

Never had Caitlin seen grown men so excited over tea. *She must make one satisfying drop of brew.*

Kayden turned to Axon. 'I'll leave it up to you, Axon. You may have other plans for your team later.'

Axon had a slight grin. 'Haven't been to one of Mrs Lekett's parties in a very long time.' His features hardened, and he added, 'and as you do, I also believe that to mingle and socialise with the Rulers is a vital essence of camaraderie when engaging in peace talks with them at a later date.' He eyed Rory, his mouth twisted in another grin. 'What do you think, Commander?'

'My first thought was, No! as a few of my team have been mucking about, but, I guess I could turn a blind eye if a certain someone, the ringleader, would start behaving.' He turned to Caitlin, and his look was, *quit your nonsense.*

Caitlin had trusted Rory never to split their team up, but that was before Bree. *Will he dump me now things have changed?* She had already grown to love what she saw so far and that thought scared her. In an attempt to loosen him up a bit she straightened her posture and her left hand came up and saluted. 'Promise to keep it zipped from now on, boss!' In all this strangeness, could she keep her trap shut? Agreement to try was all she could promise for now.

Rory moved his horse close to her so only she heard. 'Don't make me regret agreeing to stay and party, Cait.'

Kayden was the only one who heard and jumped in, leaving Caitlin's mouth open, not giving her a chance to answer and get into any more trouble. 'It's settled then.' He nodded to Woody and Rory. 'Men, it's time to get your teams ready for travel.' He gave a sharp and direct order.

* * * *

Back up in the sky above, Caitlin was happy with where Kayden had positioned her and Cassie. They were out of the line of the Supernova, yet close enough to watch all of the action. She gave Bree a wave after her friend settled into position with her equal, Ethan. Bree had been a good mate from the first day they'd met. They'd hung out after work, shopped for hours at a time, gone out to clubs at night and trained side by side with Rory and the boys, every chance they got. They were fit, happy and inseparable, well, until Rory scored with Bree. Now Caitlin was unsure where their friendship lay. For now, they were teammates, and all of her personal concerns had to take a back seat. She could see how nervous Bree looked and was worried for her.

Axon, Kayden and Rory were to her left, had earpieces on and chatted among themselves. Her own, given before they'd split up, had no sound so she assumed they were plotting a course of action if plan A didn't pan out. Cassie had already told her how unpredictable it could get out there. Caitlin watched Rory with a careful eye, knowing he would absolutely love all the power given to run his own team in conjunction with Kayden. She just hoped it didn't give him too big a head. Going crook at her in front of others was infuriating and had better not make it a habit. If Kayden hadn't jumped in she would have told him just what she really thought. They may be friends and he may now be her boss, but he needn't think he was going to start treating her differently. She had forgiven him for leaving her at the club to be with Bree, but this latest attack on her to make him look in control was pushing it. He knew her personality, and if it was so bad, he should have pulled her up about it long before now.

Disturbed by the message Kayden suddenly sent them through telepathy, Caitlin returned her thoughts to his orders.

Cassie, hold your position or both of you could end up in the thick of it, and when I do give the order, don't go without taking Caitlin with you, okay.

She didn't move a muscle and yet he put his thumbs up. 'You can talk back. Can I do that too?' Caitlin asked her.

'Secret squirrel stuff, Cait. The lads don't know I can do it. If they did, they would try to tap into it. It's hard enough for Kayden to concentrate as it is without hearing everyone's thoughts.'

'But he can hear my thoughts. I don't get it.'

'He talks to one or all of us at any one time and switches some on and some off. You have linked to me so he can hear you too.' Cassie noted Caitlin's look of dismay and smiled. 'It's okay. Rory can't. Kayden hasn't let him have that power yet. It's just too dangerous unless you know what you're doing, so keep it on the low down that you even know about it.'

'Can Kayden hear me all the time? Sheesh, I've been running off at the mouth since I got here. Thought he was only listening to my stronger opinions, not everything.'

'He can turn you off and most likely has by now. Don't worry, he thinks you're funny.'

Caitlin sat quietly without thought for a while, listening to Kayden's orders to everyone. She and Cassie were to hold steady until needed and when they were, their job was to redirect the Supernova to a location rendering it harmless to other Home Worlds, allowing time for the rest of the team to give chase and extinguish it. Kayden kept reassuring the others it was not a dangerous situation unless the Supernova exploded before they could put it out. The trainees were to stick to their equals, but not intervene, just observe the part they would play when they were on their own.

The Supernova came in sight, and Caitlin concentrated on Cassie, watching the technique she used of closing her eyes to help build up her power. Caitlin's immortal gifts were similar to hers, so she was interested to see what her equal did to control the force and use it as a weapon. Kayden had already mentioned about her ability to do exactly as Cassie did after attending a couple of sessions with Woody. However, as with everything new, Caitlin was like a sponge, soaking up what was said, always learning, always observing. She had already got the gist of how Cassie worked without his help. She may have been a slow starter in life, but since her friendship with Rory and his team, she was hell bent on never missing a trick and took pride in her own learning ability.

A sudden movement by Cassie startled Caitlin as her arms

opened out in front of her. With hands barely a few inches apart, she saw the glare of a laser flare that shot from between Cassie's hands. The force catapulted the lightning source towards the Supernova, the electrical charge spread around the lower half of the sphere, lifting it high into the sky above. The speed and accuracy of the hit floored Caitlin and all her new rider friends looking on. The split second it moved, Kayden's team sped off after it, Rory's team in pursuit, keeping close to their equals. Even though it was now only a dot in the sky, Caitlin could still feel and hear a loud rumble from the beast of a weapon that fought to destroy anything in its path.

Cassie and Caitlin, hold your positions. Kayden's order came through loud and clear. *Conor and Jason, get out of there! It's too unstable.*

Kayden was having problems extinguishing the globe of burning gas that began to break apart. The lines that appeared on Cassie's forehead had Caitlin worried. A jolt from Caitlin's horse had her hold on tightly as Kayden had them race to the rescue.

'What the blatzing hell!' Caitlin scolded Kayden as the mare turned a tight right and shot straight up, nearly tossing her off. 'Give me a blatzing bit of notice next time, you shytzer!' She screamed the last words as she steadied herself at the same time, putting Cassie off and making her slip a bit as she giggled at her.

'Don't tell me the guys have taught you to swear like a rider already,' she called to Caitlin.

Fear had Caitlin yell to her as they sped side by side towards the explosive entity. 'Conor is a crack up,' she dobbed him in. Had her in stitches when they woke up. He was giving it to Kayden for putting him to sleep on the floor. It had stuck. She liked the new lingo.

Cassie stopped her thinking. 'This is major if Kayden's pulling us up there this fast. If you heat up, it's just me, helping you control our combined magic until you can do it on your own.'

Caitlin nodded and at the same time felt Cassie tap into her, controlling her mind. It felt weird having someone else activating not only her own powers but something more kicked in. Heat within her grew, and she did feel as if she had a hot flush but nothing she couldn't handle. Already she had learnt and was helping to ignite something bigger.

'Cassie, have you got control of Cait too? I need both of you! This damned thing is about to blow. Blatzing hell! Kayden cursed.

Got it Kayden, step aside and let us girls have a crack at it! Cassie sent to him by telepathy. Caitlin was shocked she could hear everything she said too. *Man, this chick has balls.* Her thoughts flitted as the danger became apparent. The supernova was on fire and exploding shards of steel. Massive flaming flairs shot out from all angles, the giant star, hot and threatening, scared the life out of her. Never had she felt the raw emotion of such danger as she stared death in the face. How good was her equal; how good was she?

Cassie eyed her, listening to her every thought. *We're about to find out. This is where we sort out the men from the boys. Hold on girlfriend, I need you to copy me exactly. Can you feel me?*

You bet! But what are you packing me with?

Steady your mind, trust me and do as I do.

Caitlin nodded. She would learn all this, but for today, she just wanted to live. She trusted Cassie, who had done this many times over and was ready to follow her every command. Breathing deeply, she allowed Cassie control of her mind to do what her equal did best, to target and eradicate all dangerous matter regardless of size or mass.

All teams are clear, Cassie it's all yours. Kayden sounded calm, his faith in Cassie evident in the tone of his message to her. *Show that sucker who's boss.*

Cassie took over the mission. *Cait! Now!* Caitlin felt her eyes close and in her mind, saw the Supernova and measurements that tallied to the amount of energy needed to destroy it. The way Caitlin saw it she could reach only half the energy required to destroy it and hoped Cassie had a little extra. They needed to vaporise it completely before it hit the Home World it headed towards. Together with Cassie, in the same split second, Caitlin opened her eyes and threw her arms out, letting go of the pressure growing inside her. The energy was so intense she was compelled to eject it out with force, tossing it towards the offending mass. The two streams of light hit it so hard; the backdraft hurled both horses and girls in a circle as they spun out of control. Caitlin and Cassie used every ounce of strength to steady their rides. Once they stopped turning in circles and the horse's large wings were in control, they were able to view the damage.

A blue electric charge crackled and snapped at the object, covering its mass and preventing it from any further bursts out into the atmosphere. Within the confines of magic, the death star exploded, the remains literally crushed into nothingness as it closed in on it, leaving only a cloud of dusty residue in its place. The girls slapped hands.

'Well done Cait, you can ride with me anytime.' Cassie's face was alive and glowing happily. 'Sure you don't want to get rid of hunky Axon and join us?'

'Hell no! Kayden's a damned maniac. You can have him. I nearly lost my lunch back there. Your boss is one scary piece of work; wouldn't want to be under his jurisdiction if you paid me. Hey, do I get paid for this?' She continued the joking around with Cassie, her mood on a high until Kayden reached them.

'I can see I better split you two up tonight.' With a shake of his head and a smile that etched the corners of his mouth, he turned to where the supernova was. 'Job well done ladies! Now get your arses back to the Teapot before I slap you both for hanging it on me. I heard every word,' he said, his mood improved now there was no danger. 'Oh and Cait, you had better hold on, rebellious one, because I'm about to make it a lot worse for you after those cracks.'

A hearty laugh had bellowed from him before the horses jolted off with a jerk, the sudden movement and speed almost tossing Caitlin off the back.

'Shytzers!' she called out in a continued shriek.

Cassie kept up with her and cracked up at the look on her face as she battled to stay on her mount.

'You're a funny girl Cait. Do you ever shut up?'

Cait ignored her, continuing the onslaught of insult at Kayden. 'That ratfink. I'm telling you now, when we stop I'm going to give him a piece of my mind.' She squealed as he put her in another spin, her abusive language getting a little livelier.

Cassie laughed harder at Caitlin, causing her to almost fall off her own horse. Kayden came to the rescue, helping Cassie to regain control, disciplining her for encouraging Caitlin's behaviour by laughing at her.

Cassie tried to defend herself, wiping away the tears. 'She's the one doing it. She's absolutely a mess, a feral and funny as all hell.'

Kayden turned to Caitlin. 'Damned girl, you're going to give Axon a coronary when he has to deal with you on his own. He hasn't got my sense of humour you know. I best quit stirring you up. Let's just call a truce because I'm not giving in, and after gobbing off like that Rory's giving looks to kill.'

'What, he can hear me?'

'I've relayed everything.'

'Are you serious?'

Her serious, no-nonsense expression caught him off guard. The cheerful light in his eyes turned to concern. It made her laugh so hard she had to take in gulps of air to calm herself.

'Gotcha!' She put her hand out to him, 'Deal!' Think we're even now. You should have seen your face.' They shook hands.

'Why you little –? Okay, guess I deserved that, but, no more!'

'Promise.' She crossed her fingers behind her back using her other hand. In Caitlin's dictionary no more meant no more until next time.

Okay men, enough fun. Let's go celebrate. Our girls just did all our work for us. So I think the rest of us should head down and celebrate with one of Mrs Lekett's brews while they wash and pretty themselves up. They look like chimney sweepers! Come on sooty scruffs. He kept the good-humoured mood going as they headed back to the Teapot's Home World.

Suddenly the feel of a powerful surge alerted Caitlin that Cassie was up to something. Caitlin twisted her body, turning slightly in the saddle to see what. Cassie was about to knock Kayden off his horse for his comment, and even though funny, Caitlin tried to warn him. At the same time, Cassie's hands thrust towards Kayden with an energy force. Alas, her warning was too late. The magical beam that resembled a burst of light shot from his wife's hands faster than

Kayden could move. It knocked him off Zoltan, leaving him stranded in the air, the look on his face was priceless. His horse snorted to sound its disapproval as it flew to retrieve its rider. The teams laughed so hard they could barely see through the tears of hysteria.

'Call me a scruffy chimney sweeper.' Cassie eyed him, trying hard not to show amusement as he remounted his horse with one leap.

Kayden, back on Zoltan, gave an order, forcing all the horses to take off at a high-speed which, caused most of the team members to fall off and it was a mad scramble to pull themselves on to a horse that neared them, many now riding double.

Teach you lot to poke fun at the boss and that undisciplined wife of mine is going to cop it when we stop. Kayden laughed with them all.

CHAPTER FIVE

Sagittarius

On the way back to the Teapot, Kayden lost the plot and pulled Cassie onto Zoltan with him so he could keep mucking around with her while she was in such a funny mood, giving Rory control.

Caitlin settled down. She knew when to behave and it was times like this Rory looked for her support and she wanted him to know he still had it. His nervousness was obvious to her. She rode silently beside him as he used telepathy for the first time, gaining confidence, making his whole team proud of him. Landing both teams safely, she noticed that even Axon had a happy expression, shaking Rory's hand when they dismounted. He patted his back and threw an arm around him while quietly congratulating him on taking control of not only both teams, but the badly behaved one.

Caitlin knew he meant her and rolled her eyes as she passed him. 'Got a problem Boss, tell someone who cares,' she said, as she flicked her hand in the air, swaggered her hips and walked off with her nose high in the air.

Bree and Lisha caught up with her, lifting her in a sandwich bear hug, excited with what she had done. Their chatter ceased on hearing new orders. They heard Ethan getting called and put in charge of Cassie's security. Rory, Nate and Zeke were also summoned to mount up as they would be accompanying their equals, Kayden, Woody and Jason to talk to the prince.

Once on Zoltan, Kayden turned to addressed them. 'We still have some negotiating to do. My aim is to resolve the dispute amicably with the prince before discussing it with Klim tonight. For the newbies, Klim is the guardian of the Milky Way and should be arriving here anytime soon. The rest of you are free to enjoy the night but do so with decorum. Dismissed.' He watched them get out of earshot before speaking to Axon. 'You sure you want to stay? You're welcome to join us.'

Axon held his lips tight as he watched Caitlin walk away.

Kayden saw the look and put up his hand. Woody saw the command and had the men trot a slight distance away so the two leaders could speak privately.

'Talk to me, Axon.'

'I have my doubts about a particular team member and would prefer it was me who welcomes Klim when he arrives. It also gives me time to catch up with Mrs Lekett and fill her on where we are at so far.'

'It's Caitlin, isn't it? You know what I think. She's innocent and a good egg. I believe she has what it takes, just needs fine tuning.'

'I know you like her, but innocent my arse. She's out of control, and you're not helping by encouraging her antics.'

Kayden lifted his spread out hands, speaking through gritted teeth. 'Whoa, calm down.' He took his own advice and shrugged it off. 'That was a tough battle for their first time, and humour is Cait's way of deflecting her fears. It also helps ease the tension for her friends out there. They are used to her and not sure if you noticed, but she makes them very happy. Don't underestimate their loyalty in return, they are extremely protective of Cait. Even Rory jumps in and would sooner chastise her than have us upset her by disciplining her. They are a tight unit, believe me.'

Axon breathed out heavily. 'I'm no fool, I have eyes. It's clear she has won you all over but let me tell you this, I am not putting up with her potty mouth, and the gods will not tolerate her rot either. Not for one minute.'

Kayden knew his friend well. He was old school, and this girl was really pushing his buttons. He wasn't convinced Axon was angry about her swearing. He sounded frustrated, but why? Kayden wondered if there was more behind this than met the eye. Could his friend be irritated he had finally found a woman who didn't fall at his feet… *maybe!* He leant towards Axon to give him one more solid piece of advice before leaving. It was the way he saw it and he felt compelled to try and defuse the situation. 'Give it a little longer. She will calm down, and everything will work out, trust me. They're a great bunch and if you just give them time, they will sort out the rough edges and do you proud.'

Axon felt pleased to get his stamp of approval so early. 'Sorry K. I'm just blowing off steam. I do have faith in your judgement. No hard feelings?'

'None. You know we have a big job to do out here, but as leaders, we don't always have to be pricks while we do it. Cassie taught me that. So I felt it wise Rory learns that early in the piece. As for Cait, she is what Rory needs. Look how she rode beside him on the way down. I did that for a reason and was very impressed. Also, with her nature, Rory will never get too cocky from so much power. I could see Caitlin going off like a cracker at him if he dared get too big-headed. Now, are you sure you wouldn't prefer to have a break from the girls and come with us?'

'No thanks, I'm keeping my eye on that one regardless of how you try to lighten the situation. I still intend to have a word with her.' Axon strode off in a rush to catch up to Caitlin. Once beside her, he took her arm firmly and marching her away from the group and out of earshot.

'I admit you were very impressive out there Cait, but quit the antics and keep that smart mouth in check.'

'Okay.' She pulled from his light grip and stared up at him. 'I get it, you're not keen on my personality, but I was rattled to the max up there. It's the way I deal with things. Gee, you and Rory really need to loosen up. Kayden gets me better than the both of you and has only just met me. Rory, I can understand, he's trying to look good in front of everyone. But you Axon, I thought you would have known what it's like getting pumped with power from someone as strong as Cassie. To tell you the truth it was overwhelming from the moment I arrived and I have to use humour while adjusting to so much magic. I make no apologies for being me.'

Axon almost grinned. Caitlin stood with hands on her hips acting all tough, her copper red ringlets framing flushed cheeks. He found her fascinatingly beautiful. Would he tell her, *no way!* Axon tightened his lips and showed dominance. 'Have you now got it under control?'

'I think so.' She lowered her eyes.

'Good!' He removed his transfixed gaze away from her and headed into the home of Mrs Lekett. Walking away was the only way he could think of to get some space between them and stop the urge to lift her chin and kiss those plump sulky lips. *What's wrong with me!* He was shocked at the thought. This was not normal for him and he wanted distance between them from now on.

'I'll try harder, I promise!' she called to him.

He stopped and turned his head.

'Cait—' Axon didn't finish the angry spit he wished he could drown her in; instead, his arm dropped by his side. *She could be so frustrating, but so annoyingly sweet.* 'Just go join the others. I doubt you even know how to behave, but give it a go.' He turned and strode off, annoyed. His feelings were all over the place.

Left standing alone, Caitlin jogged to catch up with Conor and Ethan, deciding they might keep her out of trouble for a while.

'My boss just blew me off for the old woman in the kettle! Can I hang with you guys?'

'Sure, if you shut your trap. We're sick of laughing at you,' Ethan said, cracking up.

Conor threw his arm around her. 'You can hang with me. Stuff him. Come on dirty girl, I'll show you where you can take a shower and wash that black stuff off.'

She had him in fits of laughter as they climbed the stairs and when he left her in the bathroom, he couldn't help offering to help scrub her down, laughing again when she let out an abusive amount of cussing and slammed the door on him.

'Keep me out of trouble,' she muttered while getting undressed. *I am so going to get another tongue lashing by the end of this night.* She ducked her head under the water. *Oh well, so be it.*

After the shower, she dried herself and reached for her dress, that had mysteriously disappeared. *Oh wow! I'm with Rory on this one. That golden bridle is staying on my horse forever.* She eyed herself in the mirror and watched the magic change her dress. Once the bright glow faded it left her wearing a silver cocktail dress with a stunning pair of shoes to match. Her hair had been styled into a bun and makeup was perfect. *Hell yes! What a time saver but geez horsy out there, wake up to yourself or I'll come out there and slap you, really! A dress!* she mused, fitting right into this bizarre new life, taking pleasure in every second.

* * * *

In the dining hall, Bree claimed her as soon as she walked in and clung to her arm. As Caitlin had thought, the newest member of their group had freaked out. A scan of the room found Lisha in her element, laughing hysterically with Conor who did seem infatuated. Ethan stood with Cassie or more to the point, looked like he was on guard duty and then she remembered that was what he was instructed to do. Cassie was a precious commodity and she guessed while Kayden was busy he would have her safety foremost in his mind. *My team better not start that babysitting bull-twang with me.* Regardless, Caitlin needed Ethan to help her with Bree and steered her towards them. *He would just have to talk while he guards.* His match wanted to talk and Ethan, being her paired-off guru, was who Bree needed.

Due to the short time Bree had been in their group, it made sense she spooked easily. Where the rest of them were eating it up, enjoying every second, she was rattled. Caitlin worked out it was the spinning at such high speeds that had her on edge. She imagined it would shatter anyone the first time. To chase after shooting stars was crazy enough without the atmospheric conditions that left them feeling unnaturally heavy now back on the ground. Understandably she appeared vulnerable and a little overwhelmed. However, this was Bree's part to play in the deadly game they had all agreed too. Unable to add value to the conversation, she left her in Ethan's capable hands, to explain what it was like for him on his first mission.

Free to look around and with mischief in those emerald eyes, she sought out the food table and browsed the buffet. *That was hard work out there today!* She straightened her shoulders with pride, a little guilty that her part in all this was a breeze. She just had to sit on a horse, look whoreishly beautiful and when asked, blow stuff up. Poor Breezy, she thought as she filled a plate with a selection of sweet pastries. A lick of her finger let her know this was real Earth food. Happy with her choice she devoured a custard and cream cake as she watched a couple of men that had arrived. Beauty! She thought. Newbies! *Newer than me.*

They entered with a dark aura that calmed when they spotted Caitlin cleaning up a mess she'd made while eating a cream cake. They thought the situation amusing when yet another blob of cream ran down her chin and onto her top. She cleaned it up just as quickly with her fingers and licked them before seeing she had attracted their attention. She shrugged and grinned. The two men approached her and soon were chatting happily. Her wit and good humour had put them at ease, and intoxicated by her high spirits, they accompanied Caitlin to an unusually high table where they sat on stools and chatted. Caitlin learned they were from the Milky Way, the constellation they had come to protect. 'Good! You owe me. You're buying.' She received a couple of deep, gruff laughs.

'What!' She chuckled with them.

'You must be from Earth. The tea is grown in plenty here and not a charge so pick your poison.' They gave her the menu with the many flavours.

She learned tea was the only beverage, so they chose the aromatic essence for her. Meanwhile, Caitlin encouraged discussion by bringing up a subject that she knew would cause a debate. 'So, which are better, planet or star Home Worlds?' Of course, she was pro the planets, but during the discussion, she was caught out and had to admit she had never been to a planet yet. Also that this was the very first Home World she had actually visited. She had her new friends burst into repeated fits of laughter with her candid opinions. The more tea she sipped, the funnier she found the two men who seemed to enjoy her company too. However, all the laughter and drink eventually had her head spin. It was then she realised the tea was not traditional. Up here in the heavens, it sure packed a punch.

It was at that moment, Axon joined them, but Klim was not about to give up his time with the funny Earth girl. Upon asking Caitlin to dance, he spun her under his arm and out onto the dance floor.

Axon held back an irritated glare. Instead, he grunted and nodded towards her before he turned his back on her and chatted with the others at the table.

Caitlin enjoyed Klim's company and giggled with pleasure as he spun her around the floor, ignoring Axon's apparent effort to make her uncomfortable. Was he still cross at her? She had been behaving, well she thought she had… *Or is he jealous?* After the music had finished, she thanked Klim and excused herself.

Slightly off balance from the tea, Caitlin left her new friends talking with Lisha and Conor. Eventually, she found her way out onto a balcony. The air was crisp and clean outside and overlooking the grounds and with the lights on was dreamy. She folded her arms and leant against a pillar, thinking how lucky she was to be having this experience. Two moons, bright stars and the feeling of freshness against her skin mellowed her mood. It was a romantic setting. It made her feel at peace as if this was where she was meant to be. Out here in the universe and even though only just introduced to it, she was overjoyed in this new life. It was a feeling that even Axon's suspicious glare could not spoil for her.

As she turned to go back inside, she noticed Axon had been standing in the doorway watching her.

'What are you doing out here alone? There are dangers here that you're not aware of, Caitlin. Please let me know next time you want to head outside so I can have you guarded. Did you not see how Cassie is watched like a hawk? This is careless; another reason you give me not to trust you.'

Anger welled up inside Caitlin and she moved inches from him, hands back on hips. 'I belong here Axon, and you know it. Okay, so I don't know the rules yet and feel way out of my depth, but don't for one minute think I need protection as Cassie does. Rory has spent years training me and I reckon I could take you on if you want me to prove it.'

Off balance from waving her arm around, she fell into his arms. Staring up into his handsome face, soaking in his dark, mysterious eyes and lustrous dark hair, she was glad it was he who finally spoke. 'Is that right, bruiser?' he mocked.

'Yes,' she said her voice soft and inviting. 'You, Axon Stanton, sure know just how to push my buttons, but you know that don't you?'

Caitlin smiled, stood up on tippy toes and playfully kissed his lips, then with a giggle went to run inside. She got only a few steps before feeling his arm around her waist as he swung her back to him. She was pressed up close, and her chest heaved with excited joy as his mouth came down on hers. His warm, sweet breath she remembered well, her eyes closed enjoying every moment of the tingle of sexual lust that had her tremble with desire. The wish to have this man in her bed was stronger than the last time they exchanged such passion. His hunger for her showed when she weakened from desire, as he lifted and cradled her, deepening the kiss which sent lustful shudders deep inside her. Caitlin felt they had both tapped into yearnings neither had previously known; maybe it only existed for them. She had never read or heard of kisses to give so much pleasure. She was falling for him in a big way and going by his insatiable desire, hoped he had a place in his heart for her.

Gently, he placed her back on her feet. Goosebumps and a tingle still ran throughout her body and she stood for a moment gazing into his captivating eyes, windows to his soul… that suddenly locked her out. A calming of her desire for him lessened with the tough guy look. Caitlin straightened and patted his arm, letting out enough power to make him jump with the electric charge. The leap of his body gave them distance enough for her to straighten more, and lift her chin with an indignant look before walking off on him. She looked back and he was shaking his head. Was that a slight grin she spotted for the first time today?

The kiss was unexpected; Caitlin coming to the realisation that what he said, and what he was thinking towards her was so very opposite. She now looked forward to getting to know her boss on a more personal basis and sniggered to herself. She would have to keep this quiet for his sake. But this also worked in her favour. Rory had changed towards her and she was unsure where she stood with him during this mission. To have the boss in her back pocket secured her position in the team regardless of how he felt. In a daze and dreams of the beginning of love, she joined the others who had gathered at Kayden's return.

Rory took Bree in the circle of his arms, lifting her off the floor in a hug when she ran over to him.

'I missed you, big fellow!' She smiled up at him. 'Have you finished yet or do you still have to do stuff?'

'Just a few more minutes Bree, honey.' He grinned back at her.

Caitlin watched on. She and Rory used to be like that together. She missed him but was happy he had found someone sweet and loving to spend his life with. Bree was honest and a lovely person. If it had to be anyone she was glad it was her.

Bree almost skipped away from him. She seemed so happy now he was back and poured herself and Caitlin another tea. 'Have a beverage with me, Caitie girl.'

Axon slipped it out of her hand. 'Don't Cait, you've had enough of this tea for one night,' he said and held it up. Caitlin jumped to grab it but his height played to his advantage, the black tea ending up on a shelf. He swung her onto the dance floor with him. 'You're such a little live wire; do you ever stop and take a breath?' He waltzed her around the floor.

'Yes, when you kiss me.'

Axon bent down and whispered, 'Not a good idea to remember that, whatever it was. And, that being said, quit sleazing up to the

Rulers, it doesn't become you.' He sounded exasperated.

Her eyes glazed over. *He lied!* 'Well, whatever *that* was it has happened twice now. As for Klim, give me some credit, I was nothing but a friendly companion to amuse him until you and Kayden were ready to speak to him.' She shook from his arms and strode off the floor. He didn't leave her side until she was back with her friends. Then he hurried off and joined Kayden, his movement rushed and annoyed.

Cassie offered Caitlin a cup of Mrs Lekett's addictive brew.

'The bully boss giving you a hard time?' Bree slipped an arm through hers. 'Give her a mug of it, Cassie.' She continued to console Caitlin.

Before long the girls were joking, noisy and were having such a good time together that even Lisha joined them. The four girls together was probably not a good idea. They became louder and ended up on the dance floor, their antics having those who watched in stitches of laughter. The only time they stopped was to sip more tea. By the time the men did join them, they didn't get a look in as the four girls stood arm in arm and swayed as they sang at the top of their lungs. Eventually, they sat in a circle and had a girl power chat until they fell asleep together.

* * * *

In the morning, Caitlin found she had a headache for the first time ever. Putting a hand to her temple, she nursed her throbbing head while looking for Axon. He was asleep in a chair when she found him and she squealed with surprise when he made a grab for her and pulled her onto his lap.

'What are you up to now?' he whispered loudly, trying not to wake everyone around him.

'Looking for you to apologise. I kind of ignored your advice and feel sore and sorry for myself for doing so.' Her tone was timid.

He shuddered as she wiggled closer into him. His reaction confirmed to Caitlin that he had feelings for her.

'Your head is aching, am I right?'

She nodded, as the throbbing pain and his sympathy made her frown.

A light sparked in his eyes. 'You wouldn't listen?'

'It was a girl thing. They encouraged me.'

'I'm sure they did! Hold still while I take away that ache. Although I should let you suffer a little for disobeying me.' He gave her a touch of his magic to rid her of it, ignoring her protest that she wasn't that bad.

He held each side of her head, his touch soft and delightfully refreshing, making her eyes close. Sudden warmth radiated from his fingers and took away all traces of the pain she had felt. Warm lips touched her and left her weak and breathless as she melted into his arms. He pulled away, apologising. 'Sorry, that wasn't part of it, but your lips are just so kissable.' He stood them both up.

'What! Is that it?' She raised her hand to her head. 'Hang on, I think it hurts again.'

'Caitlin, behave! That was nothing. I'm a man that's all. Don't make anything out of it. I'm going for coffee unless you can take away my headache as well.'

'Well, let's find a room. I'll give it a fair shot.' She chuckled uncontrollably.

He ignored her and left her to follow him, or not.

Well, that went well. Caitlin collected her dignity. *He so likes me.* She trailed behind him knowing he was heading for a coffee machine and that sounded too good to pass up.

Like an annoying child, she was at his side and chatted nonstop. He was relieved once they found Mrs Lekett in the kitchen. Caitlin gravitated towards the aroma of bacon and eggs, giving him peace.

'There is tea brewed.' Mrs Lekett smiled at Axon's strained features.

He politely refused the tea offered and instead, filled the coffee maker with fresh beans, opting to make a robust antidote.

Rory and Bree joined them, and Caitlin handed them an empty mug each. 'Hi guys, want a coffee? The boss just brewed some.'

Rory ruffled Caitlin's hair. 'Just so long as you didn't make it,' he said. He picked up the pot, filled both mugs and handed one to Bree.

'Not so good in the kitchen?' Axon raised his eyebrow, glad to find a fault in her.

Rory collapsed in the chair beside her. 'Axon, never, and I mean *never*, let that woman loose in the kitchen. Even on your best day, you'll want to kill her.'

Caitlin and Bree just laughed. 'I'm allergic to kitchens. They bite and burn and cut,' said Caitlin. 'I hate them.'

Axon seemed happy for a change; it was as if he deliberately looked for flaws in her. Caitlin glared at him before deciding to ignore him. *He just doesn't want to admit he's hot for me!* The thought made her smile and feel happy again. She had him pegged.

'So, what's the status on the battle between the disgruntled lovers and the opposing stars? Did it get sorted?' She changed the subject to show she wasn't just a funny girl that couldn't cook. There was more to her than that. She turned to Axon. 'What was the verdict? Does the prince get the girl?'

Axon put down his cup and sat back. 'Well, it's not completely sorted yet! We are to call in on the prince on the run home. Kayden worked out a deal with Klim last night, only he still needed to present the proposal to the two lovebirds. He's reasonably sure after they hear the plan, the disagreement will be resolved.'

'Man, Kayden's a smooth talker. I learnt so much yesterday,' Rory confided.

Axon had on his business look, and Caitlin tried not to smile. She adored the different personalities he allowed her to see. A hard-arsed businessperson and yet protective, and someone Caitlin was beginning to feel very safe around. Even if he wouldn't admit he liked her too, she hoped one day he would.

'So tell me,' Axon said calmly to Rory, 'do you feel more confident? And before you answer, I appreciate you still have concerns and agree, there will be mistakes made along the way. But I'm sure once you have your team trained the way you want them, those concerns will lessen. Even Kayden had his share of headaches while developing his group. That said, I have to warn, unlike his, your team will be dealing with planets, not stars. Most of the fun they have here may not be what you find where we are going. Where I take you there will be gods, goddesses, and hard-core Rulers that have done things their way for many centuries. I'm not trying to frighten you off, but I expect my team to be ten times better than Kayden's due to the situations we'll be faced with.'

He picked up his cup and drank the last of his coffee. The clunk of it on the saucer was loud as the noise around them had silenced. He knew he had given them something to think about and continued. 'You've all had a good laugh together, and I allowed it because it showed me you had a keen sense of humour. This, Kayden tells me, you will need to get you through some nasty situations you'll face up here.' He leant forward and clasped his hands on the table in front of him. 'After much consideration, I agree with Kayden and do think you and your team have what it takes to be the Riders I search for, but I have to know, do you believe so too?'

Rory glanced at his friends. 'Of course we can handle it. We get it, our missions will be more intense but those challenges you speak of, us lot will take on eagerly. My team works as hard as they play. I've been with them for a long time and have every confidence in them. I'm just glad you guys can see it in them too.'

Rory held up his cup to Caitlin in a toast, and both clinked the china before the rest of them joined in. 'To the planets!'

'And I pity the poor gods when they meet our Caitlin,' Rory stirred her. 'They are so not going to know what's hit them.'

'Horrible man!' Caitlin leant over, slapping Rory on the shoulder. 'You'll keep, buddy.'

It was only then that Caitlin noticed Bree had her head cocked to one side. Pale lips curved down and the creases on her forehead showed she was still uncertain.

Caitlin placed her hand over Bree's affectionately. 'Honey, this is what the rest of us have trained for and always hoped for, a chance to use our powers for good. We love you and want you to be part of all this, but if you want out, we can find another team member. This decision will not change our friendship. You will still be Rory's girl and my very best mate, always. But in saying that, I think you're putting too much pressure on yourself to take it all in at once. We'll all learn together. Yes, there will be some slip-ups I'm sure, although not from me!' she joked to lighten Bree's grip. 'However, as a team, there is nothing we can't fix. Just try and see it for what it is; one hell of a ride.'

Rory wrapped an arm around Bree. 'She'll be right, won't you muffin? I'll keep you safe, I promise.'

'Okay, I'll give it a go, but don't expect me to be as good as you lot just yet until I learn.'

'You are as good as we are, Bree, just give yourself a little time and you'll see it too.' Caitlin smiled when Rory gave her a grin and winked for helping.

'We're good then?' Axon asked.

Rory, Caitlin and Bree nodded.

'All ready and willing, Axon. Bree here just needs a bit of TLC. The others have been with me for years and are as tough as they come. Breezy's only been with us a short time, but she'll do just fine. You'll see.' Rory patted her hand and sat back.

'That's your responsibility and I'll expect you to make the hard call if any of your team doesn't work out or follow your leadership.' He shook Rory's hand. 'Welcome to the heavens and into the Riders contingent. I'll leave it up to you to tell the rest of your group. As for me, I have to let Zoren know I've picked my squadron and hope the news gets him off my back.'

'Have we got a cool name like the Cloud Riders? Please tell me we're not going to be mini me's and be called the Cloud Riders 11.' Caitlin pushed to find out what was on all their minds.

'Your new title will be the Cosmic Riders.' He paused while they cheered. When they silenced, he continued, 'And, Rory, I look forward to watching you develop your team members to the standard I will need you to be. In saying that I have no doubt after watching you in action, the Cosmic Riders will be the most talked about, innovative and proactive team the heavens have encountered.'

'I won't let you down, Axon,' said Rory.

'I know. That's why you are here. I trusted you from the moment I met you.'

With a handshake to Caitlin and Bree, Axon left the room to touch base with Zoren. Caitlin wondered how he would contact an angel but kept her mouth shut. That would be a question for another day. She wanted some alone time with just her friends. The excitement of Rory's decision and Axon's acceptance of her and the rest of the team with all their issues had her buzzing. She looked forward to knowing so much more about this mysterious new profession and, of course, Axon Stanton.

After an hour of happy chatter, Rory let the girls go to wake the others up to tell them the exciting news. Caitlin and Bree couldn't wait and jumped on Nate and Zeke. In retaliation, the boys tickled and gently ruffled them up. Kayden opened his eyes and smiled at the shenanigans while waking up Cassie. Jason and Ethan were on armchairs. Both girls stood at the ready to pounce, counting, one and two and three, so they could land at the same time. Bree leapt at Ethan, Caitlin at Jason and before they dropped on them, both men had woken and snatched the girls up in mid-air, their speed equal to a panther chasing its prey, running with them out into the pool and tossing them in. Bree and Caitlin were out like lightning, making a grab for the boys. Rory came in, snatched Bree from them and placed her behind him affectionately, waiting for a showdown. Ethan and Jason, never ones to back down, ran at him, both taking him down and pinning him beneath them on the floor.

'We have a traitor in our midst.' Jason chuckled. 'You hold him Eth, and I'll get the girl.' He dashed towards Bree, who was too fast, so he tried to grab Caitlin but Axon was too quick and they disappeared into thin air and reappeared in the kitchen.

'It'll take them a minute before they realise where I took you.' He shook his head at her. 'You won't learn, will you? I'm not going to spend the rest of my days saving you Cait, so be...' but before he could finish Jason and Ethan ran in and snatched her quickly out of his grip and sat her at the table between them.

Jason laughed. 'As punishment for playing dirty, you're not

allowed to have her back until we're ready. So whatever discipline you were dishing out just then will have to wait and there will be no negotiating.'

Axon opened his mouth but it was as far as he got. Jason put up his hand for him to stop. 'Axon we don't care if you are a Lord of the Planets with transportation abilities. You're not our boss! Our territory; our rules!'

Axon stood for a minute and Caitlin could tell he was plotting something until Kayden put his arm around him. 'Don't even try, mate, or they'll only make it a whole day exercise.' Kayden sat down with Cassie. 'Glad it's Caitlin this time instead of you, honey.'

Rory and Bree came in with flushed faces. Caitlin smiled, knowing exactly what they had been doing. Smooching, no doubt. Nate and Zeke almost knocked them over as they burst in the door to see what was going on. One look told them.

'You lot are crazier than us.' Nate said as he and Zeke pulled up chairs.

Conor and Lisha were last to come and join them. 'What did we miss? We heard the commotion.' Conor's sentence ended as his eyes rested on Caitlin. A teasing smile formed. 'Ahh, the red-head. Should have known she would give our boys trouble. Sorry Cait, I should have warned you what'd happen if you stir us up. *Not!*'

Caitlin pointed to Bree. 'What about Miss-butter-wouldn't-melt-in-her-mouth? She helped.'

'Your Protector was the one that turned this into a game and challenged us,' Ethan said putting his arm around her. 'Your boss needs to learn, not to mess with the best of the best.' He puffed out his chest. 'Newbies!' Ethan high fived him, agreeing.

Even Mrs Lekett gave a steaming kettle chuckle while she placed breakfast on the table. The two teams put aside the games while they dug into the delicious scones, pancakes and muffins, the conversation now on yesterday, all intent on learning the outcome.

Caitlin noted Kayden seemed different today, more relaxed, and didn't tease her once by relaying her thoughts, although he did keep glancing at her as he spoke about the men she met last night.

'Klim from the Milky Way is going to allow the Royals in love access through his Milky Way if the Prince stands down.' Kayden told them. 'Delta, the ruler from the Pegasus constellation who was with Klim last night, has offered to let the love birds use one of his winged horses.'

'Good news, right.' Caitlin was pleased to hear they were nice guys and she had got it right spending time with them.

Kayden nodded. 'It does enable them to travel back and forth from their Home Worlds whenever they wish and that is due to you, Caitlin.' He surprised her, the colour creeping into her skin as all eyes rested on her. 'The reason for their change of heart was the quirky and kindly friendship you freely gave to them last night. They trusted you and so, in turn, decided to trust us. This alone made them so much more agreeable and willing to compromise. When we left, Klim and Delta asked to pass on to you their gratitude for the unusually comical and enjoyable night. This extends to an open invitation to visit them anytime you wish. I did explain this was not your domain, but they insisted the treaty would only go ahead if you promised to keep in touch. Axon has already given permission for an off-world vacation once you settle into your new position.'

Caitlin smiled while remembering the stories of their homeland and how the Milky Way had a fun park that she'd pestered them to tell her about. 'Hot damn, guys, we're going to a theme park in the stars! Wahoo!' She stood, leant over the table and slapped at her friends' hands.

The chatter ran high with stories from Jason regarding the rides on Klim's Home World. It left team two excited. As they waved goodbye to Mrs Lekett and thanked her for her hospitality, they looked back on a now familiar sight that Caitlin would never forget. *Well, not the tea, that's for sure!* she pondered, waiting for her horse to arrive. The view was quite magical as she watched rabbits walking on back legs, complete with waistcoats and caps. The little munchkins guided the huge winged horses out from the forest, holding the reins with their little front paws.

Axon's eyes soaked in her every feature as she enjoyed the

procession and, catching him watching her, she smiled sheepishly. Jason and Ethan guarded her until the horses stopped in front of them. 'Okay Red, you're free to go but remember, we are the superior team and always will be,' Ethan stirred, hoping to get in the last poke.

'Boys, I could have had you on your arses if I wanted, but damn I enjoyed that bit of fun.' She showed honour in her response to their game.

Jason lifted a happy rider up onto her horse. 'You're all right Red.' He gave her the reins. 'Word of advice, try not to stir up the planet Rulers too much. They're not us. Well, at least make an effort to behave.'

'Cripes and Rory's had me on a leash. I've been on my best behaviour.' She straightened, acting prim and proper.

Jason and Ethan both cracked up laughing, Ethan slapping the leg of his pants. 'Man, she's trouble. Wish I could join their team.'

* * * *

Landing on Altair to speak to the Prince, Caitlin had to admire the sheer splendour of how Royalty lived. The castle's centuries-old architecture was impressive and utterly enchanting. Their orders were to stay put while Kayden, Axon, Woody and Rory went to negotiate. Caitlin protested, wanting just a peek inside the incredible and most likely historical attraction.

Jason lifted her from her horse, not giving them a chance to say, either way, placing her arm on his. 'Can't take you in Red, but I can show you around the grounds if you wish to join me in a short stroll.'

'Thank you, Jason, that's very gentlemanly of you.' She patted his arm and gave him a winning smile, 'I'd like that.' She turned and shot her nose up at Axon. His uncomfortable shift of posture gave her satisfaction.

Axon sensed her bubbly chatter was an act to get even more attention. *She is trouble with a capital T.* It frustrated him how the men, even married men, seemed to rally around her giving in to her every whim. She was sure no goddess, so it baffled him. *What was it about her…* A question that continued to play on his mind as he followed Kayden into the castle.

As Caitlin watched Axon leave, she secretly gloated her snubbing act had got to him. *He is so mine.* Or had she read too much into it? *Hope not.* He had insisted she, like the others, was to wait by the horses, and she knew it irked him that she never followed instructions. Her lips spread in a smile at the stubborn set of his jaw jutted out as he set off with the others into the castle.

Rory caught her eye. *You are so spoilt!* he mouthed as he turned to join Kayden on the overbridge which led to big golden gates that slowly opened before them.

'Are the gates real gold? They look so thick.' She spoke to Jason when the others were out of earshot.

'Sure are, they're made of pure gold. The Home Worlds here have existed for many centuries, some since time began. And it's the use of commodities such as this which gives the structure timeless durability.'

Caitlin liked the way Jason could act so old and wise when he wasn't fooling around as they did on their own. Here, on a ruler's turf, he was as she would expect, a notable Cloud Rider. She appreciated him sharing this change of demeanour, and popped it in her memory bank; how to speak and get respect. He was still teaching and she liked that he had seen something she needed to correct without chastising her. No more was necessary to be said, and she felt he knew that too. Caitlin got it, and with a smile, he walked beside her in silence. Bedazzled, her eyes soaked in the gorgeous landscape of this lavish Home World and wondered if it were indicative of the worlds she would encounter from now on. As they strolled, she was in awe of the lush grounds, each tree and shrub meticulously carved into shapes that represented so much of this universe she would now call home. A moat surrounded the castle, the water clear and clean as it washed over the rocky surface beneath. He led her into a courtyard, home to many unusual creatures. They were small and furry, yet shape-shifted when annoyed. They were similar to the dogitters from the last planet they were on, only these had wings and could fly off, although not too high.

Caitlin jumped when one came near. 'What the hell is that!' She took another side step away as it hopped slightly at her.

Jason was amused at her reaction. 'Similar to chickens on Earth; they lay eggs, but don't taste like chicken. More like a rabbit.'

'Yuk, hate rabbit.' Caitlin screwed up her face in disgust. 'Shoo … weird chickrabbit.' She waved her hands about, scaring it away.

He laughed. 'Very close, they're actually called chickbits.'

The threat eliminated, she identified with the animal and glanced down, her feet sinking into the thick lawn. Above, trees spread out big, expansive branches. The leaves were a gold and orange mixture, each tree full of songbirds that struck up a noisy chatter and fluttered around at the sound of gunfire. They swung round as a huntsman moved further into the woods, his kill, a lifeless-looking lamb, effortlessly thrown over his shoulder, his young companion letting out a shout of joy.

White blossoms fell from the trees as the wind blew gently, shaking them from the branches. Jason removed one of them that landed in Caitlin's hair. Without thinking her hands went up to helped brush away the rest. Her hair and skin were a surprise to Jason. He took hold of one of her hands. 'Geez Cait, your hair and hands feel like that of a child.'

'A story for another day.' Not wanting to spoil the moment explaining why, she smiled. 'I want to enjoy this time and not talk about me if that's okay.'

She was polite but firm, and Jason knew it was just one more mystery about Caitlin that would unfold when ready. He saw her eyes dart up and close as the sunlight danced on her skin. Golden beams lit up the trees, bringing them alive. It was as if someone had flicked a switch and hundreds of fairy lights illuminated the playground of the planet's animal kingdom. Jason took a step back as he watched, sure it was her that had lit up… or had it lit up to welcome her? He would have liked to watch this new mystery girl longer, but the sight of the team who had gone to negotiate was back in sight. 'Sorry Cait, it's time we went back to the others.' He saw her shake her head, smile and move an arm. *Did she wave goodbye?* He was sure she did.

They arrived back at the horses just in time. Jason was keen to learn what happened. With all the soothing magic Caitlin had projected, he felt the outcome had to be good.

'How did it go K?' Jason asked.

'Done!' Kayden looked pleased. 'Let's go home.'

CHAPTER SIX

Riders United

Caitlin felt it a kill joy when they arrived back on Kayden's farm after the thrilling ride they had just been on; that was until Woody suggested a swim and BBQ at their farmhouse next door. Caitlin had racked her brain as to how they would all sleep in Kayden and Cassie's modest two-bedroom house and was thrilled when she learned they would be sleeping next door in an eighteen-bedroom homestead. The prospect of having her own room for the night pleased her immensely. Kayden's home was all right for two people, but just resting up before they left on the mission was a task in itself as they all pushed and shoved for a bit of space to lay their heads. Outside, Kayden's farm was as pretty as a picture and the horses were adorable, but to sleep thirteen adults; *nightmare comes to mind.*

'So what, the boss lives here in Smallville with no frills, while you guys live it up next door in a mansion with a spa and pool.' Caitlin couldn't help herself.

Conor had his arm around Lisha and started grinning. 'He won't live with us because he won't share Cassie.'

Ethan chuckled and nudged Jason. 'But we don't put up with that rot. If he doesn't share we go over and steal her away.'

The men joked around as they began reminiscing about the last time they took her for a whole day and didn't get her back until late that night.

'Kayden was so pissed,' Jason recalled. 'We didn't go near him for days.' He let out a loud *ha*! This put the rest of them in fits of laughter.

Caitlin eyed Cassie quietly standing by her man, remembering the party-girl-Cassie from last night, and could see why they loved having her around. She sure made you have a good time, yet looking at her now; she was at ease and happy with just Kayden. The fun time girl from last night was nowhere to be seen. She comfortably fitted in with whoever she was with at the time. Caitlin wondered if she'd have that talent now as well since they had done the magical sharing thing. She hoped so because, with her red hair and temper, she had never been the IT-Girl.

Once next door, when there were no bridled horses to clothe them, Cassie took Caitlin, Bree, and Lisha upstairs to get changed for a swim.

'Where are Ella and Sonia?' Caitlin sifted through bather's drawer to find her size.

Cassie chuckled. 'When those two go shopping they call in on Ella's family. While the men are off saving the worlds, they amuse themselves and stay away to give their husbands time to wind down. Somehow, Ella just knows when Woody is ready for her. Amazing lady for a mortal.'

Lisha looked at her thin frame in the bikini she wore. 'Mortal lovers, not my style.' She huffed and left the room.

Caitlin and Bree glanced at each other and back at Cassie. Lisha was just being Lisha. What could they say?

Cassie shrugged. 'I agree.'

Her honesty had them burst out laughing.

'We so love you, Cassie.' Bree hugged her and, letting her go, turned back to Caitlin. 'Her humour is so similar to you Cait; she cracks me up.'

Cassie and Caitlin grinned at each other. Both girls had become friends and found this a compliment.

'Come on girls,' Cassie grabbed both their hands. 'Come and meet the gang off duty. You'll have a blast.'

Caitlin looked forward to getting to know the rest of Kayden's team now the work day was over. She ran beside Cassie, both her and Bree raced her down the stairs.

When they got out to the patio, the guys were already in the pool fooling around. Cassie was as gutsy as they came and dived straight into the middle of them and was lifted up into Kayden's arms as if he felt her coming. She giggled and laughed with him, showing no fear of being hit by the others as they flung arms and legs and jumped around her. *Trust*, Caitlin thought. Something she had yet to learn. *Here goes nothing*. She gave herself little time to think and, throwing her towel aside, did the same. Rory caught her and tossed her up in the air, and as she dived under the water, the next to snatch her up was Axon.

Caitlin looked over at Bree and Lisha. 'Come on, it's fun; just dive in the middle of them, they can feel you coming.'

They raced each other to the edge of the pool, hurling themselves in the middle, and instantly they found protection in someone's arms. Caitlin heard Bree squeal as they tossed her about until she ended up in Rory's arms. Caitlin relaxed, glad that Bree had listened to her.

Turning back to Axon who still held her, she caught him checking out her body in the skimpy bikini. Not even an ounce of embarrassment did he show. In any other situation, she would have slapped someone ogling her in that way, but his eyes burned into hers with something she didn't expect; admiration. 'You're one impressive woman, Cait.'

A little shaky and not quite sure what to say to that, Caitlin wiggled from him and splashed at him to hide her confusion. She'd sensed by his kisses he was interested, but only now saw so much more. Holding her had left him shaken. Unprepared for this reaction, his feelings were revealed. Rather than make him uncomfortable by commenting or discussing it like adults, she decided to dive sideways and get as far from him as she could. She didn't want that moment ruined by the off-handed remarks he generally made. Something off-putting like, *I am a man. That's what we do – look!* She had little time to reflect as another pair of hands gripped at her waist.

'Jason!' she squealed, and with a wink, he threw her high into the air, a movement that put her back in the middle of the fighting mess again.

This time Ethan lifted her up and out, setting her onto the edge of the pool, somehow picking up that she needed time out. She smiled as he touched her nose affectionately before jumping back into the game.

Caitlin moved from the edge of the pool into the spa, now questioning how well they could feel her. Ethan's foresight and sweetness had surprised her. In the spa, she was joined by Axon, Kayden and Cassie and listened to them talk as she leant back and closed her eyes. The gentle stir of the jet stream moved her just enough to take her from their chatter and into the worlds where she wished to live forever. She imagined a life with a man such as Axon, in a world unlike this, her mind's eye conjuring up a lifetime of wonderment.

'Wake up Red, you're mine.' Woody broke her blissful trance.

'What?' Caitlin sat up with a jolt and saw Woody and Rory looming over her.

Caitlin already knew the potential that existed within her after Cassie's powerful influence. To have such a gift did her head in, but not at the minute, not with all the powerful and influential immortals that she for once felt at home around. A one on one with Woody wasn't what she felt like right now.

Rory offered a helpful hand, Caitlin smiled while gripping it and pulled herself out of the water. She listened to Rory intently while drying off with a towel.

'We have talked about much, Cait, but you need more in-depth awareness than I can provide to get you into prime form. Woody has a gift that we believe can help bring out the powers Cassie has inaugurated in you. While on the job, she used her inner psyche to help you, but on our next mission, she will not be there. You have to be able to do it on your own. Woody's the best there is to peel away layers to discover the magic beneath.'

'But I'm feeling okay, Rory.'

'Cait, let Woody in, that's all I'm asking.'

'All right!'

He rolled his eyes at her tone. 'Just do as you're told, short stuff, or else.'

Only he knew what she might have to divulge, things his friend had long forgotten, and with a hug, he darted off. This left Caitlin to ponder, *what's with all the concern?*

She threw on some shorts and a top, not wanting to hold Woody up. She followed him around the other side of the house where it was quiet. They talked, but it kept going in circles, confusing Caitlin. Woody continued to ask about her childhood. Repeatedly, she told the stories she had told for years. They started out as fairy tales to hide the truth, but these stories Caitlin grew to believe.

Not Woody. He kept digging, and she kept evading. 'Honestly, I lived like a princess, waited on hand and foot and that is why I have no idea how to do even the basics.' She pursed her lips, annoyed, but he persisted.

'How did you meet Rory?'

She pulled her eyebrows together and blinked as her head cocked to the side. 'Rory found me, can't recall where. He educated me, gave me homeschooling and so much more.'

'Like?'

'Well, how to cook for instance, although he didn't do so well teaching me that task. I'm an absolute nuisance in the kitchen, total klutz.'

'What about housework? Can you clean?'

'Rory got sick of patching me up and organised a house cleaner.'

'You dress beautifully, so you obviously knew about fashion.'

'Rory.' She sighed and put her head down. 'He has taught me everything I know. Yes, even fashion, although his sister, Lisha, was a great help in that department too.

Believe me; I couldn't even boil water without burning myself or blowing up the kettle when I met them. Rory has even gone as far as paying for an instant hot water tap to be installed for me, and does that every time we move.'

Woody's frustration started to show. 'Caitlin, with all that magic Cassie has shared with you, I have to say, it's epic. Because of this, I need to warn you to stop keeping the door to your past so tightly shut, or, my friend, you will become a walking time bomb. So I beg you to let me in, it's for your own good, I swear. Just give me one truth about your life before meeting Rory.'

'Why is it so hard for you to believe that I was just a spoilt princess?'

'I know the hum of royal blood. Cait, I'm sorry, but I don't believe your story. Yours is untainted, saintly. With your permission, I'd like to discuss this with Rory. Let's have a break.'

She shrugged. 'Go for it. I have nothing to hide.'

Woody watched her walk away, unable to help her until she was ready to trust him completely. She was lying and he knew it, but until she could remember what actually happened to her, it was a waiting game. He watched the proud, squared shoulders, the bright red hair, and the texture so soft and childlike. The wind whipped it wildly and even her walk showed strong will and someone who would go to great lengths to achieve total perfection. She was one extraordinary woman. No, this person was destined for much more than he initially thought. It was then it dawned on him that her childhood might be even worse than Cassie's. Maybe her secret was buried so deep even she knew nothing of it. Even Cassie worked out what she was destined for within the first year of her immortality. Cait had been immortal for a few years now, so why didn't she know? He got up from the tree trunk they had sat on, stretching his neck, realising this was far too deep to uncover in just one session, even for his magic. All he could do for now was to teach her to direct her powers using her mind instead of her body's physical strength. Her other powers wouldn't develop further until she was ready to face her past.

Caitlin hugged into Nathen. He and Zeke were manning the BBQ.

'What's up, Red? The other redhead giving you a hard time?'

Zeke flipped the biggest steaks she had ever seen.

'I don't want to talk about it,' she grumbled.

Nathen gave her a squeeze. 'Want me to thump him for you?'

'No, just want a cuddle.'

Nathen raised his eyebrows and gave Zeke one of his looks, both men working it out once they glanced over at Rory who was now deep in conversation with Woody. They knew it was about her. Otherwise, it would be Rory she would want support from.

* * * *

Ella and Sonia arrived home. They had gone to the city the day their men went on the mission. They'd met both their mothers at the Casino and the four women had such a good time, they'd decided to stay a couple of nights to go shopping in the city.

Ella and Sonia were excited when they pulled up to find so many cars parked on the lawn. It meant that everyone was home, safe and sound, and there was a party going on.

Both looked forward to seeing Conor's brother, Tremaine, as his van was parked directly in the driveway. They exchanged glances. If he was on his own, he would have come by horse.

'Tonight will be a big one,' Ella turned off the engine.

'Wonder how many backpackers Tremaine brought with him. Not sure how much fruit will be picked tomorrow.'

'The stories of travel those backpackers tell, have me so envious.' Sonia looked dreamy. 'Wish just once we could go on a trip overseas with our men.'

'One day; until then we will have to put up with each other.' Ella reached into the back seat to grab her purchases.

Sonia smiled. 'We do have fun. Guess they'd be bitchin' in no time if they had to shop for hours. Na… leave 'em home. You're right. What am I saying.' They both chuckled.

Ella pointed to a sports car and two more parked behind it. 'Look, Pam is here too. Guess she's been asked to bring some friends for the newbies. Come on, let's leave the rest of these bags of shopping for the morning. I want a hug from my man.' Ella closed the car door and both girls headed inside.

Once the girls arrived, it made Caitlin relax to see Woody busy. At least he looked more interested now in Ella than feeling the urge to dig into her past. She still had no idea why it worried him, but one thing that did come out of it; she was feeling much better after speaking to Woody, well, until Rory's name was mentioned. *Discuss what with Rory?* A little cross at him still, Caitlin huffed past the love birds to join Rory now he was free. *May as well get it over with and find out what was said.* However, to her surprise, Rory chatted about anything but the session.

Ethan joined them too, standing with his arm around a short woman, shorter than her, whom she learned was Pam, a new flame. Caitlin observed the conversation and came to the understanding that only wives were privy to the secrets about the Riders. She noted how often the subject changed quickly to cover the slips made by them. Luckily Pam seemed a bit of an airhead and didn't even notice.

'Who are those two women with Nate and Zeke? Did they come with you, Pam?' Caitlin noticed they were overly dressed.

'Oh, they are singles from out of town. When Ethan rang me a couple of days ago, he said they were expecting guests. He asked if I could arrange an extra couple of ladies to you know, entertain them.' She winked. 'He is so funny. He never wants the same girls twice, except me.' She grinned and looked pleased.

'So that sorts out Nate and Zeke, but what about Conor?' Caitlin asked looking over at Conor.

Pam giggled. 'This afternoon I was told a third was not necessary. I mean, I don't want Ethan thinking he has a choice. When I arrived, saw why, Conor is very content with your friend, Lisha. I was introduced to her earlier. She gave me the evil eye until she saw I was with Ethan. Don't think either of them needs company at the minute if you know what I mean.' Her smile gave away the obvious enjoyment of sharing the gossip.

Caitlin eyed the tall, elegant women and finally got what she was alluding to. 'They're escorts?'

'No love, out in these parts they prefer to be called attending angels. Angels my arse, they aint getting anywhere near my man the gold diggers.' Pam placed an affectionate hand on her arm. 'But hush now! That's our little secret.'

Caitlin realised Pam was no dummy after all. She just chose to keep her thoughts to herself and stay all sweet and cute for Ethan's sake. Caitlin looked forward to spending more time with Pam, the gossiper. She had much to learn about her rivals, the Cloud Riders.

She made a mental note to remind Lisha that Conor was only her equal and, when not in training, she should give him some space. It was while she watched that reality struck, that the attention they received pointed to only one conclusion; that they were still in training. The message had been received and understood, that just because they would be stuck at home most of the time, it didn't mean they couldn't have some enjoyment. Partying, for them, had always been with strangers, never allowing anyone to get close. Here, they got Conor's brother to bring his fruit pickers and Pam to organise call girls to party with them. They were never around long enough to question why they never changed in looks. Using strangers from far off places meant they kept their "never ageing" issue a secret. She smiled. *They're pulling out all stops to school us on all aspects of their operation.*

As Caitlin searched the yard for other unusual events to support her theory, she spotted Jason and Woody who looked more like little boys at the minute while their wives fussed over them. Kayden sat with Cassie by the pergola. He had a contented slouch as he ran his hand up and down her back while they spoke. Both had taken full advantage of the time they had alone.

Her eyes finally settled on Axon who leant against a pillar, his arms folded. A slight smile that touched the corner of his mouth drew her to him. His grin as she neared melted her every step.

'What?'

'There is nothing you're not taking in, is there, Caitlin.'

'I'm learning,' she said, still watching the others. 'There is so much love between them that it kind of blows me away. It's like they're all so different, yet one solid unit. Do you think our group is really going to be as remarkable as theirs?' She was more saying her thoughts out loud than really expecting an answer.

'Our group will be better! We have you!'

'That's if I can keep out of trouble for five minutes.'

His eyes swept across her lips, and Caitlin held her breath. Did he want to kiss her again? *Oh yes, yes,* she hoped so.

Her thoughts of them being together overwhelmed her and just as she was about to make a move on him, and drag him from prying eyes so she could smooch him, Jason called out, 'Are you all in for a game of cards?'

The moment was ruined as Axon held up his hand, his eyes diverted from her. 'I'm in.' He strode off.

Caitlin was beginning to have strong feelings for this sweetie and yet he confused her. There was chemistry, she felt it, so why push her aside? With a deep breath, she pulled her emotions in check and spun on her heels.

'Me too! Wait up,' she called to him, but he had slipped through the doors, leaving her to chase after him.

Groups were chosen, and every table was instructed to continue until there was only one winner. The winner of each group then played the winner of another until only one winner stood. House rules were given, but all else was approved, which included practical jokes to put the winner off.

'Let the battle begin.' Jason filled his mouth with a savoury snack and swallowed its entirety as he knocked on the table for the games to start. Mumblings of good luck erupted as the first hands were dealt. Caitlin concentrated on Cassie. She connected to her as taught and soaked in how she played the game. Cassie felt her and gave Caitlin a smile. She lifted a glass to her equal and winked.

Caitlin's nightclub days had paid off. She could still hold her own, so it was no surprise when it finally came down to her and Cassie who played each other. They were so evenly matched they ended up just calling it a night, much to the disappointment of the cheer squad that stood behind them. And, unknown to the supporters, Cassie had made a secret pact with her to end it, so neither of them looked bad in front of their team members. Arm in arm the two girls moved to the couch and collapsed, very pleased with the outcome. Kayden held out his arms to Cassie and laughed with her as he escorted her upstairs to bed.

Tired, Caitlin lay back and fell into a deep sleep.

* * * *

Next morning when Caitlin woke, the sun was streaming in through an open window. Birds chirping were the only sound that filled the quietness of the room.

'Where is everyone?' she mumbled, rolling off the sofa. Her first thought was to go and find Axon and use some excuse that she hadn't thought of yet, to wake him. To see his tousled hair and sleepy movement first thing in the morning she felt would give a lovely start to the day. The thought had her racing up the stairs.

Most of the doors were open, so Caitlin stopped at each one. The bedrooms became a blur to her while staggering up and around the twisting corridors. The last door was ajar. With a slight push and a peek around the corner of it, she found Axon. Her shock at seeing him in bed with another woman had her feet stuck to the floor. Her first reaction was to feel embarrassment from spying on him, intruding in on his privacy, but the next was fury.

He had kissed her, twice now. Had she got it so wrong that he had flirted and felt something more for her than just a fling? That passionate kiss in the stars and now he lay with another – *What a tease!* The hair prickled the back of her neck as her anger grew.

'Eeeerrrr,' Caitlin growled through clenched teeth, waking him up. A pillow on the floor was her weapon of choice, and she hurled it at him before sharply turning. 'You big fat loser,' she snapped and stomped out of the room.

Back down the hall, Rory and Bree's voices carried and she followed the sound to their room.

'What's up Cait?' Bree patted the bed for her to sit and join them. 'You're as white as a ghost, sweetie.'

'I – I thought Axon liked me.' Her voice shook.

Rory sighed, stretched and leaned on his elbow. 'I knew this was going to happen, Cait. He is our boss; surely you didn't think you had a chance with him.'

She sniffled. 'I really liked him, Rory, so don't.'

'Sorry, but if I can't be honest with you, then we have bigger problems than you and Axon.'

Bree pushed him and he rolled on his back, hands under his head, not impressed. 'Rory, stop being unkind to her. It's getting annoying. She has come to us for sympathy, not a lecture. Sometimes I worry about how you treat her. Is this how we will end up one day too?'

His head jerked to look at her so fast his neck cracked and Bree, being Bree, grinned. 'Well, that snapped you out of it. Now can we get back to Cait?'

He rolled towards Bree, took her hand and kissed it. 'I'd never get cross at you gorgeous. I'll zip it.'

She rolled her eyes at Cait. 'Pay no attention to him. He is under just as much pressure as us. Now, what happened? But start from the beginning because Rory didn't tell me about any of this.' She held her hand and patted it, consoling her.

'It doesn't matter now; Axon must have been teasing me. He is nothing but a flirt, and I hate him for making me feel something for him.'

Rory put his hand on her shoulder. 'He's not good enough for you Cait. Mr Right is out there, but for now, let's just get back to being a team again and forget about love for a while. We have much to learn and I need you. Please let it drop.'

Caitlin smiled weakly. 'You're right, he isn't worth the bother. Consider it dropped!'

Years of friendship had taught her that what Rory said, he meant. In her mind, she was programmed to listen and obey their leader. There could be only one, and he had always been it, but her heart tugged at her core. Could she forget that kiss?

* * * *

Later that morning, after more sleep and a shower, Axon came downstairs, and it only took one glance at Caitlin to see her mood had not improved. Impulsively, he called upon Rory to get his team together. It was time to leave.

Chapter Seven

A Home at Last

The air was thick between Caitlin and Axon, and yet, much to Rory's surprise and joy, Axon still hired his whole team. They had a short two-hour drive to their new base of operation. It was on acreage miles from nowhere, but close enough to Kayden's group if they needed each other.

Caitlin was super quiet on the drive. She was embarrassed, believing she had caused this quick departure. There had been whispers as they got into the four-wheel drives and even now she felt Rory's eyes on her in the rear-view mirror.

'You'll make it through this experience stronger and better for it,' Rory had said before they left Kayden's farm. He had no idea Axon was her first kiss and this was not just a kiss for her. However, in the spirit of kindness, she tried not to spoil everyone's fun. This was a big moment and something they had dreamed of for years. A place to call home was epic.

As for Axon, Caitlin didn't want to hear any of his lies; she just wanted the team to be together and for him to go back to wherever the hell he came from.

* * * *

The long dirt driveway seemed as if it would never end and as they bumped along the corrugation, her eyes diverted out at the barren sparse landscape. It was so unusual. Red dirt with tumbleweeds, big old boulders and dead trees that resembled sticks poked out of the dry soil. The only bushland was far from them. She turned her attention to the front windscreen, the heat from the ground distorting the road ahead. Her friends became silent as the vehicle's tyres skidded to a halt.

She peered out the opposite window. It was dusty but she could make out the house they would now call home. It was grand and plenty big enough for them all to live in. In fact, she could barely see the top of the second storey. *Why am I not thrilled?*

'Yahoo!' Zeke opened the door and sprang out first.

'What a beauty.' Nathen whistled as he craned his neck, taking in the entirety of the building.

'Hot damn, I'm so in heaven right now!' Lisha wiped her eyes.

'Oh Cait!' Bree gripped her hand. 'You and Rory have always said one day we would have a property and live away from prying eyes. It's finally happened.'

Rory put an arm on Axon's shoulder. 'Man, you are my hero.'

'It's yours.' Axon gave him the keys. 'Go and take your friends in for a look.'

'Do you know how hard I have been saving to give something like this to my guys? And without asking for a cent, just our promise of loyalty, you're giving this to us. I can't believe our luck.' Rory wiped away a tear of joy, pretending he had something in his eye. He turned and lifted Bree, swinging her around. 'I'm just so damned happy, sweetie; it's our very own home for as long as we want. No more moving.' He laughed with her and gulped back emotions as Bree sobbed on his shoulder, overwhelmed.

Caitlin was surprised and pleased, but there was also a pang of loss which took away some of the joy. She and Rory had many dreams together, but this wasn't quite how she pictured it; she'd always imagined it would be her in Rory's arms getting hugged. She looked around for Axon. He had hurt her too, but neither seemed interested in showing her any kind of affection. Not that she really wanted his arm around her while she was so cross with him, but it would have been nice for him to at least give her a moment of his time. Maybe a hug to break the ice between them or he could stand beside her, allowing Caitlin to say her piece so they could at least part on talking terms. This experience had taught her a big lesson for falling for someone like him. The sweetness of yesterday gone, crushed by the two most important men in her life, Caitlin was left emotional and sad. And even though Rory was not on her best friends list today, he was right about Axon. The relationship with someone so worldly would never have worked. *Anyway, I want to be a rider, not a wife who stays home. What was I thinking?* Axon and Rory had let her down; had now both made it clear, there would never be anything more to their personal relationships. They would only ever be her bosses. Acutely aware of this, she found it helped put things into perspective. From now on, she would respect them as such, but for anything more, they would have to prove their worthiness to her.

Her thoughts were interrupted as Axon suddenly appeared at her side. 'Cait, we have to talk!'

Here was her chance. She could barely make eye contact, but she wanted to put whatever it was between them to rest, once and for all. She kept her emotions out of the response. 'I apologise for expecting more than you could give, Axon. That display back there put me in my place as it was meant to; you are my boss and duly noted, message received loud and clear. Therefore, I intend to respect you as such and, I expect the same courtesy… don't ever kiss me again.' Caitlin gave a respectful nod, turned her back and with intent in her step, strode over to Zeke and Nathen to keep well away from further interactions.

Early the next morning, Axon woke Rory and they spent hours on their own in the satellite room, locked away, before he grabbed a quick bite to eat and was on his way. His departure got Zeke excited.

'Is he going to teach us how to do that too?'

Rory smiled. 'Only those with titles up there, have transport abilities. Sorry bud. I went on a secret trip with him this morning to meet Zoren and found out then.'

'Far-out! You met the angel. Was he really cool.' Nathen grinned, excited.

'You will meet him when we go up on a mission and yes, he is all you might imagine and more.'

'Freaky! With all these powerful gods and angels we'll be crossing paths with,' Lisha shivered, 'we'd best start training now. This job just went up a whole other notch.'

None of this fazed Caitlin as she was still cross that Axon didn't attempt to pull her aside and say goodbye. *I probably deserved it. I did put him at arm's length.* Still, she kicked the stones around outside as she sulked. *He could have at least tried to stay friends. But as if he would be interested in a girl from Nowheresville. I thought there was love in his kiss. There was in mine!* She turned and wiped a tear.

* * * *

Days and weeks passed. Training had consumed them, but finally, Rory felt they were ready and contacted Axon to find out their first mission. He was unreachable until the end of the week so had given the team some R&R.

Caitlin walked around the empty house. Most of the team had gone riding together, but she preferred to hang out and rest. The house had fourteen rooms, four bathrooms and the biggest kitchen ever, but none of them felt enticing enough to sit in. Outside, she walked past the lap pool and spa and wandered around the grounds. She stood and stared at the flower beds which had only just been planted, and noticed burnt patches in the freshly laid turf. The sun was hot, and both areas needed water. In the barn, she searched for a hose, and, seeing the bale of hay had been moved, stepped on the landing which took her down to the Vault. It was their underground control chamber the Cloud Riders called the satellite room, and because it was secretly locked away from prying eyes, and it was theirs, they wanted a better name for it.

At the bottom, she walked into the first office where she found Rory. 'I didn't realise you stayed. Thought you'd gone riding with the others. You gave us all the day off, and that means you too.'

'You know me.' He shrugged.

'Yes, you're a workaholic.' She folded her arms and leant against the door frame. When he went back to what he was doing, she straightened, ready to leave. 'Look, I'm going to tend the garden; sure you don't want to have a break and get down and dirty with me?'

'Gardening! Cait, you have to be kidding me. Are you really?'

'Yep. Come or not!' She waved her hand in the air upon leaving.

'Gardening!' She heard him laugh. 'Might just have to come up later to see that miracle.'

Caitlin grabbed what she needed and headed off to tend to the garden. They had a gardener twice a week, but Caitlin wanted to dig, weed and feel the earth. She didn't care if it meant spending the day in the scorching sun.

The sound of her horse grunting disturbed her at one stage. With a stretch, Caitlin lifted her head. Over in the paddock, Shargan, her magical ride, stood in the river bopping her head up and down frantically as her hoofs beat in the water, the motion splashing the new horses. Kayden's ranch hand had dropped them off for them to care for earlier in the week. The new horses were not yet used to the surroundings or to her horse. The excessive playful motion sprayed water on the others, annoying them enough that they backed away from her. Shargan sounded almost as if she laughed at them. Caitlin grinned and continued working. Her horse was a chestnut red and the mare had her temper but also her sense of fun.

It was nice to have time on her hands to enjoy these moments and to think. To reflect was something of a rarity in a house full of rowdy friends. She looked far into the distance but the others were well out of sight now. Zeke, Nathen, Lisha and Bree had taken their horses for a ride. They said they were following the river to where Axon had told them there was a waterfall. Thinking of him, she dug energetically at some tough weeds that had lodged between two rocks. Finally, she pulled them free and stood up, wiping the back of her hand across the perspiration on her brow. *Maybe I should jump on a trail bike and catch up with the others.* To swim in dark, forbidden waters somewhere cool that would scare the life out of her suddenly appealed. She had seen aerial shots of where the waterfall fell into the river below and it looked as if shapes were lurking in the depths. *That would surely take my mind off…* she wasn't sure what. She just knew she was a bit out of sorts and had felt like this for a couple of weeks. Her roommates, on the other hand, had taken to their new surroundings and had settled in just fine. Rory had commented that they should enjoy it while it lasted; it would not be long before Axon said, enough training, it's time to earn what you have been given. *Sometimes in these peaceful surrounding, I could easily forget we are actually laying our lives on the line for the planet now.*

* * * *

It had been a long day. Caitlin glanced in the mirror as she brushed her teeth. Her eyes were sunken and dark from lack of sleep, but she was hopeful that the hours of gardening would mean tonight she would be physically tired enough to do more than doze for a few minutes at a time.

* * * *

Caitlin looked at the clock. Had it really been four hours of tossing and turning? In the morning a call to Woody might help her state of mind. Maybe he could come for a visit and help with whatever it was that haunted her so. She remembered that during their last meeting, he had warned her she might feel strange due to a power overload. Maybe that was all this was and after all, he had told her to contact him the minute she felt a bit *off*. Why had she not remembered sooner? A moan passed her lips as she rolled out of bed, opted for some fresh air that would do for now and wandered outside. It was dark and a slight breeze that whipped up made her shiver. To stroll in silky shortie pyjamas was not a good idea. Caitlin cursed that she hadn't grabbed a robe and considered going back, but instead continued, her mind taking her into nothingness, her pace fast, each step stretched out until it turned into a jog, as each stride helped to ease… what? Enjoying the freshness against her cheeks, her body numb and with her mind in tatters, she pushed forward to have it feel again, any sensation would do. *I feel free.*

* * * *

The view of stables and horse paddocks blurred as she passed them and sounds blended into silence as this hazed state of mind drew her in deeper. Chaotic images left imprints and rattled her inner consciousness that was not at all in tune with her body, but deep within itself.

The new day broke, and an exhausted Caitlin plopped down on the ground to watch the sun come up and continued to dream of a time when she was back up in the stars, where she felt the happiest she'd ever been in her whole life. *Where did my happiness go? Was it all just magic?*

Her focus fell on her feet as her gaze dropped sadly to the ground. 'Oh my GOD!' Panic built inside her at the damage this walk had caused. Her head bent to view the source of painful throbbing she'd only just noticed. The right leg was dirty and scratched up. Blood seeped from gashes, some wide open, *is that bone?* An inspection brought the realisation the other leg was no better. In distress she checked her feet and pushed them away with horror, stretching them out so she couldn't see them as well. Her hands gripped at the gravel with the pain the action caused, her breaths came short and sharp, and her heart pumped at a rapid pace. She was ready to throw up, not knowing how this happened to her. *I have to calm down.* Her head moved from side to side, her eyes flickered to every direction, not knowing where she was. She gingerly moved her gaze to each arm. The scratches and slashes made her look as if she'd been attacked by a pack of wild animals with claws. *Could the bush have done all this?* She viewed the thick prickly scrub that surrounded her, knowing she must have pushed her way through it to get to this open space.

Grabbing a stable branch from a tree that had fallen, Caitlin used it to hoist herself up and screamed out with pain, 'Someone help, please, can anyone hear me?' With her throat dry and emotions running high, the sound was barely a whisper. 'Which way is home?'

Her hopes shattered, as that too was hardly a sound against the faint splash of water. *Water!* The sound perked her up and reaching out, she grabbed another dried stick for support. Delicately placing each step, her face pinched with pain as her aching torn feet shuffled towards the waft of dampness. Her immediate thought was that the guys always followed the river and maybe, just maybe they might think to do it this time. *Surely, they would know that if I was lost, this is where I would go.* She freaked out with each step, already seeing the frustrated look on Rory's face when he saw the magnitude of her wounds.

He would be cross she hadn't gone to him if she had problems and she wished now her mind had not hidden them from her as well.

Even worse was Axon's predicted response, kicking her out of the group because they couldn't trust her not to do something so bizarre again.

Overwhelmed and in much pain, a distressed Caitlin collapsed awkwardly on the ground to rest. *If he doesn't, Rory will for sure.* She was still lost in thought and confused, and the possibility of her being off her tree scared her. Rory would think it was jealousy as they had only started to argue since he and Bree had become an item. Sure it wasn't jealousy and that he was just getting on her nerves, she shook that theory off. But the concern didn't go away. That was what he would think. *This might be all he needs to get rid of me for good.* Her eyes welled up again. Her temper had been out of control lately and now this! Loud sobs sent tears streaming down her cheeks, and she snuffled into the back of her hand, wiping the sadness from her face.

After much heartache, the gloomy mood lifted as her passion for surviving stirred. *Sitting here wallowing in my own self-pity is not going to help.*

With a heave, the strain and pain of getting to her feet with gusto hurt, but that soon was transferred into positive energy, giving her the strength to move. Maybe once she made it to water and washed the blood and dirt off, it would look much better. *Yes!* Caitlin gave herself a pep talk. *A clean-up, a rest and then …* The positive thoughts as she crept along battled the mindset not to go any further. *Just one more step and then another.*

* * * *

The water was a welcome sight. Caitlin crawled the last few metres and saw the waterfall over the other side of the stream. It was stunning. *How did I make it this far?* That thought slipped from her mind as the feet she was dangling in the water hurt, the damage evident, her feet swollen so much they were twice their normal size. After a good soak and with the pain manageable, just a throb, Caitlin pulled her legs out to dry. The hot sun that bit into her skin worried her more than her injuries as she carefully dragged her tired, battered self under a lush old willow tree nearby, thankful for its large branches and droopy leaves that gave her shade from the harsh climate. Sleep had evaded her for so long and yet here, in this secluded heaven, sleep came easy and she curled up without movement until night fell again. Thirsty, she used her hands and knees to get back to the water, not even being able to stand anymore, glad for the full moon that gave light as she soaked her soreness again in the clean and refreshing water.

Huddled back under a tree, the cold breeze didn't bother her. The sun and windburn from the day left a mild sting to her skin as her eyes closed and the comfort of sleep took hold. Her last thoughts were of planets, Home Worlds and castles in the sky. Dare she imagine a new life or was it now just a dream? Had she ruined it all?

The sun was high in the sky before a sound disturbed her. Instinct and fear had her sit up and tense, her eyes blinded by the light of day. A distorted shape headed for her, but was it animal or human? Her eyes were out of focus and she couldn't tell.

'Who is it?' Caitlin cringed, and pressed her back into the trunk of the tree, her words barely a sound, although she prayed it was help. A hand reached for her, shading the light, closer now.

'Axon!' She gulped air as she heaved out a cry of gratitude as he lifted her into his arms. 'Don't sack me.' She freaked out as he checked her feet, his eyes saying what he didn't.

He bent his head, shading her face from the light. 'Shh, you aren't going anywhere. Just relax and let me get you somewhere safe.'

He held her with one hand as if she was light-weight and touched a device in his ear. 'I've found her and she's in quite a state.'

There was silence while Rory talked.

'No, just scratched up and bruised,' Axon said.

Rory must have flipped out as usual. He trusted no doctors, ever.

'I realise your doctors aren't trustworthy. I'll take her to my home and have her checked out there.'

He listened again. Rory talked so loudly she almost heard his words or could imagine them, going off his tree at her recent behaviour and now this.

'I know you want her home there with you Rory, but I have a mission for your team. You will be unable to care for her while gone. I'm sorry, but this out of your hands. She will need bed rest and my employees are well equipped to care for her.' He hung up.

* * * *

Caitlin closed her eyes, ready for the strange trip she was to experience, glad she didn't have to face Rory just yet, amazed when, seconds later, she opened them to a huge room, antique furniture, walls of murals and heritage paintings. Many she thought might be of the family. She presumed the scenery on others might depict the world outside this stylish manor. As Axon carried her up the staircase, she heard the irritated snap in his tone as he barked out orders, half in English, the other in an ancient tongue. The instructions had the servants scurrying off and out of sight. She did pick up some of it.

'Ring Doc Petersen! Run a bath! Cook a plain omelette! And bring me some clean clothes.' He held her out and viewed her. 'Size 4,' he grumbled, kicking open a bedroom door, and carried her inside. Another call must have come through. He tapped his ear again and listened with eyebrows squeezed together while placing her gently on a bed.

'Wow!' Caitlin swept her eyes around the room at the elegance.

Her frame felt tiny on the four-poster bed draped in silk. The softness was dreamy and made her eyes close but they snapped open at his stern voice. 'I need you now!' The tap of the ear again had her guess he'd hung up.

'It's just a few scratches, really, I feel fine.'

'Caitlin, you're far from fine. You're a mess, please, relax until I've had you seen to. Don't fight me on this!' His temper frayed, his worry for her health as one of his new team members was just one more problem he didn't need. 'You have given us one hell of a scare Cait. Please keep quiet and give me time to think. You were meant to go on a mission today. This has changed much and mucked up my plans. Worst is, I have to work out a way to explain all this to Zoren and a reason why I have brought you to my home. This can't be about us, Caitlin, bigger issues are facing us than petty jealousies.'

'It's got nothing to do with you, Axon.' Her eyes glared at the insult.

'Then what? Just thank your lucky stars it was me that found you and not Rory. Your boyfriend sure can swear.'

'He's not my boyfriend.' Her voice was sulky.

'Well, he sure acts like he is. To tell the truth, I got sick of watching him pull you aside and the both of you secretly whispering. Blatz, if it wasn't Bree he had hold of, it was you! It didn't look good from where I stood.'

'He is my boss, that's it. There may have been more once, but he is with Bree now. Has been since the night I first met you.' She put her hand over her face. Her last words faded with weary discord.

Caitlin turned her head from him, an apology stuck in her throat. Apology for what, though? She had done nothing wrong. The man she loved hated her and looked at her with disdain.

A knock at the door kept her from bursting into tears. In came a woman with lion-like features and sunburnt orange hair that hung down to her waist. The overly long nails, even though painted, looked like claws and her thin tapered body slunk in and viewed Caitlin as if she were prey instead of a patient. The only way Caitlin could tell this was the doctor was the black medical bag and a stethoscope that loosely hung around her neck. The harsh features dissolved when she looked at Axon. The stunning smile with pure lust meant her issue was with Caitlin. The Doc had the hots for her boss.

'This is your precious commodity?' she scoffed, directing hostility towards Caitlin. 'One of the Cosmic Riders,' she said, and smirked. 'I think this new job has done your head in sweetie. Better give a real woman a call to straighten you out.'

Axon replied in the foreign language he used earlier, and after she had snapped back in the same tongue, he turned on his heels and stomped out the door, leaving her with Doc Lioness.

Caitlin felt as if she had an aura around her lately turning everyone she met against her and so far, it didn't look as if it was lifting anytime soon. With quick precision, after a clean down with a smelly substance, a needle *'Ouch!'* and some sutures, the doc snapped off the surgical gloves.

'You will have to stay off your feet for two days and bathe in this.' She held out a phial of purple powder. 'Timewaster,' she muttered as she scooped up her equipment.

'Excuse me!'

'Look, you got yourself into this mess, so go home like a good little girl and get Mummy to pander to you. Axon hasn't time for employees who can't handle their God-given gift. Grow up and stop trying to get everyone's attention.'

'So you're not just a doctor, you read minds and think you know mine.'

'Just one look tells me all I need to know. Well, you got his attention but don't expect it will last. I've watched him sidestep many and you, my love, are not even worth the sidestep.'

Footsteps broke up their dispute, and the door flung open.

'Well!' Axon crossed his arms, standing strong and stubborn, apparently still angry at whatever went down between the two of them beforehand.

The doc spread her evil mouth in a twisted smile that an hour ago Caitlin might have thought sweet. Now she knew what the Doc Lioness was like, it was way overdone.

Again, they talked in their own lingo. *Note to self; learn that language.*

Before the doctor left, she tried to put on a friendly expression that so didn't work. 'Remember sweetie, stay off those feet, okay.'

'And when I need the bathroom, how do I get there, by shank's pony?' Caitlin snapped at her. *To snub me is one thing but this doctor was a real piece of work.* Caitlin was glad Rory had kept her from medical practitioners if this is what they were like. This doctor sure had a problem, and she realised what it was; Axon. Having Caitlin in his house for a few days really got up her nose. *It has to be that.*

'I'm sure you'll work it out. I have advised Axon to take you home immediately. Recovery is always quicker around your family and friends.'

That sneaky witch!

'That's okay Doc, you need not worry about my welfare. Axon is my boss and a friend and has already taken excellent care of me. If I need another visit from you, it's best I stay with him. Thanks for coming.' Caitlin turned her back from the doctor quickly, pulled the blanket that lay over her up around her shoulders, and hoped Doc couldn't read minds or she would hear Caitlin laughing inside. *Gotcha!*

* * * *

Caitlin surprisingly dozed off, waking at the sound of the bath water running and Axon's weight on the bed. He smiled. 'That was very mischievous of you Cait, even though she did deserve it. You see, I heard part of the conversation.'

Caitlin had a coy expression and burst into a giggle. 'How do you put up with old-stickybeak-doc is beyond me. The comments left me floored but only momentarily. Oh, that woman has so met her match.'

Axon laughed. 'You sure are a feisty one; how does Rory put up with you?'

'Don't start me on him. He is majorly in my bad books at the minute for not knowing I was a basket case and needed Woody.'

'What do you mean you needed Woody? What's he got to do with this?' He gave her a friendly smile, the one she remembered from that first night. The one that told her she could say anything. And she did.

'Woody said if I felt strange at all to give him a call and he would come straight over. I thought I was all right, it was merely sleep deprivation. You see I've barely slept since we moved to the farm. I worked hard the entire day, yet still, I just tossed and turned. I only meant to wander outside and get fresh air.'

'In your nightwear. It didn't occur to you to put on a robe and slippers.'

'I know, I just wasn't thinking. My thoughts shut the door to my senses. They didn't return until the moment I flopped down exhausted. Not until then did I find I was like this and in the middle of nowhere.'

She gave him a sideways glance. 'So what now?'

'I'm just not quite sure Woody is the answer. I believe I have contributed to your state of mind, Cait. If you don't mind, I'd like you to stay here a couple of days so we can work through what happened down there and find that friendship I carelessly threw away.'

'As I told the doc, I'm staying. It's your punishment for being such a good kisser.' She grinned.

'Well, get your gear off, slasher girl — it's time to stop stinking up the bedroom.' He was surprised when she chuckled at his humour.

She started to remove her nighty and he with a gasp he turned his head, holding up a towel. 'Man, those cuts look gruesome — and those are the visible ones. Poor little pumpkin, I promise not to tease you anymore. When you're ready, pop the towel around you and I'll carry you to the bath.'

As Caitlin flung her nighty aside, she couldn't wipe the smile from her lips until she looked down. He was correct; her feet, legs and arms looked as if they had been slashed. It was a ghastly mess, yet it didn't sour her mood. She had finally found someone that could make her laugh, even while in agony. With his eyes averted, it comforted her that he was a man that didn't just want her for self-satisfaction, but as a friend and wasn't scared to have a laugh with her, but suddenly show a softer side when realising how bad it really looked. Wrapped up, he carried her to the side of the bath and left her to bathe in private.

'There's an intercom switch by the towel rail and clean clothes next to the chair. If you need help to bathe, I'm available to jump in and lend a hand.' He chuckled. 'Other than that, call me when you're done.' He left, smiling at her infectious laughter and crude refusal. *That's my girl!*

The purple healing potion the doctor said to put in the water worked a treat. Now back in bed, Caitlin sat back on puffed up pillows and had a light meal before snuggling down under the soft bed covers to sleep.

A tinkle of china on a tray and a sudden stream of light stirred Caitlin as curtains drew back. She stretched, yawned and rolled over to catch Axon smiling at her as he moved towards her bed, repositioning the trolley of food he must have wheeled into the room.

'Hi beautiful! How are you feeling?'

'Much better thanks to you.' She warily pulled up into a sitting position while he placed pillows behind her.

'The doc says you need to eat and drink something or she is recommending drips.'

'The doc- when was she here?' Caitlin rubbed her eyes and ruffled her bed hair, trying not to look too daggy.

'She's just left. She redressed your feet and gave me some more medicine for you. There is an infection, so we have to be careful.'

'Really? She was here, and I missed her. I'm sad. Not!'

'I thought you'd be happy you missed your cat chat.' He placed a stable table on the bed loaded with foods she didn't recognise. 'Now eat and drink, or the doc will be back to put in that drip.'

'You're joking. I ate last night.'

'Cait, that was over two days ago. You were out cold. I tried everything to wake you, but nothing worked. I've pulled my hair out wondering what to do. Doc was off world. Lepius, my regular physician, has been banned from travel for disobeying Zoren's ruling and Woody's on a mission. The only reason you woke this morning is the doc freaked out that you haven't been up and about. She cancelled all her other appointments to come here and as soon as she arrived, gave you a potion to bring you around. She was honestly worried when she left but had to get back to her other patients. She's not that bad, just over-protective. I have to give her credit; she's one hell of a doctor. Knew exactly what to give you and look at you, awake and as bright as a button.'

'Well, I suppose I should forgive her then.' Catlin sipped the soothing juice. She had no idea even what it was, but it did take the scratchiness out of her throat.

'Bottoms up then!' She lifted the goblet to him and gulped it down. 'What is this?'

'It's called Moonjuice, which is velvety liquid from the moon's precious underground rivers. Moonjuice brew can be quite potent or very soothing as this one, depending on how far away from the sun it is collected.'

'What other strange drinks do you have? What is equivalent to say, rum?'

'Starstarter shots are similar to your rum and give you quite a kick but luckily not the after-effects. Although we do have one speciality wine, it is brewed mainly for the divine order. It's called Ambrosia and is referred to as the nectar of the gods.'

'I've heard of Ambrosia, have you tried it?'

'Yes, it does pack a nice warm punch.' He continued with a tale of a wild night with Zoren while he watched Caitlin played with her food. He stayed and chatted, hoping she would actually eat something this morning. The tiny nibbles taken were not near enough to sustain her. To his disappointment, she soon gave up and pushed the tray aside.

'Cait, there's nothing of you. If I can't get you to eat, I'll have no choice but to call Doc back. You're fading away. I remember what you looked like when we swam together at Kayden's. You haven't been eating much for quite some time, have you?'

She sighed and lowered her eyes. 'I just haven't felt hungry. Maybe there's something wrong with me. Did the doctor do any tests?'

'Yes, and you're as healthy in every other way except for the damage to your feet. These you need to stay off for a little longer so no sneaking out of bed without help. That is non-negotiable.'

She suddenly felt guilty for staying. Rory was used to her and it never seemed a bother for him to care for her when she wasn't well. Axon seemed worried. Maybe she should go home.

'I feel guilty doing this to you. You have planets to manage, and really, the doctor was right, you don't need some stupid girl mucking up your life. You could probably do that disappearing thing and take me back to Rory and the others. They won't mind taking care of me. Then again, Rory's going to be really pissed off with me so maybe on second thoughts…' She rolled her eyes and dropped her lip.

He put his finger to her mouth. 'Hush, stop worrying all the time. You're staying here, and that's final. Leave Rory to me.'

Pulling the pillow from behind her she lay back and sighed. 'Okay, I'll try to stop worrying. But something is not right, Axon. I usually heal quicker than this.' Her voice petered out and her eyes fluttered and dropped, feeling tired again.

Axon shifted off the bed.

'Can you stay a while; I sure need a hug about now,' said Caitlin without opening her eyes.

He stood still for a minute and she thought he would leave, but instead, she felt him lie down. He allowed her to roll into him, and his heartbeat and arms that circled around her were just what she needed. She had missed him and was genuinely sorry she'd been such a cow. Regrettably, the incident could not be forgotten, so instead, she asked for forgiveness which he gave as she drifted off to sleep.

The room was in darkness when she woke, with Axon still by her side, his breathing heavy and deep. He was asleep.

A call from nature made her fidget.

'Are you all right?' he whispered.

'How do I go to the bathroom if I can't walk? This is very

embarrassing, Axon.'

He rolled her over him and stood up with her in his arms. 'Just call me when you're done.' He chuckled at her indignant look as she waited for him to leave and give her privacy. 'Woman, you are so damned shy when it comes to something so natural.'

With the flick of her hand, she shut the door after him. She wasn't game to oh and ah with the soreness in case he came back in. *He's such a male.* She sucked in her breath as she moved tender feet on the floor. *Not an embarrassing bone in his body.*

'I'm hungry,' she said when he had carried her back to bed.

Axon touched his ear and turned to her. 'What will it be?'

'Umm, ice cream and bananas with chocolate topping.' She gave him a playful smile.

'Did you get that?' He paused. 'Make that for two.' He shrugged, not minding the idea.

Next morning he was gone and it left her to speculate if he had stayed. Could she still be not well and had only dreamed they had eaten a midnight dessert together. *Where's that buzzer?* Refusing the help he must have organised, she felt around the bedside table and found the buzzer he gave to her. Was this a crisis, *of course!*

Within seconds, Axon stood beside the bed looking worried. 'You okay?'

'Hungry.' Her stomach grumbled, and the noise had them both grinning.

'Is that all? Thought I told you that buzzer is for emergencies only.'

She leant on her elbow. 'I have been stuck in this bed for days. I want to sit up at the table and eat.'

'And you expect me to carry you downstairs, as you don't trust the help.'

She threw the covers back and stretched out her arms. 'Quit your bitching and do that transporting thing you do. It's quicker and no, they will not do. I'm fussy with who holds me.'

He shook his head and lifted her, his arms gentle and inviting, silently expressing to her that he liked the fact she only wanted him.

'Bath first though missy.' He had been busy and had organised the chamber maidens to have a bath ready and take care of her, so was surprised when she rang for him. Had she sent the others away? He guessed so as they were nowhere to be seen. He took her into the bathroom that smelled of herbs and lavender crossed with pungent antiseptic. Not even letting her get undressed first, he dumped her in the water, chuckled and walked out of the room, ignoring Caitlin's frustrated shriek.

'Call me when you're done, spoiled little redhead.'

'Eeeerrrr!' was the last sound he heard.

Clean and refreshed, Caitlin sat for the first time on the terrace of this most distinguished castle. The French doors opened wide, and she watched curiously, as three fair-haired men with pure white skin, bustled in and out carrying platters, delicate china and cutlery. They wore starched white waistcoats over blue pants and shirts and strange almost-flippers that covered unnatural-looking large, flat feet.

The waft of fresh coffee, pastries and other delicacies grabbed her attention. The table and pleasing food that had been placed in front of them were all she could concentrate on.

'Thought you might like to eat out here in the fresh air,' Axon said and poured them coffee in elegantly designed teacups.

'This is perfect.' Caitlin glanced out over the manicured lawns, lush paddocks and, farther on, the rolling hills of the forest, home to creatures she had yet to see.

Axon saw her interest and dropped heavily into the chair beside her, pointing out the dominant species of wildlife.

'This is the Home World of the constellation Ara known as the Altar. It is here the gods swore their oaths before they laid claim to their planets of choice.'

A wolf howled in the distance, with many of the pack stopping to glare straight at them. A shiver ran through Caitlin as the numbers grew. Many hundreds suddenly appeared, their eyes almost red in colour; coats of fur fluffed out on their backs as their hackles stood up in readiness.

Axon put two fingers in his mouth and whistled out an

unexpected call, almost like the one she had just heard from the pack leader. The tone dispersed them. The only wolf that stayed was the huge black animal that had initially called the gathering. He had stretched out paws and straightened his legs. He could be mistaken for a fur rug, except for those watchful eyes, and Caitlin doubted they would miss a thing.

Axon turned to her and smiled. 'Russo is the pack leader. He is harmless now he knows you are a friend. In the early days and before the gods came here, this is where the Centureans came to sacrifice the wolf, Lupus. Zoren and I came to save Lupus and his pack from certain death. In return for our good deed, he left the wolf, Russo, and his pack in charge here, always to guard my home against invaders or ones to wish me harm. I must apologise for their caution, but your red hair has confused them; it is a sign of danger to them.'

'What happened to Lupus?' Caitlin turned back to Russo who had still not taken his eyes from her.

'Zoren gave him his own Home World. The constellation's named after Lupus and he still rules that group of stars.'

'Am I safe, while you're not around? I mean, if looks could kill and all.' She shrugged off the eyes that had become quite disturbing.

'He knows now that you are my guest. When he hears you laugh it will calm him and he will move on.'

With a movement Caitlin was least expecting he tickled her lightly and she squealed out a giggle, slapped him and stopped as he pointed, and said, 'See he doesn't fear you now.'

With a sideways glance, Russo heaved up his large frame and disappeared into the woods, as had the others, his eyes still a reminder not to muck with their boy.

The conflict over, she stretched out on the chair to feel the warmth of the sun. 'Thanks for bringing me here, Axon, your home is stunning and up here, I feel that my Earthly worries no longer affect me. This happiness I have only dared to dream.' She opened an eye and grinned at him. 'Well, apart from Doc protector and Russo the bully.' Not expecting a reply, she relaxed at this new world that drenched her in a delightful quest to want more. A niggle of fear to slow down and not let it consume her totally nagged at her to remember, *I am only here while I recover.*

'I'm the one who's been the bully, Cait. To a degree, I believe my refusal to form a real relationship has added to your confused state. I broke your trust in me, showed you disrespect and I apologise. I'm not sure where to go from here now you have no confidence in me.'

Caitlin straightened her back, sitting high and proud, her hand extended, and when he placed his in hers, she gave it a warm handshake. 'Hi Axon Stanton, my name is Caitlin Warner.' Her lips parted in a slight smile. 'Yes, it was a shock, I admit, to be rejected by someone I had too many feelings for, far too soon, but it was my own fault for jumping in feet first, not getting to know you initially, or vice versa. So this is me telling you a little about me, hoping you will still be a friend at least, once I've finished.' She let his hand go and leant back, not looking at him. *Here I go.* She coughed and cleared her throat. 'I have a quick temper, I speak without thinking, I'm impossible to live with and spend far too much money on clothes and shoes. I'm hopeless in the home and kitchen and need so much attention all the time I even drive myself away. This said, I do know one thing, and that is what I like, and you, Axon Stanton, I like.'

Axon followed her movement, expressionless as she turned to him. The tilt of her head allowed her soft red curls to fall gracefully over her bare shoulder. The atmosphere had put a honey glow to her skin and within those remarkably large green eyes, he knew there were secrets, but they both had them. In his line of work he always would. 'If after what I have divulged, you still want to be my friend, you are crazier than me.'

Axon took her hand, the surprise of the honest truth she spoke reflected in his features. 'I don't like having to get up in the mornings so I can be quite grumpy. I tell terrible jokes and drink too much when I am with the boys. I have never had to share my life with anyone, and it scares the hell out of me, but it scares me more when you're not with me. I've never even tried to have a relationship so am not familiar with what is proper or not, but do know what I like… and that is you, Caitlin Warner. So, if after all that you still want to be my friend, I would love to try.'

'I would like that.' Her fingers moved over his hand. The quiver at her soft touch told her all she needed to know.

Spreading his fingers, he wrapped them around hers. 'Truce.'

'Truce.' Her face broke into a warm smile.

CHAPTER EIGHT

Calmer Waters

Caitlin enjoyed every minute spent on Ara with Axon. He entertained and pandered to her every need while she recuperated. She never remembered a time in her life that she had been so happy, and was thrilled further after Russo, the crazy-eyed wolf that stared her down the first time she saw him, befriended her. How she wished she could stay, but Axon had just arrived home from work and Caitlin knew this early arrival was to discuss her going home. The thought put a prickle down her spine that made her legs buckle.

It was on a chair he found her. Moisture dripped down her forehead and when she looked up her complexion was pale and sickly.

'Cait, what's wrong? I'll call the doc.' He touched the communication pod in his ear.

'No!' She shook her head and put her hand out. 'I just want you!'

On bent knees, Axon put out his arms, and she hugged him so tightly he battled to pry her free. It was easy to feel her stress and fear. *But why?*

'If I let go, leave here, I'm scared… not sure why but think it has to do with what happened. What if it happens again? Axon, I feel happy here, safe. I'm sorry to freak out, but I don't want to go yet, I'm not ready.'

He soothed her until she was able to converse without tears and the trembling stopped. It was Axon's first breakthrough. He was relieved and thrilled Caitlin finally trusted him enough to open up about many doubts, including her ability to do such a demanding profession. He even spoke freely about the friendship between them and asked how she felt about them now. Emotional from Caitlin's own honesty, he gave a little of him and openly admitted he didn't look forward to her not being there either. He told her he had enjoyed coming home to her but couldn't continue being selfish. The Cosmic Riders needed Caitlin and although it pained him, it was time to take her home.

Again, the following morning she burst into tears when he mentioned it was time to go back to Earth. She still sported bruises, and the doctor informed him it would be at least another week before she was healthy enough to go back to work. He wondered if the tears were just exhaustion from the previous night. They'd stayed up half the night talking, and on top of that, her grievances might have overwhelmed her again. It was that, or she was getting a premonition, but he quickly ruled that out as she was surely not well enough for her magic of foresight to be working at this stage.

'What if I come back and stay a couple of nights? Maybe I could organise for Woody to visit and get the big guy to take a look at you,' he suggested.

'No! You have work to do. I've taken up far too much of your time already.' She wiped her tears and tried to be brave.

He lifted her chin, seeing the soul inside her breaking. Could he really let her go? He sucked in his breath. *No, never.*

'I've got a better idea. What if your friends come here for a few days? That way I don't have to worry about your wellbeing as you will have company.' He paused and pinched at his chin, deep in thought. 'If anything happens with the planets this idea is perfect; the team is right here, and will get to the mission much quicker.' He looked pleased with his temporary plan. 'What do you say? Just until you heal completely and feel better?'

Axon caught a thrilled Caitlin in his arms as she lunged at him, her laughter infectious as he smiled at her delighted response.

'They will love it here.' Her eyes danced.

She didn't mean to make such a fuss, but for some reason she had such a hard time leaving. *Is it because Axon makes me so happy? No there has to be more to my apprehension.*

'I'm usually tougher than this.'

'Don't worry about it. I have learned there is always a reason for every change to a plan. I'm sure the reason you felt this will unfold shortly.' He was oddly brighter that she could stay and was pleased with this decision.

'You are so deep Axon, philosophical. I have so much to learn. But for now, I'm out of your hair in case you change your mind.' She headed for the stairs and missed the first step and stubbed her toe. She swore and heard Axon, *tut, tut* her from behind.

'I know!' She waved her arm as she tackled the next steps more gingerly. 'Quit the cussing,' she mimicked him.

One of Axon's concerns that night, when they discussed her position as a Rider, had been his expectations of her. He was adamant Caitlin's role had to change. He needed her to be the one to step up and become a role model to the other women in the group. He chastised her about the excessive fooling around and explained why it was a necessity to curb her cussing and stop instigating inappropriate innuendos and cheekiness. She had not thought about ramifications of dealings with the divine and finally saw his point. Gods and goddesses would not take kindly to such poor verbal habits, as he put it.

'You must get in touch with your feminine side, Cait, for all our sakes,' he called to her again, making a push for her to become more of a lady.

Caitlin shrugged. 'I keep getting caught. Must cuss quieter.'

'Or not at all.' Axon sighed, wondering if he had lost the battle. Time would tell. He watched Caitlin move carefully up the staircase. To carry her would have been easier but she had been vulnerable, too teary and he wondered if he had spoilt her. Never had Axon been so attentive to a female and he wasn't sure of these feelings. Was he falling for her or was this just empathy? He looked up to the heavens, unsure how the divine would handle this little pocket rocket that he had grown to admire. He hoped they would too. He recalled where she had come from; the shabby apartment, with not a care in the world, to working in the heavens. She took it all in her stride; adjusted to the new lifestyle, the power gifted to her by Cassie, and him. He had been cruel at first and yet she forgave him without ever mentioning it again. They had become good friends and each day he looked forward to seeing her lovely smile and her bright disposition. *No wonder her team thought the world of her.* He had a feeling he had lost his heart to her that night he stole his very first kiss. Now he had got to know her, he wasn't sure how he was ever going to give her up. For now anyway, Axon decided to hide this attachment. *Man! Zoren's going to laugh if I tell him that I not only accept women on the team, but I'm falling for the feisty, adorable redhead.*

Axon shook off the dilemmas that Caitlin brought into his life and transported back to work. He left some instructions with Nigel, asking him to be ready for the arrival of the Riders.

'Caitlin.' Nigel bowed and addressed her when she asked for drinks to be served as soon as her friends arrive. 'Non-alcoholic,' he said, and grinned. 'Lord Axon has left strict instructions there will be no spirits until he has had a chance to show the team around. He wants to take them up to the observatory tower and bring them up to speed on the NATequipment there.'

'He's such a party pooper. Does he ever have any fun, Nigel?' She chuckled at his expression. 'He so needs to loosen up.' She left him with his mouth gaped open.

Her movements were deliberate and carefully when hobbling outside, her nervous state building as she waited. Perspiration lined her lip and dripped down the side of her face. *What is it with this overwhelming need to have the team here with me?* In fact, this feeling was so strong, she began to freak out they might still be on Earth. *Hurry!* She closed her eyes and wished for them to appear soon.

CHAPTER NINE

Under Attack

Meanwhile, on Earth at Kayden's farm, the Cloud Riders had returned from a mission. After caring for the horses, they went back to their prospective homes for a well-earned rest.

It hadn't been long before Cassie woke with a start and rolled out of bed, her body trembling with fear. 'Kayden, wake up honey!'

Kayden sat up, making a grab for her, but she was too quick. Already she had pulled on shorts and stretched a T-shirt awkwardly over her head. He could see the panic she was in. 'What? Give me something to work with.'

'I don't know. You have to call the boys, tell them to get as far away from here as they can and - *now*!' She shrieked the last word out.

Kayden knew his wife well enough to know they were in trouble. In record time, he had dressed, snatched her up and once outside, sent a message to his men.

Team! And I mean all of you, Cassie is freaking out. She's picked up on - I'm guessing it's an attack. She wants you all to get as far away from this area as you can. I'm already putting her in the car so move it double time. Will be right behind you so head for Mt Newman…. Hang on!

'Cassie, can you talk?' He sat her on the front seat of the utility truck, doing up her buckle.

She started to shake uncontrollably. 'No! It's worse. Change of plans. I think you better get them to come here to help me. I'm going to need their power!' She shivered, and her teeth chattered.

'Cassie! What's going on?' Kayden wanted her anywhere but here. The trance she was in prevented her from communicating very well and she was about to go into hysterics, so he did what she said.

Scratch that guys, get here! Hell, I don't know what's going on but now you're moving away from her, she's worse.

The men had already started to drive in the opposite direction and he heard the screech of their tyres as they swung the four-wheel-drives back towards the farm. The howling and smoke let him know how close they were and he called to them one more time when her breathing got heavier. *Hurry!*

Her rapid panting slowed as she listened to his new orders and clicked off her seatbelt.

'It's okay, Cassie, they have turned into the driveway. What do you want us to do?' He knelt to talk to her. With glazed eyes, she stared up at the sky. He wasn't sure if she even heard him. Her hands pushed at his shoulder gently to let him know she needed to come out from the car.

Guys, hurry! I'm positive we're under attack. It's too late to go get Starburst for her. I think she knows we can't outrun it. Looks like we have to stand and fight.

Kayden held Cassie by the elbow and fed her as much power as he could. His knees buckled as she drew so much from him.

'Hell Cassie; it's big isn't it?'

She nodded but didn't look down at him, her head high, her sight fixed in the sky. Kayden heard the cars skid as they lost it when they hit the dirt driveway.

Calm down guys, but hurry; she's draining everything I've got. Oh my god, I don't believe it, Starburst is here. She's called her own flipping horse. Thank the stars this girl of ours has so many unique abilities!

Kayden groaned out as Cassie threw herself upon Starburst, the gifted stallion not needing the bridle. His wings protruded on their own; the armour that appeared enabled her to harness and encase the power she built within the impenetrable shield. Kayden could only admire the woman he loved, as her abilities continued to amaze him.

'Cassie, the men are here. Take what power you need, they are well rested and ready to help.'

Woody grabbed Kayden by the arm and the instant power surge from him had Kayden back on his feet. 'K, you had us that spun out. Since when do any of us run?'

'Sorry man, it was Cassie's directive and we know she is always right, usually, but when I gave the order and you started to move away from her, she hyperventilated. I've never seen her like this and look at her horse; Starburst hasn't even got a blatzing golden bridle on, she has her own damned magical saddle and reins.'

Woody shook his head. 'Far out, she's good.'

Jason grabbed them by the shoulders, and the movement pulled them from the awe that had them spellbound. 'Stop trying to work it out and get out of the way. With all that energy she's sucked in, she'll blow you both to kingdom come.'

A safe distance from her, Woody leant on Jason. Kayden stood, arms folded, while Ethan and Conor knelt, feeling safer closer to the ground. They guessed it was going to be some blast off and waited for the backdraft of the explosion which would surely send them flying.

The glow that surrounded Cassie and Starburst built and became so intense and bright, her team lifted their arms across their faces. She screamed as she let it out and in the blink of an eye the weapon she had created launched. Cassie's arms were spread, the silvery blue flash punched out effortlessly from her delicate hands. The noiseless beam headed directly towards the eye of the threat. Kayden and his men fought to keep in place; Woody grabbed Conor by the shoulder as he pelted backwards from the ferocity of the blast as it took off, his other arm fixed tightly around a tree. Kayden made a grab for Jason and Ethan, and the three of them toppled over in the massive shock wave the weapon left in its wake.

Kayden used his power to view the now-visible threat as it exploded. The remains burnt up in Earth's atmosphere, but was it over? She still sat poised and ready to do more.

'Hell K, there's another,' Ethan called out.

Cassie turned to him and nodded. 'I need more power, I'm drained.' Her shoulders slumped.

The men quickly circled her, and all hands now rested on Starburst. Cassie drew energy from them through her horse. The magic she captured in a transparent electrode created a lethal electric burst of energy and punched it out with force towards the second threat. The outburst of an ear-splitting war cry was the only way she knew how to pack more punch to the weapon. Even then the blue beam of light was not nearly as bright as the silver colour of the first. It fell short, missed its mark and the asteroid plummeted to Earth, the damaging sound not far from them. Maybe an hour or two away was Kayden's best guess.

'Goddamit!' he cursed out. 'I think the attack was on both teams. I'm almost positive the second one has hit Rory's farm.'

'They wouldn't have had a hope! Hell, Caitlin's up with Axon, so they didn't have ground support.' Woody's skin tone paled.

Cassie's sobs brought them out of the shock they were in. 'Kayden, I'm so sorry, I tried, I really tried hard.' Her uncontrollable gulps of air and tears shattered him. He knew by her reaction alone where it had hit. She confirmed by her reaction he was correct. The Cosmic Riders had been attacked and with the ferocity of the explosion they heard from so far away, he knew there would be no survivors, nothing left.

CHAPTER TEN

Presumed What!

Stunned, Axon and Zoren stared at the news. Pictures flashed before them of an asteroid that had hit Earth. The aerial shot showed the land had been gouged deeply by its forcible entry. The news froze them to the spot.

Breaking news! It flashed across the screen.

'Oh my god, are you getting this?' The reporter raised his voice over the sound of the noisy helicopter that gave details of the incident.

'Hear you loud and clear, Jerry, go ahead,' the NBB news commentator answered.

'Ted, I'm in the air above a farm in outback Western Australia where an asteroid hit late this morning. As you can see it has opened up the ground with a fissure a few kilometres wide by, I don't know, maybe eight k's long. Ted, there's nothing as far as the eye can see, everything is gone, obliterated in this mess of smoke and gas which seems to be the only remains of what I can imagine was once a house. I can see parts of a roof that's upside down and from the damage, it must have blown right off.'

A fumbling noise was overheard, while the view of the camera changed. Scattered remains and charred debris edged each side of the gouged track laid by what was left of the fireball of rock that now sat harmless, dug deep into the earth. 'As you can see, Ted, no one, not even the animals, could have reacted fast enough to get out of the way of this killer. It has annihilated everything in its path.'

The feed stopped as the focus returned to the studio analyst. 'That's right viewers; you saw it here first, on NBB. You have just witnessed the wreckage left by the impact of an asteroid to a property in the outback of Western Australia. Details of who owns this land have not been released, but we do have a couple of acquaintances of the occupants who have just turned up worried for their friends. It's believed that before this enormous chunk of an asteroid hit the property, there was a two-storey home complete with a massive stable full of specially bred horses. It's believed the family were home at the time of impact and are now presumed dead. We are having trouble with the audio but have just received this message via email.' He took hold of a news feed handed to him. 'Still no luck tracking down the owner of this farm, but the two acquaintances of the residents who had only just met them at a barbeque said there were three men; Rory, Nathen and Zeke and three women; Caitlin, Bree and Lisha. If anyone can help authorities with surnames or who knows the whereabouts of any of these men and women, please contact the police urgently.'

Axon switched off the feed and leant up against the bench, his mouth open, clearly in disbelief.

'How could this have happened? The location was top secret.'

'Wait!'

Zoren put his hand up. 'Kayden's on the line, he may know something. Maybe your team is with him.'

Axon shook his head. 'No, Zoren; they were meant to be at my place by now, but I called home only moments before this happened and they still hadn't arrived. Caitlin is stressed to the max. She'll be worse if she hears about this and I'm not with her.'

'Hang on Axon, I'm listening to two conversations here. What was that, Kayden? You were hit too!' Zoren's face was generally pale but now looked white, and his phone-hand trembled as he listened and relayed what happened with Kayden. 'Okay. I'll tell him.'

Axon could see Zoren took this personally, stunned that the gods were brazen enough to attack teams that belonged to him, he being an archangel. His status amongst the gods was his protection and until now, had also sheltered his peacekeepers from their wrath.

Zoren had reined in his anger to relay the conversation with Kayden. 'Cassie foiled their attack but only just.'

'Thank the stars they're safe.' Axon was pleased for them but anxiously waited to hear news of his team.

'Yes,' Zoren agreed with him. 'But apparently, after blowing up the first asteroid, Cassie tried to destroy the second, but even with the help of the team, she ran out of power. The beam fell short and missed the mark, the first time ever for her. You see, her health suffers too. While Caitlin is unwell, Cassie, her equal, will continue to deteriorate also.'

'Seriously?' Axon scarcely believed the magical sharing of the Riders could stretch so far.

'Yes,' he answered. 'I'm afraid so, and that's not the only bad news you will have to prepare yourself for. Kayden said there's no way anyone could survive it. They drove straight there and have only just been able to get through to us; the satellites are crammed by the news feeds.'

'I have to go to Cait.' Axon looked at his watch. She's been waiting hours for them and will be terrified if she is watching this news report.'

'We'll both go. Give me a minute to get my experts moving. I want answers.'

Zoren signalled to a monitor, and within seconds the door swung open and a stream of skilled experts, some in suits, others in uniform, took their place around the table to discuss the acts of violence before them.

Monitors and screens from roof to floor switched on. The room lit up with every means they had available. This chamber in their headquarters was so hi-tech even the slightest movement captured would be picked up and analysed.

'You have just witnessed, as we have, an unprovoked attack on two of my teams operating from Earth. This is an outrage! No one leaves here until I know who did this! Use whatever resources are necessary. I expect a full report sitting on my desk in an hour.' He stood fuming, and added, 'while I'm waiting, develop for me an official response to this barbaric attack – Now!'

There was a scuffle of chairs, some sitting, some standing and viewing the footage on the big screens. The sudden eruption of voices and chatter escalated as the brainiacs of the heavens began the task set for them. To find answers – fast. When Zoren said jump, they did.

CHAPTER ELEVEN

Ara Home World
(An hour earlier)

It was late morning, and Caitlin was beside herself when the winged beauties had still not appeared from the cloud cover. *Rory, please be safe.* She flopped in the chair, her feet sore and swollen from pacing. The clink of ice against glass distracted Caitlin. 'Sorry miss,' Nigel apologised for the noise. 'Your friends are running late, so can I get you a snack while you wait?'

She flicked her fingers to dismiss him. Then she felt bad as his light grey hair bobbed down as he bowed to leave. 'Sorry that was rude of me. Stay a while and chat with me.' She turned her head to the side, her lips parted in a smile.

'You must be very close.' He looked outward towards the sky.

'Yes.' Caitlin picked up the iced tea and sipped the soothing liquid she had come to enjoy. 'We have been together for a little over ten years now, except for Bree of course. She's only been with us a short time.'

More time passed as they sat chatting. Every minute felt like an hour. Suddenly a flash of light in the clouds caught her attention. 'There!' she squealed and stood with her hand shading her eyes. 'Look!' she shrieked at Nigel and leant over the rail as if that short distance would make her see better.

'I'm not sure, ma'am, it could be just lightning. It's overcast today and we do have electrical storms up here.'

'No! It's them. I know it.' She was fixed on that area of sky.

With a burst of electrical currents and the crackle of the portal opening, the first horse appeared with Rory, then another. Caitlin waved madly and jumped up and down as she screamed out their names. Her visitors had arrived and tears of joy ran down her face.

Nigel smiled. 'Excused me, ma'am but I must go and greet your guests.'

Caitlin didn't stop calling to them until the Riders were under her balcony. The procession of winged, armoured horses landed on the grass below, and the eloquent glow of magic at its finest had Caitlin's hands clasped together in awe, overwhelmed as her friends dismounted.

By this time Nigel and half a dozen of the albino men waited in greeting. Caitlin had learned that Axon's dark hair and her red hair were unusual on this planet. By the look on the horse handlers' faces, they were completely taken aback at Rory and the team who looked more like angels with the glow that shone from them. The stable hands shielded their eyes while her friends dismounted, and only relaxed their arms as they marched off looking straight ahead in unison, with the horses beside them. With the magical rides being taken care of, her friends waved back before Nigel had them inside and out of her sight. She moved as quickly as she could to join them.

'Rory!' She went straight into his outstretched arms, his big warm, friendly hug just as it used to be.

'I've missed you, Red.' Rory searched her face while he frowned at the visible marks that scarred her creamy complexion. Too moved to explain, Caitlin slipped from his grip and after lots of hugs and excited chatter, she gave her friends a tour of the twenty-four-bedroom mansion.

'He lives in a castle,' Lisha gushed.

Rory and Bree snapped up the first room they saw. It was huge and had a big living area which included a kitchenette. The boys, as she'd expected, quickly laid claim to the next two rooms that had a balcony and a spa in the ensuite.

'That's not fair,' Lisha sulked when hers was dull, nothing special, not like the others. She'd held out for too long making a decision as she thought a better one might come up.

'Ah!' Nigel bowed upon seeing her disappointment. 'For the fairest of maidens, come.' He backed away from her before he turned and stood upright, the shuffle of the elderly gent easy to keep up with as he led them to a door that opened up to another set of stairs.

As they reached the top, a heavy-set door automatically opened into an elegantly furnished room. 'This is where Zoren sleeps when he stays over. I'm sure if you don't move his antiques around, he won't mind it being used for a few nights.'

Lisha jumped on the monstrosity of a bed. The huge four-post outrageous sleeper took up most of the space in that room. There were two doors on the other side. One led to the ensuite complete with a spa that looked more like a swimming pool. The other door took them into a kitchenette.

Nigel opened up the curtains to a magnificent view of the woods far below them. 'Come, fair maiden.' He inclined his head to Lisha who had apparently won his attention. Caitlin knew Lisha was drop dead gorgeous but apart from that, she could act incredibly spoilt and insensitive at times. She wondered how long Lisha would stay polite and sweet now she had the best room in the house. Not wishing to miss a thing, Lisha kicked up her feet and struggled to get off the bed. It looked like a tortoise stuck on its back and made them laugh at her. It ticked her off. *Here we go*, Caitlin mused.

'What!' Her voice indignant and cross as she emerged from inside and peered out over the balcony. A sudden chorus from the wolves broke out. Many lined the trees on the edge of the woods and upon seeing her, they howled in unison.

'What's wrong with them? They'd better not be laughing at me too or they are so dead.' Unimpressed Lisha put her hand to her ears to drown their noise out.

'The wolves call to you and your friends.' Nigel tilted his head, confused at her curtness. 'They think you are angels that come from the sky; they serenade you.'

'Well, they can quit that racket. Shooo!' She turned to Nigel. 'Tell those stable hands to hurry up and remove the bridles from our horses. Not putting up with that howling all night.' She huffed, turned with her head held high, her attitude impatient.

Nigel closed the balcony door on the wolves to quieten them down and with his head hung and shoulders hunched stood next to Caitlin. She nudged him. It hadn't taken Lisha long to show her true colours. She had insulted his pets and showed indifference to what he thought wondrous.

'She must like you, she is generally worse.' She tried to apologise for her friend, saw his look and grinned. 'Ah, you like her. May I say you are not the only male that has fallen for her on sight.'

Nigel bit his lip to prevent a smile. 'Will that be all ma'am?' His posture straightened, not giving away any secrets.

'Yes thank you, Nigel. I'll call if we need anything further.' *He's a dark horse.* She grinned as he nodded and left.

Chapter Twelve

Friends Forever

Caitlin, aware after staying with Axon over the past days and nights that his life was all about his work, was not expecting to see him until late into the evening. With this in mind, she organised a swim before the midday meal, but her joy was soon upset when Rory spotted the bruises she had not been able to hide.

'Cait, what happened to you?' He pulled at her arm and spun her around to face him. 'You have scratches everywhere, and what the hell, your feet are a mess, they're black and swollen.' He held her two shoulders firmly. 'Why didn't you tell me you were so banged up? Hell Cait, this isn't funny. How did you let this happen and more to the point, why?' His voice rose, and his tone and reddened features made her cringe.

Axon had naturally downplayed what had happened to keep their heads in the game. The last thing he wanted was to send out an uptight team leader, worried about a team member. If she'd known he'd react this way, she would have stayed dressed. *Thanks for the heads up, Axon.*

He shook her slightly and received a stare with no response. 'Is this how he found you?' His voice was raised and angry.

Caitlin snapped at his outburst, hurt. 'It was an accident, and why do you care? You haven't even called me.' She threw her hand up in the air and released herself from his grip. 'Leave me alone!' She turned, moved as quickly as she could up the stairs and threw herself on the bed.

Rory already knew she wouldn't do this deliberately but for her to do it at all worried him. 'I'm sorry!' he apologised after following her. He dropped down on the bed beside her. 'I just freaked out. When Axon said he was taking you for a couple of days, I was ticked off, sure, but thought it necessary for you two to work things out. That's why I didn't interfere, left you alone with him and didn't insist you come home. After all, you were terribly angry with him, and he being the boss it made for a very strained visit all round. Until now, that was what I thought your episode was all about; you wanted his attention. When I first saw you, it damned near floored me, Cait. You've lost weight, your face is drawn and there's barely a spot where you're not scratched or bruised.'

'It wasn't about him, Rory, and I hope you believe me.'

'Then it was me!'

'What? How did you come to that conclusion?'

'The way I treat you. We were closer than best friends. You must have known how I felt and when you didn't return my advances and Bree came along, I threw my relationship with her in your face, didn't I?'

She sniffled into her tissue. 'Yes, it hurt.' She looked up at him. 'We both hurt each other, Rory but this didn't happen because of you two, that's silly.'

She faced him. 'Axon believes my session with Woody was incomplete. The magic he used to make me open up to him and then heal the wounds he exposed must have caused me to flip out a bit. There is no other reason for me to have been so angry at Axon. I had only just met him and yet I expected him to feel as I did. I was irrational, couldn't eat, sleep, and worse of all didn't have a clue why. My mind was frazzled and yet if you were to ask me why I would have shrugged.'

'Woody wanted you to remember your childhood, but why?'

'He feels my powers will never be fully developed until I face my past.'

'Then it is my fault. I let you close the door on it, Cait. Why remember so much pain? Maybe if I tell you how I found you?'

'No!' She put her hand to his lips. 'It doesn't work like that. I have to do it.'

Caitlin took her hand away, her features soft as she looked at him. 'Please don't blame yourself. I would be so much worse without you. I hold you so deep in my heart and don't blame you for choosing Bree. I know now it would never have worked between us and recently I worked out why.'

'Why, Caitlin? I need to hear you say it. I need to know this thing between us will not destroy our future together. I too have missed you, but on my team.' He smiled, the kindness in his eyes unmistakable.

'Rory, you hold me when I cry, laugh when I laugh, care when no one else does; you alone taught me how to live and love but as a brother figure. If you were thinking straight back then you would have seen it too.'

He grinned. 'I see that now, although you have to cut me some slack too. I was your everything until our team grew and suddenly our relationship changed. You became better friends with the other members, while I became buried in paperwork and keeping you all safe. I felt left out of all the fun you guys had together. We both had to change and grow. Somehow we both have, and you know what, I reckon we're going to do just fine aren't we?'

'Yes.' She smiled back.

'A truce, finally.' Rory flopped on his back. 'Anyway, I wanted someone who can look after me, not the other way around.'

'Oh, that's it! Hang it on me now, after ten years. What… I bet you even make Bree wipe your arse, you chauvinistic prick.'

He laughed at her indignant pose. She looked as if butter wouldn't melt in her mouth, yet she sure did have one. He blamed the way he and the boys spoke in front of the girls. He would have to stop that now.

'You're such a bitch sometimes Caitlin, but so much fun.' He got serious. 'Just promise me you will never talk like that in front of anyone but me from now on. We all have to start becoming a little more upper-class and leave the gutter talk behind, okay.'

She grinned. 'Okay, as I said to Axon, I promise to try and that's all I can do.'

'I'm your boss, not Axon. I and the team like you just the way you are Cait. Come back with us and let us take care of you at home. This is no place for you to live. It's far too stuffy. It will destroy who you are. You can be yourself around us, it's only up here you're expected to slap on airs and graces. You must know that wherever I am, that is your home and I always want you in it.'

'I want to, Rory, more than anything, but have this fear that rips through me every time I imagine that place. I don't know what it is.'

'If something at home is freaking you out, I will remove it. You get strong vibes at times and I trust your intuition, but you belong with us. Give me a chance to work through it with you, and whatever it is I promise to fix it when we get back to Earth.'

She smiled and nodded.

He grinned back. 'You'll consider it seriously for me, won't you Red? I mean we even dragged Shargan up here for you, so don't make us go home without you.'

She stood up. 'I will sort this out before you leave as I have every intention of contacting Woody about my power issues and will discuss with him this fear I'm sensing. When I feel better and my magic stops crippling me, I'm all yours.'

'Have you contacted Kayden and asked to see Woody?'

'No, but I will.'

He rolled his eyes. 'Do you want me to?'

She put out her hand to help him up. 'I have to start doing things for myself, Rory. I'm a big girl and you have too much on your plate already.'

Rory shook his head and hugged her. 'If you want to be all grown up I'll stop coddling you, but I'm serious, you're part of our team, no matter what, okay.' Then he grinned. 'Oh, and don't tell Bree I gave you a hug. She is not as forgiving as you.'

CHAPTER THIRTEEN

Safe in the Home World
(Ara)

Back at the Alpha site, Axon and Zoren discussed how to break the news to Caitlin that Rory and the team were dead. They had searched the route they usually took and watched all the footage. However, the team did not emerge from the opening portal connected. With heavy hearts, they both transported out to Axon's Home World, Ara.

* * * *

Zeke practically dropped the freshly brewed coffee pot when Axon and Zoren appeared. 'Cripes, can't you two knock or something?' he scolded them as he put the pot on the table and licked his burnt fingers.

Axon punched the air before he crunched knuckles with Zoren and turned round to Zeke. His arms wrapped around him and lifted him off the ground in a tight squeeze. As he let go, his face released the tension. 'Sorry buddy, thought the lot of you were dead! Man, it's great to see you.' He ruffled his hair and turn to shake the hand of each team member. Caitlin, he lifted and spun around with her, excited. 'As for you! I could hug you to bits. If it hadn't been for your little performance, they would still be down there.' He stopped suddenly and faced Zoren. 'Sorry, got a bit carried away; everyone this is Zoren – Zoren, you've met Rory.' He pointed to each team

~141~

member. 'This is, Nathen, Zeke, Lisha, Bree and this little redhead that saved them, with her incredible intuition, is Caitlin.' He released his hold as her words finally broke through.

'What's going on… saved who, how?' Caitlin was rattled by his comment.

'Yes, exactly Axon, what's this all about?' Rory straightened his back, his face taut.

Zoren wasted no time and with a wave of his hand and a click of his fingers, a vision appeared from nowhere with a news report of the event. Rory and his team sat with mouths open as they watched for themselves.

'Those malicious thugs!' Rory stood up so quickly his chair shot back behind him, crashing hard against the wall.

'You gotta be kidding me!' Nathen thumped the table.

'Hell! The horses!' Zeke joined Rory, too ticked off to sit.

'Our new home! Gone!' Bree sobbed on Lisha's shoulder.

'What I want to know is how did you guys get here? We searched the route you take but saw nothing, yet here you all sit. I'm stunned yet darned pleased at the same time,' said Axon.

Rory breathed out with a sigh. Everything was gone yet work came first and put his grievances aside. 'The damnedest thing happened. We were tossed into a cirrus radiatus cloud. It thrust us parallel and entirely off route. The portal we came out of was on the opposite side of the horizon. This was the reason we were so late arriving; I had to jump us through a cirrus uncinus cloud. I used the hook at the end to catapult us back to where we needed to be. Now this has happened, I understand why. We must have been thrown off course by the force field and speed of the weapon used to target and destroy our farm, and us.'

'Lucky Rory was in a hurry to come pick up Caitlin, and we had left early. ' Lisha grinned at her brother. 'And I'm so proud of him for knowing how to get us here to Ara safe and sound. All that extra study on cloud formations, hey bro?'

He gave her a wink but turned his attention back to the team member he had come to collect. The farm he could do nothing about at this point, but his friend he could. 'Are you okay, Caitlin?'

She was stunned and sat motionless, only managing a slight nod to Rory as thoughts continued to consume her. She'd seemed to know a disaster was coming, but how? This was getting too weird. Axon was right; she knew something was going down, but this… Yet as she watched the camera swing around their now destroyed property, she already knew what she would see. *Did I know?*

Zoren noticed as Rory had that she was staring and deep in thought. Her thoughts were confused and he took her hand. 'Great work Caitlin, you must feel relieved you had such insight.'

'I don't think she has any idea what we are talking about.' Axon turned her to him. 'You with us now, Cait?' He snapped his fingers in front of her eyes, which made her blink and smile. 'That's my girl.' He spoke to Zoren. 'Her eyes have been glazed over since last night, but now look.' He held her face and tilted her towards Zoren. 'Suddenly, they have cleared and I can feel she is her happy self again.'

'Ah.' Zoren grinned and spoke in a language Caitlin had never heard before.

'What did he say?' she asked Axon, who nodded and agreed.

'He thinks you channel the Congress of the heavens, who are caretakers of many universes. This is why he believes you to be a goddess that has not reached your full potential yet. As a child, you were ill-treated, and it was the Congress who gave you strength.'

Caitlin tilted her head, unsure. 'My childhood is vague, but ill-treated seems harsh.'

Zoren once again spoke to Axon in the odd dialect.

'Yes, Caitlin has asked for a consultation with Woody, but you have had him rather busy.'

Zoren shrugged. 'And now after this attack, he will be even more in demand.'

Axon breathed out. 'I know, but if you are right and she does channel the Congress of the heavens and its wisdom…'

Zoren finished his words. '…she will need more experience and although you are my best warrior, I'm not sure your team or you, Axon, can provide this level of teaching. She may have to walk this path alone. This will force Caitlin to use her divine gifts and thus sharpen her craft naturally.'

'Then she must see him soon to be in top form for what lies ahead. If he can't come to us, then we will go to him. You said yourself that Caitlin's confused state is affecting her equal. Cassie suffers too, so it needs to be sorted.'

'Yes!' He nodded. 'But let's not panic, for now, your team is safe, and I must make mine safe too.'

'What will you do?'

'It's what – we will do.' He glanced at Rory and back to Axon. 'You two I need with me. The rest of your team are on full alert until you return. Show them how to put your monitors on stand-alone mode, so you're not hacked. The rest is similar to what they already use on Earth. If they have any trouble, they can call.'

'I guess, with your transporting skills it's not as if we can't get back here within seconds if anything does go wrong.' Rory was more convincing the team than himself on how quickly they could return.

'True.' Zoren stood to leave. His impatience to get going and meet up with the Cloud Riders was apparent in his quick movement and edgy stance. 'And don't forget, your team have magic equal to Kayden's team. They only need to call on their special abilities, gifted by the Cloud Riders, and they will find an answer if anything does go down while you're not here.'

Axon fidgeted, not wanting to leave Caitlin. In a short period, he had become protective of his new friend. He smiled down at her. 'If Rory and I both go will you be all right here or do you want to come with us?'

'My friends need me, and I want to stay and help them. And anyway, I know the grounds inside and out so I know where to look if there is an attack. If I come with you, I'll be in the way. Just show us what to do up in the NAVtower and we'll be fine.' Her eyes flickered with tiny sparks and seeing this wonder made him believe all would be well. Those eyes were the key, and in the future, he would not take them for granted. For the time being, if there was something else going to happen, he was sure she wouldn't be acting so chipper, and she wouldn't be dazzling him with that charm.

'Well, come on.' She pulled at his arm, and he blinked away the daze of how well he could already read her.

'Okay, okay!' He tutted at her impatience and, turning towards Zoren, shrugged his shoulders. 'We'll be there shortly.'

With a flick of Zoren's arm, the image of what was being reported on Earth vanished and so did he with his smile wide. He knew enough about his boy, Axon, to see that the little one they called Red had significant control over him already.

* * * *

On the way up the stairs, Caitlin listened as Bree and Lisha raved about Zoren's electric blue eyes that changed with his different moods. 'How pale blue and sexy were they when he left and did you catch that smile?' Lisha gushed.

'And that flawless complexion and yes, those to die for eyes hidden behind them long blond lashes. Ohmygod he is so adorable,' Bree agreed.

'And sexy!' Lisha added.

'Okay you two,' Rory disciplined. 'Mind on the job, and Bree!'

'Yes honey.'

'You like me better, right.'

'Yes sir!' She giggled and raced Lisha to the top.

'Caitlin, this is your fault, teaching my beauty to ogle other men.'

Caitlin raised an eyebrow. 'Rory!' She gave him the birdie, laughed and ran up after her friends.

'See Axon, I tell you, girls can be so disrespectful; you're so smart living without one.'

'You love it Rory, and you've missed her, haven't you?' said Axon.

'When she's not with us, we hate it. I was going to take her home tomorrow, and now all this!' He shook his head, 'I'm gutted. What can I offer Cait now, in fact, give to any of the team?'

'Material possessions can be replaced, but you, we cannot. We will rebuild, stronger, better. As for the way we both feel about Caitlin, I think we both better brace ourselves. Does she belong to any of us?'

'I know. I heard what Zoren said about the Congress of the heavens, and her. I guess only time will determine the future, but I'm not letting go, ever.' Rory's jaw set firm.

Me either!

CHAPTER FOURTEEN

Observatory Tower

Caitlin passed by and pushed Nathen. Once he got his balance, he took two steps at a time to catch up to her. The race up the stairs was a bit more than Caitlin had envisaged. Her heart felt it would burst out of her chest as it beat so fast. She was glad when Axon was there to catch her. 'Where did you come from?' She smiled at him.

He had predicted her current state of frailty and shot up after her, making it in time to catch her as she stumbled through the open door. He steadied her. 'Cait, careful! You're still not over the worst of it.' He glanced at Rory. 'Her rate of healing has been slow and has me stumped. I'm glad Woody is coming today. If Kayden agrees, I'm going to suggest swapping a team member for a couple of days. Keep him around a little longer.'

'I'll go.' Lisha put her hand up. 'Conor! Mmm.'

'Really!' Bree eyed her.

'Done!' Rory said. 'Maybe if you go spend some time with him you'll get over the crush and shut up about him.'

'What did I miss? I didn't know she had the hots for Conor.' Nathen raised his brow waiting for the gossip.

Rory coughed, as he hadn't realised it was a secret. With a wave of his hand to stop the chatter, he changed the subject. 'Not the time buddy, button it, we're holding Axon up.'

'Sorry man.' Nathen folded his arms to listen to what needed to be said. Caitlin eyed him. As usual, he didn't back chat or show any sign of irritation toward Rory shutting him down. His loyalty to him was incredibly bonded. He was now Rory's right-hand man, with powers equal to Woody's. Caitlin couldn't have been happier with Kayden's decision to put him in that position. Rory needed the best by his side, and Nathen was that man.

It was then, Caitlin realised Axon still had hold of her. Moving from him she smoothed out her top that had twisted when he caught her. 'Sorry about that, I'm fine now.'

'Caitlin, you're still not fully well. I have eyes, so no need to play the tough girl act with me.'

She felt her hand shake slightly as it went up to brush away hair from her face. 'I guess you're right. I got a bit excited.' She moved and stood next to Rory and melted him with her sweetness that he admired and had missed.

Axon watched on, knew the juvenile sprint was to prove to the others she had recovered but she hadn't, not yet anyway. Not even his magic was working. Whatever Woody had that he didn't, he hoped he got there soon. With no more time to dwell on Cait, he moved back to the door.

Caitlin nudged Rory as Axon looked into a glass hexagon shape by the door. 'What's he up to now?' She whispered and saw his hand wave past what could be mistaken for a light switch fitting, that was until it lit up blue and green. The thing flashed and accepted his eye scan as Axon Stanton. 'Cool security,' she couldn't help saying but became silent as the lightly furnished room began to transform. A large boardroom table emerged from a trapdoor in the floor. In the middle of the table was a tower with arms that reached out, holding individual four-dimensional, touch-screen control panels.

Axon turned one on, showing they were capable of displaying a holographic image of planetary action in the centre of the table for all to view.

Wall panels rotated and converted into screens. The brightness, once they automatically switched on, made them squint.

Six sets of eyes glanced up at the sound of a motor that strained above them. With mouths open in awe, they watched the ceiling disappear and realised the glass they looked through was actually a powerful telescopic lens. The focus blurred and then cleared, which allowed them to see stars thousands of miles away, their surfaces clearly visible.

The hum of another motor starting up grabbed their attention as more desks with digital equipment far more advanced than they had ever seen, complete with chairs, ascended from trapdoors that snapped open from sections in the wall and floor. The team jumped out of the way, a stunned Nathen collected by a chair as it roughly sat him in it. Zeke laughed at him until the sofa he sat on rotated and disappeared. He only just leapt to a steady surface in time. Axon snatched Caitlin up before one next to her spun and cleverly made way for a central processing unit. Bree and Lisha were in hysterics until a workstation slid under them. Rory had caught them before they toppled over each other.

Rory knuckle-punched Zeke and Nathen and whistled through his front teeth. 'Wowee!' He enjoyed every minute of it.

Bree couldn't get the grin off her face.

Lisha put her arm around Caitlin's shoulder; both girls were speechless. Their heads turned from monitor to screen as they observed the distinct mapping system that continued to alter repeatedly.

'Got your attentions now haven't I.' Axon watched their expressions. 'All you see is kept secret, even from the servants. Only the butler and close allies know it is here, and now you lot. When not in use this room resets and will need to be activated each time you enter. The reason for this is so the townsfolk from the city of Klaxton, just north of here, don't guess what I really do for a living. Blowing my cover to the universe would evoke attacks from every fraction. It's best they consider me merely an eccentric wealthy tycoon. This way if they do go snooping when I have a party, or they come to me for their requests by the council for financial assistance, they find nothing unusual to make them suspicious.'

'Understandable,' Rory agreed. 'Same as us when we have

friends over. A walk around the property or a sneak peek in the barn would give them no clue or reason to be suspicious as to what secrets are hidden beneath the barn floor.'

'We all have our concealed resources, but I think this next one is something none of you expects. I have gone one step further, as you do when you are the right arm of Zoren. You see, if my home is attacked and we're too late to divert the danger, this is what to do.' He strode to the left wall, punched in a code on a portrait, the keys invisible to them, and the image slid up to reveal a button behind a glass case. 'Push this and it will activate this whole section of the internal castle and plummet us all deep underground. The external building stays the same, which keeps onlookers from seeing the secrets held within the walls. If danger is successfully warded off, we surface and none is the wiser.' He grinned at Caitlin when he noticed her look of astonishment.

'You're kidding me!' She blinked and went over to feel the keypad on the picture. 'I'll be blowed, really…' She ran her fingers along the lumpy section where an invisible keyboard had been embedded.

Axon glanced around the room. 'Listen up,' he said as he walked back to the main table, and leant against it.

'Concentrate! I only have time to run through this once.' He spent the next hour showing them how to operate the sophisticated paraphernalia.

Once they all had an idea of how it worked, he turned to them. 'So here it is in a nutshell. Dig in and get comfortable. It might be some time before we have another location for you to live. In the meantime, keeping all this and where you are secret, is imperative.'

Rory intervened. 'Axon has given you ample time to come to grips with this station. The ones that get it can teach the others. You will have to work in shifts! As from now, this Home World needs to be monitored 24/7. Nathen, you're in charge while I'm away, so keep your wits about you and let me know the second there is an inkling of trouble.'

Axon bent and tapped a screen that clearly showed the eight planets and Pluto. 'Until we can determine how to resolve this dispute with Hades and his brothers, these orders to monitor the sky around the clock stands.' He pressed buttons so fast they saw his hands as a blur while he searched through files on a screen. 'What puzzles me,' he said looking up, 'is this; Zeus is the only god that has the power to access our confidential data. But even then he would need to break our code before working out your locations on Earth. How did they break that encryption?' He tapped on the screen before straightening. 'The answer is in here somewhere... this is something for you all to keep working on. If we can find it, we will know if they have identified my Home World. Until this information is found, we must stay on full alert.'

He turned to Rory. 'We can also keep working on this at the office. Ready buddy? We have a lot to do.' He put his arm around Rory, and they shimmered out of sight.

Nathen's mouth was open ready to say goodbye, but all too late. 'Cannot believe the gods and Rulers are the only ones to have that gift.'

'And we get a herd of horses with sissy wings that fly us around like overly dressed circus performers,' Caitlin added and made them all laugh.

CHAPTER FIFTEEN

Woody Visits

The team had gathered to meet Woody when he arrived. He only had to take one look at them to see he had his work cut out for him. Caitlin was a mess and hearing no united power, he realised they had barely tapped into the magic they had been given by his team of Riders. He began dressing them down and before letting them have their say, got stuck into them about Caitlin.

'You guys should have felt Cait's stress and pain. It would never have come to this if you were working as one unit.' He glared at each member. 'Well you sure botched that up, Cait would be healed by now if you had listened, and used what we gave you.'

Nathen gulped, wishing Rory was there with them. He felt like a spoilt brat now, thinking back on it. They had felt superior, and sure they were the better squad. Because of this, it was now obvious some of the finer details they were taught, had been missed. He was embarrassed and feeling the vibes from his friends, he knew they felt bad too. Like his teammates, he had been too busy showing off, and like juveniles, they joked together when the Cloud Riders tried to teach them their skills. By the angry glare they were getting from Woody, he knew they were in for a world of hurt for being so insubordinate.

Woody stared into speechless faces of shame. 'This nonsense that you don't need help stops now.' He pulled out his knife and threw it between Nathen and Zeke. The movement was so swift they didn't have time to move. 'Get it.' He growled at their inability to move as quickly as he could. 'So, there will be, no more smart mouthing or self-indulgent behaviour. You are a team! Start acting like one!' Woody gave it to them straight. 'Are you ready to learn now?' He walked up close, eye-balling each member.

Nathen turned the colour of Bree's red top. 'Yes sir.' He was fully embarrassed. The others followed his lead and spoke loud and clear.

'Sorry man, we have not only let Cait and you down, but we have also let ourselves down.' Nathen turned to Caitlin. 'Sorry, Red, we'd be dead if it weren't for your intuition. Thank the heavens you were listening and learned something to save our hides.'

'I'm as guilty as you, and I don't expect to be treated with soft gloves just because my body is a bit unwell. I want to learn too.' Caitlin directed her attention back to Woody.

'And you will. But first, these knuckleheads have to get you better.' Woody scowled at Nathen. 'Cait is the one you need to protect the most. She should be as precious to you as our Cassie is to us. My blatzing oath, it was Cait who saved your arses. Her intuition brought you here, keeping you safe while your home was under attack. Yet here she stands totally messed up, overloaded with stress and her health in jeopardy. And not one of you has used your magic we gave you to even attempt to heal her. If it were me, I'd think twice about saving you lot – I would have let you bastards perish. Disgraceful – is all I can say.'

Nathen stood with his jaw clenched. He knew they deserved a bullocking and once it was over, he unfolded his arms while Woody stared him down. 'Okay I'll wear that, and yes, you're right, maybe we were acting a little like spoilt brats.'

'Maybe, you say, *maybe* you've been acting like brats. That's an understatement and not harsh enough. You have been arrogant,' Woody spat out.

'All right, I agree we have been arrogant and acting irresponsibly. But point taken and we are ready to listen and learn. If you give us a second chance we won't stuff up this time, Woody.' Nathen put his arm around Caitlin's shoulder. 'We've learned our lesson, so how do I fix her and prevent this happening again?'

It was a few minutes before Woody spoke. His look of disapproval was enough to make them all hang their heads. He sighed and rubbed a hand through his curly red hair. 'Has Rory linked you all?'

'Yes, but we're not sure how it all works yet,' Nathen answered with readiness and hope that was the end of the lecture. He felt bad enough being Woody's equal. It was worse that he hadn't picked up all he needed to know to run his team while Rory was away. Rory had been so dedicated during training, had been a sponge while learning how to use the equipment and travel procedures. This side of it, Nathen was meant to learn along with the rest of the team. He was to pass on to Rory the group's area of expertise. He mucked up, they all had, but this time he wasn't going to be cocky or let the team miss a second of this time with Woody. *They had better be on their "A" game and listen or they will answer to me.*

Woody scratched his chin, staring at them, 'You're serious, and you haven't used any of it yet. Goddammit, you guys. Why didn't you ask?' Once again, he looked into deadpan eyes. 'Blatzing newbies,' Woody grumbled and shook his head. His eyes shone like chips of emeralds as he lost his temper, telling them they had better listen up this time and listen good, or he'd give them all a taste of his size fourteen Gucci's.

Nathen gave one last ditch effort to speak on behalf of the team. 'Woody we really do apologise and promise we are listening to you this time. You're right; we thought we were ready, but losing all we had down there and then being left to protect this fortress without Rory is overwhelming for us. But as you say, if we were working as one unit we'd be more than confident we had this and wouldn't need the boss's help.'

'Finally, you are getting it. And the other reason you feel besieged, is because Cait isn't well. With one team member down, especially one so important, you will feel like a bat trying to fly in the daylight. Your vision and senses will be way off. So before we start, let's get her on the road to recovery and then by god you lot have some training to do.'

It was then, once they all gave in and looked helpless, that he softened. They had been headstrong, impertinent and smart mouthed. He needed them to take him seriously and knew the gods would not put up with a bunch of impulsive cowboys. He sighed. *This is going to be a long day.*

* * * *

Out in the barn, he had them bridle their horses and sit on them to give them more power. He mounted his own horse. Once comfortable, Woody combined the energy from each rider and directed healing magic towards Caitlin. The glow around her was blinding, and once it dissipated, Woody quickly dismounted and lifted Caitlin off her horse. The surge of healing made her so dizzy she almost fell. The rest of the team was stunned at his speed. The improved connection between them allowed each member to experience the energised boost, but before the healing begun, they felt her pain. The relief on their faces was noticeable once her soreness eased. Still feeling the effects of her injuries they now understood what she had been dealing with so they sat still in the saddles, their hands firmly wrapped in the horses' manes until Caitlin had improved. Then came the best part; they felt her joy at feeling better.

'Do a spin for us Cait.' Woody put her on her feet. Suddenly her eyes snapped open, as her energy flooded back. The instant jump and joyous hands in the air made them all happy she was okay.

'Look, we did it, she's healed!' Bree clapped her hands.

Woody was pleased to see Cait's improvement as she danced around. Her eyes drifted as she searched for marks on her legs and arms. He was amazed that even the deep scaring was gone. *Maybe these guys are more powerful than I give them credit.* This gave him hope that with a little more work, they might just be the right fit to work amongst the gods.

'How do I look? Can I train with the team now?' Caitlin's eyes were still dull, but only Woody noticed that. He knew there was much more to her condition and he would work with her later, in private.

First things first, he rationalised. *This motley crew needs a workout.*

He turned to the others. 'Today will test you both mentally and physically. Your collaboration as a group and reactions to situations will determine the outcome.' His tone stated his objective. This time he had no intentions of pandering to them; nor would he be letting them off lightly. Without warning, he launched into the first rule of being a Rider, staying connected to their ride. With a single swipe of his hand in the air, he knocked them off their horses.

'You had better learn how to stay steady on your rides and become quicker at picking up magic threats that could send you flying. Now get back on your horses and ready yourselves, or you will have more than bruised butts.'

* * * *

By the end of the day, they had trained well, and Woody could tell they were brain wrecked. He had been bossy but needed to be the hard taskmaster he was, as he tested their reflexes, aptitude and their universal mind control. He made them sit and defuse before allowing them to go inside for showers. Nathen and Zeke, who decided to take the next shift, waved off a happy Nigel who had covered for them while they trained.

Axon's butler had tried to get out of the duty, but Woody didn't take no for an answer, and his last attempt at getting out of this chore was met with Woody's pointed finger towards the staircase. 'Now man— stop whining.'

Caitlin opted for a spa first; tired yet proud of the team for her healthy body that floated weightlessly in the bubbles.

Bree stayed with her, enjoying the warm water on her muscles, too exhausted from the day's activities to stand in the shower. 'That last exercise was the bomb,' she told Caitlin. 'Nearly spun myself out of control, that last bolt of light came at me so fast, and what was with that! Geez, Cait he had you doing stuff I've never seen you do, ever.'

'Me either. I didn't know Cassie had given me that sort of download. I'm so all that.' She lay back with a smug expression and jumped as she felt a slap.

Bree hit her one across the shoulder good-humoredly. 'That's for getting me good that last stint.'

Caitlin lay back again but wore a grin. Today she'd learned how to let out a mere sliver of power, just enough of a beam to zap the team if their reflexes weren't quick enough, and enjoyed her ability to exercise authority. 'That was one great experience.'

'For you maybe, Cait. We were the ones spinning like a top to deflect it. You just sneaked up on us. Man, I hated you a couple of times. That hurt.'

Caitlin thought that hysterical and ended up with a mouthful of water, coughed and sat up. 'Sorry, *not!*'

Bree was glad they could talk about anything again but wished she wasn't the butt of her joke.

'Breezy, honey,' Caitlin saw the look at her seriousness. 'It worked though didn't it? You and Lisha don't get dizzy now, and Zeke has stopped hesitating.'

'I suppose so.' She finally grinned. 'Woody's a good egg isn't he?'

Caitlin agreed as she stood up, grabbed a towel and wiped the excess water from her bathers. 'Come on, girlfriend, let's go doll up to impress our men.'

'Cait, you like Axon, um – lots don't you?'

'Shush, our little secret, okay.'

Bree grinned widely, her fingers held firm to Caitlin's as they ran up the stairs. Caitlin confiding in her again proved they were still best friends and she had forgiven her for taking Rory. This thought gave her a shudder of joy *or was it Cait's magic?*

* * * *

Later downstairs, dressed, pumped up after a great day, the two friends fooled around dancing. Bree and Caitlin leapt away and squealed, then laughed when Axon and Rory shimmered into the area they were in, both getting a surprise at their sudden appearance. Bree jumped up into Rory's arms.

'What are we celebrating, beautiful?' He grinned at her. 'You look stunning.'

'Look.' She pointed to Caitlin. 'We healed her.'

Caitlin opened her arms and spun in a circle. Her short skirt and loose sleeveless top showed off her figure. Suddenly she flushed crimson as Axon's eyebrow lifted and a slight grin softened his mouth.

Rory stared at Caitlin, speechless, and broke into a grin as he spoke to Bree. 'You guys did well, so how about you fill me in on the rest of it while I take a shower.'

'Woody taught us so much cool stuff today.' She grinned happily at Rory as he dragged her off, making her giggle as he lifted her again into his arms and ran up the stairs with her.

Axon caught Caitlin's hand as she brought it down, and transported her into his study.

'That was trippy. Kidnapper!' She chuckled. In comforting arms that wrapped gently around her and warm lips that claimed hers, Caitlin's head swam in the dreamy embrace.

'You look stunning. I couldn't help myself.' He lowered his head to steal one more kiss.

'Can you stay here a minute, beautiful? I want to hear about your day but just have to duck up and get changed.

She agreed and sat over on the couch waiting for his return. At the speed he could move, she knew it wouldn't be long before he came back.

It was just a kiss, she reminded herself, bewildered by the affectionate move he made on her and glad he finally did. Her eyes dropped to the low-cut top and tight leather skirt and she pulled at the hem. This didn't change the position, so she shrugged and smiled. She figured it worked once, so maybe it might just get her one more kiss before the night ended. She felt wistful as she waited. While thinking of his wide grin and come-to-bed eyes, pleasurable warmth built inside her. They had only just started to kiss again, nothing too serious, so she stood up and paced. He had broken her heart once, and she must stop falling into his arms every time he wanted her there.

All thoughts left her as he transported back into the room with his shirt undone. Her eyes widened, and her heart happily hummed as she watched him do up his buttons. His shoulders were massive, a buff chest tapered down to a trim waistline and the slight hint of manliness on the pants line made her blush. Luckily, he missed her checking him out, or had he? There was definitely a sexy drone in his voice as he asked about her day. Caitlin averted her eyes to catch her thoughts while he tucked in the shirt.

'Well, it started with Woody giving us a dressing down for not taking enough notice of what we had learned from the Cloud Riders. After he had thoroughly made us feel like spoilt brats, the drill master, no that's too pleasant, the tyrant, spent the day training us. I, of course, ended up the teacher's pet and had the pleasure of handing out the disciplinary measures. The guys are still annoyed at me.' She giggled.

'So he sounds like he gave a bit of tough love then.'

'Yes! He is so cool – but strict, you have no idea.' She rolled her eyes as he sat opposite her and bent to tie his shoelaces.

There had been two calls for dinner before Axon was satisfied he knew the day's events, and stood up. 'This has been, as usual, very enlightening but you must be starved. Shall we?' He gestured for her to go through the door first.

Caitlin had never been wooed by a man before but was sure he should have at least taken her hand or stolen another kiss. She'd miss-read him again. *Maybe he just wanted information and knew the kiss would loosen my tongue.* She sulked as they joined everyone at the dinner table.

Woody was the first one Axon headed for. He shook hands with him and thanked him sincerely for the work he put into the team. 'Welcome. I hear you kicked arse with my lot today. They're a good bunch but did need guidance; hell, we all do.'

'Well, I won't say it was my pleasure because I was pretty ticked off. Yet, give them credit, even though I gave them what for, they took it on the chin. I expected a bit of attitude back but they surprised me. I was pleased with each of them for the big effort they put in after.'

'Glad to hear that! The gods will eat them alive if they dare argue with them.' He searched the room and spotted Caitlin. 'How did you go with the feisty one today?'

'I'll try again tomorrow. Cait put a lot of heart into the training session today but still needs more work. Is this how she's been over the past few months since I saw her?'

'Worse.'

'Mmm, thought so!'

Axon shrugged. 'Shouldn't be a problem if you need her again tomorrow. I'm sure Nigel would love to help out and do a shift or two for her.' He grinned. 'She tells me you had him on duty today; interested to know how you got him to do that. He has been with me for too many years, and I have rubbed off on him. He can be one stubborn cookie to handle if he doesn't want to do something.'

Woody laughed. 'Thought I'd have to hog tie him to the chair he gave me so much cheek. 'Where is he?' He laughed heartily. 'Butler or not, I'm having a beer with the funny man.'

Woody snapped his fingers. Nigel looked up while still serving drinks and smiled.

'Get over here you!' he commanded and ruffled his knuckles on Nigel's head when he got to him. It was then the team relaxed and during the night saw what Woody meant in his gruff voice, when he said, "you work hard, and I'll show you wimps how to party." And, did they party, all but Caitlin. She volunteered to go on watch. The day had been exciting for her, but the session with Woody the next day was on her mind. She hoped to get some clarity and give him something other than a dumbfounded look this time.

It was just before sunrise when Axon joined her. He had showered, and his light aftershave lingered as he passed her to check the activity within the planets. Chatting to her, Axon scanned the solar system. While searching the surface of Pluto, he told her of its ruler Hades and the role he played, as God of the Underworld. She shuddered at how cruel he could be and out of all the Rulers, he was the one she least looked forward to meeting.

Next, he focused on Jupiter, the ruler of this planet being Hades' brother, Zeus. Caitlin asked many questions about Zeus. He, being the King of the Gods, fascinated her.

Last was the eldest brother Poseidon, ruler of Neptune and God of the Sea. The titles of all three brothers were overwhelming enough, without the fact that she and her team were now the peacemakers to these ancient lawbreakers.

'Axon, are you sure we have the clout to control such divine characters?'

'Not the way you are, Cait, and I assume you look to rectify this by your offer to do the night shift. I hope it gave you time to reflect on your upcoming appointment with Woody. But just know I'm here for you and will be beside you every step of the way, helping any way I can. As for the planets, if we are to have any kind of peaceful outcome, we need to do this as a team, with you in prime form.'

'I agree I need more tweaking if I want to be anywhere near as good as Cassie. So yes, it was the reason I chose this shift, I did need to think. I also gather from what you have said so far, it was Hades' brothers who put the hit out on our farms. If this is true, it means we'll be facing these gods head on.'

'Correct.'

'And you honestly believe that I'm to the planets what Cassie is to the stars. That… my friend… is a big call. I just hope I don't let you down.'

'Caitlin, as unwell as you've been, it was you who felt something was wrong and that fear alone, forced my hand into bringing the team here, hence saving their lives.'

Her eyes widened and she raised her nose in an uppity pose. 'If that's so, I believe they're all indebted me.'

'Maybe I should have kept that quiet.' He found her amusing. 'I can only imagine what they will have to do to make it up to you.'

'Mm, yes, they will be at my beck and call, that is for sure!'

'Okay, I can see this is not going to go down well with Rory, but your call.' He grinned. 'In the meantime, Woody's waiting downstairs for you. Just remember what I've said and why it's imperative to let him into your psyche. Allow his magic to make right what is needed. Then you will be a force to be reckoned with young lady and will need none of us to give you the confidence you currently seek. But in saying that, these immortal men are ruthless, yes, but don't forget, they are just men. That power we seek is just a weapon and should only to be used as a last resort. Work just as hard sharpening your peacekeeping skills, and I'm positive you will have them wrapped around your little finger in no time as you have me. No magic needed.' He pulled her to her feet. 'Call me when you're done.'

Axon breathed out as the door closed behind her. He had started to wise up that she had a power that was unlike anything he had come across. It was the scent of a goddess, aromatic and delightful. This morning, however, it was exceptional. He closed his eyes and groaned. The aroma still lingered and his will against her charms, the fight inside to keep their relationship platonic, had weakened further. *Stay tough!* his mind warned. *She has a stronger connection with Rory and will leave you.*

* * * *

When Caitlin arrived downstairs, Rory and Bree were in the kitchen cooking breakfast while Woody sat at the table sipping coffee. His hair was ruffled, and his usual spark, flat. Caitlin hadn't slept but felt better after her chat with Axon. He had a way of uplifting her spirits which put her in a cheery mood. Her smile lit up her face as she grabbed a chair to put next to Woody.

The chair squealed on the tiled floor as she dragged it closer to him making Woody grunt. 'Sore head, shh,' he muttered.

Rory put a plate of food in front of her. 'Here, cooked this especially. The boss told me you'd be down about now.' He took both her arms and, treating her like a puppet, he moved them so she could pick up her knife and fork. This had her and Bree in stitches. Caitlin had missed him and the games he played to have her eat whatever he cooked.

Woody leant on his arm and watched, fascinated.

Rory shrugged and grinned at him. 'Unlike the rest of us, Cait has little interest in fine cuisine and I guess has plain taste buds. She's been like it since we met her.'

'What, not a lover of herbs and spices, Cait?' Woody asked.

She swallowed down a big mouthful of food with a gulp and poked a fork towards Rory. 'I eat what they cook for me.'

Woody glanced at Rory who smiled. 'We look after our own, Woody, and it's not an issue for us. Cait asks for nothing and gives us much. To cook for her is a delight and the least we can do.'

Woody watched Caitlin devour breakfast and then glanced at the pleasure on Rory and Bree's faces as they looked on. Making a meal she enjoyed was their way of showing her how much they cared. By enjoying it, she reciprocated their love. This was much like what Cassie did for their team, only this was in reverse.

CHAPTER SIXTEEN

A Friend in Need

Woody said nothing until he found a spot outside where they could be alone. As they stretched out on the grass, he moved his head from side to side and cracked his neck.

'You okay?' Caitlin said. 'I know all that rah rah and party boy you showed us last night was to reveal you're just like us. We get it, though, you have a job to do and we did need a good kick in the pants. But have to admit it was fun and glad you let them locks down and dropped the tough guy act for a bit. You fully won them over.'

'And you?'

'You've always had my respect, but now I know you are fun too. It's made me like you more.' She nudged him and grinned. 'I dig your style big Red.'

'Don't miss much do you, little one.'

'Nope, and one more thing, I bet after you finish with me, the session yesterday will feel like a walk in the park, right?'

'Mmm, maybe too astute.' He gave her a grin. 'You know then, that you exhibited cracks in your magic during training.'

She nodded and put her head down.

'If I don't fix it, the planet Rulers with their godly powers will identify your weakness, single you out and target you, possibly try to kill you. So yes we have a bit of work to do. Now quiet.'

'Yes sir.' She saluted him and sat up straight, ready for whatever exercise he was going to get her to do.

She was surprised when he requested hush and, turning her chin, stared into her eyes.

With her full attention, Woody was now able to create a bridge between them so his magic could search and find the grief of yesteryear. She had blocked him last time but he hoped to peel more layers from those walls this session and release her hidden fears, turning them into positives. He allowed his magic to flow from him to her. It gave her a sense of peace. Caitlin flopped backwards, eyes closed, but her mind far from quiet. Her forehead wrinkled with worry.

'Talk to me,' he said.

'I stuffed up.'

'Yes.'

'Can you fix me?' She squinted at him.

'Shush now. Let me see what's going on.' He moved his hand above her, and a blue flash was the last thing she saw as her eyes slammed shut; her mind his.

* * * *

Woody was almost in panic mode when her lashes fluttered. He had put Caitlin in a deep trance, the hypnosis needed to unlock the past. The secured bond of secrecy stayed dormant in a mind that had held firm. He was relieved when the comatose body, that had been out of it for many hours, finally moved.

'What happened?' She woke, refreshed.

'I had to go pretty deep to bring out what was troubling you. Do you recall anything we spoke about?'

She shook her head and shrugged. 'Nothing.'

'You will.' He dusted off leaves that had blown on his trousers as they had been there so long. 'I'm here for a few days, so if you are up to it, I'd like to try again tomorrow.'

'So we're finished? That was easy. Can I go?' Her energy levels had spiked and she wished to go use some of it up. 'I feel great.' She was bursting from within.' Lifting her arm, she checked the time, and her eyes widened as she stared at him. 'What! We've been out here all morning.'

'Yes, it was an exhausting session and after, you slept for a very long time. But no, we have not finished. How do you feel?'

Caitlin stretched. 'Like I've just been reborn, so energised.'

'The mind can forget, but the experience stays. I have set off a seed of truth in your memory. The magic in the seed will seek out hidden truths. After you recall that which upsets the flow of your power, it will dissipate and it won't bother you to mention it in the future.'

'So you can magically wave away the pain of the past that I can't even remember yet.'

'Yes!' He smiled. 'Now young lady, I have to see what this session uncovered.'

'Another test!'

He put a hand to her forehead. 'Cheeky! Now close your eyes and relax.'

She did as he commanded, still under this very powerful man's control, and she heard him communicate with her team. 'Zeke, is that you on watch?'

'Sure, what's going on?'

'Ignore the explosion you will see shortly. Cait is ready to power up and do an exercise for me.'

'No probs; will alert the others.'

A grin spread across Woody's lips. 'Ready.'

'Ready.'

'Caitlin, you have the power to do many things, but today I want you to launch a rocket-style projectile into space.'

'What! Are you serious?'

'Concentrate. This exercise, Cassie can do without thinking, so now focus on my orders and quit the negativity.'

She breathed out heavily. Woody knew stirring her up about Cassie would change her tune. *Both so competitive.* He grinned at her sulky expression.

She closed her eyes and let his words flow through her. 'Twist the top off the invisible casing I know you can see and fill it full of your own magical explosives. Secure the top with a tight turn before sending it out to the desolate sky to the right of us.'

Caitlin completed the task in her mind. When ready she opened her eyes and picked the target. The powerful bomb shot out from within her hands as she held them out. First, it was like a silver flash of light, and as the beam whizzed through the air and at a certain height it began to illuminate. Once the glow of the beam dulled the magical weapon moulded into the perfect shape of a rocket. By this time, they were both standing while Woody held her. The backdraft alone was incredibly powerful as it whistled towards its target.

'It's easier to fire these off when I'm on my horse,' she had to yell so he could hear her over the noise.

'Our rides sure are resilient, I know,' he shouted back.

As it hit the mark, Woody let her go. 'Better cover your ears Cait.'

'Won't need to— watch!'

Worried about the power she had stored and the damage it might cause, she ignored his last instructions and filled it full of something a little less harmful. Woody squinted, his lips squeezed firmly, realising she had strayed from what he asked. Caitlin giggled at the look he gave her and made him laugh when she pushed him. The glow from the exploding fireworks that popped and shrilled through the air, a total crowd pleaser, softened his mood towards her.

Lisha and Bree heard the sound of fireworks and knew their friend was putting on a show for Woody. Both girls appeared on the balcony above, jumped around and high fived each other while they took delight in the colourful display.

Woody smiled. 'Not what I asked for, but very creative.'

'Can I go now?' Caitlin itched to join the girls and have some fun with them. With so much energy she wasn't sure where to put herself.

Woody touched his ear pod, and listened to Nathen. 'No, that's not us. Our session is over.' In one swift movement, Woody had snatched up Caitlin and put her down facing the stables. 'You're up Red; you aren't going anywhere. There's trouble coming. Which stable is your horse kept in?' He looked around at the twin barns big enough to house twenty-five horses at a time. 'I have to get you up in the sky, pronto. This is not a drill, now— move it!'

Caitlin ran in front towards the barn on the left.

'Quick!' He hoisted her up and then fitted the golden bridle securely over Shargan's head. Her horse transformed, her armour cool against Caitlin's skin. A new outfit replaced her shorts and top as Shargan stretched out her massive white wings. The armour was decorative and bright in colour, and she patted him while waiting for Woody. His black stallion showed its age when shaping. The white wings were tinged with grey and the armour colours had faded. She could see they had been together a very long time.

Zeke was nearly out of breath as he, Bree and Lisha got to them. He talked fast as the girls raced to get their horses. 'At first, we thought it was you guys mucking about. The explosive matter slipped past Zoren's team, and we didn't pick it up either until it was in sight. It looks like a comet heading straight for us.'

Hearing it was so close, Woody and Caitlin headed off in flight while the others bridled their horses. The three riders still on the ground mounted quickly and were only seconds behind them. Caitlin could hear Woody as he communicated with the tower below, her ear pod cutting in and out from the power she built. She did get, however, that Nathen and Rory had to stay until relieved by Axon who had just arrived. Nathen headed down to get the horses ready while Rory waited in the tower, anxious to mount up and join his team.

Rory talked fast, leaving the channel open so his team could hear what he said to Axon. 'They must be tampering with the satellites, for us not to pick up anything. The only chatter at the minute is coming from Pluto and Jupiter. Hades and Zeus are following it, we're sure of it.'

Woody broke in. 'Can you hear what they are saying?'

'No, they're talking in an unfamiliar code, and it crackled so much we only heard parts, but it's being taped. Zoren is attempting to decipher it. We should hear from him soon.'

'Hang on Woody.' *Silence.*

'Okay, we're on our way. Axon has decoded some of the words, and it's not favourable. He's reasonably sure they are calling it a Dwarf Nova, so we'd better get up there quick smart to help.'

'Orders!' Woody tapped hard on his ear pod.

'Caitlin is to destroy it if she gets a clear shot. But tell her she will need everything she's got. Axon thinks it's too unstable to try and move it from the solar system, so it will have to be blown up.'

'Caitlin.' Woody's voice was firm. 'The rocket exercise I just showed you, give it a shot. Has more grunt than what you have been using and this one is huge and needs something big.'

She took a deep breath, closed her eyes and concentrated hard while the explosive magic began to take form in her mind.

Woody turned from her. 'The rest of you, get into position. Cait's already used a lot of power in the exercise. It could shatter and shoot out in all direction. Get ready to clean up the mess before it hits other Home Worlds.'

Zeke spoke to Woody. 'Counting you, Woody, we have four of us. Without Cait, we leave the fifth quadrant exposed.'

'Rory and Nathen are on their way, so until they do get here we will have to manage.' said Woody.

Zeke nodded in agreement. 'Just hope Cait's got something left to help until they reach us.' He knew how dangerous it was to drain Caitlin's powers entirely. He could already feel her straining now they had been connected correctly. He nodded to Bree and Lisha who could also feel it. 'You girls know what I'm thinking.'

They both nodded and put thumbs up.

'No use learning something if we can't use it when we need to.' Lisha was impatient to get started. They had been training for just this situation, although they had never used it. Being Rory's sister, she knew he would approve. It was he who came up with this manoeuvre to get more power from their spin. Instead of cleaning up just one spot at a time, they were possibly able to stretch the circumference to cover the entire cluster of debris at once.

'Glad you're on board because I see no other way around this if we are to stop the damage this will cause.

'No probs.' Lisha gently shook the reins and moved off. 'Come on Bree, he'll be here any minute. Stop being so co-dependant.'

Bree looked uncertain.

'Bree,' Woody broke in on the conversation. 'It's loyalty that makes you wait, not love, I can feel that, but don't confuse your work ethic by reflecting on Lisha's comment. Keep your head clear and do what you know to be right. Rory trusts you, make the call he would insist upon.'

Bree's face lit up, her smile cute as pie. 'He would want me to wait. He puts me at the tail end; less spin allows me to use the extra power to push or drag the target where he needs it to be. Actually, it's a trick Caitlin taught me.'

'Then you know what to do.'

Bree stayed where she was, glad Woody allowed her to make this call.

Woody turned back to Caitlin. 'I don't want to see fireworks like your piss-poor, half-hearted effort earlier.' His cheap shot annoyed her. Yes, she deserved it. Woody had been in service many centuries and to have someone alter his orders would have annoyed him. He sounded ticked off, and she would have relished retaliating with a wisecrack, but kept her cool, something she was also trying to master. Instead, she shook it off and took a breath, determined to show him that when on the job, she was trustworthy. With this in mind, she packed this missile being created with a little extra.

Tuned out on further influences, she opened her eyes and focused on the Dwarf Nova. There was no way she would fail. If she could prevent her team from involvement and possible harm, she would have to punch through this bad boy. She shoved the giant ball of burning flares and gas high above her. The thrust she gave it sent it spinning far into open space and at the same time launched the explosive missile. Both finally connected in a deserted sector of the universe.

Cheers went up around her, for the execution was spot on, and the explosive blast that lit up the sky left sparks that looked like shooting stars.

'Now that was impressive.' Woody gave a whistle and stilled. Lifting his strong jaw, he squinted and focused ahead with one ear slightly tilted, while the floating embers drifted from them.

Rory had arrived and joined Woody. The intensity of his stare was a worry. 'What's up Woody?' He tapped his ear pod. 'Axon, can you hear anything?'

'Oh hell! Look out guys, it's a comet, and the blatzing thing is out of control. It will reach you in seconds. Has Caitlin got anything left?'

Woody answered for her. 'That was her second one in a short space of time. I'll make her try, but even our rider, Cassie, can't pull three out in a row.'

The comet was in sight. Aware how fast it moved, Rory left Woody and, using telepathy, shifted him and the rest of the team into position. The clean-up if they couldn't stop the comet would be huge and he readied them for the worst possible outcome

Have news, Rory relayed to his team using telepathy. *The comet won't totally blow up the Home World, Ara, when it hits, but will destroy Axon's home and take out most of the city of Klaxton. Cait, if you do have anything left, direct it and see if you can't push this sucker up and away from here, or at least push it off course to save the town. Us guys can handle it from there. Axon said he can rebuild, but Klaxton is a poor community and he fears for their survival. As a last resort, he will transport the villagers away from danger, but his cover will be blown. Our boss has faith in us so I for one will not be letting him down.*

Caitlin called upon her gift one last time, her hope dashed upon firing up, for it felt like a drained battery. Not even a spark of magic left her when she threw her hands up high in the air. She had shown off in front of Woody and used too much power on the last rocket. Unable to save Axon's castle and the villagers horrified Caitlin and tears streaked her face as she strained to draw from within. The smidgen of magic conjured up was weak, which made her effort useless.

Rory was impatient when nothing happened and communicated his concern. *Woody, what's happened? She should have moved it or slowed it down by now, not sure if we can stop it in time but we'll give it all we got—*

I call to the light! He shouted out a plea. His voice vibrated out as he put himself in a perilous spin, the quickest and only way to battle the oversized speeding threat.

'They won't stop it in time, will they Woody.' Caitlin's heart thumped hard in her chest as he agreed. Her lips were so dry from stress, and licking them did little to ease the sticky sensation.

'Come to me, Red.' His powers drew her horse sideways to him. He lifted his leg and got on behind her. 'With my help, we might just defeat that sucker. Let me teach you a trick of Cassie's. She draws power from her horse all the time and has worked out how to use us when she needs to as well. The thing is, this is dangerous, and if not careful you could kill both your horse and me so be forewarned. Never use this on anyone else unless you really get how this works.' He tied his horse loosely to Shargan's saddle. He knew she needed her horse's magic. Woody's stallion was far too old for such a power up that would be necessary. 'Afterwards, I will be helpless, so you must get us both back to Ara. My team will feel my loss of life essence and come to my aid. '

Tears poured from her eyes. 'This sounds dangerous; what if I kill you? Woody, isn't there another way?'

He shook his head. 'Cassie did this in her earlier days too, but when her powers reached their full potential, as yours have already, she nearly took Kayden out. It was touch and go for a while. Thought we had lost him so only take what you need, okay, just enough to do the job.' He whispered in her ear, 'no pussy fireworks. Use it wisely.'

She wiped her eyes. The comet was in sight. The team had barely moved it; the gases sparked with the Rider magic, but it being so unstable, it was not enough to steer it off course. Caitlin took a deep breath, and touched her earpiece. 'Clear the area, I'm giving it another shot.' She made the call while calculating the size of the comet. To concentrate better, she closed her eyes as she only had seconds or all their efforts would be futile. Woody used his magic to begin the sequence and, learning quickly what he had done, she took over. Her plan was to build up enough explosives to stop the menacing fireball in its tracks, but the entire time she kept in mind Woody's warning.

'I won't let you win, Hades, you evil tyrant,' she heard Woody growl through gritted teeth as she drew the power from him and her horse. As she did so, Woody opened up the floodgate to his magic, and the magnitude of his power shot through her like an electric jolt. Snatching what she needed, she closed off the magic feed from Woody. His eyes rolled until only the whites were visible. Caitlin held steady as he slumped against her, and screamed out as the horse dipped too.

'Don't you dare fail me Shargan!' The horse shook its head and kept them steady. She knew Shargan had got a fright. 'We can do this girl.' She pulled Woody's mount closer. He would keep them all in the air until help arrived. This was going to take all of them if it was to succeed. Caitlin swung her arms up and down with vigour, shook all the power to her hands, and when she could handle it no more, shot out a wave of energy that congealed around the comet and froze it dead in its tracks. Lifting it quickly from her team and out of harm's way, she shot out the rest of the emission and blasted the frozen comet to pieces. The soft coldness that remained dropped on them like snowflakes.

Rory and the team sat stunned with what she had just accomplished, yet freaked out when they saw Woody slump sideways, and half his body fall over onto his horse. He looked as if he was out cold.

Caitlin spun around and held the buckle of his pants, to prevent him completely falling from her horse. He was heavy. Exhausted, she tapped her earpiece then put her hand up for help. 'Hurry guys, he's too big, I'm dropping him.'

Rory put the horses into full flight, leaving the Riders to use their own magic to push them faster. He flew with supersonic sped towards her. *Oh my god Cait, what did Woody just get you to do? Is he alive?*' He didn't get any more from her after her hand went up, and knew she was in real trouble. They had only just arrived as Caitlin too collapsed.

# Chapter Seventeen

Cosmic Riders Prevail

What am I doing in bed? Caitlin tossed the covers back and threw her legs over the edge of the bed. 'Whoops.' Her giddy head spun.

The door flung open, and Rory swaggered in. 'Bout time you woke up, had me worried sick.'

'What? How did I get here? I feel like I've been eating rug!' She smacked her dry lips together, picked up the goblet on the side of the bed and sculled it down.

Rory opened up the curtains, and the sun streamed in. 'You've been out of it for some time, delirious most of it. How are you feeling?'

She put out her arms and swung her legs; all seemed to be intact. 'Fine.' She finally recalled what happened, and her words were almost a whisper. 'How's Woody?'

'You did well Cait, he made it just fine. He couldn't believe you returned the power that you didn't use back to him. It saved his life, and the guy's done nothing but rave about how talented you are. You're Axon's golden girl at the minute. Trust you to win all their hearts.'

He bent down on a knee. 'Axon wants you to stay here even after we leave. Thinks it's dangerous for you on Earth and doesn't trust that we can look after you.' He looked worried, his frustration at the situation apparent. 'I want you to come home with us. You're one of my team, and this is just too hard. I need us to train together. It's the only way we can become spontaneous, to be one unit. Please tell him you're coming home with us.'

'Geez Rory, he's the boss. Anyway, that won't be for ages. We haven't got a home, remember?'

'Caitlin, you've been unconscious for nearly three weeks. The farm has been rebuilt, furniture and equipment went in yesterday, and it's ready for us to move back in. I came up here thinking it was to say goodbye, but now you're awake you can tell him your home is with us.'

Caitlin threw her arms around him. 'You look so worried Rory. You know whether I'm here or there, you are and will always be my most favourite person. I miss you guys too when you're not around. Look, help me to the bathroom, and once I'm dressed let's discuss it over coffee. I'm parched.'

After a relaxing bath, Caitlin looked more refreshed. Rory was pleased when she kept her promise and sat o u t on the balcony with him so they could talk in private. Here, he caught her up on the comings and goings of Hades and his brothers. 'Since they saw their plan had failed, the brothers have not been seen, not even visiting their usual hangouts.'

'So we can assume they are planning something even bigger.'

'That's why I want us all together. To tell the truth, after that last attack and not being able to pick it up, I don't even trust the security here.'

'I doubt we will be safe anywhere until this is sorted out, Rory.'

Rory sat with a sullen expression.

Caitlin had been with Rory for what seemed like forever. She hated to see him worried, never mind how upset he was at them possibly living in different households. But to her, she didn't feel as if they were parting as she would simply meet up with them at the rendezvous point from Ara and had already got Axon's okay on this if she did decide to stay. But still, she and Rory did have a connection even beyond her understanding so at this point, for him, she was leaning towards going home.

Her mind skipped to Woody and how he had opened up some

past memories in their last session. Not remembering much of the session, she did sense it was Rory who had healed her painful past. He did this by giving her purpose and a new family. The new life he built around her allowed Caitlin to move forward and leave whatever it was that scared her, even now, to think about, far behind. She owed him much, but there was also a part that had matured, made her want what he had found… *love and happiness*. Could she live without Rory and the team? They had been her world, her joy. But Axon had a piece of her heart now too. It missed a beat, and she blushed as the need to see him heightened. Could she say goodbye to the Home Worlds, Ara, Nigel the amusing butler, the crazed wolf Russo, or the man who was stealing her heart? Axon, the only man who made her melt, and in his arms had shown her she was no longer a girl. Her mind stuck on that for a minute. Why didn't she say he made her feel like a woman? She had not been a girl for a very long time – yet she was thinking of herself even now as a little girl. It tugged at a memory, forced her to look away while trying to shake the feeling, but it kept repeating in her head, *girl – little girl*.

'Where's Axon?'

'Are you telling him goodbye?'

'I'm a Rider and belong with you.' The grin she received was worth every sacrifice she was about to make.

* * * *

Axon's smile widened when Rory walked her into the den. 'Caitlin!' It was a chilly night, the fire which had just been lit crackled and spat sparks as he poked at it. 'Sit!' He puffed a cushion on the couch for her.

Rory helped Caitlin sit down, and could tell she was still a little weakened by the experience. He couldn't wait to get her home and take care of her. Nobody, he believed, could care for her as well as he could. He bent to speak with her for just a minute. 'I'll give you time to talk and say goodbye, and then I'll be back to collect you.'

He stood up to a surprised Axon and decided to use bluff. 'She wants to come home with us, so we're taking her when we leave.'

Not allowing Axon to respond, he trod heavily out of the room, leaving the door to close with a thud.

Axon, stunned, moved and sat in the chair opposite Caitlin, taking it slowly to give time to collect himself. He had already made it clear to Rory it was best she stayed with him, for safety reasons. Had that been the motivation for the decision? Now she was actually leaving, his mind was in tatters. He didn't want her to go and was speechless.

'You look tired, Axon.' She stared into warm, kind eyes set in dark shadows. His face wore a frown.

'I have missed you.'

'And Rory's comment has upset you?'

His head was down, and the slight shake of his curls made her want to get up and run her hands through them, and ease his worries. He cared for her too, it astounded her he was only just seeing that now. It was time to choose; she would hurt Axon if she left, Rory if she stayed. Caitlin loved them both. Rory, she trusted with her life. Did her trust run as deep for this gentle man that had become entwined in her life? The vision of her grown-up self making this decision faded into a girl, no – I'm not a girl but a woman. *There it was again*. Caitlin closed her eyes. The dark scared her, so strained to open them, but darkness was everywhere. *Have I fallen asleep? Did Axon turn off the lights? What happened to the fire; did it go out?*

It had strangely turned to night. She could barely see and feared everything – feared the hours of darkness, loneliness. Memories flooded back of her childhood, she was but a young child. She had a doll in her hand as the light went out – pitch black.

'Where is everyone?' she cried out. *But alas, there was no answer,* 'I am here on my own, please come back!' Her gulps of sadness had her fall to her knees.

She screamed. *Was that me or was that the little girl?* 'Why can't anyone hear me? I don't know where my bed is,' she cried, 'and where is my doll I held?' *That girl – that is me?*

Caitlin was locked underground, alone. Memories flooded back, and once again she was that little girl and tears ran down her face.

'Someone, help me.' *She's so scared, and the sobs break my heart. I can hear them so clearly.*

Arms were holding her and now she wasn't alone.

'Don't cry little one.' *I kept hearing that.* 'You are not alone anymore, so don't cry.' *Did I say that, or did someone else?*

Her heart broke as she recalled the dark nights that sometimes lasted longer than the light. Meals left, but no contact. *Doesn't anyone care just a little?*

'Yes, we care, come back! Come back to us. You're loved now and have a happy home, many friends.' *I hear a voice through the terror and yet now I run through the bush. I am grown, but I see a little girl that looks like me. I follow her through the harsh scrub, scared for the child that sobs and runs from me.* 'Wait!' *I call to her as I stumble over bushes and rocks. I have to get to her and even though I am hurting, this little girl is all I care about.* Exhausted, Caitlin drops to the ground; she hears the girl no more and is at peace. She looks up and sees the sunrise of a new day and wonders where she is and how she has become such a mess. Cuts, bruises and exposed bone freak her out.

'I remember everything!' She cries on a shoulder only too willing to be there.

'The little girl is better; she is grown up and loved so very much by me and she is finally happy,' the person that holds her says.

I want to stay in sadness, but there is a happy ending for me. It is there, where I see the light shining through the cracks.

The brightness opened wider and wider until the glow of light illuminated. Axon cradled her gently, and it was he who had talked to her, and loved her. Without question, she wanted to always stay with this man, the man she loved. She knew for sure the little girl was happy, for she had the life she dreamed of all those nights. The little girl had finally poured out all her terrifying years of darkness to *this* man that cuddled her so-caringly in his arms.

Axon kissed her tearstained face and hugged her gently. 'I love you. I will always love you, so please stay here and let me show you how lovely your life can be.'

Rory came in while Caitlin had her meltdown. Axon was with

her, and by his words and how carefully he handled her return to realism more than impressed him. He wished while watching, it was him, but she chose Axon. *However, this changes nothing, I'm still taking her home.*

The three of them sat and talked through the night; Rory relented and promised he would leave it up to Caitlin to decide when she was ready to go home, and then he would come and get her.

'I'm not entirely a controlling monster, Cait.' He lightened the conversation in the end. 'I can see you need time alone with Axon, and to tell you the truth it's probably for the best. I want you in the right headspace for the next mission.' He turned to Axon. 'This is a one time offer so don't expect it all the time. How about us lot stay an extra day to look after Ara so you can take Cait somewhere special tomorrow?'

Axon's eyes widened. 'Really, you would do that for us?'

'No, I'd do it for Cait. I have upset her lately which is something I don't intend to ever repeat. So to make it up to her before she fully dumps my arse, I want to do something to make up for my behaviour towards her. I see it's you she has chosen for this so I will back down on this instance, but only because I want her to take off somewhere relaxing and unwind after what she has just had to go through.'

'You knew about her past and yet kept it secret,' Axon guessed.

'Again, it was for her!' He stood up. 'I could have killed the mongrels when I saw how she had been living. But all I could think of was to get her out of that stinking pit of an underground basement. I don't know how she survived. When she forgot, I let her. Right or wrong of me, I didn't care. I hate that she has had to relive those memories.' He moved her hair back off her forehead. 'She is my family, my friend. Don't hurt her.'

'Never, I love her too!'

Axon held her. *You're mine!* He grinned happily as Rory left to get some sleep.

Rory had a big day ahead if he was to handle things while Axon was off world.

CHAPTER EIGHTEEN

Fate has its Own Plan

Axon smiled. 'You look beautiful,' he said before transporting them and poof! Caitlin stood on a beach of what appeared to be a tropical island resort. He landed them in the water. They laughed as the waves lapped gently at their feet and then they ran up on the beach, where both plopped onto the sand and sank into the softness, kicking off wet shoes. With loafers in hand, Axon stood and helped her up.

'Hungry?'

'Starved.' Caitlin took his arm as they strolled along the water's edge until they reached a restaurant. A waiter fussed with napkins after they were seated and gave a hearty welcome, but the name he called Axon confused Caitlin.

'Ah, Mr Wolf, just in time. Would you and ma'am like to try Delphinus Ambrosia? The grapes are from my grandfather's very own vineyard, the young crop gives it a fruity yet robust flavour.'

'Yes, thank you, Garston.' The waiter poured a small amount for him to try. Axon swirled the Ambrosia in the goblet, sniffed the bouquet and sipped it. 'That's perfect.'

After both goblets had been filled, and their orders were taken, Garston left to organise their meals.

'Mr Wolf – what?' she whispered to Axon once they were alone again.

'The name is homage to the wolves on my Home World. An

alias is necessary when off world without security.'

'Yes of course. I hadn't thought about it, but now I'm a Cloud Rider I will, won't I?'

He reached out for her hand. 'For the moment it isn't an issue. If I have to introduce you to anyone here, I will call you Red.' He grinned.

She was happy with that and glanced around. 'I still can't believe I'm here and, with you.'

They had been seated under palm trees. The fronds on the branches quietly rustled in the delicate warm breeze. Axon poured her more wine, which they sipped it in silence while Caitlin took in the ambience of loveliness that surrounded her. 'Are we still in the stars? Has this island a name?' She turned back to him.

'I hinted to you that the stars were an exuberant place to live and I'm so pleased you are finally well enough for me to prove to you just how much you would enjoy it if you chose to stay. This is Dolphin Island on the Delphinus constellation.' He directed her attention to the water where a few dolphins had come close to shore and, once noticed, they began to make a ruckus. 'They're friendly if you want to pat them.'

'Hell yes!' She stood up quickly, wanting to make the best of it. She had no intentions of wasting one minute of this chance to experience something new.

In the water, they swam around her legs, rubbing themselves against her. If one missed out on the attention, it made a funny clicking sound that made her laugh.

'They talk to you, how cool.' She was fascinated. 'They feel soft.' Her hands ran across them before Axon dragged her back to the table when their meal arrived.

'This is just what I needed. Thanks for giving up your day for me.'

'My pleasure, but I have a lot planned so eat and let's go and explore.'

Three islanders played soft music to them while Caitlin used her fork to push the food around her plate, preferring to chat. With a movement so fast that she held her breath, he stood, picked her up in his arms and swung her around, smiling. 'Wine, music and still I can't get you to eat. Maybe a day in the fresh air might just do the trick.'

Caitlin giggled uncontrollably as he stomped up the beach with her still in his arms and sat her in one of the island explorers, a Dolphin buggy. A dig in his pocket produced notes that he gave the attendant. With a tug of an electrical lead that charged it, they set off, the chunky wheels churning up the sand. Caitlin coughed as they became consumed in dust and gravel.

'Stop!' She got out when he pulled up, walked around to his side and made him move over to the passenger's seat. 'You guys up here have become far too complacent with your transporting powers. Have none of you got a licence?'

He joked, 'What's that?'

They stopped at the edge of a thick forest, preferring to take a stroll through the freshly scented woodlands.

'Well, now I know how the person in the land of the giants felt.' Caitlin stood with her head back trying to see the tops of the trees.

'Giant Delphonie trees,' he told her. 'You see, many years ago this was all water, the Island did not exist. The story goes that the Boto breed of Dolphins found a special magic that enabled them to become shapeshifters. Unbeknown to them, being able to shape into humans changed everything, even where they lived. They started to die off; the only ones that stayed healthy were those who lived in fresh water. King-Sea, the King of all Dolphins, fell in love with a Boto breed, Princess Delphinus. When she became ill, King-Sea could not bear his beloved to die but wished her to stay near so instructed his royal guards to called upon all dolphins to help save the princess. The dolphins swam around and around in the shape of a dolphin, sucking up the ocean floor, and created this very island. After the heavy rains had gouged out river beds and filled them, it is said her royal court of Boto dolphins struggled through the sand and planted sea seeds. This was to encourage vegetation on the sandy island. After the flood had subsided, the King ordered the Dolphins to circle the entire island. This time they sprang up on tails and sang to the seeds to set growth in motion. These are the trees they first planted to give cover during the hot months, and to this day if you listen hard, you will hear the song within the trees. Legend has it that if the Boto Dolphins leave, the trees and vegetation will die.'

'I love that story.' She smiled and moved gently in the breeze; sure she heard the song.

Back in the car, she pulled up as they came to a dead end. 'Where now?'

'We walk to that rock.' Axon pointed to an enormous rocky mountain to the left of them. He turned and pulled a bag over from the back seat and rifled through it.

'What are you up to and where did that come from?'

'My little secret.' He grinned. 'Come on, time to gear up Cait. We're climbing to the top.'

'Oh my god! You're kidding me, right?' The tall, steep and rugged rock surface loomed above them so high; the top was out of sight.

'Scared?'

'Me! Hell no. Give me them.' She wasn't going to show him how crazy she thought this idea, but instead snatched at the gloves he held up for her.

Climbing the uneven and crumbly surface, Caitlin wished she hadn't been so gung-ho, as showing off had worn her out. 'This is hot work.' She wiped the perspiration from her brow.

'Nearly there.'

'You said that half an hour ago.'

He smiled and gave her a hoist up to a ledge. 'See, we are here.'

Eyes open wide, she was in awe, for the view was spectacular. Ocean surrounded the entire island that seemed to be situated in the middle of nowhere. Goal accomplished, they kissed and sat to enjoy what they had achieved. After some time she stood up. 'So how do we get down?' The climb had taken its toll, and although she didn't want to have to admit it, she didn't look forward to the descent.

Axon stood beside her. 'I have enjoyed every minute of the climb up here with you but am finding greed prevents me taking the two-hour trek down. I missed you while you concentrated so hard. So, this is how we are getting down.' He grinned and transported her there.

'Hey, isn't that cheating?' She chuckled.

'I'm not always the good guy, especially when it comes to going after what I want.'

That was the first time he'd mentioned how he felt since her meltdown. She liked it and needed to hear more.

'So does that mean you've finally fallen for my charms?' She fluttered her eyelashes at him.

He snatched her up in his arms and plonked her in the driver's seat. 'Drive.'

Back on the bumpy sandy track, the subject was changed and deep in conversation, they arrived back at the resort far too quickly.

Caitlin dropped her lip when they pulled up. She wasn't ready to go home. 'Do we have to get out? Can't we drive somewhere else? This has been amazing.'

He smiled. 'I wasn't going to leave just yet. You don't come to Dolphin Island and not have a cocktail at sunset. The night sky here is quite spectacular, something you shouldn't miss.'

'I love you doing all this for me.'

He grinned. 'There's a reason for all I do, and from here on in it's about you, Caitlin. I want you to start experiencing all the things you missed. You won't see any of it, locked up in my arms.'

'But that would be pleasing too.'

Her sexy tone made him shake his head. 'Cait, behave. I'm trying to give you a memory to cherish. Something to take back and get you through tough times that may be ahead.'

She chuckled and made him smile. She had been stirring him and poked him when he got it. She wasn't prepared for his sudden attentive and inviting look which drew her in too. They had almost kissed when a light shower came down on them from nowhere. Arm in arm they looked more like happy lovers on a honeymoon as Axon ran with her into a restaurant close to them.

'This is a bit posh.' She started to back out of the door. 'I should have brought a change of clothes.' She felt underdressed.

'You look adorable. Stop worrying, woman!' He held her close to prevent her leaving while waiting for the maître d' to tend to them.

Seated in a private booth, he passed her a menu. 'See, no one even noticed us come in, and now we have privacy. Feel better?' He grinned.

'Guess so.'

Next thing an islander came from behind her and placed a string of flowers around her neck. He grinned like a schoolboy. 'You beautiful woman.' He backed away and tripped over the table behind him, unable to divert his eyes, apologised and scurried off.

Axon shook his head at the young man who had no hope with the woman he had every intention of spending the rest of his life with. He relished that she never gave the young man with bright blue eyes a second glance, pleased her eyes stayed fixed on him only.

She shrugged. 'Guess I don't look as frightful as I feel.'

He pointed to a poster. 'The theme tonight is Hula of Delphinus. See, your bright floral sundress will fit right in.'

She eyed him, unsure what Hula of Delphinus meant. 'Hula is…?'

'Similar to the celebrations from your world, they dance to preserve traditions and the culture.'

'Oh, I see. You mean islander grass skirts and bright body painting, stuff like that?'

'Yes! You like?' He raised a brow.

'No!' She grinned. 'I love it.'

He laughed heartily.

Caitlin had grown accustomed to his sense of humour and the more they grew to know each other, the more opened up and relaxed they had become. After ordering Moonjuice for two, Axon took her hand. 'Would you dance with me, Cait?'

'Sure.' She tried to sound confident and worldly. She had taken only a few lessons but was not about to let an opportunity to be in his arms slip. To dance with someone like Axon, a gentleman who was both honourable and exciting to be around had her floating on a cloud as they walked to the floor.

'Dancing, as well as staying for dinner. I feel very spoilt and honoured, but shouldn't we eat up and leave? What about your work? Won't Zoren be annoyed you wagged it?'

'Wagged it?' He sounded confused.

'It's an Earth term; if you skip class, you wagged it. Sorry, not that funny now I know you don't get it.'

'Cait.'

'Yes, Axon.' Her mind was dreamy from dancing so close.

'Just dance.'

'In our world, a man would pretend it was at least a little funny if he was expecting more from the woman he held.'

'Cait.'

She chuckled. 'I know, dance and zip it.'

'I was going to say, that was funny. Now can we go to bed together?'

'Axon.'

'Yes, Cait.'

'Just dance.'

They both cracked up laughing.

They swayed effortlessly to the music, their bodies moulded into one another. Caitlin felt as if they had danced together for years. *Is there nothing he's not good at?*

'I didn't know you brought perfume with you, it's quite intoxicating.'

'I have no handbag, so I carry nothing.'

He held her at arm's length. 'It drives me crazy, you wear it all the time.'

'No, I never wear perfume. It's just me. Rory thinks it's a power. It seems to get stronger if I feel threatened.'

'What, with me?'

Caitlin glanced around. 'We could be in for a rocky night. Can you handle it or do you want to leave?'

'Umm…' He eyed her. 'I think I'd prefer to see this play out Cait. It will give me insight into what this magical scent attracts and what it does if anything. Assuming Rory is correct and trouble does find you, I'll transport us home.'

'Don't believe me, do you?'

'Cait, just dance.' He pulled her in, having a feeling the only trouble she would find was him not being able to keep his hands off her. 'You are one big mystery, Cait. And trouble with a capital T.'

'Axon.'

'Yes, Cait.'

'Just dance.'

His smile was broad, his eyes bright as he spun her around and dipped her, his kiss light and deliberate.

She hoped he knew it wasn't him she feared as a danger. Did he make her feel her virtue was a little at risk? No, it was something else, *but what?*

Back at the table they ate from a fresh seafood platter and watched the first performance of the night. Female islanders, dressed in traditional costumes with their tops painted on, danced out stories of old. After dinner, Axon moved Caitlin closer, and she leant into him to watch more entertainment, this time from the men. One of the over-eager bucks hit on Caitlin, first serenading her, and then inviting her to join them on the stage. She refused, wanting to stay in Axon's comfortable arms, but laughed and surprisingly went with him after three others came to help. As two of them lifted her onto the stage, she hoped she didn't embarrass Axon as she had enjoyed a little too much Moonjuice during dinner.

To inspire her to learn their native dance, they wrapped a grass skirt around her waist and a halo of flowers around her head. She had fun with it and enjoyed every minute of the lesson, giving them as much cheek as they gave her. The laughter at the table beside theirs was the loudest. The entire table stood and gave her a standing ovation when she finished. She curtsied towards them and clapped with excitement when it was over.

'That was entertainment at its best.' The one with the curly dark hair stood up and asked for her name so he could introduce her to his family.

She winked at Axon. 'Call me Red if you like.'

The dark-haired man eyed her. 'Mind if I call you, Glow Girl?'

'Why?'

'You're glowing, girl.'

'And you?'

'Anything you like.'

'Then I will call you Jett.'

Some of them at the table heard and laughed. 'Jett. Jet black hair… Funny.' The woman next to him chuckled.

'They like it.' He stood back and played with his goatee. 'Jett it is then.'

She gave him a warm smile. 'Nice to meet you, Jett.'

'Same.' He shook her hand, turning it over. 'Your skin is so soft.'

'No! Don't even think about it.' She chuckled. 'No calling me soft touch or I swear I won't speak to you for the rest of the night.'

She could see by his expression he was hanging on her every word. Maybe he thought she was an actress and was a paid part of the act. Rory and her friends invited and made performers welcome at their table all the time when they went out at night. It made the evening more fun, so she didn't find it unusual to be the centre of attention. It was a buzz that she was the one getting fussed over for a change. What could it hurt? They didn't know she wasn't a star and she soaked up the attention. In a fabulous mood, she turned and put her hand out toward Axon. 'This is a dear friend of mine who goes by the name of Wolf.'

Jett shook his hand and invited them to join their table. 'Your friend has us wanting more of her impressive good humour. I hope we are not intruding on your plans for tonight.'

Axon was all for the development of communications with other Rulers and knew by the hum of their magic that these were powerful and influential individuals worthy of breaking into his alone time with Cait. It would be beneficial for her to start forming friendships with those she may one day have dealings with.

Axon smiled. 'Maybe just for a drink,' he said, turned back to his table, and picked up their two goblets and the jewelled carafe. Caitlin held on tightly to his arm as they moved across to join the group next to them.

'Everyone, this is Wolf and Glow Girl.' Jett grabbed the rest of the family's attention. 'Oh, and my alias is Jett.' He grinned as he pulled out a chair for Caitlin.

One of the men laughed heartily at his pet name. Caitlin was almost sure he was a brother. Even though they had different hair and eye colour, the features and build were similar.

The brother stood and his blond hair fell forward as he reached over to shake Axon's hand. 'Hi, I'm Calyx, pleased to meet you both.' He smiled and spoke to Caitlin.

She was so absorbed in Calyx's baby blues that she blushed when not catching a word he said. 'Sorry.' She giggled. 'Can't hear anything over the music,' she fibbed.

'I said, this is my wife, Zuri,' he shouted a bit louder.

'We also use code-names.' Zuri shook Caitlin's hand. The leggy blonde with the stunning looks tossed her hair back and lowered herself delicately back in her seat.

Next to be introduced was Jett's wife, Melita, who looked quite amused. 'I think I like Melita better than my own name.' She took Caitlin's hand gently. Her personality radiated sweetness, and the pitch-black hair and eyes gave her more of a cultured mystic appearance.

On the other side of the table, yet another sibling looked nothing like his two strikingly handsome brothers. He had long blond hair and a beard that she wondered if he had ever shaved. Caitlin laughed with him. His personality was loud, yet he was easy to get along with and during the night, Caitlin changed his alias to Razor, because he needed one. His wife, who never got a word in edgeways around him, he called Angel, and Caitlin thought she looked just like one.

The last man at the table was the brothers' father. They called him Ted and their mother was Honey. During the evening he kept giving Caitlin bear hugs and grunted a lot, so she amended his title to Ted Bear. He scowled every time she called him that, but didn't ask it to be changed. His wife then became Honey Bear. She was sweet and snorted lightly when she chuckled, which made them all laugh even more. If she got Ted started, his big belly laugh shook the table. Caitlin took to him and sitting at one stage between Ted and Razor, spent the time to get to know them better. She found they had big personalities and were very similar. Even more amusing to her, they both had beards. These she pulled and teased them. 'Even these things are the same. You both need a good shave.'

They laughed, their eyes telling her they enjoyed every minute of her playfulness. It surprised Caitlin as she never usually made friends this quickly. Yet this table of fun-loving individuals made her feel comfortable and at ease as if she'd known them forever. She was having a delightful time with them too.

During the night, Jett enticed Caitlin to dance, and it was the only time she saw jealousy in Axon's eyes.

'If he wasn't married I'd worry about my competition,' he whispered to her when she came back to the table.

It made her night that much better to have him show her how he felt. *He's mine.* Her heart leapt.

He calmed when she finally sat beside him. 'Enjoying your night?'

'I've had a blast, A— I mean Wolf,' she said, and leant into him.

'I think it's time we left. You're worn out.'

'It's all the dancing. Can we stay if I sit here and catch my breath?'

'Of course we can.' He stroked her hair.

She was getting drained, and he was beginning to agree with Rory that her perfume was a power and something or someone was draining her. Yet he felt she had not yet done what she wanted to do. His magic worked, and suddenly she was back her eyes were alight, and she looked gorgeous. Her perfume grew stronger, drawing them all back in. Energised again, Caitlin jumped up and moved around the table to chat with the women this time. Axon blinked hard to snap himself out of the daze she kept putting him in when near him. If she was doing this to him, he wondered what this power was doing to them.

Chapter Nineteen

Goodbye Delphinus Island

At the end of the evening, they said their goodbyes to their new friends and wandered back down the beach. 'I guess we should go home.' Axon held her hand.

Caitlin dropped down onto the sand and sat smiling up at Axon. 'You know what I have always wanted to do?'

'What?' He humoured her. 'Lie on the beach of a magical paradise, with the man of your dreams and gaze up at the stars?'

'Yep.'

He eyed her. *Why did I say that?* He knew they should be getting back. 'I was just kidding.'

'I'm not! She lay back on the sand and looked happy. Not wanting to spoil the fragile innocence he saw in her eyes at that moment, he lay beside her. Caitlin rolled into him, comforted by an arm that held her protectively.

* * * *

Daylight shone in their eyes and woke them. They had fallen asleep under the moonlight sky. Sunshine had Axon sit up with a start. Caitlin felt his movement and scrambled to her feet.

'What!' She looked from left to right.

'Hell, I fell asleep. Sorry Cait, I didn't mean to startle you!'

'Startle me! Geez, I thought we were under attack.'

'What were you going to do; blow these up?' Amused, Axon held up pillows someone had put under their heads while they slept.

'Guess not.' She looked around at the empty beach. 'Where did they come from?'

'No idea, but let's find out.' He glanced around.

Their new friends from last night sat out on their balcony far in the distance. A BBQ sizzled near them, and the aroma of bacon and eggs wafted in the slight breeze that blew suddenly towards them. They waved at Axon and Caitlin to join them. Without Caitlin having him under her spell as she had last night, Axon saw through their magic and realised who they were. These undercover gods and goddesses had fooled him last night, but not in the light of day. Careful to prevent confrontation, he waved back to them politely.

'Can we join them?' Caitlin's puppy dog eyes he found hard to refuse.

'Just for another hour and then I have to be at work.' He fiddled with his watch, unsure why he didn't just say no. Caitlin had given him no chance to think and had him by the hand. Her impatience to get to them made him feel uneasy. He suddenly realised Caitlin had no idea why, but she had to cement the relationship with these people before they left. Something more was going down here, and all he could do was support her until the mystery unfolded.

As with last night, Caitlin provoked the royal treatment with her cheerful mood. The perfume that was stronger today had Axon fight to control further thoughts as her strange mystic charm forced them all to forget everything, and just enjoy the moment. He shook his head and tried to remember if there was something else he should be doing. Forgetting about his work commitment, he took the coffee they handed to him and slumped down in the chair next to hers. His legs sprawled out, suddenly calm and relaxed.

'Ah this is the life; woke on an island with a beautiful woman next to me and now, with coffee in hand, who could ask for more?' he said to them when asked how he was this fine morning.

The father that Cait had named Ted Bear lifted his mug in a friendly gesture to him. 'Coffee and breakfast are the least we can offer you both for so much entertainment. This has to be one of our best weekends here.'

They all agreed, and the conversation then turned to the mystery pillows and how Jett had gone to wake them.

'He went to offer you two a bed for the night, but when he saw you were out cold, he put pillows under your heads,' Ted said.

Jett came around the corner, tongs in hand. 'Ah, you're awake.' He placed an arm around Caitlin. 'Come, talk to me while I turn the bacon.'

'Don't get her to help you,' Axon called to him. 'I want to be able to chew it.'

'Ha ha funny!' She poked her tongue out at him and catching Caitlin's cheeky retort, Jett smiled down at her. 'No good in the kitchen?'

She shook her head.

'Well, you can't be beautiful and cook too.' He said.

Her face lit up, and she glowed with the compliment.

'Glow Girl, it suits you, lovely one.' He touched her cheek softly.

CHAPTER TWENTY

Mission Tragedy

Axon and Caitlin had arrived home and after a shower sipped coffee while recapping their time away. It was in there, in the kitchen, Rory finally caught up with them.

So what happened to one day away?' He scolded. 'Not a word from either of you and you turn up out of the blue and decide it's okay to sit and have coffee. Neither of you thought to let me know you had returned.'

Axon looked over the rim of his cup. 'Only just got back, I was just about to head up and check in with you guys.'

'Doesn't look like it to me. This cosy little huddle doesn't seem as if it was about to break up anytime soon. Well, I have news for you two. You're both on duty. It's our time to have some R&R… seriously.' He shook his head, his hands still on his hips until he pointed. 'To the Tower!' He was banishing them for their sneaky extended trip away. 'Guess we can't trust either of you. I should ground you both.' He finally joked but was still insistent they do as he said as their punishment.

Both stood with their coffee and eyed him.

'Now! Go!' he ordered one last time. His strong jaw held fast, and there was no fun in those eyes that could light up a room.

Giving him a solute, Axon transported them up to the tower. He was surprised Rory hadn't been overly angry, pleased to make amends by only having to do one shift. It was late, but both were far from tired and still energised from a couple of days away, and enjoyed a bit more time alone.

* * * *

On Zoren's orders, Rory and the team stayed on Ara to continue monitoring the sky. It had been a couple of weeks since Caitlin's weekend away, and after two more sessions with Woody, she felt much better. In fact, after the last one, she felt so good while on watch that she was sure the heavens reached out through a psychic message and cautioned her of imminent danger. She immediately woke Axon and Rory. Both raced up to the tower and manipulated the equipment to project a larger circumference as they searched the sky.

'There!' Rory pointed.

Axon punched heavily on the keyboard as he fed more data into the superior mainframe, and the object finally came into view.

'Got it!' He contacted Zoren while Rory hit the alarm.

The ear-piercing sound screeched through the castle.

'That's it mate, let's get out there.' Axon snatched up Caitlin in one arm and grabbed Rory by the elbow, and transported the three of them into the barn.

Rory began to bark orders. 'The rest of the team will be here any second. I'll organise the horses if you two can collect the bridles. I'll meet you both out front.'

By the time Axon and Caitlin got outside, Rory had lined up the rides and was ready to help put the magic golden leather around the horses' heads. The display of armour and wings always caught Caitlin's breath.

Bree and Lisha arrived first and in too much of a rush to mount. They scrambled oddly upon their stallions and giggled at each other. 'We need to work on this, hey stupid!' Lisha pushed at Bree, which made her chuckle more.

Caitlin was tiny compared with Shargan, but the powerful animal had chosen her and no other would she ride. Because of this disadvantage, her mare lifted her hoof as she always did, which allowed

Caitlin to step up on her leg and get up easily onto the saddle without assistance.

Zeke and Nathen ran towards them. They grinned at each other, somersaulted, gripped hands in mid-air and changed places before landed on their own horses.

Rory and Axon sideways glanced at each other. 'So these are the cowboys I've hired.' Axon crossed his arms. 'Just hope Zoren never sees how this unruly bunch mounts their rides.'

'I blame their horses.' Rory tried to lighten it as he mounted his own horse to take the lead, pleased when he heard Axon laugh. He was glad his boss had a sense of humour but his face showed something different. Rory knew he had a lot more training to do with his team and had to shake it off. *At least they are on their darn horses...* But for now, they had work to do and he ignored the doubts of his superior.

Axon waved them off with a wistful expression. He wanted to go with them, but his position was on the ground. They needed a set of trained eyes to search the sky and pick up anything they hadn't. The equipment was being tampered with and couldn't be trusted. He worried this wasn't the only projectile heading for them.

Rory immediately opened up the channel of communication, using telepathy to prevent outsiders who could possibly be listening in on their plans. *Okay, riders, from the tower we spotted three comets. The gas coming from them alone, if ignited, could blow outwards and cause massive damage to surrounding Home Worlds. Caitlin you will need to focus and send them to the coordinates I give you, but be careful as a single spark could set off an explosion.* Rory could see Caitlin's concentration. He directed his question to her. *Is it possible to gather the three targets and move them all at once?*

Caitlin put both thumbs up. The no talking rule was something she wasn't used to yet. Excited to try out her newfound powers on the three comets, Caitlin's multitasking had her adrenaline at its peak. Already powered up and calculating the ratio, she was confident she could match the matter.

Rory split the teams into two. After placing them in position, he concentrated back on Caitlin. *Steady now sparky, all I want you to do is push them off course. The team will take over once they are out of the danger zone. If we go out of sight, stay where you are so I can direct floaters to you if it gets too hot up there for us to handle.*

Caitlin nodded, her eyes quickly spotting the three faint lights that came towards her. She targeted their location, closed her eyes, visualised, but still needed a bit extra. Using a new trick Woody had taught her, Caitlin nudged at Shargan and now had ample power. Her horse understood, and the spirited animal kept her steady as she opened her eyes, aimed and thrust her hand in the air. The boost of power that ejected from Caitlin's hands split into three. The blue electrical bolts of lightning encased the brutal comets and, with little effort, turned them and sent the gas giant and matter into outer space.

Rory had his hand up to give her the thumbs up when he saw a dark mist settle around her and Shargan.

* * * *

From the tower, Axon felt helpless as he watched a faceless figure appear, arms enclosed around the woman he loved. He immediately transported to the spot but missed the mark as Caitlin and Shargan faded. The only sound was his own agonising plea as he got a glimpse of the captor. 'Please Jett, don't hurt her!' And the captor's curse as he swore when he saw who he had. Both vanished in an instant.

* * * *

Caitlin had been seized, and Rory, who had also raced to her rescue, picked up a devastated Axon. 'Blatzing Hell, Rory, that was Hades. If he takes her to Pluto she's either already dead, or he'll keep her so deep in the Underworld, she'll never be found.' His heart bled, and his voice cried out for the safe return of the only woman he had ever loved. He knew only the gods could grant him his wish. *How can it come true when it is a god who has taken her!* His optimistic spirit sank, but he still had to try.

Nathen and Zeke had arrived to assist.

'Rory, jump on with Nathen. I'm going after her. I should be able to catch up to Hades before he reaches Pluto. Talk some sense into him!'

A cloud with ear-splitting thunder and lightning darkened above them. 'NO!' a voice bellowed.

Axon knew only one archangel who could project such angry vibrations in the atmosphere surrounding them.

Zoren's voice quietened. There was no sight of him, just the voice; firm, commanding and holding Axon to the spot. 'Your personal feelings towards this peacekeeper must not prevent the predestined mission set before her. To live or die is now in the hands of Hades and the Heavenly Congress will come down heavy upon any who dare interfere with their order of impending proceedings.'

Axon sat motionless and stunned at the directive from above.

Rory leant towards him and using telepathy spoke so quietly only those closest would have heard.

I will know if she is hurt or in trouble and orders or not, if it happens, we go in!

Axon nodded. His features hid this new plan from Zoren; the only telltale sign was the fire that burned brightly in those eyes. If she was hurt, Axon agreed that the team were to ignore orders from above. Their mission would then be to save Caitlin, and he would be right by their side.

CHAPTER TWENTY-ONE

Icy Home World

Caitlin panicked and shivered with the sudden change of temperature that felt well below sub-zero. The arms that held her were unusually warm against her skin that had felt ready to snap freeze. Fortunately, though, Shargan used magic and instantly changed her outfit to suit the environment. A white fur coat fitted snugly around her, and a hood warmed her head. Boots of bearskin with white fur spilt out from the tops of them replacing her previous pair and, suddenly toasty-warm, she stopped shaking, her teeth stopped chattering, and she calmed her fast-paced heart as she waited for whoever it was that had her, to speak.

They were motionless on her horse, and she speculated why he stayed there and allowed the magic of her horse to clothe her more sensibly. Did that mean he would keep her alive and for what, *to be tortured?* Already she knew this person had removed her powers, for try as she did, her mind couldn't conjure up weaponry or resistance to his harmful control that squashed each thought she had.

She sighed and gave up. He had won this round but while still alive, she would keep the spirit of the Cosmic Riders within. *This fight is far from over.* Just the thought of her team gave her strength and the will to stay alive. It replaced the sheer panic of the potentially dangerous situation.

She was lifted off her horse, thankful the person that held her in a tight grip didn't remove the bridle, as it was Shargan that kept her warm.

This place is worse than a day in the snow. There was hardly any light and even coated up, it was bitterly cold. She saw the outline of a person take the lead, and her horse stayed as quiet as she did while taken elsewhere. Her hope was that Shargan had ended up in a stable, or somewhere out of this weather. As for her, a cold, musty smell and a cell replaced the chilly winds and the slightly visible outline of an eccentric old castle she had squinted to see.

Placed on a bed, Caitlin kept still, glad it wasn't a stretcher in the corner or worse, a hay bed. She preferred not to struggle as her eyes adjusted and she saw who had her. Axon had told her who Jett was after they left the island and it left her shaken to look upon the god Hades. The feel of the bed sagged as the mattress took his weight, and the deep breaths alerted Caitlin to the stress he was under. She didn't know why but the urge to hug him overpowered her and she flung her arms around his neck.

'Jett,' she whispered desperately in an attempt to appeal to the compassionate man she had met and she let out a heartfelt sob before she let him go.

No reaction came from him; not even a change of breath indicated he was her friend anymore. Without a word, he glared at her with cold dark eyes before he strode out and slammed the cell door. She could feel his troubled emotional state and kept quiet. He was too close to losing it, and she didn't want to wear his rage. He'd had no idea the two holidaymakers he had befriended would be his archenemies. She preferred him to go away and think. So far, he hadn't hurt her. *This can still be resolved amicably.*

* * * *

Caitlin lay for what felt like hours before big steps on cement floor interrupted the silence. Then there came the turn of a key in the lock and the squeak of hinges, and slowly the heavy door groaned open. The one thing she knew Jett had lost in her was trust. If he hadn't come to hurt her, then she hoped her silent stillness would impress on him the loyalty she was capable of, that it might ease his hatred of her abilities and position within the Cosmic Riders.

The aroma of fresh roasted beans filled her senses as china clattered on the wooden sideboard. The darkness of the room prevented her from seeing clearly, and she jumped slightly as he touched her hair. His fingers rubbed a lock before he turned and left the room. She could feel his torment as to what to do with her and knew in her heart that he'd brought her there to kill her. Something stopped him and she had no idea what and suddenly wanted to know why. With a thrust, she lifted herself up.

'Jett?' The whisper fell on deaf ears, for he was gone. Thirst had the better of her, and eagerly she gulped the sweetened coffee down. Seconds later, she cursed silently when she felt suddenly tired, and realised she'd been drugged. Her heart thumped with fear of why he wanted her asleep. With a sway of her head, she fell backwards, with no choice but to yield to the nothingness.

Dazed, she woke, stretched and knocked a tin bowl from the ledge beside her. Dizzily she moved off the bed and onto the floor, where she felt for the spilled contents. The room was too dim to see clearly, so Caitlin had to rely on other senses. Feeling it was bread, she sniffed the air, surprised to smell the aroma of bacon and egg. Starving hungry, she stuffed an entire half or the roll into her mouth as she retrieved the scattered remains. She was unsure how long it had been since she ate, but by the sound of her rumbling stomach as she gulped it down, it had been some time ago.

'Not again,' she said, as she fell flat on her back just as the last bite went down.

In and out of consciousness, she wondered how she got back onto the bed. At times when she woke she made out a shape that sat on a chair outside her cell door, his head leant back against the stone wall. At other waking moments, he was gone, but had left food and drink.

A noise startled her, and she sat up, squinted and scanned the room. *Nothing.* She found herself alone but no longer in a cell. A door ajar had her on her feet. She was busting and had to go and find a bathroom. *How long have I been here?* Her head spun from the drugs, and her groggy state had her grab at furniture each step of the way glad to finally use a real toilet.

I'm still alive. She contemplated that as she splashed water on her face to ease her throbbing head. Clearing her mind of the haze of drugs, she was overwhelmed with relief that her aromatic calming power still worked; a power that was apparently saving her life. She wondered how this gift was not connected to her mainstream magic that Hades had stripped from her already. How it had continued to work was a mystery to her but she was very thankful at this point it couldn't be taken from her.

With an aching head Caitlin staggered back toward the bed.

Jett made it just in time before she hit the floor as dizziness overwhelmed her. The unexpected feel of another person shook her senses and revived her. She viewed him with eyes wide and frightened.

'I... um needed to go to the bathroom.' She felt suddenly overwhelmed. He was so strong; his powerful vibration was equal to none she had ever known. She was no match for this giant of a man.

He frowned as if he heard her thoughts. At the same time, he turned her to face him, and his hand moved to her forehead.

Caitlin gently pulled his hand down. 'It's just a headache. Guess it's from all the drugs you keep giving me. I'll be okay, but I'm telling you, it's not necessary. If you don't want me to leave this room, I won't. Just put me where you want me to be, and I'll stay and not annoy you, I promise.'

A palm touched her back, and the gentle nudge moved her back to bed where she lay down quietly.

'Okay, so it's here then.'

He didn't answer. His hand went to her temple this time. The warmth of magic instantly removed the pain in her head, and then he pulled quickly away.

'Thanks Jett,' she whispered while watching him leave.

There in the endless semi-dark her idle mind questioned if there were day and night here. Would her eyes ever capture another sunset or sunrise?

The next time Caitlin moved was to have a shower. The warm coat disappeared when it was removed, and her teeth chattered as she rubbed the towel briskly over goose bump skin. The coldness of the room had her shiver uncontrollably while making her way back to bed. She was glad someone had heard her having a shower and had put heat packs in the bed. It radiated heat as the covers were pulled up tight against her neck. The welcome feeling of warmth calmed her immediate fear of freezing to death, but she knew what he had just done; removed the bridle from her horse. Her last link and hope of her friends finding her was gone.

The bed was warm and, grateful for small things at this point, she snuggled up, clean and comfortable for the first time in days. Caitlin even managed to smile when Jett brought in a mug of hot chocolate. She was thankful that for some reason he had let her live. Thirst quenched, she closed her eyes and drifted in and out of sleep.

Every time she woke, Jett would still be there, in the corner of the room where he contemplated her future.

The creaking of his chair as he leant back in it woke her. The fright of being alone like this forever overpowered her need to be close to someone, even him. As a woman possessed with fear and yet determined to end this crazy situation, Caitlin threw the bedcovers aside and scampered over to him. They had been friends once, and she needed to find out one way or the other if they could be again, or if this would be her demise. The latter she gave little thought to as she sat on his lap and hugged him. 'I can't stand you not talking to me. Growl, get cross, but no more silence, please,' she begged.

He didn't move for a minute, and her mind raced with embarrassment that he didn't feel the same. The slight movement had her sigh with relief when his arms wrapped around her and hugged her against him. They still had a strange connection, and Caitlin knew he couldn't hurt her as she couldn't bear to hurt him.

The warmth he exuded amazed her. He wore very little and yet his body didn't seem to be affected by the cold. A thought crossed her mind of how cool his skin felt when they danced together on the island and she realised his powers enabled him to adjust to the weather changes. The music they danced to and the fun they had replayed in her mind. How sweet he was and the mood he emitted then was far from that of the man she had seen of late. To herself, Caitlin hummed the tune and kept the image of Jett firmly in her mind. As she did it, she felt him move slightly with her in a rocking motion to the sound. *He hears me.* She lifted her face to his.

'You remember too.'

He too had kept the memory of their lovely time together.

He stood up, lifted her with him and put her back in bed. His footsteps left her unsure of his mood as the door closed and locked behind him. She fell asleep with a sense of relief. To have found the courage to see if the bond they had was still there, and for him to show her it was, made her happy.

The juice beside the bed made her aware it was morning. The slight adjustment of light now enabled her to tell day from night. Caitlin figured she must have slept deeply not to hear the unusually big lock that clunked on his return.

A yawn and a stretch put her in an upright position. She eagerly gulped down the freshly squeezed orange juice he left. A daydream of the warm beach at Dolphin Island on Delphinus kept her entertained rather than dwelling on the cold and eerie quietness of where she sat. The vision of how much fun she had with Jett and his family made her smile. She wiggled her toes and imagined the water and sand beneath her feet. How she wished they could go back there and start again! They could introduce themselves as they should have and put all this madness aside. She'd thought they were going to be friends forever. *Was last night a dream or did he show me we were still friends?*

Still deep in thought, she was startled when Jett shimmered into view beside her bed.

'Dreams of sun and surf will do no good here. Ice and cold are all that is offered on Pluto.'

He can read minds! All stress of how miserable the last few days were, slipped from her thoughts. He had finally spoken.

She could feel his eyes take her in and hoped it was in a better way that he now viewed her. He poked her skin and lifted her hand as if he looked for something, but she knew why he did it. Her skin was soft as a child's, and it confused him.

'I never had daylight touch me in my youth, and it wasn't until I transformed, you know, into immortality, that Rory found me. It was then I saw the sunshine for the first time. Only after being introduced to adults did I see how different I was to others.'

He frowned, and shook her hand gently for her to tell him more.

If they were to become better acquainted, she had to talk, be truthful, and in return hoped he would open up too. Caitlin knew he could read her thoughts.

'I am still suffering from the drugs you gave me. Sit and allow me to create that moment in time, and you can see it for yourself as you read my mind.'

He stiffened, let her hand go and the air around him thickened.

'Yes Jett, I may be female and without powers, but I'm not stupid. Please, pull your chair over so I can begin.'

He turned to the chair, and with his eyes aglow, their magic within dragged the seat across the room to him.

'Impressive.' She smiled.

He was all powerful and grumpy but sat as she asked.

'Before I spill all, I also have a question, one for my future security. Can the rest of your family read minds as well?'

His indignant expression almost made her smile again. 'They wish! And a god should not be made to wait.'

Not using her own will, his powers rolled her to face him, and her eyes shut tight. If she hadn't lived in a world of magic, this would have frightened her.

'Tut tut! Patience, Hades,' Caitlin said before she allowed the secrets of her past that he craved to flood her mind. Her memories took her first to the darkness in her earlier years that she spent locked in an underground basement. Then to her late teens when Rory heard the cries of a teenaged girl, broke in and found her, uneducated, dirty and with nothing but a worn doll and a torn and dirty, baby blanket tucked under her arm. This blanket she had believed was magical and that it had protected her from night-time evil.

Jett's eyes widened with pity as her recollections showed him how a frightened Caitlin covered her eyes and came out into daylight for the first time with Rory, petrified and clinging to a man she didn't even know. Although trusting this person, her steps were shaky as cars whizzed by, people shouted, and horns blew. All were loud strange noises she'd never heard before. At his house the television had her cringe behind him, shaking uncontrollably.

Nervousness had her pull out of the trance she was in. She woke to the kinder features of Jett who leant on an elbow, his face close to hers, staring at her intently with a look of shock on his face as he read her thoughts.

'Anyway.' She spoke and squirmed, uncomfortable to have revealed so much and yet feeling it important. 'To cut a long story short, I guess my skin is my only reminder of a lesson I'm yet to understand, and as for how soft it feels, well maybe I'm normal, and everyone else is weird with their thick skins and olive complexions.'

For the first time, Caitlin saw his mouth at the corners nearly give way to a smile, and his eyes were bright with compassion as they had been the first time they met. He was still in there somewhere, and even though he got up quickly, cutting off any further communication, she remained hopeful he was still her friend.

He opened the heavy curtains and flung open the window. The cold snap had Caitlin pull the covers tight around her neck. He looked out with a confused stare; his thick dark curls blowing across his forehead, his black eyes dark and worried. He fretted for something and although unsure of him, Caitlin wished she could relieve whatever ailed him.

After a while, he closed the window and without another word left the room.

Alone again, Caitlin was pleased how concerned for her he seemed, but as he stared out the window, she wondered if he still debated killing her. She hoped not. To kill her now made no sense.

Chapter Twenty-Two

Friend or Foe?

In five days Caitlin had not seen Jett or even heard his familiar footsteps. *What went wrong? Had she told him something he had not appreciated?* After coming out from the bathroom, she contemplated this while sipping warm milk that mysteriously appeared on the night table. It also amazed her how food and drink only ever came while she showered. How strange was this behaviour? Was it to ensure there was no contact even with servants? She could be killed and disposed of with not a soul knowing it was her locked away.

Before this, Jett had kept a watchful eye on her as she slept and as creepy as it first seemed, Caitlin had got used to it, even comforted by the thought he may be protecting her from his family. Weirdly, even tonight as she woke dazed, her eyes scanned the room, but again he wasn't there.

On waking her instincts were to stick her head out of the door, even bang against it to get attention, but she decided against it as this would anger him. Consistently being where he put her gained his trust and at this point Caitlin had no intentions spoiling this earned achievement. After a good workout, a routine exercise plan Rory had taught her, Caitlin wondered if this was a test. To escape, which would be tricky since she didn't even know where to find her horse, would give him reason to end her life if caught. To shake the crazy ideas from her mind, her attention was sucked up in a crime novel she found. This story, unfortunately, made her even more suspicious of where he had gone. The notion he was at war and possibly out in combat with her team, or her man, had her pace the floor.

Stop it; she stood still coming to her senses, realising if any of the team were injured, she would, herself, be consumed and crippled with pain. *What about Axon?* If he was hurt, she would never know. With a violent shake of her body, she brushed away the negatives and kept her thoughts positive. Comforted the connection with her team worked both ways, she took three deep breaths in a row. If she kept busy the team would not become concerned about her own safety and attempt a rescue; this she feared would only end badly, and not just for them. *After all, I'm not in any immediate danger*, just very lonely.

It was the afternoon of the sixth day when Caitlin's stress from not hearing from him accelerated. What if something happened to him and nobody found her? The thought freaked her out and to relieve the stress she decided to have the bath that someone had filled earlier while she slept. It was cool enough to get into now and she added a sprinkle of the tranquil aromatic bath salts left on the vanity. It completed the antidote she believed would calm her.

'Ah! Sweet.' Her eyes rolled in bliss as the hot water and fresh fragrance lightened her mood. 'I am so over being indoors.' The words were lost as her head ducked under the water and came up with suds dolloped in her hair. Under the water reminded her of the situation she was in. No light or sounds that would even make her feel the world outside of this existed. It was hard not to feel miserable, but the days seemed to elongate as her biggest fear started to become a reality. Was this going to be her life from now on? To deal with living as she did in adolescence, an eternal strength had to be found. The promise to Axon and Rory, to stay alive no matter what, was foremost in her mind. If she behaved and didn't annoy anyone, she would keep that oath and with some luck, see them again one day.

The door flung open, and Jett stood there with a frown. She jumped out of the bath, grabbed a towel and pulled it in front of her. His eyes were almost pits of murky dimness and there was a shadow of darkness that lurked around him. Panic-stricken, the outburst of an apology for whatever she may have done poured out.

'I'm sorry Jett,' she squeaked out, as her eyes darted around the room for a protective weapon. 'I – I'm not sure what's been going on but honest, I have been here and had nothing to do with it.'

The more she rattled on, the angrier he became. He made a move towards her and only for the size of her petite frame was she able to slip past him and run into the next room. She headed for the door, but he had locked it so she searched the room for a place to hide. With only the bed in sight, she jumped on it, cowering away from him. It was where he insisted she stay but at the moment it didn't feel at all safe. As he stomped towards her, Caitlin pressed her back against the bedhead, scared to imagine what he had planned for her. Fumes seemed to flow from him. *What the hell changed his mood?*

As he came closer to her, she leapt from the bed and scrambled into the corner of the room where she cringed in a foetal position. The towel she held covered little, and she wished he would go so she could at least put clothes on and regain some dignity and control. What was he going to do to her? She was shaking uncontrollably.

Suddenly he vanished and reappeared, scooping her up into his arms. *Shyte, forgot he could do that!*

He startled her, and she shrieked.

'You can't escape from me so stop it!' He pulled her in tightly to warn her he was serious.

Tears ran down her face. His grip didn't ease off, and the thought ran through Caitlin that her time was over. Something had gone wrong. Had he fought with her team and lost? Maybe he wanted to take it out on her. There were no more words to help with her defence. If he could grab her so easily with his magic, he was right, there was nowhere she could run or hide. She was at his mercy.

The image of her imminent death ceased as he dropped her and water splashed around her. He had dumped her back in the bath.

'You're going to freeze to death, so sit there, warm up and just listen to me Glow Girl. I'm angry for another reason, so quit it.'

Caitlin shook and sank into the bubbles as he took two strides from her and dropped awkwardly on the vanity chair that was far too small for him. Obviously uncomfortable, he got up and threw it aside. Effortlessly he hoisted his large body up and sat on the wide ledge of the vanity.

'Where I've been is none of your business. I can tell you this. I looked forward to coming home and seeing you until I spoke to the servants. What's going on, Glow? They say you haven't eaten and getting a look at your thin body, they aren't exaggerating. Is it your plan to starve yourself to death? Is that what all this is about? No lying.'

Embarrassed to learn the reason for his mood wasn't what she thought; Caitlin slid under the water and washed her teary face. He was in no mood for the run-around, and as she came up, she wiped the water from her eyes. Her fear subsided as suddenly as it started.

'Okay, you want the truth. It's simple; the food they give me tastes revolting. There's no nice way of saying it. You made me simple things like bacon and egg sandwiches, Earth food. I never see anyone to ask for what I want!' Her lip dropped in a sulky pout. 'I've been starving, waiting for you to come home. They should have asked me! You should have, instead of giving me the silent treatment and making me feel like a dog that just gets stuff thrown in my kennel.'

He actually smiled and that made her smile too. 'What would you know about dogs? You've never owned one have you?'

'I can read.' She eyed him. 'And how would you know that?'

'I know.'

Deep in thought as to how aware he was her head tilted to the side. Maybe he hadn't been fighting at all. Had he checked out her story to validate her sincerity?

He looked amused, verifying to her the ability he possessed to read minds. That confirmed her suspicion; nothing would be private around this man.

'So to be rid of me, you are not attempting to starve yourself to death.'

Suddenly stunned, Caitlin was staggered. *That's really what he thought?* She flushed and became annoyed. 'Why would I take my own life? I know I've been miserable and have missed the company of you, hell, of anyone. But you read my mind and know I've lived like this for many years already.' She sighed, frustrated with the poor communication between them. If he wanted honesty, he would get it. 'I know when you stole me away, the plan was to end my life, but you didn't. You could have left me in that cold dungeon, but here I am in comfort. No, Jett, if my life is to end it will be by your hands, not mine!' She was firm and held his stare, for her temper, once ignited was hard for her to control. Caitlin had a sudden pang, had she gone too far? His mood change told her to button it as his eyes diverted to the floor, giving them both a moment to calm down.

He lifted his head; it was Hades that addressed her. 'I guess I deserve that but don't ever speak to me like that again. This snappy, rude behaviour does not become you whether I am friend or foe.' A dark shadow surrounded him again and his eyes glowed red.

Caitlin put her hand up. At this point she knew he wouldn't kill her and, starved, she was in no mood for Hades' temper. 'Hold on there, god of fire eyes. If you can't handle honesty, then don't ask me a question. You're one scary individual when you don't hear exactly what you want.' She held her breath, just as annoyed.

He stood, even angrier. 'You are right to fear me, Glow Girl. You must know by now, I am Hades, God of the Underworld, and take no rubbish from a half pint smart mouthed redhead. And you are right, I did want you dead.'

'Did! Ha! But didn't, so bad luck. You're stuck with me now and only livid because you don't know what to do with me.'

It was Hades' eyes that calmed, and it was he who was able to contain his anger. He gave a half smirk and picked up a hand held mirror and turned it towards Caitlin so she could view herself. In the lighting flickering from the lantern, her hair looked as if sparks of red ambers spat from her, and her green eyes glowed golden.

'You're kidding, it's just the lighting, right.' She started laughing, and hysteria had her almost drown. 'That's so funny.' She came up, coughing.

Jett was back, not laughing but with his mouth slightly twisted in a grin. 'You are one temperamental redhead. I guess I'd better rustle up some food then if I want to get rid of the hungry psycho girl.' His mood had unexpectedly improved.

'I'm so sorry, it must be this place. I thought you took my magic from me.'

'I believe you fed angry magic off me, so we both had better calm down, Glow. I don't want to hurt you.'

'Or I you.' She smiled. 'Hey, can I come with you to the kitchen.'

'No!'

'Please.'

'Keep that temper in check and I'll think about it.' He held a towelling robe up for her and at the same time turned his head.

'I'm not scared anymore.' She slipped into it and pulled it around her.

A chuckle came from him, a sound she thought she would never hear again.

'Caitlin, you're naked; be scared, be very scared.'

She couldn't believe Hades was gone and he joked with her. They'd had so much fun when they first met and he was back, her Jett was back. 'You're so full of it,' she replied with a giggle. 'Your wife is absolutely gorgeous, so there is no way a naked me, after looking at her, would do it for you.'

'Well, you have a point, Glow. I'm not really into short, skinny redheads, but you'd do if I was hard up.'

'Thank goodness it's so cold here then. Being hard is something you wouldn't see very often, I'm guessing.'

He turned around and grabbed her by the shoulders. 'You stirrer, you! What do you want to eat – you whinging little pest … *I don't like your food,*' he mimicked her. 'I'll give you fussy, even my manhood is at stake with you around. I mean, I could have taken any one of the girls but no, trust me I had to snatch the redhead.'

'Yes, that's true, but redheads are definitely more fun.'

'Well I would have preferred someone sexy, but I guess kidnappers can't be choosy.'

'Sod, I give in. I have no comeback for that one!' She grinned as he hugged her.

This was how they were on the island when they first met, fun and light. She was so glad he had come back to her.

'Can I ask you something?'

He let her go. His mood changed; the air now thick with annoyance. 'The answer is no!' he snapped. 'Don't even go there Glow or you'll get me pissed off at you again.'

'Shish grumpy bum, I wanted to ask who the hell took the bridle off my horse. I'm freezing to death here. My horse clothes me, and now I've got none.'

He threw his head back when he realised he got it wrong and laughed good-heartedly. He'd jumped to the conclusion Caitlin was going to ask him to take her home.

'Oops.' He turned his head slightly with an apologetic grin. 'About the horse, it needed to be stabled, but the wings were in the way. I thought … well, I put heat packs in your bed and instructed they be changed each time you got up, but guess I didn't really think about what you'd wear if you didn't want to be in bed. I don't feel the cold.'

She put her cold hand on his cheek, and he playfully jerked away. 'Guess I better go raid the wardrobe upstairs. My wife keeps warm clothes for her mother when she comes to visit but I'm not sure if there is anything small enough to fit a pixie.'

Caitlin slapped his arm. 'I'm so going to mess up your hair if you keep picking on me.'

'I told you my hair is just naturally curly and this colour.'

With her hand, Caitlin moved the curl that spiralled down his forehead. 'Nothing can be this perfect and be real.'

His charming smile generated a natural response and overwhelmed with happiness she stood on her tippy toes and kissed his cheek.

Gratitude that he'd been forgiven flickered in his eyes.

'Thanks Glow.'

'You're welcome. That's to show my appreciation for being you. Well, the you I know.'

'Then I have big shoes to fill. I was on my best behaviour the day I met you.'

She smiled widely, amused. 'Oh, I think I can handle you either way. You're not so tough, even as Hades.'

'Little witch!' He grinned. 'You weren't scared of me at all, were you?' He tickled her.

'In your dreams, bully boy.'

CHAPTER TWENTY-THREE

Snow Cabin

While Jett went to find her something warm to wear, Caitlin sat smiling by the vanity brushing her hair. He was so much fun, they just clicked. Rory had warned her to zip her rough edges around these gods, but Jett brought the worst out in her. She could only be herself around him. If he didn't like it, they wouldn't be getting on so well. Hades, his other side, was a different story altogether, sense of humour… nope. But after spending time with him as Jett, Caitlin believed he would work out a way, to one day take her home, and it thrilled her. For now, to have time alone with one of the most powerful gods, to get to know him, was a marvel to appreciate and enjoy. Her intentions were to enjoy every minute of this gift of time. She had only just finished her hair when he arrived back with pants, a top and a gold coloured woollen jumper.

'Oh wow, these look so expensive.' She held up the large sweater that on her was going to be more of a dress, but this didn't faze her. What counted was him going to such an effort to please her. Holding it against her cheek, she smiled. 'It's so soft.'

'My wife has good taste. Only the best quality lines her closets. I'll leave you to dress and be back to collect you soon.' He closed the door to give her privacy.

Alone, a cheery Caitlin danced around with the warm ensemble before quickly dressing when her teeth began to chatter. The thick socks and fur boots were pulled on last and, energised, she jumped back to her feet and continued her jolly movements, stopping abruptly with the turn of the door knob.

'Can I come in? Are you decent yet?'

'Yep, ready to go.' She felt lost inside the oversized clothes.

He grinned.

She wiggled and posed for him. 'Maybe now I don't look so skinny you might think I am a bit of all right again.'

'You could never look sexy to me, Glow Girl.' He put out his hand to take hers. 'But please, kid yourself. It amuses me.' He laughed as he transported them to the kitchen to check out the pantry. 'Okay Glow Girl, cook me up a feast. I can eat anything so whatever you're used to eating will be all right by me.'

'You're sure in for one big disappointment.' She put her hands on her hips. 'Maybe you should have killed me when you had the chance. I hate to tell you this, Romeo, but I never learned to cook and am quite useless with pots, pans and heat. Rory never lets me in the kitchen. My position is on the bench. There, I talk while they cook or I shout takeaway. So unless you have a fast food outlet around, I got nothing.'

'Then I guess if I don't cook we starve.' Amused, he picked her up, sat her on the bench and headed for the pantry.

'Hell! You better be a damned good talker, that's all I can say.'

He disappeared into the pantry, his voice raised so she could hear. 'Then tell me what you like, little miss, *I can't cook,*' he mimicked her in a put-on girly voice.

Her stomach grumbled at the thought of eggs. 'What about quiche and salad?'

He stuck his head out of the pantry and rolled his eyes at her. 'You think I'm chef blatzing Sharman,' he mumbled, making her laugh. Chef Sharman was one of the top pastry chefs in the hemisphere, so she had recently found out.

'I though gods could snap their fingers and food appears.'

He popped his head out. 'Would you eat it if I did?' His eyes were wide in hope.

'Nope, but good try.' She chuckled as he went back into the

pantry continuing to bellyache while he retrieved the rest of the ingredients.

* * * *

The meal had been a hoot to watch him prepare, and Caitlin had to admit it was one delicious quiche. But now it was over and, looking weary, he took her back to her room.

Jett went in after she was comfortable and tucked up in bed to say goodnight and saw her frown.

'I ate too much; that's why I'm tired.' She yawned.

Caitlin looked sweet, like a little girl, but he had to try not to overly spoil her while she was staying with him. *Easier said than done!* 'It's not my food that tuckered you out, admit it Glow; you just can't handle late nights, can you ol' girl.'

'Pfff.' She rolled over. 'Give you ol' gal. Return my powers, and we'll soon see who can outlast whom.' She closed and rubbed her eyes before slipping into a contented slumber.

The next morning Caitlin rushed to be ready. Jett had promised to show her his Home World and take her skiing.

Once she was ready, the housemaid took her to the den to wait by the fire for him. 'The divine god, Hades, will be with you shortly.' The maid paused. 'And yes this is where he eats his breakfast, madam.'

How did she know I was going to ask that? Caitlin pondered. Everything was so mysterious and wonderful here.

A quick turn of a handle and the door swung open. Jett's entrances were always so noisy. Caitlin turned to face him, and his presence overshadowed all else. He filled the room with his masculinity and poise. A proud man, a man with many faces and in that second he was Hades. Eyes of steel, mouth set stubborn on a strong jaw. A man no human would dare defy, his power willed all that stood before him to heed his words. Even she trembled slightly at the sight; not from fright, but from the enormity of who he was. She had befriended one of the universe's most feared gods.

'Are you okay?' She tossed aside her coat onto the chair and walked towards him, worried.

'Don't.' He put his hand up, his temper evident.

Caitlin had seen Axon like this when he had problems that were too secret to talk about but which he needed to share with someone or explode. This was easily fixed if he truly trusted her.

'Coffee?' She picked up the pot.

He nodded as his body sank into the big armchair by the fire. Picking up the newspaper beside him he began to read.

Once he sat, it was with a confident and steady hand she poured out coffee for him. Caitlin's senses spiked when hearing the paper pages rustling as he turned them roughly in his blatant attempt to ignore what was on his mind.

Jett's hand reached for the mug offered, his eyes not diverting from the article he read. Caitlin was used to Axon and understood these moods went hand in hand with such powerful men. She sat quiet and sipped her own coffee, her mind consumed with thoughts of her working years on Earth, snippets of humorous happenings between her and her five Rider friends.

Jett gave her a start when he threw the paper aside. 'Glow Girl! Do you ever just sit quietly and not think? My goodness, woman, since you've been here I've been unable to have one thought of my own without yours consuming me.' He leant forward with an amused stare. 'I have an idea. To tire out that overactive mind of yours, how about we hit the slopes? What are you like at skiing?' It had worked, he was Jett again, playful and approachable.

'Can't ski for nuts.'

'Here we go again. *Don't like the food, can't cook and now, can't ski.* He mimicked her in the girlie voice. 'Well, it's time you learnt. That team of yours gives up too easy with you young lady. Today my intention is to prove to you there is no such word as *can't*.'

'Fine! But don't feel bad later that there are some things one can never achieve.'

'I am God of the Underworld, ruler of Pluto and I never fail!'

'You have already. You failed at the task of killing me.'

'That, young lady, can still be rectified.'

She drank down the last of the coffee and placed the cup gently on the stand next to her. *If I had my powers back, I'd dump him on his backside in the snow for that comment,* she smirked to herself before turning back to him.

* * * *

Jett's eyes widened after reading her thoughts. The glint of amusement in her face made him smile. 'Is that right! You would dare dump a god in the snow? We'll see about that.' He reached across and snatched up her hand, transporting her into the snow. Once there he let her hand go, knew she was feeling unbalanced getting taken from a sitting position and waited for her to end up in the freezing slurry. Only she was quick and gripped him with her other hand. Using the angle of her body and unsteady legs, she managed to knock him off balance too and both landed backwards onto the soft wet snow.

Shock first, then laughter broke them both up as he transported them into the cabin high above them. He restricted the time he had her in the sub-zero conditions, as just those seconds were enough to snap-freeze the fur around her soft cardigan.

High up on a hill, Caitlin peered out through the window but wasted her time as it always looked dark outside to her. She turned instead to watch Jett. The logs in the fireplace lit up as he put flame to them with his magic. Her teeth chattered while she waited for the room to heat up and she sat on the floor in front, with legs crossed, while warming her hands.

Another glance outside told her little about what time it was. Caitlin had thought that, once outside, there would be a noticeable change. It was as if time was of no consequence here. Night and day almost rolled into one and not often could she tell the difference.

Neither had eaten, so Jett checked the pantry and freezer. Before long, they sat each side of a coffee table by the fireplace, carefully sipping hot infused tea and eating tasty muffins, thawed by the heat of the fire.

After that, Jett did give her lessons on how to ski. However, Caitlin proved to be a poor student, falling down more times than he cared to count, and he did start out counting. Finally, she showed some improvement so he took her down one of the smaller hills, but each time he had to catch an out of control Caitlin at the bottom.

After the umpteenth dozen time he shook his head. 'Glow Girl that's it, I'm done!'

She had knocked him over for the final and last time and his patience had run out.

Caitlin laughed hysterically and lay helpless in the snow. 'Just remember it was you who gave up.'

'Even a god has his breaking point. I had enough an hour ago.' He helped her to her feet.

She eyed the hill. The moon was up high and gave light to a chairlift nearby. She tried to see where it went and guessed it would take them up to the veranda of the cabin. There was a warm fire up there, and she much preferred to be there than to be transported to her room. To have this time with Hades as Jett come to an end, saddened her.

'Can we go back up the hill in the lift?' she pleaded.

'You look frozen, Glow. Sure you don't want me to transport you to your room where the help can heat you some water for a nice hot bath?'

'Soon.'

'You don't want to miss a thing do you?'

Her smile lit up her face. 'Not one thing.'

He helped her onto the lift that took them back up the mountain. 'How you ever manage to stay on a horse is beyond me,' he teased.

'Magic, smarty pants!' She playfully slapped him. 'I'm just there for the fireworks. I'm hopeless at everything else.'

'You put yourself down too much Glow Girl. You have a characteristic to be envied. You didn't give up, not even on me. This has become a quality about you that I admire tremendously.' Jett helped her out of the lift when it stopped on the veranda of the cabin.

'Awe, golly gee Jett. Don't go all gorgeous and gentlemanly on me now. I was just starting to hate you! Get me to freeze my boobs off and bruise my rear end and then what? You give a girl a damned compliment.'

He raised his eyebrow at her and smiled. He had no comeback, just pure joy on his face for the good time they'd had.

Inside the cabin, warmth rushed at her and drew Caitlin to the fur rug in front of the fire. Gloves off and warming up, she took the hot chocolate Jett offered. The liquid warmed her with each sip and sitting so close to the fire she heated up quickly and removed her jacket.

Jett sat with her and poked at the burning logs, causing the embers to spark in a frenzy. It was he who finally broke the silence. 'You never mention Axon or seem to fret. You two are so much in love, so how do you manage to stay so calm?'

'You never mention Melita either, and I know you love and miss her too.'

'Touché.' He grinned.

There was silence again until Caitlin finished her drink, and then the thump of the mug as it clunked on the coffee table disturbed Jett's thoughts. He took advantage of her not holding anything and wrapped his arms around her. Both leant back and rested on the couch. It was an innocent hug, not feeling at all sleazy. A hug you would get from a friend. She felt comfortable enough to enjoy this new level of friendship he gave. They didn't talk for a long time, but just sat quiet, comfortable and listened to the crackle of fresh-burnt wood as the flames flickered light on them. Somewhere during the ordeal, they had renewed their friendship, and neither had expected it to develop into the kindred closeness it had. She figured the way it happened mystified him too, and was the reason he needed the hug. They had been through a lot. She had confused him, but he, coming at her as Hades, had scared her and made her mad too. Yet he was also Jett, and he didn't frighten her at all.

She finally broke the silence. 'I know you don't want to discuss anything personal, but Melita, she is well?'

She was worried about where Melita was, but Jett opened up and surprised Caitlin with his honesty.

'Not a fan of cold weather! Melita stays at her mother's during the winter months and doesn't come back here until the spring.'

Caitlin turned and found Jett's eyes raw with sorrow. Every emotion surfaced in those eyes as they had when first they met him. 'You must miss her terribly.' An honest sadness for the both of them was expressed by the quiver in her voice and the caring look.

'That's why I need to move to a planet closer to the sun. I hate her leaving and me with no choice but to stay here to deal with the Underworld on my own.'

Caitlin finally got it. This was the reason, the desperate urgency to take over Mercury. It wasn't about the need to move back with his brothers but for the love of his woman. This she could understand. It all started to make sense.

'Jett, you have the best planet for both of you right here. I've had so much fun today, and I bet this is only just a little piece of it. If I can be honest with you, you have the money to buy anything you want. The technology at your disposal could be mind-blowing with all that cash.'

'Okay, little-miss-I-can-figure-out-anything. What would you do if I gave you my chequebook?'

She waved her hand over her head. 'Cover your entire castle, and as much of the grounds as you can figure in that would include a pool, spa and tropical garden.'

His back went rigid. 'Go on.'

'A dome cover could completely encase the castle and however far out you want as grounds. You could then fill it with warmth and artificial lighting to imitate a bright sunny day. Grow seasonal flowers and trees, and in the spring when Melita comes home, I bet she never leaves again. There is nothing one can't achieve if one wants it badly enough.'

His eyes were bright, alert and she had his full attention, yet in the next breath, he had doubts and questions. 'You've got to be kidding me. I'm not sure you understand the responsibility I have in overseeing the souls in the Underworld. You see I have many other priorities and a project like you suggest, well, that would take months.'

She raised her eyebrow. 'You talk of priority and you feel these other things are greater than Melita? Are you telling me these are more important than having the woman of your dreams with you forever? You can't spare a lousy few months out of all the hundreds of years you will live, to make her feel the most loved woman in the universe?'

'But if I take over another planet, I'll have her without the fuss.'

She shrugged, turned her face away from him and concentrated back on the fire. 'You asked.'

'You think I'm taking the easy way out?'

He watched as she held his hands and studied his fingers, turned his hands over and looked carefully at them. 'These are not the hands of a man that has ever taken the easy way out. It's the thought behind what we do that brings love banging at our door. I am a woman, Jett, so I will share with you a little secret. If you had a modest house and I want one that faced the sun, and you went out and found one, it would still be just another house, but I wouldn't whine anymore. Would I love you more for it, probably not, but for my man to change his whole kingdom to accommodate me as his woman, that would be impressive, and I would fall into his arms for his thoughtfulness.'

He reached over to the coffee table to pour a strong Starstarter from a gold embossed decanter. In his hand, he swirled the liquid around in the goblet as he contemplated something.

At least he hadn't moved from her, so he wasn't cross with her honesty.

'I can almost feel the cogs as you churn over something you want to ask me. If we are to be friends, you must trust me enough to confide what it is you are struggling with.'

'I'm not sure how else to say this so will spit it out.' He turned to face her. 'I need you, Glow Girl, more than I've ever needed anyone in my life. I'm drawn to the extremely ordinary way you look at life. There is a childlike simplicity you use to resolve problems whereas I see war as the only redemption. If I promise that you will not come to any harm, will you stay with me a while?' He searched her face as if he was trying to read her thoughts.

'As your prisoner or as your friend?'

'As my friend.' His soul was exposed, sincere.

'As a friend, I would expect to have some requests met.' Her smile radiated warmth and caring.

'And what would they be?' His frame stiffened.

She spotted his change of mood and decided to lighten the tension. 'Only Earth food is served to me; no more planet creatures.'

'And?' He waited for her to say something he knew he couldn't give her.

'And when you've finished with me you will let me go home.'

'Is that it?'

'Almost! A question really. Does any of your family, including Melita, know that I'm here?'

'No, they think you're dead. That is something I was meant to do and the reason why I can't let you go just yet. I have to work out how to handle this from here on in. If my family finds out I let you go…' He didn't finish although Caitlin knew he wouldn't be in good stead with any of them if they uncovered his lie. After meeting the powerful deities, she could understand his anxiety. They were one solid family unit, but she would not like to cross them either.

'Do they know that the Glow Girl, who they befriended, is really Caitlin and is one of the Cosmic Riders?'

'I never gave away your identity, or Axon's. None of us had ever met Axon before, only Zoren, so both your aliases are still safe to use.'

'Why did you save me? It would have been so much easier for you to have blown our cover and destroyed us both.'

He shrugged. 'It was one of the happiest times in many years when you came into my life, although that changed once I found it was you who dared fight against me.' He flashed a friendly smile. 'Truthfully, back then I wanted to hurt you for deceiving me, but you just lay there, doing all that was asked of you, not even giving me a hard time for taking you from your loved ones. I admired your strength and that's why I kept you and your secret safe.'

She moved her head from side to side and stretched her neck, the tension relieved and her features softened. 'You scared the bejesus out of me at first because you came at me as Hades. The man with me here, now, is my friend Jett. The two are like chalk and cheese. Hades knows what he wants and goes after it. Jett, on the other hand, has chosen to have me in his life and that changes things.' She reached over and put a gracious hand on his arm. 'You haven't hurt me and have been a charming gentleman, so as far as I'm concerned, you have broken no law, yet. Therefore, if asked, I will tell only of the enjoyable break where I explored a planet and a friendship of much significance.' She smiled. 'What sort of a person would I be if I couldn't forgive you for something as simple as a misunderstanding? After all, you didn't know I was Glow Girl. I doubt you would ever have snatched me if you did. I think you would have requested a consultation and talked first, am I right?'

Her affection radiated to his softer side, and his hand slid roughly through his hair with uncertainty as he still contemplated the hopelessness of their future together. She wondered if he would answer, or, if she had it wrong.

Finally, he faced her. 'You are correct, I would have done that. Not sure about my brothers though. They had you targeted for more reasons than I can ever say. You see it was me you attracted that night; me that lost my head where you were concerned. When you left us that day at Dolphin Island, I had a horrid feeling of loss. You can imagine the shock when the next time we met was at war, on opposite sides.' He breathed in deeply. 'Well, you know how poorly I handled it at first.'

'You felt betrayed. I know, and yet I had no idea who you were, Jett. I swear it on our Riders' oath.' Her lips quivered with the hurt she had put him through.

'That's why you're alive, Glow. I believed you. What I can't get my head around is why your team has not come for you.'

Her grin brightened her face and made her glow as if she was an angel. His face melted with a special bond he already had for her.

'My team would know if I was in trouble, but while I'm happy they will wait for my return.'

'I'm glad of that. You see there is a calm that comes over me when

I'm with you, the anger and frustration disappears, and I find myself wanting to re-evaluate my actions. I want to find a diplomatic way to settle this, and yet it hurts my brain to think of anything other than spending time with you. I love my wife, Melita, more than life itself so I know I'm not in love with you, but it's something else, something I don't understand. When I'm away from you, I am Hades, ruthless and hackles are up ready to fight with my family. But you wear me down with your sweet, peaceful thoughts. I have never known a soul that knows no hatred or bitterness. And yet for so many reasons you have good cause. More and more I want to find another way a more peaceful end so you can stay in my life. So until I can find the answers and approach my family with who you are, I must keep you with me. As for how long at this stage Glow, I'm not sure.'

'You'll know when it's time, and by then I'll be ready to go. Today is not that day.' Caitlin beamed; glad he was honest with her. To stop this war, time together was paramount. He, in turn, pulled at her heartstrings too and she was still yet to work out why she didn't want to leave him either.

He lifted her hand and kissed it. 'Thank you, Glow, for giving me a second chance. I promise to let you go home as soon as I'm able to!'

Now they felt better, and differences talked through and set aside, they lay back against the cushions, both deep in thought, where the warmth of the fire lulled them to sleep. Both woke in darkness a few hours later, but with a flick of Jett's hand the fire was once again alight and burned brightly.

'Let's eat dinner up here tonight.' He stood up from the chair where he'd slept. 'I'll grab a couple of steaks and be back in a flash.'

'Sounds great.' She rolled off the couch he must have put her on as she slept, and standing up, stretched.

'There's a hot tub through there. The water is heated by the pipe system laid under this fire. It should be lovely and warm by now.' Jett opened a door and pulled off the cover to a steamy pool of water that smelt of lemongrass. 'Feel free to take a dip and freshen up, while I raid the guest wardrobe for some warm night attire. Melita is always prepared, and for once, I'm pleased she is a shopaholic.'

'Don't forget the steaks you promised,' she called to him, but he had gone.

CHAPTER TWENTY-FOUR

Time with a Friend

Caitlin walked into a lovely ivory tiled room with a dark blue roof where tiny down-lights gave the impression that bright stars glimmered overhead. Moons and planets on the walls were formed from coloured tiles, carved impeccably. She put her hand in the water and found the silky warmth and the faint aroma enticing. The prude in her left her underwear on, and she now hoped he might bring back a change of them too. The enormity of where she was and how to handle this from now on slipped away when her body slid into the amber liquid. Her eyes half-open, she lay back relaxed and let the charm of the embossed planets on the wall take her mind off all else. Curiously, there were more planets than she was aware existed; odd shapes with names Ceres, Haumea, Makemake and Eris. Intuition told her to take note, but to her, this was a solar system, and it meant nothing more.

Caitlin's mind went to the day in the snow, this spa and how happy she felt. *Jett should be proud of what he has, yet his eyes cannot see it.*

When he came back, she dressed in the tracksuit, slippers and toasty warm robe he gave her. Jett had started cooking so joined him in the kitchenette where they chatted while he made dinner. To her surprise, he had thought already about the dome to cover his kingdom, and the reason why he would go ahead with it sat uneasily with Caitlin. It was a devious diversion to give him time to work out how to tell his family about her. She chipped him on it, and he continued to try and explain.

'I promised not to fight while you are here and this will give me a cover story as to why I have to put the war on hold; the excuse is that I have to be here to oversee it.'

'You still intend to move from here, even after you do all that work.'

'Don't think this changes anything. I still intend to honour my family's legacy and rule a planet again. The plan to take over Mercury is a done deal.'

Caitlin felt disappointed he hadn't taken the project seriously. He was unable to see the modern construction would enhance his entire existence and bring great happiness. She rolled her eyes. 'You have so much to learn, grasshopper.' She shook her head and gave a look a mother would give a child that didn't get it, but would.

'Give me trouble Red, and you'll find yourself in my Underworld with the pests of my past,' he teased.

She laughed at his threat, her clean hair glossy as she tossed it back, her green eyes bright and mysterious and her face vibrant. At this very moment, Caitlin caught his breath with her beauty, and he knew it would not matter what he did to her or said; she was his always. And even though it scared him, he would never betray that trust he saw in her.

Caitlin was aware that to push it further at this stage would have been pointless. He had promised to stand down from the war for the interim. The project for him would be life changing and at least it was going ahead. It meant peace for a short time, and that was all she could ask of him for now. Since joining the Cosmic Riders, life had been gruelling, and lessons left no room for error or fun. She had learned much, but nothing had prepared her for this. She was running on instincts and knew if there was to be a peaceful outcome to this war, she was in the right hands, and it was going to take time. With a stretch, she felt better and was going to enjoy every minute with this man who had worked his way into her very soul. He kept her alive and safe from his family's clutches and for this alone she was deeply in his debt. Time here with the god that passed judgement on the dead, did sound scary, but he called her friend, and for that, she wished him happiness and intended to direct him towards the happier future she saw for him.

When they moved to the table, still mulling over what they had been talking about had him hesitate. He picked up his knife and fork and then placed them back on the table. 'Gees Glow, I don't know what the hell I'm doing. If my family finds out I have lied and you're here with me....' His voice was soft, almost a whisper.

She felt his stress. 'Yes, your family will be cross, but they will forgive you.'

'What about your friends and Axon? Will they forgive you for staying?' He raised a brow.

'I'll just have to leave that up to fate. I have no crystal ball to see into the future. If our families do forgive us, I'd say the worst case scenario is we'll be kept from each other. It may be centuries before we can revisit this friendship again. So we might as well make this moment in time together, worth it.'

He held up his goblet of Ambrosia and touched it to her glass of chilled water. 'Let's not worry then and just deal with it when the time comes.'

She nodded. 'Good plan.'

Jett talked about his wife and the love he had for her while he devoured his steak.

Caitlin listened to his dilemma and decided to change the topic to keep him in good spirits. 'Now Jett, the way I see it is you're with a gorgeous redhead who you recently spent time with, naked may I add, yet still, you miss and pine for your wife. Awe sweetie... does your family know what a big softy you are?' She received a flick on the arm with his fingers for her cheekiness.

'That will bruise.'

'A good reminder of your evil dinner companion.'

'Sod.' She grinned, rubbing away the sting. 'I will never wash this arm again. Ah, bliss! To eat with a god, I'm just all in awe!' She fanned herself.

They both laughed, but it set the mood for the rest of the evening. Jett would growl, and it egged Caitlin on to stir him further. With his constant laughter, it was easy for her to see he enjoyed her company. She guessed his position as, deity and Ruler of the Underworld, would keep many from kidding with him. It dawned on her what had attracted Jett to her that very first night. Not her power? No! He liked the way she treated him like a normal person.

As they ate, they discussed many ideas about the dome project. Some were sensible, but a lot were crazy notions that broke them up into hysterics. Jett was light hearted and nothing like she imagined this so-called severe tyrant would be. He did have a few devilish ideas though and saw quite a lot of the real Hades came through as the Starstarter he gulped down took over. He didn't frighten her, but she did take a little step back and calmed the situation. There were two sides to Jett, and she would keep it in mind not to stir him when he drank that divine elixir.

At her noticeable silence, his shoulders sank. 'I'm sorry Glow,' he apologised and held up his goblet. 'I think I've had way too much of this tonight and maybe shouldn't drink so much while around you.'

'That can be easily fixed.' She nudged him as they sat side by side on the couch. 'Give me back my powers so I can dump you out in that snow and cool your wheels if you try anything on me, and you can have as many glasses of that star brew as you like.' She grinned and stood up to fill her glass with infused tea from the jug.

He thought about that for a moment before taking her glass and tossing it in the fire. Laughing, he playfully lifted her and sat back down keeping his arm around her so they could talk about it. 'There will be no arse kicking given around here, young lady,' he joked and made her feel comfortable with him again.

Still in his gaze, she felt his torment of whether to give her powers back, but she knew he wasn't ready. He needed her to stay until he worked out how to handle his family. For them to find her alive would cause issues for him, and she wished, as he did, to prevent discord where possible. His family had made peace where other kin would feel there was no hope. Her entire being yearned for this to be preserved for others to follow. The other reason, the one she now saw in his eyes, was a need to have her friendship. This, she didn't get. He could have any friend in the world. Many would bow down and give him their total alliance. She could never do this but she wished they could always stay friends. As for her powers, it was a cheap shot and she didn't even need them. *In time he will see and trust I wouldn't run from him, not ever.*

He pulled a pillow up from the floor and placed it under her head. 'I won't hurt you Glow Girl, but I can't give you what you want because it might take away what I need at this moment.'

'It's okay, but if we sleep up here, I am at your mercy. Without my horse's magic to keep me warm I am like a weak mortal.'

He kissed her forehead. 'Sleep, funny one. I will care for you always, awake or asleep.' He used his powers to make her sleep. He was unaccustomed to such challenges and, worn out, reclined the chair beside her to rest.

Chapter Twenty-Five

Pluto
(A month later)

It had been a month since Caitlin agreed to stay. The days were getting colder in the castle, and Caitlin gave thanks to the small generator that ran the electric blanket Jett had purchased for her. Jett was building a power plant to operate the electrical side of the showy outdoor dome but hadn't been keen on running the electricity to the castle to heat it. During breakfast that morning she had stirred him about being an old fart, telling him it was time he came into the twenty-first century. Yet it was after dinner before he answered her.

He had come in to say goodnight, and even in the candle light, Jett could see her lips were blue. 'I guess if I want you to ever visit again I'd better look at installing ducted heating.' He tucked the covers around her neck, seeing her shaking under the bed covers.

'Not for just me, what about Melita?' Her voice shook.

'I keep her warm enough.' He smirked.

'Then come and keep me warm.' She got a smile from him as usual but tonight was colder than any other night and she was pleased when he at least sat beside her and rubbed her back gently to try and warm her.

'It's the dead of winter,' he said as he heard her teeth chatter so loudly it made him laugh.

'Seriously, I know I can trust you. Stay for a while, keep me warm.' She patted the bed beside her.

His laughter was light-hearted as he lay beside her and lifted an arm so she could hug him. Before long she was hot and able to toss off the bed cover and lie comfortably with only the blankets. That night they talked for hours.

Jett knew all he had to do was give her powers back, and she could use her own magic to keep her warm, but it was complicated. Her boss saw him as the enemy, and Axon wasn't wrong, to them Hades was. Every time this came to mind, he would sigh and struggle to cope with not ever seeing her again, so he would push the notion aside.

Instead, Jett had a fire installed in her room and made sure it kept burning day and night. During the day if he wanted her to come and look at where they were up to he walked with her arm in arm to keep her warm. He enjoyed these strolls as she had a way of taking his mind off problems and giving him the pride needed to carry on.

Lately, there had been a blizzard and he had been reluctant to take her outside. He was pleased when he woke to a break in the bitterly cold winds. He picked up Caitlin from her room and headed outside.

'Wait until you see it today!' Jett walked beside her, liking how she was already noticing every single detail. He looked forward to her thoughts in case he had missed something they had discussed.

'Oh, my goodness, Jett!' She put her hand to her mouth when she saw the massive half-ball dome that had taken shape above them. 'I had no idea this would be so far ahead.'

'That blizzard was a doozy, but surely now the dome is up you must feel much warmer.' He grinned.

She moved closer to him, her coat pulled up tight around her neck. 'It's so warm, Jett, I could pop on a bikini and sunbake.' She chuckled and shuddered with the cold.

'You're such a bad liar.' He transported her back to her warm room where a fire burned brightly. 'I have a business meeting but I promise to be back in time to have dinner with you. Keep warm. I'll see you tonight.' He kissed her forehead.

'I've got plenty here to keep me amused.' Caitlin picked up

a novel she had started reading. 'This one from your library, it's a sizzler, so don't rush.'

She saw him shake his head and smile.

'Don't get any ideas. I'm a married man.'

'You're not my type. I like my men grumpy.' She chuckled and threw herself on the couch and wiggled into the pillows to get comfortable.

His laugh was cut off as he transported out of the castle.

A thought niggled after he left. *Was it a family meeting*? She shook that off. He had promised no more wars while she was there and she believed him. Caitlin also admired his loyalty to Melita. Last night he had explained his idea to heat the vast space within the roofed area. She liked the plan that in years to come when she was off probation and allowed to visit him, she could do so without freezing to death. It was a bittersweet offer. Both knew that at the end of this time together, the war would begin again and they would be back on opposite sides. But would they? She had won him over and not often of late had Hades overshadowed his image. She hoped the two of them had something more than just friendship, that together they would find a peaceful solution. These were high expectations on her part, but she would not give up on him or what she believed would bring him happiness.

* * * *

Some days later Caitlin woke to a voice, a familiar tone that put a shiver through her. Jett's brother Calyx had visited to see how the works were going. Her first instinct was to look around for a place to hide. A few deep breaths helped calm her, and, comforted by the locked door and Jett's determination to keep her secret, she stretched and threw the covers back. *Jett would never let it slip I'm here,* her inner voice told her as she dressed in warm clothes. For the first time since being there she understood why Jett continued to lock her door at night. It wasn't to keep her in; it was to keep those inquisitive visitors out. From the bookcase, Caitlin selected a book that took her fancy. Covered in a blanket, she sat by the window on the sofa and read.

The sound of a key turning in the lock and the door opening had Caitlin rattled but she breathed out in relief when she saw the butler.

'The master ordered breakfast for you this morning, ma'am and apologises that he won't be joining you.' A gruff, harsh voice broke the silence.

'Just here on the coffee table will be perfect thanks, Marco.' She shifted a couple of magazines. 'Yes, I did hear him speaking to his brother. You must hurry back, so you're not missed. We can't have him curious as to where you went, can we?' She smiled.

'I was very careful ma'am, although it may be a while before I can come up and collect the dishes. Possibly I will wait for them to go outside if that is okay?'

'It's more than okay; it's been cold out lately so on the quiet, could you let Jett know I'm perfectly happy to stay here rugged up all day if need be.'

'Yes ma'am.' His big hands fumbled as he positioned the tray, noticeable worry lines creasing his forehead.

'This looks yummy.' The wink she gave softened his expression. They too had become friends although it took a while. He had been colder than the snow and only thawed when he noticed how happy Jett had become.

She ate slowly. Knowing the activity in the dome was almost at the end, worried her. Men and machinery worked feverishly to complete a project far too quickly. *There is so much more I wished to achieve.* Her heart sank. It was almost done. The roof reached all the way to the outer wall.

She glanced at the Galactic newspaper on the tray, and got up to pace when the date jumped out at her. It was only another couple of weeks before Melita would return from her mother's home. Jett would have his wife back, and she would go home to Rory and the gang, back to Axon. Caitlin walked over to the couch and cuddled up with the throw rug and a book. Her concentration wavered as she wondered if Axon still waited for her.

The thud of heavy strides and a loud outburst outside froze any further thoughts. Scuffled footsteps sounded before the key turned and the door swung open. Jett's brother moved towards her, his body rigid and forehead creased. Faced with his fury, she responded with a gracious calm and smiled. Her mind was in turmoil; how did he know she was there? Had Hades' vindictive self re-emerged while with his brother, and given her away? How was she to convince Zeus, the King of Gods, she was not an enemy? Her first reaction was to show no fear.

'Calyx! My goodness. It's so lovely to see you again!' Using his alias to throw him off, her tone was unhurried and welcoming as she faced one of the most feared gods. Today he looked livid.

He sucked in his breath, suddenly taken aback, and looked confused. 'Glow Girl! What are you doing here? I thought you were…'

'Were who… Jett's lover?' She giggled and tried to remember what they had discussed doing if his family found her. 'Sorry. Weak attempt at humour, but I can't think in this weather.' She gripped the novel hard to prevent him seeing how uncontrollably her hands shook. She fiddled for a second with the book as she laid it on the bedside table and searched her memory for Axon's code name, a word that signified the sacred animal of his Home World. She looked up with confidence again when she remembered. 'Actually, my boyfriend, Wolf, is on a trip off world with work and dropped me off for a visit. If I had known you were here, I would have come down.' She shivered more from his slightly icy look. 'I'm afraid I feel the cold so have spent most of my time here, reading in the warmth of this room.'

Jett was now at his brother's side, his eyes wide and alarm written in his features. Caitlin saw the relief in his face when Calyx went from antagonist to socially approachable in a millisecond and put out his arms for a hug. Caitlin tossed the blanket aside and responded quickly to his change of mood. 'Sorry if I worried you about who was here but I've always wanted to learn to ski and Jett was kind enough to offer to teach me last time we met,' she prattled on.

A sudden push on her shoulders had her at arm's length to him as doubt and suspicion bothered him. 'How did you know where to find my brother? On the island, we used only aliases and didn't speak of our Home Worlds.'

Jett butted in. 'I ran into them back on Dolphin Island. They were at a beach party, and me, well I was just there to you know, dolphin watch.' He winked at him, and Calyx smirked. Caitlin figured it was a private code between them. 'Anyway, I got chatting to them and asked Glow Girl to come for a visit while Wolf was away, so I could teach her how to ski. The delicate little one feels the cold terribly though so I have given her a rest today.'

Calyx looked over at the breakfast tray, a meal for one, but even so saw his distrust was still evident in his expression, so she continued to talk.

'How's Zuri? Is she here with you?' She peered around him.

He looked down at her happy face, his softening with the mention of his wife, Hera.

Caitlin had been careful to use the alias Hera had used on Dolphin Island and noted it pleased him.

'No, Zuri couldn't make it but will be disappointed she missed you. She took a real liking to you.'

She sat and patted the cushion on the couch beside her. 'Sit and tell me how everyone is.'

His weight caused Caitlin to lean into him as they chatted and her charm gradually cooled his uncertainty about her. Jett sat on the edge of her bed with a watchful eye as he waited for his brother to go. His only hope was that they got through this without incident.

'Honey and Ted Bear, are they well?'

Jett noticed how Calyx answered at first cautiously, as if he was under a spell, and noticeably relaxed the longer he sat next to her. Although she would have known it to be mostly fabricated, Caitlin looked delighted in his tales of the family and was pleased Calyx laughed with her when she chuckled uncontrollably at his humour. After some time he watched Calyx take her hand in his.

'It was a pleasure to see you again, Glow Girl. I hope you enjoy your stay and if my brother dares treat you poorly just let me know and I'll sort him out for you.' Calyx looked genuine.

'Jett has been a perfect gentleman and teacher, very tolerant of my ignorance towards snow and skiing.' She smiled brightly.

'That's a shock to hear. I think you must be talking of someone other than my brother. He has zero tolerance for anyone that shows even the slightest fear.' He rolled his eyes and glanced at Jett, baiting him. 'Brother, I can't believe that! I think she must be the one with the patience.' He stood up. A strange expression flitted across his face. 'Sorry guys, I've just been summoned. Congress waits for no man.'

'You are a legal man?' Caitlin asked, acting dumb.

'Something like that.' He casually eyed Jett. If she hadn't picked up on it, he would have thought her mindless. Yet acknowledging it made him slightly suspicious. Whichever way, she had to earn respect and show she was no fool.

The surprised tone gone, he had accepted her curiosity as that of any woman's and spoke kindly. 'Well, I must be going. No doubt, Glow Girl, we shall meet again.' He inclined his head, kissed her hand, and turned and followed Jett. His voice still had an uncertain tone as they conversed on the way out.

Caitlin paced with worry while she waited for Jett to come back.

The door flung open on his return, and he stomped in and sat heavily beside her. 'Phew, that was close. He heard one of the servants talk about the young lady upstairs and demanded to know who it was. He immediately thought you were who you really are. He was taken back when it was Glow Girl he found and not the Cosmic's explosives expert.'

'Is that what I'm labelled as?' Caitlin sat beside him and crossed her legs. 'That is so cool.'

'You're a mighty warrior, and the entire family was staggered with your abilities. We discussed brainwashing you, to turn you to our side.'

'And?' She was interested in the plots against her. His other side, Hades, answered her. His voice was depleted, almost exhausted. He had something more on his mind, and she hoped it wasn't what she thought.

'With your unique magic we were unsure it would work on you, so the vote was to terminate the threat.'

'Just like that!'

'Just like that!' he repeated, 'and if we had not used an alias when we first met, it would have been on, right there in that restaurant.'

'I'd be dead without question.'

'Fate works in mysterious ways.' He had a slight shake as he moved his hand through his hair. Hades' eyes softened as Jett's kinder side returned. 'Yes Glow, you'd be dead now, and I would never have had this time with you. What are we doing? Calyx knows you're here now and once he tells the others, I know them, they will put two and two together. They dissect everything and every day I keep you here now will endanger your life, again.' He put his head in his hands. 'Believe me when I say that my brothers will kill you if they find out who you are. They didn't connect with you the way I did.'

Caitlin knelt down and removed his hands from his forehead. They'd left prints, making his concern for her evident. 'If you send me home they'll snatch me as easily as you did and kill me anyway. I'm afraid I'm doomed whichever way.' The fear for her future was in overdrive. 'I've spent most of my life hidden underground and the rest of it I hid from humans in case my gift was uncovered. I feel a freak that doesn't belong anywhere. Only when I became a Cosmic Rider did I finally feel worthy.' She stood up in a panic. 'If you send me back I will have to hide again, change my name and give up my job… my friends.'

'Sorry, Glow, you are no longer safe here.'

With a spin, she turned back to face him. 'Then send me to your Underworld, because without my job, my friends and Axon, I have nothing.' Her eyes were wide and angry.

'You cannot be serious,' he bellowed at her, as Hades' temper surfaced.

He felt her fear beg him for a solution. He shook his head, his only idea ludicrous, but he had to try. 'There is a way. Let me turn you evil. This is the only way you can stay. Renounce your position with the Cosmic Riders and give up your useless pledge to save humans. Why protect that which has hurt you so terribly? It seems to me, those mortals have never loved or cared for you, yet you work so relentlessly to save them. For me, Glow, turn from all that keeps you pure and stay.' Jett's tone grew soft and caring. 'I'd treat you like a princess for the rest of your time. My family already loves you, and there would be nothing you would ever need or want again. We would give you the world. Please think about it.' His broken emotions made his voice quiver.

She stood strong, rigid, yet her own voice was soft and full of compassion. 'Why don't you turn good for me? Come and live with us, and protect me so they can't remove my powers and get rid of me.'

'Now that's just panicked discord. You know how much I adore you, but I could never leave Melita or my family for you.'

She grinned through tears. 'And there lies our dilemma because I feel exactly the same.' She turned and walked over to the bed and sat on her own.

'The only choice is to let your family try to protect you now Glow.' His kind words finally broke the silence. 'It's the right thing to do. I must take you back and let you live your life out, however it might end up. You told me I would know when it was time and I believe it is now.'

He stood up, strode over and put his hand on her shoulder. 'I'll never forget you Glow. Please forgive me for not helping you, but I'm not willing to change for you either.'

The room before her disappeared and the sight of Axon's castle welcomed her. 'Goodbye, Glow Girl, and thanks for the memories. I'll cherish them always.'

She touched his face, barely able to see through her own tears as an emotionless Hades stared back. The faded image burned into her mind and he was gone.

CHAPTER TWENTY-SIX

All Hope is Gone

Her stomach in knots, she was utterly shattered at how her time with Jett ended. Though elated to be home, Caitlin felt torn not to be with a man she had grown to adore, a friend she might never get the opportunity to talk with again. He had given up on her, sent her packing at the first sign of trouble, and wiped his hands of their friendship. *He didn't even try.* She let out a sob.

The alarm rang loudly and muffled the sound as she cried out to him, but it did no good. She was home, and he would never come back. Nor would she be allowed to ever see him again. *We are enemies again.* Her heart sank.

Nathen and Zeke appeared, and both waved madly as they ran towards her with a manic spring in their step to make it to her before she vanished again. She wiped her eyes and made an effort to cheer up while holding her stomach that stabbed with gut-wrenching pain. This was all wrong. She'd solved nothing and had not only let herself down but her friends too. She was a peacekeeper now, and her job had been compromised because she had become too attached. They had become more than friends, spiritually connected, and it had frightened him that she would come to harm. *Idiot,* she cursed herself. She knew the Riders' number one rule; never get that close, or they might do something stupid. *Like, save me.*

The strain to thinking of how to solve the war now gave her a massive headache. Jett knew her, and now she knew him. Could they take up arms against each other or would Hades take over the soft side again and destroy the charming man she knew him to be?

Nathen snatched her up in his arms in a rush to have her back inside the house. It left her head spinning, and once inside, he stood her on unsteady feet.

'You right, Cait?' He held her elbow and with the other hand tapped his earpiece. 'She's safe, let Rory know.'

The alarm ceased its noise, and the quiet gave Caitlin time to gather her wits. Zeke bent, concerned with the amount of stress she seemed to be in and rubbed her back briskly. His worried features and soft words were welcoming. 'You're okay now kiddo, it's okay, you're home.' He gradually calmed her just as Axon and Rory shimmered into view in front of her. Rory pushed him aside to get to her. Not being aware of how messed up she was feeling, he wrapped his arms around her. 'Thank goodness you're alive. What happened? How come he let you go?' His eyes reddened with unshed tears. 'I was right, you were okay. God Caitlin, we never thought we'd see you again.'

Now in Rory's embrace, Caitlin didn't just cry, but sobbed sadly, confused and unable to pull herself together to answer him. Her eyes opened at one stage and saw Axon. Missing him, her arms went out to him. She blubbered and wept for him, the heartache real that he might not understand why she had decided not to come home. Would he forgive her? Had he trusted her? All this sadness she had created and yet it was for nothing. She had lost a dear friend, maybe ruined the relationship with these two men and hadn't managed to stop the war. She wept without words, utterly heartbroken.

Rory poured shots of vodka that they took eagerly while they looked for an ounce of humour to settle the emotional rollercoaster. After the third, she calmed, and Axon pulled her down onto the sofa to talk. He held her so tightly Caitlin was breathless and got Rory to give Axon another one.

'I'm not going anywhere. They can't get me in here.' She kissed his lips.

That set him off, and he disappeared with her, taking her to their room and kissing her back, with fear and urgency. The reality he still loved her lessened her sadness.

'Sorry.' He released her. He sensed she was elsewhere in her thoughts.

For Caitlin, the room was still warm, and embers glowed in the hearth which took her back to winter on Pluto. It reminded her of the nights she spent with Jett. Memories of the frozen planet flooded her thoughts for only a moment, yet long enough to cause Axon to give her a questioning stare. Caitlin attempted to cover her idle foolishness by giving him a cheerful smile. 'I wasn't expecting that,' she kidded him.

'Come, you must be exhausted, sit with me for a while.' He shook off the unresponsive kiss he got from her. 'We were beginning to give up; thought he might have turned you evil and had decided to keep you.'

'Jett would never do that.'

His arm dropped from her. The defensive straightening of her body and something more he saw in her eyes, had warning bells go off. 'You slept with him, didn't you? He has won.'

'Don't, Axon!' She looked indignant.

'I deserve to know. We had something before you left and you can't blame me for wondering if...'

She put her fingers to his lips.' 'Hush now, that's ridiculous. Yes, he stole me from you but hell, only to kill me! He was angry and to be feared. I don't mind telling you I thought my life was over, but somehow I won him over, and he became Jett again.'

'You got sucked in by the sounds of it. What did he want in return for letting you live then?' His tone was nasty, but she ignored it and continued to explain why she had stayed with him.

'It was when he opened up to me about Melita that everything changed. I went from his captive to his guest.'

'Cry on your shoulder did he?' Axon threw in a sarcastic comment, and again, she had expected it. She hoped by telling him everything he would see it was innocent and ease the jealous innuendos.

'No, it was in a conversation. I asked where Melita was and he said how she spends the winter months with her mother. I suggested a dome for the castle grounds which would keep out the cold and savage windstorms they get. He thought it a good idea and asked me to stay to help him with design and ideas. I agreed, and it was then while working on the project that we became close friends.'

Axon straightened, not taking the news well. 'So if you didn't stay to help he would have brought you home?'

'No, that bit is complicated.'

'Please enlighten me.'

'He couldn't let his family know I was still alive. He was working on how to fix that. Sorry Axon, but some things I still need to get my head around before discussing them.'

He stood and went over to the fire, to prod it with the poker. 'I kept imagining you sleeping with him, but hoped you were the girl I fell for.' He turned to her. 'I love you, Cait. I thought you knew that. He is your enemy, our enemy. There is no future in friendship for either of you.'

Caitlin rolled her shoulder, trying to un-stress. 'I said friend! And as for my relationship with Jett, I think that is over now too. Calyx saw to that. Jett ran scared after his visit. Letting me go has dropped him into a world of pain with his family who could turn against him when they see me up there fighting and still alive.' She sighed. 'He turned against me, and I have disappointed you. I'm not sure how I can fix any of this, Axon. But I do still love you if you are willing to put this behind us.'

Caitlin's eyes filled with tears as Axon sat and held her hand. Her commitment to love was what he needed to hear at this moment. 'Cait, my beautiful Cait, I am so sorry I jumped to conclusions. I should know you better than that, and I do, so please accept me being a pig-headed, jealous sod.'

He wiped her sad tears with a hanky he pulled from his pocket. 'It sounds as if you did the best you could. But see it for what it is; Hades used trickery to confuse you into thinking he was different. Jett, you related to, so why not be him around you. Only the deception didn't last, did it? Caught out he showed his true colours. What happens from now on is out of your hands and from here on in you must wipe Hades from your thoughts.'

She nodded. 'I will try,' she said, and tears ran down her cheeks again.

Axon mopped them up, annoyed at her reaction every time that name was mentioned. 'Honestly Cait, he is evil itself. You were a captive, and at the end of the day, Hades has only let you go because his sneaky, underhanded plan to have you all to himself for whatever-the-hell reason has been uncovered. He is a ruthless kidnapper and not worth these tears or the friendship you gave. If he thought about you at all, he would have brought you home once he decided to let you live or had the guts to clear it with me before just assuming it would be okay for you to stay with him.'

'Would you have let me go with him?'

'Hell no! Never! We now have plans in place, and the father and his sinister sons will never touch a hair on your head, ever. I can promise you that. It is the last time Jett or any one of his brothers will get anywhere near you for eternity.'

This revelation didn't sit easily with Caitlin. Axon had said his piece but had not convinced her. To put plans in place to make her disappear was not an option but that was an argument for another day. Neither he or the team would ever understand what she accomplished or still wished to. Yes, Hades was evil, but Jett was the real deal, kind, considerate and a good friend. She smiled politely, but on the inside didn't give up the search for a way to mend the malicious rift between the two worlds. Her efforts to explain fell on deaf ears. She knew if Jett's family found out about her, he would face the same distaste and hatred. She stood up, needing to be around those who appreciated the work she had put into the god, Hades.

'Please don't leave just yet, stay a little longer. I have missed you.' Axon's eyes pleaded as his hand went out for hers.

'I know, I have missed you too, but the rest of the team will be gathered downstairs by now waiting to see I'm all right. I'm also sure you have much paperwork to fill out and file.' She kissed him lightly on the lips and pulled away with a giggle. 'Come on boss, there will be plenty of time for us to canoodle now I'm home.' She tugged at his hand to get him up.

Reluctantly, Axon followed. She had rejected him and saw by his expression he was upset, but she needed to think and heal her heart that ached for – for what? Wasn't that her wish all this time; to have Axon's love? One thing she did know, it was unwise to give in to lust when she was so confused.

Throughout dinner, Caitlin's nerves were on edge as the team drilled her extensively about her stay with the notorious villain, Hades. They were even less understanding than Axon. It annoyed her the way they referred to Jett as Hades which encouraged her to fill her glass more times than she could remember. And even though they were lovely in every other way and gave her accolades for the miracle of her survival, Caitlin could see no marvel. She still felt so terribly disheartened, knowing her chance to win the war peacefully was over. She talked until exhausted, but this did not change how any of them felt about Jett, or get them to acknowledge the work she had put in while there. They felt as Axon did, he had conned her and used her, and that was that.

Next morning the sun shone in the window, and she rolled over to find her bed covers on the floor. Pillows lay as if tossed over the other side of the room from a restless night's sleep and although she had no recollection of that, she did recall not being very agreeable with anyone. She figured that was why it was daylight and she had not been woken to attend training or breakfast. *Time to make amends.* She felt much better. Gazing out the window, she sat up with a start, as the light that streamed through told her it was mid-afternoon. With a heave of her body and a groan of a head that throbbed, she showered in record time and started out the door to find out where she should be.

The stairs to the tower she took two at a time, her mind heavily on Jett. Even though there was a part of him that continued to tug at her inner self, she had to focus and forget him. In the light of the day and all the advice from last night, she now accepted he had chosen his path, and it didn't include her anymore. She just hoped he was happy and hurried to finish his project so his wife could be there with him always.

A dig in her pocket found the ear-pod she once wore, but it proved useless and she could hear nothing. The door to the tower was locked. *What the!* Where was everyone? Her code didn't work, *why?* She entered Rory's code which she had watched him enter many times. She figured Axon and Rory had gone to work, but where were the others? Was there no threat anymore? They should have told her last night. Inside, she grabbed a juice from the fridge. The computers automatically switched on, and as her head went back to take a sip, she spotted something. With a calculation of the distance, she sighted in the satellites and now in focus could easily see the Cosmic Riders. Her team was out there without her, battling an out-of-control star. *Why didn't they want me to help?* Was she not part of the team anymore? Had they labelled her untrustworthy for socialising with the enemy?

Frustrated and annoyed at the position this had put her in with her friends, she almost switched everything off. Her inclination was to go back to bed and to hell with them. A final glance to go crook at them one last time stopped her nonsense. Far in the distance, two inflamed stars headed their way, too far out for them to have seen.

'Someone should have been here!' She scowled at their stupidity for leaving her out of it. They were a team and needed her, and it was then it dawned on her why she wasn't included. *The fear of having me captured again.*

'This has to stop!' she called out to them and tapped the screen to where she needed to be. Her body trembled with worry as she ran downstairs and out the front door to the stables. Her legs dropped under her as she sank to the soft grass while she remembered her mare was still at Jett's. Only wolves were visible as she scanned the paddock in the hope another horse had been brought up to the Home World of Ara. She tried to see if she could spot them, torn as to whether to send up a projectile of her own. Her naked eye, even though super-strengthened with magic, was unable to depict the specific marker to hit, as the team fought the death star that spiralled out of control. They were in her line of sight. *What if I hit one of them?*

CHAPTER TWENTY-SEVEN

Help from a Friend

Caitlin's eyes squinted against the brightness as the fight came closer. She had just made a decision to try and send up a rocket when a crackling n o i s e stopped her. Someone was transporting near and, hearing a horse snort, she turned her head to the sound.

'Looking for this?' Jett held the reins of her horse.

'Shargan!' She hugged the mare and then wrapped her arms around Jett. 'You came back?' She was full of smiles, but he seemed confused.

'Why aren't you up there? You could have ridden with any one of them.'

'I only just woke. I guess they didn't want me to be kidnapped again. Or maybe theory thought I wouldn't fight against you. But enough of their hang-ups. You're here! Does that mean I haven't lost you as my friend?'

'I'm here aren't I?' He looked almost boyish.

She smiled and punched his arm. 'You had me freaked out. I'm so happy to see you.' Noises above had them both looking up. 'Damn them. That was a dirty trick to leave me behind for whatever the reason.'

Her eyebrows drew together, and the look almost put a grin on his face. 'Well if you're going to save them, I would advise you to quit chatting and get moving. Your friends are in big trouble out there.'

'I know. I was watching and came down here to grab a horse, but there weren't any in the stalls or in the paddock. I thought they would have had a back-up at least.'

'Maybe they hid them from you so you couldn't follow.' He lifted her up on Shargan. Her transformation surprised him, and the bright light forced him to step back slightly while the magic altered the image he had of her.

'You are a real vision when you go into battle, Glow.'

Caitlin glowed more from Jett's warmth. He had changed so much since the day Hades stole her with the intent to kill. 'I don't understand why you helped me. I am fighting against your family.'

'This is true, but your own family are losing the battle out there, and if I were about to lose one of my family members, I would hope you would be friend enough to do all you could to help me too.'

'You know I would.' She put out her hand to him. 'I will when that time comes.'

He held her hand. 'I believe you would. Now go! Help your other friends, or I have wasted my effort.'

'Thanks, Jett, you're the best.' She blew him a kiss as his figure faded. Shargan moved swiftly, the mare's wings high and swept out gracefully as her horse lifted them from the surface and headed for the coordinates she had already communicated.

Closer to the action it was apparent why the other two missiles were kept hidden. The magnitude of squealing, gas and flares that shot out from the surface of the first massive nova made it almost impossible to see or hear what was coming behind. Parts of the exploding death star shot out unexpectantly. The danger from the blazing hot iron-like shards caused the team to duck and weave to avoid them. Caitlin's adrenalin surged with the scene, and her power crackled from her as she flew to save her team. Her concentration was on the two inflamed stars behind the one they battled. A controlled hand went up and let out a calculated stream of ear-piercing energy towards them. The electrical feed engulfed the balls of molten rock and, acting like a slingshot, hurled the two stars in a spiral towards each other. The collision released a tidal force which instantly ripped each star apart. The eruption left a gash in the atmosphere, and both collapsed into a big black hole. Rory waited for Caitlin to cap the offending abyss before he opened up a nearby portal that led to outer space. The black hole vanished as the portal snapped shut.

Her power exhausted, she sat and watched as the team took control of the massive star they battled. It too was dead in the sky; the remaining danger came from the exploded shards that sped towards Ara. The team immediately switched to clean up mode, horse and rider quickly encased in bright light, as the action put them in a spin that left them a blur of colourful electrical surges. The bolts they projected smashed and pulverised anything in their path. The only remains looked like fairy dust glitter that floated delicately down to the surface of their Home World like soft flakes of snow. It always amazed her, the exquisiteness of the team, as her method was quick and deadly. She shrugged. *Show-offs.*

Once it was over, they headed for her. Rory instructed her to stay still while they covered her with their magic until they got back to the surface. In a swirl of colour, very similar to that when they are in the clouds, they escorted her home. *Let them try to steal you from us now; our new kung fu is strong.* He winked at her.

On landing, Caitlin felt smothered with her over-protective friends. *What sort of life is this to be?* Axon waited while she dismounted and headed for him. She intended to give him a piece of her mind if this was his doing. That's if she could get a word in edgeways, as he was already hurling questions at her.

'How did you know about the other two death stars? And where did Shargan come from? I gave orders to leave the other horses in the far paddock, so you had to stay home and rest.' His temper was evident.

Her eyes were alight with disappointment in him as she answered. Her voice was as calm as she could keep it. *Why he wasn't just happy all had ended well?*

'I had a little help from a friend. I saw the other two stars hurtling towards them from up in the tower. The guys had trouble with the first one, so I didn't know how they would have handled the others that encroached on them. The stupid headset didn't communicate that far and to send up an explosive blast looked too dangerous. Once exploded, the debris may have hit them. All I can say is thank goodness Jett arrived with my horse.'

Axon blinked in shock and his features became almost porcelain. 'If Hades thinks he can just come here and mess with your head anytime he wants, the blighter can think again. He is the enemy, Caitlin. Destroy him! That is an order!'

'But – '

'No buts! He had his chance to change for you and he didn't! He chose to oppose us, take up arms against us, so this, whatever it is,' he waved his hand in the air, 'ends now! That goes for the rest of you too. If Hades comes here again, I want him dead.' He vanished and left her with her mouth open, so much unsaid.

Head hung, seething with unshed emotions, Caitlin helped put the horses away before they made their way back inside. Her mood was sullen and she went straight to her room. The rest of the team had nodded, and all agreed with Axon, *good friends they turned out to be*, did none of them care? She kicked the door after closing it and hurt her foot. After not being called for meals that day, her mood continued to escalate and now upset at everyone, she paced back and forth. Her energy plummeted to zero and, finally fatigued, she gave in and slept.

She could hear Axon's voice, his footsteps and the door hinge squeak as he checked on her after work. In no mood to face him, kept her eyes closed and pretended to be asleep. His plea to discuss what went on that afternoon was met with silence, so he left.

A night of restless sleep did nothing to lull her fury, and again, she kept her eyes closed tight when the door open and warm lips met with her cheek as he whispered goodbye. Overnight the plan to escape for the day ran rampant in her mind. They were wrong about Jett, and he had to be forewarned. After that, Caitlin promised herself, she would do as ordered and never see him again.

Out of bed, the intention was to get ready and sneak out, but instead, her feet kept a steady pace back and forth as her mind ticked over the events since her return. A commitment to sever ties with Jett would not stop them freaking out every time an actual mission was given to her. *Would this goodbye change anything?* She didn't think so. Her future looked bleak; the reality was they would send her out less and less. Her worthiness as a powerful immortal was in question. Why was it her, only, that the gods hated? Panic-stricken thoughts plagued the thrill of being home and, for the first time ever she wished that her powers were in line with the other members of her team. The sadness of friends that once cared yet now had no trust in her, hurt more than anything. She cried most of the morning, ignoring the knock on the door and a breakfast call.

At midday, Caitlin woke thirsty and hungry, her mood a little better. Weak from lack of nourishment, her clothes were left in a heap on the floor as she slipped on a dressing gown. The house was quiet. No doubt they were on another call out, and it offended her not to be included. Sulky or not she would have gone if asked. *Well, to hell with them!* At least there would be nobody here to stop her departure. *A quick bite to eat before I go and find Jett,* she consoled herself.

The bottom of the stairs seemed further than normal as her foot missed the first step and with her equilibrium way off, rolled her ankle and misjudged the next. She grabbed the rail too late as she lost her footing and toppled off balance, feeling the sharp pain as her body hit step after step as she plummeted to the ground — then nothing.

The first voice she heard was Rory's. 'Cait's been like this for the past couple of weeks and doesn't seem to be getting any better.'

Really! Her conscious-self returned as it had done many times. She recalled drips in her arm, faces, hands that held hers, needles and sponge baths. Yet her voice was stuck in her throat. She was sure she'd just spoken, answering Rory. Did he not hear her? Confused and disorientated she heard Axon. *There you are,* she said to him, but again no answer came. Her eyes closed on Axon's tortured features that looked on. He had been determined to rule her life and distrusted her judgement. As a boss, he had let her down and didn't believe in her. As a man, his devotion had to be stronger, or their love would not survive.

They can't hear me. Caitlin wanted to cry, but no tears would come.

In and out of consciousness, Caitlin tried each time to lift her head from the pillow but finally gave up, her mind in tatters as she lay there looking up at the roof. Axon had just left. Zoren was with him. Her guess was the archangel was his last shot at getting her better. The stream of endless faces in white coats with concerned looks had lately made her feel like an animal in the zoo. Prodded and poked, a bright light in her eyes, a lot of talking, but not one word did she understand. Her eyes were all that moved. She'd developed a defeatist attitude and felt she would get no better. Her time awake became less each day.

It was during one of these conscious episodes that a hand slipped into hers. It jolted her with a magic that reminded her of an ice world, a happier time and she looked into Jett's caring face. The room had emptied out, and they were all alone.

'Jett,' was all but a whisper as tears ran down her face like a flood of emotion.

He pulled back the sheet, lifted Caitlin's frail body in his arms and sat on a chair with a blanket that he laid gently over her. 'What have you done to yourself Glow Girl? Have you fallen for my charms and can't live without me?' He smiled.

'You wish,' she whispered.

It was the first time in weeks that words had made sense to her.

'They tell me you won't eat or drink and I guess those are the first words you've spoken. I miss you too, but we have to move on with our lives. My wife has come home, and you have your Axon and a family here.'

'I don't like them anymore. Axon never wants me to talk to you again.'

'Axon asked me to come here, Glow. He is beside himself and doesn't know how to reach you.'

Her eyes widened.

'Yes we fought, both of us pissed off for different reasons. However, once I found out what had happened, we talked. For you Glow, and only for you, are we on speaking terms until we sort this out.'

She frowned, and he rubbed his thumb gently on her forehead. He saw how hard it was for her to communicate being so weak.

'Let me talk and stop worrying. We are grown men and will sort out our own issues. Glow, he told me what he said and did. You have to forgive him. I would have done the same; he was jealous, that's all. You have to give him a break. He had been without you for a couple of months, and on your return, you talked non-stop about me. From what Axon said, to keep him at arm's length you spent your waking hours with the team. Apparently after that, you got angry, wouldn't talk about it and cringed from him when he reached for you. What did you expect? He thinks you're in love with me now and has offered to give you up rather than have you sick like this.'

She cried and to allow her time to get it out of her system, Jett rocked her gently, back and forth in a soothing manner.

'I just want to keep you as my friend. I'm not asking for the world, am I?' she sobbed through tears.

'We are on different sides Glow, so can't you see he's right? It would never work.'

'Then put me back the way you found me and leave. Why should it matter to you what happens to me?'

He stopped rocking her, taking his time to answer. 'Because I care for you as you care for me and need to know you are happy too. You're breaking my heart to see you like this.'

'Then make it work Jett. Find a way.'

'I will, but you have to give me time. This is my fault. I kidnapped you and then just dumped you off when I was unable to deal with the consequences of what I was doing. My decision was so instantaneous it never gave you a chance to have a say in it or time to adjust without me. Me, well, the project consumed every hour, and it took my mind off you. By the nightfall, exhaustion overwhelmed me and left me too tired to think. You came back and felt alienated from not only me but your friends. I've been terribly cruel to you, Glow, and even now you give me nothing but your friendship and love. I told you I was a monster.'

She dried her eyes and smiled. 'But you're my most favourite monster in the whole world.'

He laughed and kissed her. 'Yes, I guess I must be.'

He ran his hand through her hair and down her cheek, feeling her skin that she knew he loved so much. 'What about if you and Axon come and stay in the snow cabin? Have a holiday with me until you get well again. You loved it there, and the privacy might give you both the time to rekindle what you had. Please, Glow. I want to give you some of the same happiness you have given to me. Find love and enjoy your life with a partner that loves you in return. Give him a chance to make you feel happy again.'

'And you and him. You are at war.'

'So are we. Glow, I haven't got all the answers, but for you, I am willing to try with Axon.'

She gave him a weak smile. 'You will.'

He nodded and shook his head, his expression amused. 'To have you smile again like that and to me of all people – yes. I give you my word.'

'You know I love your planet, but what about Melita? Won't she mind us being there? She may side with the rest of your family.'

'No, I told her everything. She knows who you are now and would never disclose your identity. She loves me too much to get me into trouble with my family. I told her you helped me build a new world for her and she's chuffed you cared so much. You were right. She has come back to me with so much love it blows me away. I have a happy wife now, and I have you to thank for it.' He laid her back on the bed. 'Stay here and rest. I'll go and talk to Melita and Axon. I can't promise anything, but I'll see what I can do. It has to be up to our partners now. We both know this is out of our hands if they say no.'

She felt for his hand. It was big, warm and wrapped gently around hers. 'You're a good friend Jett.' Her voice was tired as she closed her eyes.

* * * *

She woke being lifted by Axon's loving hands and turned her head to see Jett had his arm around her man, ready to transport them all. She smiled, closed her eyes again and knew she had won. Axon and Jett had worked out an agreement, and even though it was because of her, at least they were on talking terms and in time, who knew. She had done her best for Jett to be allowed in her life too. Her job now done as the mediator the universe had instructed her to be, it was time for her to live again. She could feel her body heat up, not with the Cosmic Riders' magic this time, but sent from higher above. She shone brightly, and when they got her to the cabin, Axon laid her down where they both watched her body as it glowed.

At last Caitlin understood as the power from the heavens healed her broken body with a message attached. *A job well was done, and your reward is time out with a man who with just one kiss, stole your heart.*

The gift of time alone with the man she loved and being here on Pluto with the other man she wanted in her life now, lit her up more.

'Are you sure she's not an angel?' Jett turned to Axon.

Axon, barely able to take his eyes from her, shrugged. 'If she is, she's our angel. She's healing herself for both of us. I can feel her love.'

'Me too! It's such an incredible sensation.' Jett touched her face, and Axon could now see the love he had for her. He wasn't going to be a threat any longer. His love may once have been filled with lust, this Axon would never know, but it was not that sort of passion or hunger now. He could see Jett clearly. Hades was gone and the love in those eyes was not just affection but much more, a soul connection, a friendship that was eternal. How had this happened? He was floored.

Jett ran his hand over her forehead. 'Rest sweet angel, for now, it's time for the teacher to be taught.'

He turned to Axon. 'When you're ready, buzz the intercom, and I'll have a meal sent up. Maybe tomorrow if she feels up to it you can both join Melita and me for a tour of the grounds? Come and see what Glow helped create?'

Axon had been so angry and jealous when arriving on Pluto. What was accomplished did not interest him nor did he want to talk about how happy she made Jett. It infuriated him more at the time. 'On the last visit, neither of us even thought about what she achieved, only what it caused.'

'Yes! Be thankful the Underworld is full.'

'And you – that I held back!'

'For Glow – we shook on it!' Hades rolled the words off like thunder.

'For Cait.' Axon cooled his temper as they both eyed her. He gave in. 'We would love to join you both, and I'm sure Cait will be more than okay by tomorrow.' Axon shook the calmer extended hand of Hades.

* * * *

Caitlin slept a long time and when she woke it was to Axon, and they were alone. He knelt beside her and kissed her. 'Your lips are so soft and delicate, you taste divine.'

She had missed him terribly and shuddered with joy as he gathered her tenderly in his arms. His mouth claimed hers again, and in her vulnerable state, she knew if she didn't stop him, he would take her as his own. His hand moved unthinkingly down her neck and over the hardened nipples, and he moaned. With the same slow gentleness, he let it slide further to a place she had dreamed him to be, but she was not giving in so easily. His impatience pleased her. *He wants me finally!* She stiffened, her eyes snapped open, and she grabbed his hand. 'We can't.'

'We can't,' he mimicked her and smiled, before his lips moved to suckle on her neck and earlobe. 'Are you sure?' His voice was dreamily seductive as his hand moved again to where it wanted to be.

She pushed at his chest. 'Axon, we have spoken about this.'

'I know, I know.' His voice was still relaxed, soft. 'So you've said, you save yourself, but that was then, you've had experience now. Let me show you who the greater lover is.'

Her hand moved fast and swiped the side of his face. 'Take a shower Mr.' She rolled away from him and sat with her arms wrapped around her legs.

He rubbed his stinging cheek. 'Caitlin, are you for real? Stop the act. I believed you when you said nothing happened with you and Jett but for you not to want me sexually has me wondering if you were just pulling the wool over my eyes. I mean let's be real, nobody sleeps within the realms of a god's lair and walks away with such a friendship as you two have, well without being intimate at some stage.' He sounded his usual bullying self. His arms went out to her, pleading. 'Come back here gorgeous, I promise I will respect you in the morning.'

She threw a pillow at him. 'Is that what you say to your lovers? Hell, Axon, no wonder you're still a bachelor. Now it's my turn, are you for real?'

His glare was sulky; he was unsure what else he needed to do to have this woman in his bed.

'I love you, isn't that enough?'

She chuckled and stood up. 'You have so much to learn before we consummate our love.' She started to shed her clothes as she walked into the spa room, and Axon followed, unable to be further than a metre from her. Naked, she stepped into the hot spa that bubbled up when the sensors felt a presence. Axon quickly removed his clothes and climbed in beside her. His bare nearness excited her, but if he really wanted her as much as she did him, she wanted commitment, loyalty and long-lasting love. To let him have his own way so easily meant Axon might discard her as he had many others over his time. No, she would keep him on edge, wanting yet just out of reach until the day he said, *I do*.

He moved up beside her. She was a tease, but she was his tormenter, and even though it drove him insane, he intended to wait for her and never give up.

'So you want the whole deal, the ring, and the works.' His tone was sexy and alluring.

She took in a deep breath and smiled. 'Even they won't seal the deal if you keep accusing me of being promiscuous.'

'So, you still hold those mixed up good values you believed in.'

She splashed him. 'You should know me well enough not to even have to ask that.'

'Then marry me and allow me to protect your ethics for eternity.' He lowered his mouth to hers, taking her in; her sweetness and the gift of her confirmed innocence made her taste all the more delicious. She held him at arm's length and her face broke into a smile. 'Yes.'

'Say again?' He grinned from ear to ear.

'I said Yes! Yes, yes, yes.' She wrapped her arms around him. 'You are who I have wanted since our very first kiss. You are who I want to spend my forever with.'

'You will… I am!' The water parted, spraying droplets everywhere as he punched the air with excitement. When she was back in his arms, his eyes were soft and loving. 'Come to me, my sweet loving goddess. Let me show you how it really feels to be loved.' His voice was croaky with lust. His hands moved to her bottom and he pulled her into his hardness. She shuddered, wishing she could let herself be loved, but he still didn't get it; when it did happen, she wanted everything to be perfect. She gently pulled them back into a more respectable position. 'Not so fast, stud. You can show me that on our wedding night.'

He stopped moving, realised by her tone she was not joking. 'What, you're really going to make me wait?'

'You bet I am. You have Buckley's and none of trying to squeeze out a quickie without completing the transaction. I want to have the engagement ring, a traditional wedding, the whole package, sugar. Not just a wham-bam-thank-you ma'am.' She folded her arms with a pout.

He had laughter in his voice. 'You little tease of a fiancée. Okay, I will organise the ring ASAP, but after I do that, I want a date for the big day confirmed from those beautiful lips.' He moved and held her again. 'Waiting is not one of my strongest points but I guess I have no choice, have I?'

'Oh, my poor hard-done-by intended.'

She finally gave him the smile he wanted more than anything at this moment. He was actually glad she'd knocked him back. He too wanted her first to be anywhere but here on Pluto. He wanted her to be on his own Home World with the memory so good she would always want to come back to him. He drifted on a cloud, and it was after a much-needed petting session that he allowed her to leave his arms, and the spa. He was waterlogged and frustrated, but so very delighted.

'I guess if I'm not getting any hanky-panky, food will have to do,' he teased her. He wrapped a towel around himself and rang for dinner.

Dried and dressed, they cuddled up in front of the fire waiting for Jett to arrive. He shimmered into view with waiters that fussed over them with wine and hors d'oeuvres while others set the table.

Axon made a toast; 'To my fiancée.'

'What! That was unexpected. You two worked out your issues, then.'

'Sure did.' Axon beamed. 'She's going to make an honest man out of me. If I could organise a traditional wedding in a day, I'd marry her tomorrow.'

'Glow, I didn't know you were looking at settling down. What about the Riders?' Jett sounded confused.

'I'm not sure, we haven't discussed that yet. I do know one thing though. I want kids, lots of them.' She smiled at them.

'You what!' Axon's eyes widened. 'Honey! That can surely wait a few years though.'

She shrugged. 'Maybe – It's that or stay a Rider.'

He pulled her into his arms. 'If I have to have a tribe running around to keep you off that darn horse and by my side, it's a done deal. Kids it is.'

Hades replaced Jett. 'You can't be serious. Kids. Zoren will not go for this at all and neither will I. If Glow isn't on the team, don't expect me to work with any of the other nose wipes. You'd better re-think this Axon, right now!'

Caitlin pulled from Axon and stood directly in front of Hades with her hands on her hips. Her eyes were glowing, and the glossy hair shone a brilliant red with gold highlights. It was a sight Hades was used to when she got cross, but Axon was not, and his stunned look showed it. 'Don't start with me. I'm going to have kids, and you are going to be the first godparent and better be a damned good uncle or else.'

He melted. 'Godfather.' It was Jett that smiled and held her hands. 'Me?'

'I have no other real family, only you and Melita.'

'Then if it is the wish of the gods and a child is born to immortal parents, I would be honoured.'

'Jett.'

'Yes.'

'I will always be your Glow Girl and help you when you need me.'

'Then I welcome the news of your engagement.' He kissed her forehead. 'Congratulations to you both.' He shook Axon's hand. 'Sorry to be a buzzkill. But I need her too.'

'I know, Hades – I don't like it, but for Cait, I will honour these wishes to have you in her life. I hope we can put aside our differences out there long enough to both keep that promise.'

Jett stared down at Caitlin. 'You have me wrapped around your finger. Let's hope my family is just as understanding as your man.'

She stretched up and kissed his cheek. 'The two men in my life are trying. I couldn't ask for more. Thank you.'

'A toast!' Jett opened the champagne, and they drank with him. The meal was put off as they sat around the fire and chatted. Jett was interested how their romance came about and listened to Axon's side. He could see Axon was more than thrilled to finally talk about Cait's and his time together. Jett laughed with Axon, as he could clearly imagine Caitlin throwing him out after their first kiss and giving him a hard time after finding him in bed with another woman. After hearing Caitlin share how Axon had cared for her after she got lost in the bush, he understood their deep connection. Until then Jett was a worried mess as he had waited for the call for dinner. He hoped he hadn't left her in the hands of a monster. Jett had already seen Axon's other side as well, and it wasn't pretty. But how Axon was with his Glow, made Jett contented to finally leave Caitlin in the hands of the man she was in love with, and who he now saw as the right fit for her. 'Sure you don't want to come and spend the night in the castle?' he asked again, before leaving.

Caitlin shook her head. 'Here is perfect,' she said and leant against Axon as she watched her best friend transport out. *This moment is just that, perfect.*

With an arm around her, Axon moved them over to the table, and as they ate dinner, they talked honestly. Axon was over the moon their relationship hadn't been affected by past events, and in fact, was more confident now Cait had promised to marry him. It was because of this he felt comfortable about discussing what was on his mind. 'You now know Hades well, yet I am at a loss as to why you both continue to call each other by your pet names from the island.'

'It's how I got through to him, and he *is* Jett when he is with me. He's Hades when he is not.' She shrugged. 'For him, he has happy memories of Glow Girl and hasn't shown any interest in calling me, Cait. Even Zeus brightened up when I called him Calyx. The change was quite noticeable.'

'That may be so, but you are a Cosmic Rider, Cait, and all the names in the universe will not change that fact. Be careful of the fantasy you create because when his family finds out who you are, the dream of friendship will almost certainly crash down around you both. That is unless he's got a plan, but still, it is an awful risk he takes to bring us back here to Pluto.' Axon played devil's advocate. 'I'm sorry to be blunt, but you seem unable to see the problems attached to this arrangement.

'Maybe!' she admitted. 'But today I asked Jett to find a way so we can stay friends, or leave me and walk away. He knows if he wants me in his life, it is up to him to find it.'

'That's why he said it's time for the teacher to be taught.'

She put out her hand and held Axon's across the table. 'Jett has never allowed his heart to feel. As you know, Venus and Cupid fooled around one day, and Cupid's arrow accidentally pierced his heart. Persephone, or, Melita as we call her, was the first maiden he laid eyes on, but I believed that love to be mostly magic. My mission was to stop the war. I had to open his heart to me, have him call me friend, and do a good deed to prove his loyalty. This he has done, and the action will change his life.' With her free hand, she patted the back of the hand she held apologetically. 'I'm sorry Axon, but you were part of it, and so was Melita. You and Jett had to be on talking terms, and that's happened. With the improvements to the Castle, Melita is content to live here all year round. Jett has now opened his heart fully to Melita too and has told me how wonderful his life is now with her. My work is done, and I have been released.'

Axon looked troubled. 'I wish you could have shared some of this burden with me, love. You have put yourself through so much for this final outcome. Are you sure it's over? There are so many loose ends— his brothers, the family—'

'For now maybe, but later…' She sighed.

He squeezed her hand tenderly. 'It's all right sweetheart.' He felt her pain for the secrecy. 'I know from doing this job for so long that there are many things you cannot share, as there will be times the team or I will be unable to share t h i n g s with you. Just know that next time I'll remember your integrity under no circumstance wavers, and because of this, you and I will be okay. I promise my jealousy will not ruin your homecoming ever again.'

'Remember always Axon, the universe can take what they need from me, but they will never take the love I carry for you. Have patience with me, because as you have seen, I have evolved yet again and with these new powers, I guess there will be a future circumstance where they will be warranted.'

He knelt before her. 'I trust you completely. You don't ever need to worry about us again. This experience has changed me too, and I promise, next time the universe calls on your services, I will back you one hundred percent. This will come easier for me now I know you only leave in spirit, that your heart you leave with me.'

She nodded. 'And now you have given me yours I can take it with me.' She wrapped her arms around him and slid off the chair and into his arms.

He ran a hand down her long red hair and closed his eyes while he inhaled. 'In the meantime, until you are needed, I'm going to enjoy every minute with you,' he said in a husky voice. He lifted her easily and took her back over to the fire. Wrapped up in the warm furs they talked until they fell asleep.

A noise woke them, and Caitlin stretched and smiled. Jett had arrived and handed them each a freshly brewed mug of coffee.

'Do you two wish to sleep the day away or can I tempt you with an outdoor walk and maybe some time on the slopes afterwards?'

Caitlin sipped the hot beverage and nodded at the same time, her fingers working to straighten out a bad case of bed hair. Suddenly remembering both men had seen her look worse, she gave up and tossed it over her shoulder and out of her own view.

Axon rose from the floor where they had slept and flopped onto the sofa, which caused him to spill a drop or two. He smiled at his clumsiness and awkwardness in knowing that Hades, a god, waited on him. But at that moment, he realised he had to see Hades as Caitlin did, as her new friend Jett. 'First decent sleep I've had in a long time. It's so quiet here; you must love it.'

It warmed Caitlin to hear Axon's light-hearted manner towards Jett. She waited for the response. Could she wish both men were going to be civil from now on? Behind her back, she crossed her fingers in hope.

Jett positioned himself opposite. 'Thanks to Glow Girl here, I'm starting to. She's made me look at Pluto through her eyes.' He shifted in his seat, obviously uncomfortable about sharing his time with Caitlin.

Axon wanted there to be peace for his girl's sake. This was the start of a new day for all of them so, to make him feel at ease, he put aside differences and openly invited him to speak about whatever came to mind. If that was about Cait and Jett's time together, Axon was, funnily enough, okay about that too. 'Yes, Cait did tell me a little about the project you both worked on while she was here and the concept fascinates me.'

'Here on Pluto, to invite friends to spend time outdoors was impossible, until now.' He stood up straight. 'Look, how about I show you, and after that we can have a bite to eat, if Glow's up to it, of course.' He looked amused as he eyed Caitlin. 'Sorry, I mentioned you might come for lunch, so Melita has been in the kitchen most the morning baking.'

Caitlin glowed. 'Really, fussing for me? We'd love to join you both, wouldn't we?' Her eyes were soft and loving as she looked up at Axon.

'Of course, no way am I going to miss out a bit of home cooking. My fiancée has no idea how to cook, so I'd better get decent food whenever it's offered from now on in.' Both men laughed.

Caitlin jabbed him in the ribs. 'You'll keep, sweetheart!'

Axon turned back to Jett. 'Just give us time to freshen up and change, and we are all yours.'

* * * *

After another relaxing spa bath, Caitlin stood with a frown, dressed in linen pants and a light summer top. 'Is this all he left me to wear? I'm going to freeze,' she said, and pulled one of the furs around her while they waited for Jett to come back and collect them.

Jett grinned when he arrived. 'Don't worry, Glow.' He smiled at her when she complained and threw the rug aside before transporting them. 'Where I'm taking you both, what you have on will do just fine.'

The instant bouquet of blossoms and the warm sultry air was a pleasant surprise as they changed locations. Melita waited for them in a bikini with only a light floral wrap on. She had been swimming in the pool and wrung out her wet hair while coming over to meet them.

The dome was complete, and they had heated it. Palms and plants flourished in the warm climate, and the entire area looked more like a resort now, rather than the cold ice surface Caitlin had become accustomed to. The curved roof stretched out for as far as the eye could see. They had added lighting that gave the impression you looked up at blue sky complete with fluffy white clouds. Caitlin was so pleased to finally see the finished result.

Melita met them with a warm hug. Her enthusiasm for the first visitors in their newly renovated home overwhelmed them. She was delightful as she tugged at Caitlin's hand and showed her the outdoor kitchenette in the BBQ area. It left their men alone to discuss the logistics and practicality of the entire development. Later, as they all strolled around the grounds, Melita pointed out the location of a proposed tennis court and received a smile from Jett when she told them of the playground where they envisaged their children would play.

'Children! You too? And you picked on me for wanting them?' Caitlin teased Jett.

He shrugged with a look of superiority. As if he could do whatever he wanted, and he could. Caitlin actually welcomed the idea and was really excited. To have such news signified their future would be here on Pluto. She had made a difference and couldn't have been more satisfied with the outcome that just kept unfolding.

Melita smiled, patted Jett's arm and hugged him. 'We're trying, aren't we?' She smiled lovingly.

'This is just the best news ever.' Caitlin hugged them both.

Melita kissed Jett, who spun her around and caught her in his arms. 'Your happiness is so infectious.' He smiled down at her.

At last, Caitlin could relax. Jett had genuine happiness here. He would find Pluto a very hard planet to leave now he finally had all he ever wanted.

That afternoon, Axon and Caitlin ended in hysterics after they joined Jett and Melita on the slopes for a toboggan race, the second part of Jett's organised activities. Both drenched and cold, they ran through the door of the cabin, discarding clothes, and shoved playfully at each other to get into the hot spa first. They left an amused Jett and Melita after promising to join them for dinner after they warmed up.

'I have a surprise you won't want to miss, Glow,' Jett had called to her before transporting himself and his wife back to the castle.

'What do you think he meant?' said Caitlin.

'You mean about the surprise?' Axon's tone was calm and relaxed; this break was also doing him a world of good.

'Yes.'

'We will have to wait and see. The man has me mystified. He adores you, and yet he is obviously very much in love with his wife.'

Caitlin waited for him to say more, but that was it, he was done with any uncertainties he had now he'd seen Jett with his wife and he laid back in the spa relaxed, his eyes closed.

Later, warm and dressed, she stood by the window, where a silky light lit up the snow, a sign the day was over and night had come. Even the stars hid under the extreme cold sheet that added to the blackness of the view. She pulled the cape of fur around her shoulders tightly and closed her eyes as she sent out a wish all would end well, and she could always call this her second home.

CHAPTER TWENTY-EIGHT

United we Stand

Axon raised an eyebrow when Caitlin finished dressing for dinner. Unable to help himself he made a grab for her, a motion that earned him a slap.

'Behave,' she disciplined him.

He positioned himself on the sofa so they could talk while she warmed by the fire and both turned when they heard Jett's voice.

'You scrub up fine, Glow. First time I've seen you in an evening gown.'

'You sweet talker you.' She enjoyed the sound of Jett's rich dark tone. The black evening gown Melita had lent her flattered her figure. The back fell delicately down to her tiny waist and on Pluto, with its chilly weather, felt very revealing. Her typical attire here had been basic tracksuits. It gave her confidence to wear something else when she saw both men seemed to approve.

'I agree with Jett.' Axon got off the couch and stretched. His arm came down around her so Jett could transport them out.

Jett moved in close to her. 'You not only look good, Glow, but that fragrance you have on is so delicate, intoxicating.'

'I haven't got any on. Maybe it's the spa water.'

He eyed her. 'Hang on, didn't Axon have a spa too?'

'Yes.' She breathed in her man's scent of aftershave only. 'He does smell divine, doesn't he?'

'Glow, your aroma is nothing like the scent of aftershave, trust me. The bouquet is a delight. It is what drew me to you in the first place. I have wanted to say something for quite some time, but it was barely noticeable after I stopped being Hades while with you. I have something going down tonight and Axon, you would agree that it is extremely difficult not to want to snatch her up and have her all to yourself. I'm guessing it strengthens with whoever is near and yet she is oblivious to it. It's a hidden gift; a shield of protection against powerful men.'

Axon nodded. 'I noticed it started to get heady this afternoon when we got back from skiing. I've had a hard time keeping my hands off her. So, what have you planned that has set her off?'

Jett seemed pleased Axon agreed but wasn't yet ready to disclose what was about to happen. 'I noticed it the day Calyx arrived and I believe I know why it has flared up now and it isn't us two men flexing our muscles at each other.' He winked.

'Why then?' Axon asked again and understood once Jett transported them to his home why he was reluctant to say. The first vision when materialising was that of three of the most powerful, ruthless and dangerous of all gods. *Oh, shyte!* There were his brothers, Zeus and Poseidon, their parents, Cronus and Rhea, and chatting together in the garden were the goddesses, Persephone, Amphitrite and Hera.

'Honey and Ted Bear!' Caitlin opened up her arms to welcome Jett's parents. She seemed not at all alarmed as she played the part of a friend that had missed them, and did it so well that even Axon believed it. Had she just changed in character? Was she still his Caitlin or someone else? He pondered how her sweet yet quick-to-judge temperament could have suddenly changed into this audacious life of the party. It was at that moment the penny dropped; he understood how she could be away from him and her friends and not fret. He had heard of it before. An entity, or angel force, controlled her, and for now, she was theirs, and he had to let her work. He stood back to give her space.

'Dear, you look divine.' Honey put out her hand to Axon. 'Wolf, so lovely to see you again.' Her eyes glazed slightly. Had Caitlin done that? Was she powerful enough to put them in a trance?

'Calyx and Zuri!' Caitlin hugged them, grabbed their hands and dragged them over to Axon. 'You remember my boyfriend, Wolf?' She beamed up happily at them. 'He is now my fiancé.' Then with a flick of her hair, she left them to congratulate him and ran over to the last brother. She jumped at him, and he snatched her up in his massive arms. The action made her look like a little girl. 'Razor!' She pulled on his beard. 'I swear this woolly mess has to go.' She grinned at his wife, Angel. 'How you even find his lips is beyond me.'

'Cheeky minx.' His jovial chuckle rocked his large belly and made her collapse against him, laughing. She lifted her chin up, kissed his forehead and slipped from his arms. The big fellow pulled his shirt around his stomach to hide it. The wobble worsened, and both ended in hysterics.

Axon glanced over at the pair. Even her laugh was different which confirmed his suspicions that on the job, Glow Girl dominated Caitlin.

Razor's wife, Angel, joined in and linked arms with Caitlin.

Axon was amazed at servants that doted over each god. This morning he had spotted only a few when they had walked the grounds with Jett. On their own and standing away from the others he mentioned this to Jett.

'Did your family bring their personal servants? Even I don't keep this many.'

'Over the years my needs have simplified. I have evolved, unlike my family, and need little help as I enjoy doing things for myself. My family brings an entourage as lifting a finger is considered absurd and ungodly. We do not see eye to eye on this at all.'

'But you have an army, I know, and yet there is no sign of a township or barracks.'

'Ah, forever on the job. You worry about Glow's security with my family. Don't concern yourself, my friend, I need only snap my fingers and help is at my side. Now enjoy your night and try to worry less.' He snapped his fingers, and immediately there was a servant beside him; not a word did he say, and yet the table hand tipped a pitcher of Ambrosia and filled their goblets.

'Cheers!' Axon grinned.

Jett responded, 'to a night of new beginnings.'

At the table, Caitlin was seated next to Jett. She was elated to have another chance for the family to get to know and accept her and Axon for who they were. She was glad they still knew nothing of where they came from. She was not powerful enough to take on so much might, only just powerful enough, for now, to control the temperament of these superior individuals as they joked, drank and ate together. The atmosphere and ambience underneath the dome were warm and inviting and made it easier. So did the liquid Ambrosia that they drank.

'Wine of the gods,' Ted Bear had toasted.

Caitlin picked up the vibe of pleasure in them and instantaneously Axon felt the toning down of energy that she'd put out to influence the initial convening. His mind went into overdrive as to exactly what Caitlin was capable of and was amazed. He had fought most of the evening to keep her goddess essence from stealing the wits he needed to keep her safe. But she had finally worn him down too and he gave up the struggle as the party spun out of control, and everything beyond tonight became insignificant. Enjoyment of the moment with great friends dominated further speculation.

* * * *

After the entree, Axon had an idea and moved to the opposite end of the table, to engage in conversations with others. A little away from Caitlin's influence was where he was able to become more alert. He heard Caitlin laugh and, now watching her, hoped she didn't get hurt. She believed in Jett and sat beside him enjoying the festivities. Axon, aware of her genuine adoration for the family, put aside his worries for her for the moment as he had to concentrate on this perfect opportunity he might never get again. A chance to get to know the Rulers of half the planets he was now accountable for was gold, and he wasn't about to miss this opportunity Hades had given him.

It was a great night. They all ate, watched the entertainment that was brought before them and after, sat out in the garden. The men smoked cigars and chatted while the ladies opted for the spa. Once back in the cabin, Caitlin and Axon flopped on the sofa, exhausted. Axon put a couple more logs on the fire and shut off the air vent so it would burn gently through the night. He put the cushions onto the floor and, after pulling the fur rugs around them both, he cuddled up with Caitlin and slept.

Next morning, Caitlin stretched and stood up to stare out the window. Axon woke and joined her.

'I miss Rory and my friends.' She hugged him.

'Last night sorted out a lot for you, didn't it Cait? You've seen how happy Jett is now and you're contented to leave him?'

'Yes. There is still the issue of the family spotting me when I go back to work, but somehow, I feel safer now. I believe they will think first before wielding the final blow towards me.' She smiled up at him. 'Last night was perfect, and you're perfect. You can take me home now.'

'What, before breakfast? I thought we promised to stay, but just say the word and we're gone!' He would do a runner now if she let him. Away from them and without Caitlin's power that kept him calm, he was agitated, worried that they pushed their luck too far. What if at breakfast and in the light of day, they guessed who it was that they called a friend? She didn't see them the way he did with their dark evil temperaments that showed in every crease on their skin. He knew even now by the shocked look she wore that she didn't understand his need to want her away from them, his need to hide her and not just now, but for all time. He had every intention when they got back, if they got back, of seeing Zoren about finding another Rider to replace Caitlin. She was to be his wife, and around these dangerous tyrants she would not live another day, never mind a lifetime.

Caitlin watched Axon's expression of concern. 'Please trust me to do the job I'm trained to do.' She ran a hand over his creased brow, and her touch eased him almost instantly as his body melted with the pure essence of love she saw he had for her. 'After breakfast, my love.

Yes, we did promise we would join them and it would be rude to run out on them. But after that, I'm all yours and, yes, then it will be time to leave.' Caitlin smiled.

After a heated spa and a change of clothes, Axon transported them to the patio where the family had already gathered.

'You're like a little ray of happiness. They are very taken by you Glow,' Jett whispered to her, as he took her hand and seated her between Calyx and his dad. Then he turned to Axon. 'Got a minute, Wolf?' He walked off, and Axon followed. Away from prying ears, he turned to him. 'Axon, or should I say Wolf?'

'Axon is fine, while we're on our own.'

'I wanted to speak alone for a minute as I know Glow wants to go home.'

'How did you know? She only asked me before we came to breakfast.'

'I know.' Sadness flashed for just a second across his face. 'It is you I wish to speak to though. You have befriended me, and my brothers. Last night you let your hair down and enjoyed the evening with us, and I believe it was sincere. Caitlin had toned down her power, so it was all you. I want to know why. If it's a ploy to take her from me, us, I will be so disappointed, as I too, fell for your jests and kindness and would like nothing more than to call you friend.'

Axon breathed in deeply, exhaled and eyed him 'Truthfully, I wanted to run with Caitlin. It worries me she is so small against such power and yet when I looked into her eyes when we spoke this morning, I saw her strength, her willpower and her love for you and them. I could no sooner take her from you than I could turn my back on the friendships that have begun to develop between us.'

'I am pleased to hear you say that, Axon. When listening to her thinking, it was about you both leaving. I immediately blamed it on you, and jumped to the conclusion you had talked her into it.'

'No Jett, Cait is not that easily persuaded. You must know this by now.' He grinned, remembering the performance they had just been through with her so she could come back here to Pluto.

'Yes, you are right!' He grinned back. 'Your fiancée is such a damned handful.' He gave Axon a slap on the back in recognition.

'Our handful?' Axon agreed.

'I will miss her more than I have missed anyone, anything, yet do not understand the connection. Glow has nothing I want, and yet I can't get enough. Crazy.'

Axon shook his head. 'Oh, how I can relate to that but from the opposite perspective. I want it all and can't get.' Both men cracked up laughing. 'Jett, let's just call this for what it is. My two-timing girlfriend loves us both, so how about we call a truce. As far as I'm concerned I too have had to change, as you have. As for your home, you have welcomed me into it and given me a chance to win Caitlin back. I have thoroughly enjoyed your hospitality and commend your mediation skills for setting something like this up. It has been a pleasure getting to know everyone. I don't know where we go from here; that's up to you and your family. For now and for Cait, let's at least keep the door of communication open and see where it leads.' He put his hand out and Jett took it eagerly, and the two men shook.

'Agreed, and thanks. That's how I'd like to leave it too. I've done all I can to get them to know you, Axon. I don't know what my family will do the day they finally find out who you are, but when the time comes, I hope the uniting of us this second time will at least stop them ever being able to hurt our Glow. Just promise she can visit here from time to time.'

'I will; she will make sure of that.' Axon smiled.

'Glow said we would both know when it was time to let each other go. It feels right this time.' The two strolled back to the table, the conversation light and sociable after the pact they formed for the one they both loved.

Axon noted double the number of people present. Razor commandeered the BBQ, sending the servants scattering with his thunderous growl. The rest of them sat back in the lounges, chatting and being waited upon. Axon had always wondered what it would be like to hang out with gods and this was everything he expected. Even Caitlin, surprisingly, looked comfortable as one of the servants fed her grapes, and she giggled and slapped Jett for hanging it on her. He blinked. Of course, Cait fitted in here, because the controlling side of her was a goddess. Funny how he didn't feel odd or on the outer either. The family included him in every topic, eager to hear what he had to say, amused at his normality for one that lived amongst the stars.

At the table, Caitlin won Razor over completely when she made a fuss of his cooking. 'I'm having seconds.' She leant over for another scoop of marinated wings.

'That's my girl.' Razor grinned. 'You'll need that energy from it to help you stay on your ski's and keep you warm out there. I imagine it will be bitterly cold on the slops today.'

'Skiing?' She glanced at Jett to whom she'd already confided she would be leaving straight after the meal.

Ted Bear caught the look. 'What, you're leaving early?'

'Ted, you haven't seen me ski. I'm hopeless. Ask your son who's spent many days trying to teach me.' Her words were a little desperate. She felt worn out from the power she used to keep the questions about their lives to a minimum.

'Just a couple of hours,' he pleaded.

She glanced at Axon who was no help. He too had enjoyed the last hour or two of their time there and seemed in no hurry. He puffed on a cigar, his legs stretched out comfortably as he settled into the chat with Calyx.

She plonked herself down between Calyx and Ted, the two most powerful of them all and here she would stay with them until they were ready to go. She recalled her equal. Cassie used her horse and even her team to draw power if needed. Therefore it stood to reason she too had this gift. If she could take just a little energy charge from both, they would never know, and she figured these two could well afford to lose some. The way they ate, they would gain it back in no time.

Feeling better, she filled her plate and forced in more food. Jett had not included the ski area when putting up the dome. The gods possessed powers to adjust with the weather, and he didn't feel it necessary. This Caitlin thought of when powering up beside Ted and Calyx. The extra food and fuel would help her survive the icy slopes. It was times like this she cursed her delicate skin. Her team would have no trouble adjusting to these conditions. Even with all this, without the magic of her horse, she would still feel the cold. Unable to say no and let down her new friends she decided to rug up and brave it.

'Well?' Ted nudged her once she finished her second plate of food.

'Only because you are so hard to say no to and because I would love to see what a bear looks like on his arse.' She giggled, and everyone cracked up, amused.

Thrilled she was staying and not even slightly agitated, yet wanting to provoke more laughter, Ted touched her nose. 'You, stirrer, have triggered the animal in me so don't even think for a second that this mammoth girl-eating monster will be taking it easy with you now. You're going down.' He put his head back and roared with laughter as she slapped him on the arm in good humour and called him a bully.

Caitlin turned to Honey and asked if she was skiing, but she declined. 'I've never had the patience to learn, love,' she said. 'Ted tried to teach me in the earlier days, but I have always had a fiery temper when it comes to sport, so he gave up. I have other qualities that keep Ted still very interested in me.' She chuckled and rolled her eyes at him.

'Honey!' Caitlin stood and shook her head at Honey and Ted who were smiling at each other. 'You two are so naughty, and at your age.' She tutted and sent them both into a hearty laugh.

* * * *

Later, on the slopes, the icy cold wind was bitter, but Caitlin was determined to brave it. Ted was insistent she went with him for her little wisecrack before breakfast. 'I am so going to enjoy watching the spills as payback.'

His laughter echoed, as time after time he would help her up, only to have her fall a little farther on. Once she got into a slide towards him and was just about to hit the ice when he grabbed her and laughed so hard the bear ended up on his behind as well. Caitlin fell about giggling when a dripping wet Ted called it a day. 'Just shake it off, that's what bears do, don't they.'

Flinging her over his shoulder, he headed for the cable car and sat her on it. 'No more, bad Glow.' He shook his finger at her, and the tears of laughter ran from her eyes.

All in all, they had a blast, Jett commenting he had never seen his father have so much fun. 'You've won him over Glow.' Jett hugged her good-bye. 'Thanks, Glow, you're good for me. My life has changed since I met you and now, I know real happiness, I want to grab hold of it and not let it go, not let you go. But I know I have to.' He grinned slyly. 'Maybe the evil side of me will be forgiven for preferring to just steal you away right now instead of letting you go.'

She laughed and smacked his arm. 'You will turn my man grey with worry, my little evil friend.' She chuckled.

He laughed and then got serious. 'I'll miss you and…'

'And what?' she asked.

'I want to give you something.'

'Like what?'

'A free pass for a couple of days, that means no war games or any kind of fighting. I'm doing this so you can be with your friends and make amends with them after choosing me over them to make you better.'

'Seriously! That would be so wonderful, are you sure you can do that? Won't your family ignore your plea? They may have other plans.'

Jett grinned. 'They plan to spend another few days with me. The remodel has them intrigued. They want to discuss it further, and maybe take away some ideas to use on their own Home Worlds. But this will cause great debates as they do not accept change easily. I figure the arguments on what materials I should or shouldn't have used and what they would sooner have for their own design, will take them at a minimum of two days, so no more than that, okay.'

'Thank you, Jett, you're a good friend. I have missed the gang and know I will need to eat quite a bit of humble pie, well, with Rory anyway.'

'Call me,' he said and looked as if he didn't want her to go.

'No, ring me, so I don't disturb you. Your family might still be here.'

Jett gave her one more hug. 'Talk to you tomorrow.'

Goodbyes over, Axon took her hand, and their image faded from sight as they transported back to Ara.

'Home, sweet home!' She sounded her old self.

Axon picked her up and swung them both in a circle. He was on such a high at the smile that lit up her face. Glow Girl was gone and his Caitlin back. He now knew the difference.

Chapter Twenty-Nine

A Deal is a Deal

'We're home!' Caitlin sang out.

'In here,' Rory answered from the kitchen.

'Cait.' Bree squealed and ran to her, arms spread out, and gave her a hug. 'I thought we lost you. I'm so glad you're okay.'

'I'm fine now. How's it been with you guys?'

Bree didn't get to answer.

'Come here, young lady!' Rory grinned and hugged her too, his arms shaking slightly, his emotions evident. They had gone through a lot while she played mediator and it was now time to take Rory aside and talk about it. He was the one person in the world she could tell anything to.

'Got time for a chat?' Rory was not just her boss, he was and always would be, the one man she would always trust with everything. He deserved an explanation for her recent behaviour.

'For you, all the time in the world.'

'Sorry guys, I just need a minute.' Caitlin excused herself and followed Rory out into the garden. Here they sat, and this time Rory made sure she told him everything.

'Cait, you had me so worried. I wish you didn't have to do these missions alone. I want to be there, but you closed me out.'

'I have no idea how to handle this Rory, the goddess takes me over and yet I feel it's me.'

'Then next time, know I have your back. I can help in other ways and from now on I will. My powers are growing too.'

'I appreciate you offering and hope next time I get a chance to give you the heads up because honestly, I hated us fighting, and don't ever want us to fight again. Rory, you must know how much I look up to you, I am your friend first, always.'

'And I am yours and was long before becoming your boss. But always remember you are also family; geez Cait I love you the same way I love my sister. Never forget that, okay.'

'So…' she smiled, 'that means I'm annoying most the time.'

He laughed and pulled her up from where they sat. 'You said it, not me.'

* * * *

Inside the kitchen, Axon was pleased to see Caitlin was okay after her chat with Rory and stood beside her while she talked to Bree. Rory took over cooking breakfast from her and was kept busy flipping the bacon and eggs while buttering the toast.

'So spill,' said Bree. 'I want all the goss. Leave nothing out about your holiday… nothing.'

Axon folded his arms and smirked. He couldn't help but stir the pot. He was ticked off Caitlin had grabbed Rory and possibly spilt the beans they were engaged, without him. He wanted to tell everyone. 'Well, maybe you better leave out the make-up sex.'

Caitlin dug her elbow into Axon's ribs for lying and at the same time had to smile at Rory's reaction as his head swung around so fast it cracked.

'I know Cait better than that so how about we change the subject.' Rory wasn't amused.

Bree leant into Cait. 'It's okay. You can tell me that bit later when we're on our own.'

Rory flicked her with his tea towel. 'No you won't, Breezy. I don't want you talking to our innocent Cait about any of her personal stuff and influencing her any more than the boss already has. She's not a bad girl like you. She's pure and sweet, so just behave.'

Bree winked at her. 'He loves me, but still has you up on the pedestal.'

Axon didn't look surprised at Rory's reaction. 'I vote she learns from Bree.' He grinned at her. 'You go girl.'

Rory eyed Caitlin. 'Don't listen to them Cait, stay you.'

Axon was curt and annoyed. 'She's my fiancée now and listens to what I tell her.' Axon's arrogance and confidence bit at Rory. His cheeks flushed. Caitlin hadn't mentioned the engagement when they talked.

'Sorry Rory, I should have told you.' She glared at Axon. 'But I thought we were going to wait until everyone was here together before the news broke.' She screwed up her mouth at Axon for being stroppy and overly bossy with Rory.

'What!' Axon smirked, enjoyed having a claim to her and letting Rory know it. 'He should be the first to know.'

'Yes, I should have been, Cait. I would have talked some sense into you. Axon, are you sure about this? What will Zoren say? It's not too late to admit this was just a crazy moment, a holiday fling and a mistake.'

'Rory!' Axon was annoyed. 'This is no mistake, and Caitlin is old enough to make decisions for herself. God, sometimes you sound just like her father.'

'I might come off as being fatherly, but someone has to have some common sense around here. Caitlin is part of my team, and sorry if this upsets you, but I didn't train her all these years for Cait to laze around and become all wifey and soft.'

Axon had his mouth open to fly more insults and pull rank on his stubborn commander when Caitlin sobbed. Hearing them fight after the feud she'd dealt with between Axon and Jett, was more than she could handle.

'Don't Rory, I love him.'

Rory immediately dropped the spatula and went to her. 'Sorry, Cait. I should be having this talk with him in private. I know you love him, but you're both putting a lot on the line. What if you lose some of your special powers once your innocence has gone? What if Zoren sacks him for marrying you, an employee? I lose you both.'

Caitlin leant into him. 'I think my power will stay intact if we are married first. He is the man I chose, who I want always. Am I selfish for wanting some kind of a normal life?'

Rory knew her life before him had been hell and he did wish for her a beautiful future that he thought he was giving her as part of his team. However, he had not realised she would find love so soon. He breathed out heavily. 'No, it's not selfish, and I shouldn't have upset you when this should be a happy moment for you. Sorry Cait.'

Axon twisted his mouth in anger that he had upset her. 'It's my fault, I should have waited as we planned.'

Rory turned to him. 'No, it's both of us. In future, when it has to do with Cait, you tell me first. A private word between us would have saved these tears. She has been through enough. I knew when she came home it was not over and stayed patient. Coming home now, her mission is over and we should be welcoming; not fighting about who likes her more. Yes, she is your fiancée, but Cait is family to me, and if you intend to join our family, I need a bit more respect from you if you want to be a liked brother-in-law.'

Axon grinned. 'So it's okay by you?'

'If Zoren approves, shytzer, I'll even throw the goddamned wedding for you.'

Caitlin hugged him. 'Thanks, Rory, knew you'd come through for me.'

Axon shook Rory's outstretched hand. 'Welcome to the family, big guy.'

Axon put his other arm around Caitlin. 'And by the way, Zoren knows. He's no fool and picked it up before I had admitted it to myself. When I did, I told him I was going to marry her. He warned me as you have that the Caitlin we have now could change. This might be a turning point, and without her innocence, the goddess influence could possibly leave her. But to tell you the truth, what that influence does scares the hell out of me. It attracts evil, and I don't know about you, but I'd sooner just have Cait, the one we had before all this madness started.'

'We can at least agree on that.' Rory picked up a serviette and patted Caitlin's face. 'You okay now?' He smiled when she nodded. 'But I warn you, Axon, you ever hurt her and hell—we revisit this conversation.'

Axon smiled. 'Knew you'd be a pain in the arse about it.'

'Glad I didn't let you down.' Rory went back to dish up breakfast.

'You never do, Rory, you never do.' He shook his head.

Suddenly Rory was calm again; his glowing eyes had settled and this time he stirred in jest, making her laugh. 'Seriously Cait, I think you could do better.

He touched his earpiece and called in Nate, Zeke and Lisha. 'Guys, the boss has proposed to Cait, and she has said yes. Get in here and slap her for me.'

The cheers and yahoos were heard long before the door swung open and the three bounded in with enthusiasm. The noise was ear piercing as they eagerly wished them every happiness and praised Caitlin's choice in a man. 'With you being her first boyfriend we have nothing to compare you with.' Nathen shook Axon's hand. 'But you'll do.'

Axon, accustomed to the team and their playful spirits, an attribute that attracted him to them from the beginning, smiled from ear to ear, pleased that in their own way they accepted him into their family unit. He stood back watching the fuss they made of Caitlin. She was a much-loved member and even though what she had gone through must have confused them, not one of them showed any resentment or judged her. They displayed genuine friendship as they hung on her every word, listening to the story as it unfolded to them. They all needed a break, time with each other, so he went upstairs to the NAVcom to contact Kayden. With Hades and his brothers still busy on Pluto for the next couple of days, this was the perfect opportunity to kill two birds with one stone. Woody could work on Caitlin while a training session with Kayden wouldn't hurt the rest of the team. They had struggled with the last mission while worrying about Cait, and he wanted to get them in the right head space again.

'Kayden, my man, would you mind a motley crew that needs a couple of days R&R? Woody was good value and gave my team a good shake up on his last visit. Feel free to provide one more if they have forgotten what he showed them.'

He heard Kayden cover the mouthpiece *not well enough* and swear as he informed Cassie, whom he heard squealed excitedly. 'Looks like I'm outvoted, so come on down. The men will love it, and Cassie is still jumping around tugging at me to find out when.' He sounded amused.

'We'll head off after the guys have eaten.'

'Did you want Woody to work with Caitlin? I hear she's been through a lot lately.'

'That would be great if it's okay with Woody. I know his training abilities and would hate to take away from him the pleasure of getting up in my team's grill.'

'Don't worry, he will do both, you can be assured of that.'

Both men laughed heartily.

Chapter Thirty

Kayden's Farm

It was quite a reunion when they arrived on Earth. After the horses' bridles had been removed, they were left in the barn to be washed down and fed by Tremaine, their horse handler.

After the back slapping and hugs, the team were ushered into four-wheel drives. A dusty mad dash and the sound of tyres that skidded on gravel brought them to a sudden stop outside the stately home next door. Woody and Jason awaited the team's arrival and reprimanded Ethan and Conor for racing each other.

'Guys!' Woody chastised. 'You're lucky K's not here yet.'

The pair got out of the drivers' seats and high-fived each other, neither the winner but both having enjoyed the hell out of it. 'Sorry.' They grinned while they helped the girls out of the cars.

'Like we believe they're sorry.' Jason glanced at Woody. 'Show-offs.'

Woody grinned. 'Oh well, here we go again. Let's go make the newborns feel welcome before we spank them and bring them to tears.' Both men chuckled and strode towards the team.

* * * *

Once Kayden and Cassie arrived, the riders were split into their prospective teams to begin training. The rest of the day was spent in rigorous sports activities to enhance their psyche and build their vital strengths. Kayden was old school and didn't ease up on them until late evening. Meanwhile, and reluctantly, Woody left them to it so he could coach Caitlin. She looked exhausted after Kayden had finished with her, but knew she would be worse off in the morning if he didn't sort out what was causing her lack of energy.

'Cait.' Woody approached her as she leant against the fence gulping down a bottle of water. 'While Kayden's busy with the others, maybe we could take off for a few minutes.'

'I'm all yours.' Her smile was bright, but her eyes and body language told him how she really felt, dull and lethargic.

They drove to the local water hole. The lake at night took on shapes as the mist moved upon it, the blackened water only visible when the moon shifted from the clouds above. Caitlin shivered at the eerie quietness. The slight lap of water as it licked the banks was the only sound once the engine cut out.

'Come, let's talk.' His voice broke the silence as he flung out a blanket on the ground. 'Sit, I don't bite,' he coaxed her.

She wiggled to get comfortable and even though Woody felt her walls go up, she did do as he asked. He felt her struggle with the mixed emotions of wanting to keep her past locked up. She was a tough one to crack and with no other alternative, he used magic to relax her. Like last time, it took a while for her to succumb to him. Once she was submissive enough, he began to unravel the years of torment. It was even more of a challenge this time as Caitlin's powers had strengthened extensively since their last session. Her amplified magic had exceeded Cassie's, but her gifts were all over the place. He feared they would become a danger to her if she didn't allow him to help.

'Cait, if you don't let me in to resolve your past, you're a magnet for the other side.'

'I could turn evil.' She was stunned by the news.

'Yes.'

'I'm trying, cross my heart. I've been able to open up to Axon and even told Jett.'

'That so, you've still not dealt with it. You push it aside as if it were someone else. I have to help you face it and resolve it.'

'It hurts.' Tears sprang to her eyes.

'I know, it's because your past stays fractured, with many years missed. I can ease your pain, so let me.'

In a great deal of emotional anguish, she finally gave in, lay back on the blanket and through tears, found the sadness he prompted from her. 'I hate them for what they did to me. They treated me worse than an animal,' she sobbed.

Woody watched carefully for signs. Divulging some things made her so angry she would squeeze her fists tight, baring white knuckles as she angered over the memories. As other times she would come to tears. During these moments Woody was able to seal the cuts with magic and after a moment he saw her breathe and unclench or stop crying. It was then he would prompt her to continue. 'Did you ask them if you could go outside to play even?'

'In the earlier years, yes. I would wrap my arms around their legs, crying and begging for them to take me with them. On other times I hid by the door and would attempt to escape. They would shake me off or throw me on the floor and make me starve for a day or so before they came back. In the end, I knew there was no one coming for me and nor would I ever see the light of day, so I gave up. I didn't bother acknowledging them when they came, not that they would stay long. Mostly they just sat reading. It seemed to suit them fine that I went quiet. My meals came on time, and they stayed a little longer if I was good.'

This time she was vulnerable enough to allow him the use of magic to recollect the finer details she struggled to remember. She broke down in the end, and in her negative emotional state, he was able to erase the sadness from her mind and mend the many cuts they had carved into her heart and soul.

As if a great weight lifted from her shoulders, she sat up and blinked, taking a big long breath, and when she breathed it out, she felt completely recharged. Better now and able to talk without the pain, they sat for a long time while she spoke of her life before and then her most recent mission with Hades; the kidnapping, the friendship, the betrayal and the camaraderie formed in the end.

He scratched his head. 'The forgiveness for such a criminal act and the empathy you showed that man leaves me mystified. When our Cassie was kidnapped, she forgave the kidnapper because he was her father. The god you call Jett was nothing to you. It must have been difficult to complete such a mission with a stranger as powerful as Hades.' He rolled his shoulders and chewed on a stick of grass in thought. 'What you did took real guts.'

'Not so much.' She pulled her hair back and clipped it up above her head. 'It wasn't as if he harmed me. Just had me spooked at first. After all, he is a big man and potentially dangerous. Just his presence in the room had me shaking in my boots at first; well, until I worked out he stayed true to me as Jett. Hades, on the other hand, reared his head a couple of times, and I can tell you, it was chilling.'

'You have linked him to you. I can feel it.'

'Yes, although I'm not sure how it happened. I noticed it the first night we met. I think it has something to do with a calming power I project. He knows about it, and so does Axon, and neither worries as it isn't strong enough yet to do any real harm.'

'I think there is something more at work here, Cait. This power the universe gifted you with makes no sense. It should be gone while danger is at bay and yet even now, I battle it, and I'm one of the good guys so I'm not sure why you project it towards me. It insists I probe further to bring it out fully and my intuition tells me that this is about more than the battle to force Hades into giving up on the fight for the Planet Mercury.'

'I don't understand. Until the dispute was sorted, I wanted to stay on Pluto. I was sure the feud was settled as the essence had toned right down and I was over the moon to be home.'

'This is where this job gets tricky. You have formed a bond and Hades not only wants you, but he also needs you. It is you, Caitlin, and you alone, that have set him on a path that includes your friendship. Without you, he'll go back to his old ways and become the tyrant he used to be.'

Woody left her to ponder while he grabbed two bottles of water from the car. When he returned he handed her one before his massive bulk lowered beside her again. 'You know, Cassie had the same learning experience with the warlord Conom, who kidnapped her. And believe me, Kayden was not impressed when they became friends. He's still not happy about it. Axon is even less patient, and I warn, he is not going to like this relationship at all.'

She put her head down, unsure what to say. He told her nothing she didn't already know.

'Also, after chatting with Cassie before we came here, I feel I need to give you the heads up about another gift you may not be aware of yet. Cassie is picking up from you that your journey is far from over with this family. That there is still much work for you to do before you finally achieve your goal. Because of the evil that surrounds them, she believes you have a new power, but as her equal, it is not allowing her access. It is a one-off power to erase a link to a moment in time and undo an injustice inflicted upon you, but she cautions that if you use this gift, you may lose all memories of the entire event.' He sat quietly while she took it all in.

'I've got so much to learn, Woody. I worked really hard, yet felt as if I fumbled through that mission. I damned near stuffed it up. Then I had to fix it and thought I might even lose Axon because of it. You don't know how hard it is when nobody understands why you are doing something because what I am given is for me alone. Not to be shared.' Caitlin pressed her face into her hands and sobbed into them.

'Cait, I get it, and Axon gets it now. The Cosmics are a new team and have a lot to learn in the trust department but believe me, they get it too, and if they don't, I will speak to them before you leave.'

'No!' She sucked back a sob.

'Then no more crying; you did the best you could at the time. What I want you to remember is none of us is perfect.' He grinned at her. 'Well, I am,' he teased and chuckled with her. 'Mistakes are made because we deal with perfect imperfection. Gods and Rulers have lived so many years they are almost impossible to change in character. They have belittled and bullied their way through life. To have gained even a little ground with Hades is a great feat.'

'I'm learning I can't change anything in a day, but do see the progress when I look into Hades' eyes and find Jett,' she said and gave him a sidelong look as she spilt that she also knew there was more to come. 'In saying that, as Cassie has picked up, I'm also getting vibes this is far from over so Axon and the team, well they had better strap in and give me a break, cause if Cassie and I are right, my work is not done.'

'In that case, I would make the best of the next couple of days. Rest up for when the universe calls once more. You will need to be in top form.'

'Agreed.'

He had earned her trust, and consequently, she confided secrets she had never disclosed to even her best friend, Rory.

Woody watched her dig into the earth with a stick. His admiration for this little redhead was intense and deeper than he thought he would feel for any female. In fact, he battled with his feelings for her. The urge to snatch her into his arms and kiss her lush lips tempted him. *What the …?* He shook his head as he fought back with his own power to stop her taking him over. He was falling, and hard. *What is she doing to me?* The seductress emitted goddess control as she unknowingly began to steal his heart.

'Hell!' He shook himself and threw himself into the lake to cool off the desire that came over him. She gave off some sort of powerful love potion and sucking in a gob full of water, he nearly choked with an outburst of laughter as he surfaced.

She stood up with hands on her hips. She had no idea why Woody had thrown himself into the lake and laughed. 'Have you gone mad?'

Unable to fight the feeling off, he used the water element to re-freshen his powers, he swaggered out of the water. 'Damn, girl, that was weird. I thought for a minute that I was a lovesick puppy. That is some crazy awesome magic.'

'Really! Is it that strong?'

'That essence you release, the one that Axon and Jett believe you use to calm evil— well now your walls have come down, it's at its peak. On a good person, it works the opposite way. Instead of the calming effect, I wanted to make love to you. And I mean cave man love, drag you into my grotto and never release you.'

'Oh my god. How do I stop it? Are you okay?'

'I'm fine now. I have a barrier between us, but girl, until the magic I used to heal you breaks down in your system, we'd better stay right here and away from the others.'

Caitlin breathed out deeply. 'This power isn't something new. It's been such a pain to live with. The guys have commented for years on how my perfume lingered and yet I never wore any. They would cuddle up close, unable to go. Can I tell you how weird it is to wake up with five friends so close, and the strangeness we all felt when it toned down. The funny looks they gave when they realised they had spent the whole night on my floor instead of going home.'

'There must have been trouble around. Maybe you were a target, watched, and it was a night unsavoury characters may have tried to get into your apartment. With so many staying the night, they would rethink the odds. The team possibly saved your life.'

'Maybe. I did live in rough neighbourhoods. Rory was always going crook at me for picking the cheapest apartments as they were usually located in the less desirable districts.'

Woody took off his top and squeezed the water from it. 'I have to warn you about this, Cait. You're working with evil, and this power has been heightened so be careful, try to learn how to use it, or at least control it now you know you have it. This magic could confuse and frustrate an evil egg, okay.'

'Yes, I will.'

'Your team are also your guardians now, look to them if you need help.'

'Rory will come up with something. He always does when it comes to me. We have a bond neither of us gets but thankful we have.' Caitlin stretched her shoulders, a little more relaxed as the image of Rory calmed her.

'All I know is that men like us that are not evil, feel the effect differently. Axon's going to freak out when I take you back. The effect is starting to dull a little but wow, girl, the wish to make mad passionate love to you was ripe on my mind. I give you the tip.' He chuckled and nudged her. 'My Ella would castrate me if she thought that I even looked at another woman, so for goodness sakes, keep that bit of information secret, okay.'

'I will.' She smiled. 'I do understand, you telling me is to let me know how serious it is, and I do get it. Mum's the word.'

'You, my little love goddess, just radiate, and there is no stopping what comes naturally. Stay close to your man tonight, and if the other boys or I get a bit over-excited, a good whack will sort us out. I'll warn them so they can control it, but you're on fire, honey.'

She giggled. 'Axon will be pleased then.'

He laughed with her. 'You're going to blow his mind when I take you back. Guaranteed!'

He got up, took her hand and helped her up. 'I better take you back now. And I can bet you a dollar, my Ella will pick up on it and not be happy I have gone all gooey over you.' His amusement at the whole situation made it painstakingly clear she wouldn't live this down for quite some time.

She punched him in the arm. 'That's for any further thoughts you might have on the way home.' She laughed at him nursing his arm and the pretence that he would even feel the light hit.

'That's not fair, I wasn't even thinking …' He raised his eyebrow. 'Well okay, maybe I did deserve it, but it's not my fault.' He jumped in the driver's seat with a mischievous grin that made her laugh louder.

When they reached the farm, he stopped the car and moved over towards her, put his arm around her and gazed into her eyes, searching.

'Do I have to slap you again?' she cautioned him.

'Just checking! It looks as if your subconscious is sorting it out. That's one powerful weapon. With all my magic, it brought me to my knees. Jett is a tyrant, and Ruler of the Underworld, in other words, a real bad arse, so I hate to think who you still must have to deal with.'

'More powerful than Hades? Now that's a challenge.'

He tickled her. 'You have no fear have you girl.'

'Yes, just one.'

'What might that be?'

'Losing the ones I love because of this.'

'Just be careful how many you use it on, or you'll end up with a following of males that are smitten by you and can't live without you. Axon won't share you with the whole galaxy, Cait. There's a breaking point to any man's patience. Even Kayden had his with Cassie.'

'I'm new at all this. Cassie is so controlled and understanding of what powers she has. I'm all over the place and feel like an amateur against her.'

'Just heed my warning and let the universe lead you. It will give you time to learn how to control some of the gifts you have received. Cassie's been at it a lot of years now. When learning to control her magic she was just like you, so don't be so hard on yourself.' He put his hand on her forehead. 'Enough of this worry; close your eyes and listen. What can you hear?'

'Nothing!'

'Relax further, deeper. What can you hear?'

'Heartbeats and breathing.'

'Deeper!'

'Lots of noise and whispering, laughing, but I can't make it out.'

'Stop at the noise and concentrate on one sound only, push all the rest away and head for the one closest to you. What is it saying?'

'He's just thinking that he's the happiest person alive, sitting in a car with the prettiest girl he ever saw. Her red hair drives him insane, and her creamy smooth skin is to die for. She has power over him tonight that he is finding hard to resist. He needs her to move away from him now before he steals a kiss that will get him such a slap.' She chuckled, opened the door and ran from him. It was Woody's mind she read, and he was having a bit of fun with her. He caught her just as she reached the path to run around the back. He laughed, swung her around and put her down, then both walked arm in arm around to the backyard. They had become close, and it lifted Caitlin's spirits to know she had earned the admiration of one she respected and had placed on a pedestal from the minute they met.

Woody whistled loudly, getting everyone's attention. 'Listen up teams. Somehow our session has over-developed one of Caitlin's powers. This is an essence, and while up so high is sure to make any men her slave, most likely make the devil himself bow at her feet. So a warning to all males here tonight, until it settles, I've given the love goddess here permission to slap any of us that may happen to fall under her spell.'

Axon's grin was wide as he put out his arms to her. 'Come over here, beautiful, I'll protect you.' He was aware and could handle this now.

'Axon, I'm serious, man, you will need to control yourself and keep the others away from her. I still have her wrapped in protection.'

'I'm used to it. Don't stress.'

'Okay, but if you get slapped don't say I didn't warn you – ready?' he said to Axon, and he nodded.

Woody let her go and the arms she went into with joy, were Axon's, and she shuddered as she was so glad to be back with her man.

The reaction from her caused his whole frame to quiver. 'My god, what was that?'

Woody laughed. 'I told you, she's on fire, but it should wear off in a few hours. It's already toned down heaps. I had to throw myself into the lake and get away from her when it first cut in.' He shook his hand, shaking off her magic. 'Good luck mate, I'm glad it's you holding her now. That was some session.' He glanced over at the bar. 'I'm going over there, as far away as I can and intend to pour a really stiff drink.'

Kayden and Rory were still standing with Axon.

'Couldn't be that bad; she's always had that power over men when it suits her.' Rory put an arm around her and then backed off quickly. 'Eek, he's right. It's escalated, and it feels weird to want to race off someone you view as your sister. I'm with Woody! I'll catch you guys later, much later.' He practically ran and threw himself into the pool by the bar.

'I seem to force the men around me into the water. Are you okay, Axon honey?' she asked and when he didn't answer she looked up at him. His eyes were glazed and gazing at her lovingly.

'You'll have to excuse us, Kayden.' Axon spoke dreamily. 'I do believe Cait needs to be separated from the men for a while.'

Kayden also looked confused with his thought. 'I'm not that close, but she's irresistible. You better get her upstairs before we all fall at her feet.' He shook off the sensation. 'I'd better go and rescue Cassie before her perception picks up on the power and she turns all love goddess on me as well.' He stomped off grumpily. 'That's all I need! The boys to hang off her more than they already do.'

Axon picked Caitlin up and quickly took her upstairs to their appointed room. He placed her on the bed, sat in the corner on a chair and put his hands up in a gesture to stop her moving towards him. 'Just give me a minute honey, I need to calm down.'

She eyed him. 'Surely not you too! You should be immune to my charms by now.'

'Sweetie please, just stay where you are! I'll come over to you when I can.' He gripped the sides of the chair with his hands, his knuckles almost white.

The session with Woody had exhausted her, so she drifted off to sleep the minute her head hit the pillow.

It was early morning when she woke and found Axon still in the chair asleep. She tossed aside the cover, crept over and curled up in his lap.

'Are you all right now?'

He kissed her passionately. 'I love you like crazy, beautiful, then add the extra boost of the goddess thing you have going on, and be blowed if I'll be letting you go anytime soon.'

She wiggled out of his grip, laughing. 'Go get under a cold shower Romeo, we have things to do today and pre-wedding hanky-panky isn't going to be one of them.'

'Honey, can't you bend the rules – for me?'

'Axon, shower now!'

He got up and grumbled all the way to the bathroom. The sound of her singing to herself eased his disappointment. With the knowledge she would soon be his, he turned on the taps and whistled the same tune she sang. His mind imagined what their first time would be like. He couldn't wait to make her feel his love, for him to feel her innocence, and to make her his forever.

* * * *

After a hearty breakfast, Kayden and Woody drove them to a quiet location for some fun while they trained. When they arrived at a beachfront, the guys went ballistic, pushing and shoving to get out of the cars and wrestled each other to make it to the water first. As they were about to hit the salty waves, the sound of Woody's sharp bellow stopped them in their tracks. 'We're not there yet. Get on the ferry and stop mucking about.'

Finally, the ferryboat stopped next to a jetty.

Woody stood in front of them, preventing them from leaving. 'For those unaware, this is Thevenard Island, and even though it looks enticing with its lovely beach and those waves, we lads are going out on that fishing boat to catch dinner first. So pick a shack, drop your gear inside and let's head out. You can unpack when we get back,' Woody instructed. 'Ladies, you are welcome to join us,' he said as he turned to them, 'Or you can enjoy a few hours on the beach. Maybe relax, sunbake, swim, whatever you feel like.'

'If we're fishing, you can count Cassie in.' Kayden had his arm around her. He knew she would love it.

'And Cait and me,' Bree said.

'Not me!' Caitlin shook her head at Bree. 'I'm going to lie here on the beach and suck in the sun and sand for a bit.'

Kayden glanced at Axon who stood tense, his eyebrows furrowed in a frown. 'Come with us. Cait will be okay. Look.' He pointed up the beach, 'We have the island to ourselves, and we're only going around the tip to the other side where it's deeper.'

'Go, Axon. I know you want to. I'll stay with Red. No way will you get me handling no smelly fish.' Lisha moved over to Caitlin and swung an arm around her. 'I don't feel like sunbaking but will keep an eye on her.' She grinned and using both hands, banged on her chest like a monkey. 'Me start a fire, me protector.'

Axon turned and viewed the area and smiled at her silliness. 'If you're sure, but stay in earshot of her in case she needs you.'

Caitlin was about to go crook that Axon had made such a fuss, that she now had to be babysat, when he was pulled down the beach by Cassie. 'Bye!' she called back. Have fun, Cait.'

Caitlin smiled and waved back. Alone, she was chuffed. Lisha had taken off and dressed in a bikini, so Caitlin laid out a towel and settled down on the sand. Ignoring Lisha's terrible singing voice as she belted out a tune while traipsing up the beach to gather firewood, she squeezed sunscreen from a tube and spread the creamy lotion over her legs, arms and face while she watched as the others squeezed into the small fishing boat. Lisha and the vessel disappeared from sight at the same time, leaving her at last in peace to enjoy some alone time. The sun was bright but not hot, just right for her tender-aged skin. She heard Lisha call out, 'the wood's damp here, so I'll have to go inland.'

Caitlin waved in acknowledgement and lay back, bunching a towel up to form a pillow, her mind elsewhere. She had Jett on her mind. He'd said he would ring today and she kept her NAVear piece on in the hope it would work in this remote area.

As if he heard her thoughts, a call came through. She touched the pod in her ear and rolled onto her stomach to have a chat. He sounded his usual chirpy self until he heard the water lapping the beachfront.

'We've come to Earth, and I'm on a beach sunbaking.'

'Alone?' He sounded strange.

'The guys are fishing, and Lisha is collecting wood, so I guess you could say I am. Why?' The connection severed and Caitlin rolled over, annoyed the satellites had lost the signal, and she couldn't finish her conversation. There was so much more she wanted to tell him. A shadow over the sand had her turn and expect it to be Lisha back to annoy her. Her hand went up to shade her eyes to see.

'Jett!' She sat up and leant on her elbows.

'Hi, Glow.'

'How did you find me? I never told you where I was!' She was surprised, yet happy to see him.

'I have ways and means of finding you, little red riding girl.'

'A friend in wolf's clothing. Do you have big teeth too?'

'No, but I have big ears that hear you and a nose that knows your scent, my dear.'

'Then next time I go anywhere I will insist you wear ear and nose plugs.' She giggled.

With a grin from ear to ear, he positioned himself beside her on the sand. 'I was worried you were lying on the beach alone and then when the connection broke, I imagined bodybuilders sniffing around you, or even something more sinister and thought, Damn that, she's my girl – and came for a look.'

She laughed and pushed him, making him laugh more. 'Really.' She shook her head.

'True. It really tripped me out that they might have been sleazing up to you while Axon was fishing. He needs to take more care,' he huffed. 'Leaving you here alone. I should take you the hell from him.'

Caitlin slapped his arm. 'You're so full of it! Now, what is the real reason you're here?'

'Truth!'

'Yes.'

'Okay truth, I ring you, and here I am surrounded by ice on my planet, and you're sunbathing here on a beach. It was a spur of the moment thing. You were having too much fun so I figured I'd come and spoil it for you.'

'You're a mad friend.' She grinned. 'Okay, it looks like I'm not getting any truth from you today, so either join me or get back to your godly duties while I go hit the waves and maybe do some snorkelling.'

He glanced up along the beach and screwed up his face. 'Well, no chicks worth perving on, so I'm out of here.' He stood up and brushed the sand from his pants, ready to leave.

'Hey, what's the rush, roadrunner? Rest your chook legs here for a second and stay for a bit. I didn't mean for you to leave right this minute.'

He laughed. 'Give you chook legs. I'm definitely leaving now.'

She fell back on the sand, laughing at his indignant expression.

'If I didn't like you so much, I'd so hate you right now!' he growled with a grin and checked his pocket time-reader. 'Anyway, as much as I'd love to stay and drown you…' He made her laugh harder. 'I really have to head back as those brothers of mine can't be trusted.' He pulled her up, giving her a hug. 'Wish I could stay too. A dose of you is what was needed, and I'm happy to now head back. I'm glad I got to see where you are and that you are in no immediate danger.' His serious tone unnerved her.

'What do you mean? Is there a problem?'

'No! Just me being over-cautious where you're concerned.' He faded from her sight, and his disappearance left a question as to why he worried about her now she was well again. Both he and Axon needed a reality check. She could look after herself.

* * * *

After Jett's visit, Caitlin's mind hung on every word he said. Was there a meaning to them? She went for a swim and after that, curled up under a tree to sleep. Axon woke her, dripping wet as he flicked water over her. 'What have you been up to, sleepyhead?' He plonked down beside her and kissed her forehead.

'Jett dropped in for a visit.' She thought nothing of telling him all about Jett, now they had become friends too. 'Don't ask me how he found me. I was just talking to him on the phone telling him you had brought me to a little beach on Earth and within a few minutes the conversation cut short from bad communication on this island, and he was here.'

Axon frowned. 'Kayden's not going to be happy he tracked you to one of his private spots.'

'Really–I never considered that a problem as my mind was too full of what he said and the way he said them, but you're right. I'm a security risk if he can track me so easily, but you also know what a good friend he is to me. He would never disclose my location to his family, you know that, don't you? He just mucked around with me having a bit of fun, made mention he only came to check out where I was and pleased I wasn't in any immediate danger.'

'That seems a strange comment.'

'Yes, that's what I concentrated on most but came to the conclusion he might have meant because I was here on Earth and not up there fighting.'

'Or have they got something planned for Earth, and he was checking you were far enough away from the danger?' With the strangeness of Jett's words, Axon felt very unsure about his reason now for a visit.

'I'll have to report this to Kayden. I trust Jett with your life Cait, but that's as far as my loyalty goes. Remember the stories about Cassie and her father. He protected her but still did sneaky things to the rest of the team. He even used magic potions to break them up so he could have her for himself.'

'But I don't believe he would ever deliberately hurt you or me.'

Axon sighed. 'I know honey, please don't fret. I believe in him too and in your judgement. But the others don't know him, and Kayden has his own rules to protect his team, and I have to follow them while we are here.'

Axon left Caitlin on the beach. Aware now that her friendship with Jett would endanger others she worried for them and wished she had never taken the call. Stressed she had ruined everyone's time here, Caitlin stood up and walked over to the water's edge. Her sickened stomach rumbled. How could she have been so stupid? She shuddered with fright to imagine everyone was now in danger. Fear gripped her so badly she screamed out in pain.

Axon had her in his arms within seconds of her call and sat with her on the beach. He tried to calm her as rants of what a bad person she was for endangering everyone's lives, had her cry and grip her stomach in pain.

Woody knelt beside her. 'Something is about to happen. You'll have to let me work on her quickly to see what it is.'

Axon picked her up and laid her under a tree in the coolness. Woody stroked her forehead gently, used his magic to take away the vile episode and covered her eyes.

'Caitlin, use your senses. What can you hear?' he whispered.

'I can hear branches rustling in the wind, and waves slapping the shoreline.'

'Deeper!' he urged.

'I can hear hearts beating and breathing.'

'Deeper!' he whispered so quietly Caitlin could hardly hear him.

That's when the vision appeared.

'It's a meteor, heading for Kayden's barn.' Her breathing quickened as she whispered, 'My horse! Our horses are all in the barn. I have to save them.'

Her eyes were as wide as saucers. 'They're all going to die if we don't get back there now!' The last few words came out in a shriek. 'Woody, hurry, pull me out of this trance. I need Axon to transport Cassie and me there immediately, or it'll be too late.' She was unable to move until he released the grip that bound her tightly to him.

Woody took his hand from her eyes and snapped his fingers above them. Her eyelids shot open and with a quick roll and push off the ground she was on her feet with an eager hand out to Axon. Kayden had tuned in and listened to all being said and had already retrieved Cassie to help. Both ran from their hut to them. The three men exchanged a worried glance.

'I'll take the girls and come back for the rest of you as soon as I can,' Axon said to Kayden. He knew Kayden didn't possess transporting powers but needed them all together to shift them back to the farm.

'No, stay with the girls in case you need to get them out. I'll get everyone ready here on the beach for your return, now go,' Kayden yelled, worried.

An arm went around Cassie and Caitlin and in an instant, Axon had transported the girls to Kayden's barn, getting there in the nick of time to see a meteor heading towards the building.

'The horses,' Caitlin yelled out over the noise of the fireball that screamed as it whizzed through the air. They could see hot lava spew from it as it got closer. The sphere of unstoppable fire had not broken up or slowed even slightly as it entered Earth's atmosphere.

'Caitlin, hold my hand.' Cassie put her arm out and the two held each other firmly.

Caitlin could feel Cassie's power run through her own as if a switch was turned on inside, giving her a sudden burst of power.

'Hurry girls.' Axon was anxious as he felt the heat from the gas exploding fireball close in on them. He was ready to swoop in and take the girls away if they couldn't create the energy needed to blast it from the sky.

The instant Cassie said *now*, Caitlin let her hand go and both threw the electrical charge towards the fast-moving asteroid. The force of their magic hit it so hard it smashed to powder.

Caitlin's head spun around towards the barn. 'Axon, I'm still feeling danger. The horses; we have to get them out of the stables.'

'I can't see anything.' Cassie eyed Axon. 'But to make this quicker, go get Kayden to help. He can communicate with the animals and move them to safety faster than us. Caitlin and I can open up the stalls while you're gone and at least start to move them out.' She saw his hesitation. 'Don't fret, I can't hear a thing and don't feel anything coming, but Cait is freaked, so let's do this quickly.'

'Reluctantly, Axon went to pick up Kayden. He hoped he had everyone gathered so he need make only one trip.

With Axon gone, both girls ran in, opening up the stall doors and began to shoo away the stallions and mares out of the barn. There was only one stall left to open when Caitlin called to Cassie, 'go! Get the others as far away as you can. I'll let the last one out and meet you over by the old gum tree to the left of the house.'

'Is that far enough away, Cait?'

'I think so. Can't tell how bad this explosion will be, but it's nasty.'

'Hell Cait, I can't pick up anything. How are you doing this? Nothing is coming from the sky. Are you sure there's more?'

'I'm sure, now please go!' Caitlin had tears streaming down her face. Cassie knew the look and turned, whistled and clapped her hands to move the horses that had stopped.

'You sure you're right, Caitlin?' she yelled to her from the barn door.

'Yes, go… please! We must save the animals. I'm right behind you! I'll ride this one out,' she called after her.

'Hurry Cait, you're scaring me.' Cassie ran outside calling to the precious breeds as she did so.

Back inside, Caitlin opened the door to the last stall and using the pen, climbed up the rails and onto the horse. 'Move it.' She dug her heels into the mare. The stubborn horse stood firm. 'You must be used to your rider, but if you don't move it horsey, we are dead. That means you will never feel him on your back again!'

She wasn't sure if the horse understood or felt the looming terror but with a snort and a shake of its head, it bolted out with her holding on tight to its mane. The thing bucked and tried to get her off.

'I scared you. Good,' she growled at it. 'Just get us the hell out of here.'

Her anger and need to rush this mare and get it out quickly came from deep within her, urging her to flee quickly. With a sudden jerk that almost threw her off, the horse stopped and stamped its hoof as if in a tantrum.

'Move it you stupid-stubborn-blatzing-horse,' she yelled, and this time gave it a swift jab of her feet into its ribs. It was cranky now, and if they got out alive it would hate her always, but she'd sooner that than leave it to die. The head flew up, nostrils flared, and this time there was no mucking around, it bolted. However, just as they hit the stable doors, there was a sound of grinding cogs, silence, and a shockwave that sucked at them. She knew the blast was all that was left; the final stage of a bomb that was about to tear them and everything around her apart.

'Move!' she screamed at the mare, knowing already it was too late. The whole barn exploded, the inferno engulfing the structure, and she was thrown into the air.

Chapter Thirty-One

Dealing with Evil

Axon transported back to the house with Kayden and Woody as the barn exploded into flames. Shargan had seen Caitlin in trouble and broke from the pack to protect her. The shard of steel that headed for Caitlin hit Shargan instead, and the mare collapsed and fell on her side whickering in pain.

Caitlin took the rest of the impact on her back as it blew her off the horse and through the air. Her chest plummeted into the ground as she landed. The black smoke consumed them quickly, and the blast was so powerful, Axon and the others were propelled back a couple of metres. Crashing against the house, Axon used it as leverage and gripped firmly to the veranda posts. Kayden and Woody were thrown out wide, and both slammed into a tree. The aftershock easing, they jumped up, squinting through the black residue and flames that still burned fiercely, getting a fix on where Caitlin had ended up. They raced to her side. Cassie was kneeling, holding Caitlin's lifeless body, and screamed with frustration when her magic didn't work. She was distraught when she realised Caitlin was dead.

It was a while before Axon realised he now had hold of her and it was him that screamed and cursed the evil that had taken his Caitlin. He couldn't feel her pulse or hear her heartbeat no matter how much CPR he did. He blamed Jett immediately. 'I'm going to kill that bastard.' He could feel vengeance and hate build inside him. 'A life for a life!' he stormed as he rocked her, his incoherent rant indecipherable as he broke into an ancient dialect.

Unable to help Caitlin's situation, Kayden left her healing to the real professional. His expertise was mending bones, and only Woody had powers enough to bring someone back from hell's door. Kayden could already tell by the silence of its heartbeat, that one of his prize horses was dead. But Caitlin's horse lived and raced to the injured horse's side. He knew if Woody could save Caitlin, she would be devastated to find her horse was gone. This worry for her had him work fast and accurately as he removed the shard of steel and closed the wound with a handheld laser to stop the bleeding. He kept watch as Woody created a healing cocoon around Caitlin, using his magic to mend the wounds, but it looked as if nothing any of them tried would work. Kayden was almost sure she was gone as Woody had used that technique with them all, over the centuries, and it never failed. *Why is it not working today?*

He heard Woody calling to her spirit. 'Caitlin, you can call on help to live. I know first-hand how powerful your gifts are,' Woody insisted and checked again for a pulse. 'This is ridiculous. We can't just lose you like this. It doesn't make sense.' He eyed Axon. 'Between Cassie and me, we have all the magic we should need. It's got to be the universe, it must have an agenda, and it's not letting us fix her.' He yelled to pull Axon from his shock.

His words finally broke through Axon's torment and his glazed eyes cleared. He laid Caitlin on the ground so Woody could concentrate on her alone without his anguish. After a while, he saw tears of rage threaten to run down Woody's face as nothing he did revived her.

Axon watched and prayed. 'Please, heavenly angels, help Woody work a miracle. This can't be the end of such a brave young soul.' He held one of her burnt hands. 'Please don't leave us, beautiful,' Axon whispered to the lifeless love of his life.

'Caitlin.' Woody shook her. 'I know you can hear me. Your work here is not complete so take a breath. I want you to fight for your life and heat yourself up. I know you can do this. You're strong, and I'm strong. Together we'll mend your broken body, do you hear me, Cait?

Your work here is not yet done! Now concentrate.' Woody persisted as if she were still in her body.

Woody believed she had not gone and it gave Axon faith. In an ancient tongue only used by the highest of divine order, he pleaded for her life and watched and waited.

Woody's healing made her glow a little, something Axon had seen her do when she healed herself for him and Jett. She'd been given that gift for a reason, and he trusted it was for now. He tried to stay confident the supremacies of the heavens saw this coming and they wanted her to live through it. *Please let that be true.*

Cassie wiped her tears when she saw what Woody was attempting. She sat opposite him and lifted her hand, holding it above her friend's lifeless, damaged chest. Caitlin had shared this healing gift with her yesterday, and Cassie believed this was the reason why. It had not worked moments before but she had to trust using it together with one so powerful, they had a good chance of at least getting Caitlin to breathe.

Axon was optimistic at first when his girl began to glow, but it didn't hold and continued to weaken along with hope, which faded fast. As they tried to control the glow, Axon saw a shadow overhead come and go. He knew someone was watching; one of the gods. Maybe it was Jett or one of his brothers. He didn't care who it was, he just wanted his girl back. The glow started to dull. Axon cried out again for help from the gods above; he knew they were there, somewhere.

Another shadow appeared. It was a man he had heard of but never seen before. He had red skin, cinder black hair and he swooped in and knelt by Caitlin. A mere touch of his hand to her head forced her to take a deep breath.

He stood up. 'I am Apollo, sent by my father, who begged me for this favour. He tells me her name is Glow Girl and to tell someone he calls Wolf that his family sends their apologies.'

With no more words, Apollo, God of the Sun, healer and the son of Zeus was gone.

Axon dropped to his knees, unable to believe the evil bastards had even bothered to bring her back, but so very thankful right now that she had made a big enough impression on them that they had. She was breathing.

Woody picked her up and headed for the house. Axon was so weak from the heartache of possibly losing her, that Kayden had to pull him to his feet. Putting a strong arm around him, he walked Axon behind them. There were dark shadows all around Cait. Axon knew it was probably Jett and possibly members of his family that had not entirely transformed to this atmosphere and watched, just out of view, to see if she would live. Axon yelled at them to leave her alone that they didn't deserve her. He was going to make them pay dearly for what they had done to her. An energy burst came from somewhere inside him, and Axon appeared at Woody's side, snatched her, transporting her inside the house so they could see her no more.

He stood shaking with her in his arms. When Woody, Kayden and Cassie came inside, they tried to comfort him, seeing the mood he was in.

'I am taking her home where I can keep her safe. I have better technology there and as soon as my team arrives, send them up. It will take us all to protect her until she is back on her feet.' He looked around the room. 'I don't even trust it in here Kayden. You guys are welcome to come and stay at Ara too; at least until both your properties are scanned for more bombs. Zoren would not be happy for you to stay here, you know this.'

Kayden folded his arms and agreed with a nod.

'Sorry K, I can't apologise enough for bringing my evil planet gods to your door.'

Kayden unfolded his arms and rubbed his forehead, feeling the stress of what to do next. 'I don't believe it was your gods. I know they have taken responsibility for it, but I'm getting a different vibe. Something's not quite right, Axon, so before you go accusing Cronus and his family, let's do a little recon and see where that bomb actually came from.'

'If it was the gods I'm battling with I have to leave now. Zoren needs to be informed that Hades has lied to get us to relax so he could plan this uncalled for attack. What about you, K? Can I expect you and your team to join us too?'

'Have you got room for all of us?'

'Yes, I have plenty. It's not an inconvenience at all.'

Kayden pinched his chin, thinking it was possibly the best option but wanting to ask Cassie first. He still found this a conundrum but he did trust her instincts. 'What do you feel, honey?'

'Not safe, that's for sure.'

He nodded to Axon. 'That's good enough for me. We're in.'

'Will you be right to bring both teams?'

'Not a problem, Rory knows the way so it will be an easy trip.' He went quiet… 'I can hear their cars in the distance. Woody can bridle the horses we have here while I set up the carrier to bring up the injured horse. We can drop it off at Pegasus on our way. The vets there will get the mare back on its feet. I know how much Caitlin is connected to Shargan, so tell her we have it under control.' He went quiet before giving Woody an order. 'Prepare the horses. I've just told both teams to drive straight to the paddock, and we'll meet them there.'

Woody snatched up the golden bridles, keen to get them all out of the danger zone as quickly as he could manage.

Axon frowned. 'No hanging about here. I'm still picking up an odour of some sort. I'll have my staff ready your rooms and anything you need they can fetch from town.' He could feel Caitlin breathing a little more easily and wasn't about to jeopardise her recovery by staying a minute longer. 'I'll take Cassie with me to keep both women out of any further danger.'

'Good idea.' Kayden hugged Cassie and when she complained, calmed her. 'I need you safe, sweetheart. I promise to see you in a couple of hours.' He kissed her and as he let her go, Axon moved beside her and touched her shoulder. All three shimmered out of sight.

The second they faded out, Kayden and Woody exited the building and quickly started to gather the horses and move them out into the paddock.

Chapter Thirty-Two

Riders' Sojourn
(Ara)

Axon transported Caitlin directly to his bedroom. His security was better here than any other room in his castle. 'Cait honey, keep breathing,' he whispered to her, and each lungful of air helped him believe she would live.

He laid her gently on the bed to free his hands, pulled a small NAVpod from his pocket, and inserted it in his ear. Worried she would still die, he sat beside Caitlin so he could continue stroking her hair.

'Nigel, you got me.'

'Yes My Lord.'

'Cait has been hurt again, badly this time. Get me the doctor and some help up here.'

'Right away My Lord.'

'Nigel.'

'Yes My Lord.'

'We have Riders on their way. Two sets; so get an extra five rooms ready.'

'Doctor first, then rooms. Consider it done, My Lord.'

'And Nigel.'

'I know, don't switch off.'

'Good, now move it and get up here as soon as the staff are organised and the doctor has been contacted.'

'Yes, My Lord.'

Anxiously waiting for Nigel to join him, Axon didn't tap out but instead, listened as his multi-tasking butler summoned the staff while on the phone to the doc.

* * * *

Nigel arrived in a fluster, worried after he heard the tone of Axon's voice. One thing Nigel had learned while working for this noble was that, when he was upset, there was a damned good reason.

'Organised, My Lord.' His words caught in his mouth when he saw Caitlin in a terrible state. The smell of burnt clothes and skin made him shudder. Beside the bed sat Axon and standing next to him was a pretty young lady, looking sad and wet-faced from so many tears.

Axon started to bark orders at him and wanted to know what the doctor said. It took a couple of seconds before any of the words made sense. His eyes hadn't left Caitlin, the friend he had made, the girl he adored.

'Doc Petersen is over in sector12 dealing with an emergency,' Nigel coughed out, controlling his voice.

'Then contact the physician King Lepius.'

'My lord, last we heard, King Lepius had his off-world travel revoked by the Cloud Riders, until further notice.'

'Yes, that is true, but let me introduce you to Cassie, one of the Cloud Riders.' Axon turned to her. 'This is Nigel, and you may say at times, my right-hand man. If he takes you to the NAVcom, can you contact Zoren and get the King clearance to go off world, just this once? We need a doctor and let's face it, he might now be a King of his Home World, but to us, he is still doc Lepius and the best we know.'

'I agree and he's the only doctor I'd want if that was me.' She glanced at Caitlin. 'Nigel, point me in the direction of the NAVcom mains, and I'll contact Zoren for permission. I'm positive he will allow King Lepius travel when it's for a Rider.' Cassie was more than willing to help in any way she could.

Axon gave the nod to Nigel. 'Stay with Cassie in case she needs anything and after that, show her a couple of rooms she can choose from before Kayden arrives. And Nigel, make sure theirs has an ensuites. I want them comfortable.'

It was only then that Cassie inspected herself. 'That would be appreciated.' She wiped at the blood smear on her arms from holding Caitlin. 'I might take a shower if you don't need me here.'

'No use both of us waiting for a doctor to turn up. Nigel will organise you a change of clothes.'

She gave a weak smile. 'Miss my horse! Starburst would have dressed me to save the hassle. But thanks. Appreciate your hospitality, Axon.'

'No need to thank me. You have done so much for my lot. Once the physician has been, I will come and find you and let you know how Cait's doing.'

Although she was communicating well enough, Cassie's eyes were glazed, and Axon could see she was still in shock. Not wishing her to be left alone, he turned to Nigel. 'Once she is settled in her room, have a maid stay with her until Kayden arrives. Cassie will be poorly while Cait is ill. The two girls are different to the rest, they have a strong connection even though they are on different teams.'

Nigel lowered his head to Axon. 'Will that be all, My Lord?'

'Just get some help in here now!' Axon scowled at his butler.

'Yes My Lord, I can hear the staff coming now.' He stood with the door open waiting for them. 'They are to fill the bath, light the fire and will warm nightwear for Caitlin while they help bathe her.' He looked back at Caitlin, the sadness for her condition apparent when he went quiet and stood still.

'Come on Nigel, she's not dead.'

The butler bowed. 'No My Lord, I just hate to see her so poorly,' he said as the two chamber maidens he had organised bustled in with fresh towels, nightgown, bathrobe and toiletries.

Axon saw Nigel still hesitating. 'Yes?'

'I will have a team waiting for the ten Riders. Will there be other horses?' He glanced over at Cassie.

'There will be an extra horse, Cassie's stallion, Starburst. Tell the stable-hands the Rider's horses get priority.' Axon made a hand gesture to have him leave.

Nigel turned to the guest. 'Miss Cassie, are you ready?'

'Sure.' She gave Axon a friendly pat on the back. 'She will be okay now I know it's our King Lepius coming. I thank the lucky stars his title didn't go to his head and he has stayed our physician.' She followed Nigel out.

Axon wholeheartedly agreed and once they left, he gave the two chamber maidens a hurry up as his impatience grew. While they worked feverishly running a bath, lighting the fire and laying out clothes, he opened his mini NAVcom. He had given Cassie time to speak with Zoren, and now it was his turn. On the private NAVline, Zoren picked up straight away. The entire time Axon spoke he continued very lightly stroking Caitlin's hair to let her know he was there with her.

'Zoren, they almost killed her this time. I want her out of the Riders. She is to be my wife, and I won't keep putting up with these "accidents" as you call them.'

'Axon! I knew it was wrong to sanction your mateship with this woman. You have become too personally involved! As far as I can tell, this didn't come from the gods. The chatter we are picking up is mostly them in shock, finding out who you and Caitlin really are. This cloak and dagger game has to stop. It was your idea was it not, to hide behind aliases. It has only made this situation worse.'

Axon's temples throbbed as his annoyance built. 'That may be true. I did continue with the pet names, but only to keep Caitlin alive. Yes, and it is evident now, that it did not work. Even so, I'm pulling her from the team.'

'No you will not; get in here now!'

Axon tapped his earpiece to lower the sound from the vibration and loudness of Zoren's angry reply.

'Zoren!' His tone matched that of his boss. 'I'm waiting for Kayden, and when I have settled "your" team of Riders and made sure they are safe… then, I will come straight in.'

The mention of him looking after the Cloud Riders calmed Zoren. Anger turned immediately to concern. 'Was anyone else hurt?'

'Just Cait.'

'I appreciate you putting them up, Axon, you're a good man, but as for this hysteria regarding Caitlin, that isn't going to happen no matter how big a tantrum you throw. Not her, mate. Sorry!'

Axon went silent to calm down. Zoren had his own way of defusing situations, even from far away.

'You still there, Axon?'

'Yes!'

'You okay?'

'What if she wants to leave? Will you let her, Zoren?' Axon heard him exhale deeply.

'Maybe.'

'Then we will leave it up to her.'

There was no answer at the other end of the line and Axon didn't expect to get one. Zoren had grown to admire Caitlin and would not tolerate the subject being brought up again, but he had to give it one last shot. He knew she belonged to so many, and he wondered if, at any time in their lives, she would ever just be his.

'The bath is ready, My Lord.' The chambermaids waited to help him. He nodded and both quickly and yet skilfully, barely moving her, undressed Caitlin.

'Here!' He pulled a bottle out of his side dresser and handed it to one of the women. 'Pour half of this mixture into the water.' It was the potion the doctor had given him to use when Caitlin was cut and bruised the first time he cared for her. While the chambermaids were busy warming towels and her nightwear, Axon undressed, went over to the bed, picked Caitlin up in his arms and carried her to the bath. This the reason for choosing his room. His bathing tub was huge. He walked down steps into the water and lowered them both into it. He was so glad she was unconscious and couldn't feel the pain of the water against her wounds. Yelling out to the women, he had them sit on the edge and gently sponge the soot and dirt off her skin while he held her steady. They didn't wash her enough to hurt her, but just enough so the doctor could see the damage.

'Enough!' He worried it had taken too long. 'Out of the way.'

He had little patience. 'While I dress, only place the robe on her until after the doctor has been. He will need to look at her wounds.'

Both maids straightened, stood and waited for him to place her on the heated towel they had laid on the bed for her. Here, they dried and carefully put a robe on her while Axon sipped on slacks and buttoned his shirt. He turned to see them drying her hair, which lay around her like a copper glow. Her angelic features, even though puffy, still astounded him. To him, she was the most beautiful of all women.

The door opened, and Nigel entered. 'The physician is here, My Lord.'

'We are ready – send him in.' Axon nodded to the man who entered. 'King Lepius, so glad you could make it.' He extended a hand.

'Doc Lepius will do.' He shook Axon's hand. 'You know I hate formalities while on the job.' He looked over at the patient on the bed. 'Heard about the bombing and as soon as the call came through, grabbed my medical bag and came straight over.'

'Did you hear Zeus sent Apollo to revive her?' Axon stood with arms folded.

He nodded, already digging in an opened bag for his NAVoscope that he inserted into each ear to hear her internals. In his hand, he held a body NAVscan that doubled as a healing device; this he moved slowly above her skin and did a thorough examination of her internal system. The thing beeped and made noises enough to wake even the heaviest of sleepers as it began to find problems and repair them.

'Has she regained consciousness at all?' Doc Lepius asked.

'Nope, it's scaring the hell out of me, but I'm trusting Apollo is good at what he does.'

'Mmm.'

'What do you mean by, *Mmm*?'

Axon understood doc Lepius had zoned out to care for his patient. Soon enough they could talk. In the meantime, Axon paced, worried and watched. Lepius still had a lot of work to do and apparently needed quiet to pick up all the problems. It was an hour later before he sat on the bed beside Caitlin and patted her hand.

'I'm sorry, but I have done all she is allowing. There is a block, a reason she is not responding as well as she should.'

'Did the gods do something to her? Has someone put a spell on her?'

'I don't know. I think it comes from Caitlin.'

'Why would she not want to be well? This is ridiculous. I'm losing patience with this goddess or whatever continues to possess her. I want my fiancée back – for good!'

'She is a powerful woman.' Doc Lepius faced him. 'I doubt there is any man, human or immortal that will ever totally own Cait. If you continue down this path and insist on marrying her, my advice is to learn patience. You have to let her go. If she is truly yours, when her work is done she will always come home here, to you.'

'You know me, Doc, I am what I am. I will not change for any man never mind a woman.'

'Then if she lives, end it. Send her back to her own Home World with her team.'

'Hell no!'

'Then it is you that must change, Axon, because she will defy you to do what she needs to. This will put you in a world of pain if you are not accepting of the person she has become and is still becoming.'

'Becoming? There is more?'

'She is only young in our world of magic, Axon. You know this. You also feel her power, or you would not be this attracted. I always told you it would take an incredible female that would capture you because of your own supremacy. You need equal or more. In her, my friend, you have found a perfect match,' doc Lepius said.

Axon ran a hand roughly through his hair as his gaze fell on Caitlin. 'She is my opposite and at times feels like my nemesis yet I melt when I look at her. I hurt here...' he rubbed his chest over his heart, '...when I hurt her.'

'And now you understand how Hades feels. She has given him her love too. Not as she has you, but a friendship that will last aeons.'

'Like hell! That ends now! That ended when he did this.'

Lepius stood up. 'I will leave you with this thought. If Hades feels as you do, could he have done this? He is no fool and sees how perceptive Cait is, that she'd have picked up the danger from wherever she was located and found a way to be there.'

Axon was flushed and livid. 'He knows nothing of Cait and, he is a fool! I hope he rots in hell for what he has done.'

Lepius packed up his medical gadgets and ignored Axon's outburst. He had known him long enough to see his love and possessiveness of this woman was clouding his own astuteness. 'Call me if there is any change.' He patted Axon on the back as he left.

Caitlin had groaned, and he hastily sat on the bed to soothe her. 'Honey, you've broken some ribs, and your insides are a mess but could only be partly repaired. You have to let the doc help you,' he pleaded, but she was still unmoving and back in a deep sleep.

He ran a hand through her hair. 'Don't worry, your team are on their way. Maybe they can do what you wouldn't let the doctor do.'

The feeling he was alone had him look around and notice the doctor had gone. He mentioned he'd met the Cloud Riders on several occasions. Said they were a scary lot when they had a member down. Most likely that was the reason he had departed so fast. Axon didn't blame him, Rory and his team would be in a right mood with Caitlin injured again. It was probably for the best the doc didn't witness their wrath. Rory on his own was someone not to muck with when annoyed. Just his eyes alone would scare the bejeezers out of anyone the way they electrified and glowed when he was pissed off. It gave him comfort to recall how Caitlin, half Rory's size, ignored it and gave him attitude anyway.

'Keep fighting, Cait, just like that. Don't you dare die.' Axon tapped his earpiece, 'Nigel – send in a chambermaid to dress Caitlin.'

'Yes My Lord, she is on her way.' Axon heard him bark an order and within seconds the door handle turned and the chambermaid arrived.

Caitlin looked so little and helpless, he wished he could get into bed with her and hold her but had too much to organise. He kissed her. 'I love you, sweetheart, thanks for staying alive for me, for us. I promise I will try to change, please stay,' he whispered.

'Sorry to disturb you, My Lord, but there is a caller on Navcom that insists on speaking to you only,' Nigel's voice interrupted him.

'ID?'

'System didn't register a place of origin, My Lord.'

Axon was pretty sure who it was and didn't want Caitlin to hear what was going to be said. After leaving instructions to be called as soon as Caitlin woke, Axon slipped quickly out from the room. He had been waiting for Hades, the traitor, to call.

'How dare you lie to me, to her? You nearly killed her; what the hell were you playing at?' He went quiet… 'Yes, she is breathing, but that's about all at the minute. If she dies, Hades, I'll hunt you down and kill you myself. And when I've finished with you, your brothers will have the same fate.' Axon shook with rage. Although he didn't answer, he knew Hades had not hung up even after the onslaught of words that spewed angrily from him. He could hear him breathing and… was that him choking back emotion?

'Can I see her?'

'When hell freezes over and even then, not over my dead body!' Axon gritted his teeth.

'Axon please, I didn't know. It wasn't us; well it was a family member, but none of the gods from our planets. We wouldn't do that to her, you know that. Please! I have powers. I can help. Don't shut me out. I'll give you any information you need.' His tone pleaded with Axon and weakened his better judgement.

'Hades, don't damn well lie to me. You came to the island, checking she was away from danger, she told me!' he yelled.

'I didn't mean it that way, Axon. Dammit! I just meant I was glad no other men were hanging around. I was jealous, that was all. I imagined her on a beach with Earth men, bodybuilders, maybe. She said you were fishing and she was sunbaking. When I saw there wasn't another soul on the beach but her, and that your boat was heading back, I relaxed and left. That was all. It was innocent on my part, sort of. Well, you know how I feel about her, Axon. I love her too but differently from you. Please, Axon, let me come see her. I won't stay long, I'm hurting too. I know how angry you are with me, but you have it all wrong.'

Axon really did feel he was telling the truth. The words rang true, for he believed Hades would have been jealous. His love for her was new, uncertain. Hades also knew who the culprits were and needed his help. He had to calm down, or he would blow his chance to uncover who it was, and the motive behind the attack. Kayden and Cassie had also felt it wasn't the planets. Anger had blinded him, and he had jumped to conclusions. It was time he did start to trust the friendship that was offered.

Hades was quiet on the other end of the line, waiting for Axon's answer.

'Hades, are you sure you're prepared to help me?' His anger was now under control.

'Anything you need, Axon, just don't close the door on me, on us, please.'

'Give me a minute to get rid of the help. I assume you can track wherever Cait is in the house.'

'Yes, somehow I'm connected to her subconscious. I feel her wherever she is.'

'I see!' Axon huffed, and although annoyed she had made Hades part of her life like this, it helped him understand the connection they had. 'Cait is very clever and has apparently connected you to her as the Cosmic Riders are connected. Can you feel only her, or the rest of the team as well?'

'Just her!'

'I'll be blowed.' Axon was amazed at her ingeniousness and capabilities. As Lepius said, she was becoming one very powerful woman. Should he be scared of this new ability? *Hell yes!* But on the other hand, he knew the universe was one big mystery. The plan it had for her, for him, was something he would just have to ride out. Although he did hope one day it would all be over and the two of them could find peace alone together.

'Hades, I can't believe this has happened. I want answers when you arrive, an no stalling.'

'I know Axon, and please, around Caitlin, it's Jett.'

'She knows you are Hades.' Axon was confused.

'She sees Hades as your enemy; I have worked hard to earn her friendship as Jett. If she hears you refer to me as Hades, she will think we are still enemies, and I fear it will all start up again as she works to make peace between us. Axon, you are angry, but it is not Hades this should be directed towards. My friendship is still sound between us. I'll see you shortly.' He closed off the port of communication.

Could Axon trust him? He had no idea. All Axon did know was that he had to believe in Cait, and she trusted him. He went back to the room. Cassie was sitting with Caitlin and shook her head in disbelief at the announcement of the soon to arrive god.

'I have promised Hades, I mean Jett, privacy.'

As they moved out of the bedroom, Axon discussed with Cassie the reasons why he relented with Hades so she could let the others know.

Axon had a call and tapped his ear. 'Yes.'

'The guests have arrived, My Lord,' Nigel said.

'Settle everyone in and keep them from this level. I want total privacy on this floor and tell Rory I want a meeting with him, Kayden and Woody in the tower ASAP.'

Axon turned back to Cassie. 'You right to find your way down to meet them?'

'Sure you don't need help blowing up that – that blatzing rotten god?' she fumed, still not convinced Hades was the good guy.

Axon didn't answer for a moment, considering the proposal to get rid of one of his biggest headaches. He smiled. 'Not today. But I'll take a raincheck.'

She gave a slight grin, but behind it was real anger. Axon was glad she was on her way to meet up with Kayden. He would help her harness the power from it, use it later, and Axon almost felt sorry for the next evil that crossed her path.

Chapter Thirty-Three

Judgement Day

Axon stayed to watch Caitlin until Jett arrived, and worried for the stillness of her body.

Jett shimmered in, eyes going straight to Caitlin. He sat but made sure he lowered his heavy weight gently beside her, so not to cause her pain. His hand found hers without even looking, his eyes still focused on her face. To speak just yet, Axon knew would not be easy as he watched Jett gulp back emotions that threatened to break through his tough façade. Axon for the first time actually felt for the guy. His friendship with her was way beyond normal, yet Axon also knew how much Hades loved his own wife, the goddess Persephone. Cait would only ever be a much-loved friend. Axon had never seen this much devotion before. He knew the difference now, Hades' harsh features had gone, and this was Jett, her friend who meant her no harm.

He put his hand on his back. 'I'll give you privacy with her but after, we are going to have a brutally honest chat.'

Jett looked up at him gratefully. His eyes had dark circles around them and were dull with worry. Axon understood his emotional state. He would be feeling exactly the same if he thought he would never be allowed to see her again. It was soul torturing to love this woman for both of them.

Axon went and stood outside and could hear Jett talking to her. It was mostly just a mumble, but his sorrowful voice was shaky and sad.

He waited a little longer than he should have, jealousy pinching at him even though he tried to push it away. He wished he was enough for her, but what drove her needs caused her to stretch out to yet another. He listened to Jett softly pleading then heard Cait speak faintly. He opened the door. Jett had her in his arms, rocking her. He ran his hand down her face and the magic he used on her crackled and spat out golden sparks from her skin. He glanced up and grinned, before dropping his head back down, talking to her again.

'Glow, why did you go there? You would have stayed safe if you didn't leave the beach. You can't go putting yourself in danger like that. You have too many of us that love you. Please don't frighten us all like this. Poor Axon is beside himself, he thought he lost you.'

She put a hand up to touch his face and traced his frown while she spoke ever so quietly. 'He's not the only one,' she said and dropped her arm.

He took the hand she touched him with and kissed it. 'Don't go giving me cheek young lady, you are meant to be getting growled at, not making me smile.'

He was lovely with her and Axon could see why she was so attached. Thank goodness theirs was only friendship and even though he had another twinge of jealousy and wished it were he who could have woken her, he was thankful she was at least awake. This was the second time Axon had seen Jett use his powers to bring her around. His magic was incredibly capable, and right now, Axon was thankful he was at least using it for good.

Jett laid her carefully back in bed and told her to sleep, promising he would return to visit her a bit later.

She looked at him for a minute and closed her eyes. There was no smile, but she was on the mend.

* * * *

When they entered the computer tower, Woody and Rory sat scanning the sky for trouble. Kayden was standing impatiently. His barn and one of his prize horses were gone. There had to be a massive rebuild, and until then, they had to live away from home. He was furious behind the mask of politeness when he shook the hand offered by the god who had just entered.

'Hades,' was all he said.

'Kayden.' Hades response was in the same tone.

Not a good start. Axon noticed the tension already. It was unusual for Kayden to show how rattled he was by the situation. He gestured to Rory. 'This is the commander of my team, Rory.'

'Mmm... Glow Girl's saviour.' Hades eyed him up and down but kept his arms folded.

Axon continued quickly, seeing there was no friendly handshake offered by the god. 'And this is Woody, Kayden's right arm. The wizard of the sky.'

'Boys.' Hades nodded, not extending a hand to either of them.

Axon wasn't surprised and gave Rory his look of, *don't take offence.* Unless it was of their choosing, those the gods looked upon as lesser in status were barely acknowledged; a trait Hades needed to change if he ever wanted Rory to allow him time with Caitlin while he was in charge of her.

Rory shrugged and offered around bottles of Moonjuice.

Axon noticed that if not looking directly at Hades, Rory's eyes flickered with annoyance. Axon guessed the juice was more to settle him down rather than those he offered it to. Using the team, Rory had attempted earlier to send Caitlin healing, and when blocked, suggested it had something to do with Hades. For this reason, he was holding his temper in check, only, by the look of his body language as he leant up against the wall, he was ready to take Hades on there and then.

Woody had stood to welcome the god, his attitude so different to Rory's. Condescendingly he sat, locked his hands behind his head and leaning back eyeing the god. 'Is it Hades or Jett?'

'Hades to you, lad!' His voice boomed, and his eyes flashed dark and marbled. Black smoke curled up and around him. To these men in this room, he was a god and Ruler of the Underworld, and this was showing them they were not friends. The change surprised Axon. Hades had only ever appeared to Axon and Caitlin as Jett. It was only now Axon got the extent of Caitlin's powers. She had done a remarkable job, and suddenly Axon felt so proud of her he wished she was here so he could hug her with thanks. Jett was so much easier to handle. It was the first time any of the men had met Hades, and the tension was suddenly thick as Axon invited them all to sit down at the NAVlit table and talk.

Straightforward in his questions, Kayden was relentless as usual.

Hades put his hand up and refrained from answering, firstly requesting negotiation terms. 'And furthermore, I insist that none of this leaves the room and that the situation is to be discreetly handled and without bloodshed.'

To reassure him but not to sugar coat it, Axon intervened. 'As peacekeepers, the men here are bound by codes to handle this situation strictly by the law and for your sake, discreetly. However, if all negotiations fail during follow-up of what is said here today and the culprits persist in future attacks, this will be out of our hands. They will suffer the consequences, and can expect to feel the full force of our Celestial Laws.'

Hades gave him a nod in agreement, and Axon leant back in the chair. 'Kayden, continue.' Axon gestured to him. His own anger for what happened to Cait still had him seething so to keep emotions out of it, he allowed Kayden to uncover the reasons for the attack. Rory gave Axon a death stare, showing he wasn't happy; he wanted to be the one firing off the questions, but Axon ignored the directed anger. He understood one of his team members was hurt, almost killed, but still, he was young and not ready this day to handle a god like Hades.

Even though Hades knew of Kayden, the no-nonsense god was direct and at times quite arrogant as he answered the question fired at him. It was moments later, when Hades revealed the plot was to kill the Cloud Riders and why, that he saw how unprepared Kayden was to find out the truth; that the hit on them was from one of his own star Rulers.

Hades stared directly at Kayden. 'You should know who hates you, lad. Do you want me to spell it out?'

Kayden leant forward. 'Who? Don't tell me it came from Orion's

Belt! – are you serious?' He scratched his head thinking. 'But Orion is the son of Poseidon.'

'Yes.'

'What has our star Home Worlds got to do with the war going on between the planets? That's blatzing bullshit!' Kayden stood up, knocking his chair backwards, and it smashed loudly into the wall.

Axon stood up calmly and picked up the chair. 'Kayden, sit man; let him finish.'

'I will not sit here and put up with my Home Worlds taking the blame because you lot can't sort out your own backyards. Hell, Cait's nearly dead, was dead and my boys and I are practically homeless.'

Hades stood and bellowed so loudly they froze. 'Sit, fool!'

He flicked a finger, and the chair slipped under Kayden which forced him to sit. It then pulled in close to the table.

'Axon!' Hades gestured for him to sit too.

Axon put his hand up defensively and sat as ordered. It left the men at the table speechless.

Hades continued once he had their attention. 'Now,' he sighed, and his voice was less boisterous. 'Orion, the son of Poseidon, has been well aware of the war going on between our planets. He has personally attended many of our meetings, willing to lend a hand.'

'But why us?' Kayden may have been made to sit but was still vocal.

'He's still stewing as it was your Cloud Riders that stopped him and his dogs hunting for cattle on Taurus. He feels he was robbed in the treaty.'

'You're kidding!' Woody spoke up, receiving a stern look from Hades.

'I will address leaders, Kayden and Axon. If you have to be here, please refrain from comment.'

Woody was about to open his mouth when Hades flicked a finger towards him, and his mouth closed shut. He blinked and eyed Kayden and shrugged. Woody was a man with much patience. His love for magic would find this fascinating and most likely he would be trying to figure out how to harness it, to use it on others that annoyed him.

It was about then that Axon wondered if he should go and get Caitlin to keep the god calm. He had never seen him in action before, and his magic seemed equivalent to Zoren's. Axon could hold his own against the archangel, but with Hades, in this mood, he wasn't sure. The god struggled with a need to stay in touch with a friend that he had to have in his life. This made him a dangerous man.

Hades sat forward and eyed Kayden with contempt. Axon could see he had become annoyed with Kayden interrupting with petty grievances. Gods don't concern themselves with possessions and material items. Kayden's concerns of rebuilding were tiresome and an unimportant statement. Hades spoke with authority. 'What can I say? The man enjoyed a good steak and I agree with him, there's none better than the taste of that breed of cattle. Anyway—' He shifted in his seat. 'Orion stayed reasonably calm until Axon here went down to Earth and sourced what Orion refers to as "the planet posse". That's when things heated up. He vowed revenge because there were going to be two sets of law-abiding do-gooders, and he felt that was two too many.'

Axon couldn't help but grin at what he called his Riders. Hades noticed and in his expression was a glint of amusement in recognition of his reaction. It confirmed to Axon that Jett would always be in Hades somewhere for him. They had become mates, and it felt good. Seeing Hades' response to the others and then to him made what they had special. Now he understood why Caitlin worked so hard to make it happen. Being enemies with Hades and his family would never have solved anything. Gods don't give in.

Hades sat back, speaking again. The pauses gave them too much time to reflect, or was that his strategy? 'Orion coordinated the first strike on both farms, and yes, our family sanctioned the first hit but not this one. The first was more of a test of the waters to see how well the Riders could deflect and destroy. We didn't expect the leading female to be so gifted. Therefore, we knew the one we would get must have to be a lot stronger as she would be dealing with us. This was a big problem, so whoever was the lead female could possibly put a stop to our future plans. That was when we decided to kidnap her, take her out of the equation. We thought, at first, we could turn her to our side but in the end, the vote was to take her life. As you are aware, I could not do that!'

Axon nodded. 'Yes, it must have been quite a shock when you realised who you had kidnapped.'

Hades saw Kayden's look and explained. 'You see, there was a twist of fate that none of us expected. I was away with my family, and we met what we thought were tourists, Wolf and Glow Girl, on one of your holiday resorts, Dolphin Island on Delphinus. In fact, we all lied and introduced ourselves with an alias, for want of a better word. Glow Girl sprinkled my family and me with joy and who would have known the smallest package of us all would turn out to be the most powerful weapon in our planet system.' His eyes softened as he spoke of her and Kayden saw the change and gave a slight grin. His Cassie has done the same to tyrants in his star system. Hades ran his hand through his hair as if clearing Cait from his mind. 'Anyway, it has changed a bit for us now. My family, after today, now know Glow is a part of the Cosmic Riders. They're not happy with the revelation.' He turned to Axon. 'To be truthful, for my part in keeping you both a secret, I've been put on the outer for now. Not confided in or trusted.' His face became emotionless as he continued. 'Axon, you must understand my position, that even though they are cross with me, I still back them with this move. They have been insulted by not being involved in the decision making of Dwarf status, and it has become a pride issue. They will continue in their quest to have me back in the planets with them, so our plans haven't changed. However, what has changed is that they have no interest in eliminating your team.'

Axon inhaled, and stress had him on his feet. 'Phew! I'll drink to that. Anyone want one?'

'Ambrosia,' Hades said.

Woody put his thumb up, and Hades removed the magic held over him. Woody grinned, showing no disrespect towards Hades. Axon was a fan of Woody and more so now. He was made of good humoured genes.

'Yes, thanks,' Woody said.

Axon poured the gods' elixir in a goblet and passed it to Hades. He flipped the lid off two bottles of Moonjuice and handed one to Woody. The other, Axon sipped while contemplating his next move. He wanted to go in guns blazing and wipe Orion from the universe but had promised to handle this discreetly so he needed to settle down.

Once Hades felt Axon was back in control he continued. 'To cut a long story short, Orion attended our last summit where I persuaded the affiliates to stand down for a few days. Unbeknown to them, it was to give the newly engaged couple some time off.' He glanced at Axon. 'It wasn't opposed by immediate family as they had talked about spending a couple of days at an Island Resort in sector 7. Only there was a cowboy in our midst. None of us expected my nephew to go it alone. We were stunned when we found that Orion would take this opportunity to avenge his loss of privileges on Taurus. His plan was to put the Cloud Riders out of action first. He hoped to tie up the watchdog of Taurus, meaning the wizard Aldebaran and his other rival, the warlord Conom. He felt sure they would head to Earth to assist Aldebaran's daughter, Cassie. 'With no interference, he could go to war with the ruler of Taurus. His army has never been stronger, and the intention was not to kill the ruler Aurus but to bring him to his knees and win back his right to hunt there. It was pure luck his father called in to see him, and Orion confided in him.'

He shifted in his seat, his body language revealing how stupid he thought it to be. 'Orion had no idea the Cosmics had gone down to stay with the Cloud Riders when he had put the hit on them. Or that Glow would see it coming and try to save the horses. Poseidon told Zeus.'

Axon butted in, 'who Cait calls Calyx.'

Hades nodded and changed to the alias. 'But Calyx didn't worry about it until I told him Glow was on holidays on Earth. Somehow, Calyx put two and two together. That's when he confronted me, and I had to share that the two he knew as Glow and Wolf, were actually,

Caitlin and Axon, both affiliated to part of the team that made up the Cosmic Riders. Calyx, even though angry I'd kept the secret, liked Glow and Wolf enough to do his best to prevent the blast taking place. He wasn't quick enough, as we know, to stop the attack or the explosion. By the time he got there, it was over, and Glow Girl's lifeless body was lying on the ground. That's when he summoned his son, Apollo, to fix his "stupid nephew's mistake", as he termed it. He's furious with me for lying to him and Orion's banished from further involvement in our war.'

'Your family; what are they going to do about Orion?' Axon asked.

'I have no idea. All I know is they are up in arms with me at the minute, and I don't blame them.' He stopped and got up, looking out of the window. 'But I can't stop what has come about between Glow and me or you, Axon. Even if I could, I don't want to.'

Hades turned to him. 'As for the future, I have no control. But for the moment I can and would like to help. Axon, you'll be busy every day now with Kayden sorting all this out. Glow needs around the clock nursing and must be kept safe. You know there is nowhere safer than with the tyrant who started all this in the first place. You've seen first-hand my healing capabilities and are astute enough to know I can care for her far better than anyone. Let me take her and keep her safe until she's well again. You know where she is if you want to visit her any time of the day or night.'

Axon stood up and stretched. 'My men are just as capable as you are and will make sure she's well looked after while I'm at work.' He would not even entertain the idea of her going with him.

'And if you call them out on a mission, what then? Are you actually intending to leave her here on her own… unguarded and trust servants to care for one so valuable to us? I beg of you, let me keep her from those who mean her harm, at least until she is well enough to fight her own battles again. As soon as she is better, we both know she'll be back by your side fighting against me as before.'

Kayden surprised Axon when he stood suddenly and crossed his arms, with a determined expression. 'You have a point, Hades.

My Cassie is connected somehow to Caitlin, and while she is unwell, Cassie will endure this burden and also need protecting. It seems both our women have become targets until they are in top form again. For her, there is no safer haven than with her father, Aldebaran.' He turned to Axon. 'We have two sets of Riders, the best of the best. There's no reason we need to put the girls in harm's way unless this can't be settled peacefully.'

Axon swore, knowing they were both right. He wanted Caitlin safe and knew only too well that Jett would protect her with his life, as he would. Axon had pledged his allegiance to Zoren and knew his loyalty to keeping the peace with the solar system must always come first. 'Blatzing Hell, Kayden, that's stuffed up my argument. I hate you being right. Of course, our Riders are more than capable, that is unless something more sinister is coming.' He glared at Hades.

The god shrugged. 'As I said, I'm not privy to anything at present so don't go off half-cocked at me if something heavy does come up. What I have told you is all I know.' He spoke kindly.

Axon relaxed his shoulders and turned to Hades. 'Just give me a moment to speak with Cait. I'd like her to have a say in this, but I'm already sure of the answer. Just keep this in mind, Jett, if any of your family even looks like turning against her, you bring her straight back here to me or else, and it's a big or else. Am I making myself clear?'

Hades sat down to wait, relieved. 'My father and brothers will not harm her, Axon, and while I am on the outer with them, I do not expect a visit. Glow is safe on Pluto, please trust me. But even so, I do promise that at the first sign of danger I'll be out of there so fast with her, they won't see it coming.'

Axon could tell just by looking at him this was true. In his eyes was a kindness he saved for only one, his Glow Girl. Even so, Axon had a twinge of jealousy and felt annoyed that it would be Jett making her well. Still, his hands were tied. He actually needed Jett, and even though it angered him, he was quite grateful that she had such a dedicated friend. His mind flitted to Melita. This relationship between the two of them must also get to her and yet she never showed any animosity towards Cait whatsoever. She radiated the same caring for her as Jett did. He was the only one trying to stop the friendship, and from today, he was going to make an effort to change his mindset. He was proud of Cait for the relationships she was already cementing with these planet Rulers and he had to stop his urge to strangle the lot of them for being the catalysts behind this mess they were all now in.

* * * *

Caitlin slept peacefully, but Axon needed to wake her so lay on the bed beside her. 'You smell divine,' he said quietly when she stirred. 'You know Jett wants to take you to Pluto, don't you beautiful?' He smiled when her eyes flickered in response. Her goddess essence was building, and he shook his head in wonder. She would hold Jett at her side now until he made her better.

With a slow movement, her body rolled gently into his arms, and she sighed, letting him feel how happy she was to be there. He allowed the tingle of love to wash over him, knew it was her unspoken way of letting him know how very much she loved him and his heart sang as she hugged him.

'Cait, as you already have guessed, Jett's going to take you for a couple of days while Kayden and I address the culprit who did this to you. I don't want to let you go, but I know Jett's magic will help you get better much quicker. Also, he seems to be the only one who can break through the block that is stopping any of us healing you. I don't want you to go, but I'm not sure what else to do. It's up to you, but I need you safe while you recover and out of harm's way while we work through this mess.'

A twitch at the corners of her mouth showed and a faint voice spoke. 'Pluto's power heals all.'

Axon's eyes widened. Only by using magic was Jett able to make Cait speak and he heard her, it was his Cait that talked to Jett. Yet this was not that voice. He wondered if this was the goddess within and breathed out heavily. His girl was sure a mystery but he'd work her out; he would make this his mission. For now, she had chosen, or it had been selected for her. He was about to ask her what she meant by that when her lids dropped, and she drifted off to sleep. 'I will miss you terribly gorgeous one. I promise to visit as much as I can.' He got up and wrapped her in a thick, warm blanket. It always amazed him how someone who could pack such a powerful punch, could be so light and soft. Her body was actually so delicate when she first fell into his arms for that first time on Earth, he really had to adjust his powers for fear he would bruise her. As he transported her to the tower, he admired the person she was, so frail in his arms and yet not one ounce of fear to be going with Hades, the most dangerous of all gods.

Up in the viewing tower, it was Jett's arms he placed Caitlin into, and before letting her go kissed her sweet-smelling hand. 'I love you, honey.' He put her hand inside the blanket. She looked up at Jett and Axon watched as she snuggled into him and closed her eyes. Jett knew she was happy to be with him and smiled down at her.

'I'll keep our girl safe, and feel free to contact me every day to find out how she is progressing.' He watched her intently. He looked up at Axon, with the gentleness back in his eyes and a happy grin, and then they were gone.

Axon felt like a part of him was just ripped away, so he grabbed the bottle of liquor and took a big swig. At least she was alive and safe. When she was better, he would get her back.

'You okay, boss?' Rory slapped Axon on the back in a friendly manner. 'You did the right thing, I even liked the Jett side of the arrogant old tool.'

Axon rolled his eyes, growled through gritted teeth and took another swig of alcohol.

Rory smirked. 'Axon, ease up on the guy. He will never have her love like you have.' He laughed cynically. 'Shytzer, I know how that feels.'

'You two were just friends though, right.' Axon glared at him.

Rory punched his arm. 'Though that was just jealousy eating you up… far out, man, Cait and I were always best mates and always will be. Trust me, you have no competition. She took one look at you and all other males became invisible.'

'Well, I'm pleased to hear that!' He turned to Kayden. 'One down, one to go! I need a minute.' Axon faded out of sight, holding the bottle to his lips.

Kayden nodded and left, knowing the same fate was just in front of him too. He hated not having Cassie by his side. But he knew at least he and Axon could both feel lousy together. There was one significant difference, though; Cassie would be with her dad, not an ancient god who loved her unconditionally. *And man did he change when he held her.* He didn't blame Axon at all for hitting the turps.

With Axon gone too, Woody and Rory sat back in the chairs taking a moment to relax. 'We immortals can be so insecure.' Woody lit up a cigar and handed one to Rory.

'Axon shouldn't be.' Rory lit it up and puffed out some rings. 'With all that powers we felt today from Hades, that man could have controlled her for a lifetime, maybe stolen her heart the first day he kidnapped her. But she fought when it may have been easier to give up and choose him. She was gone for months but came back here, to us; her loyalty did not waver.'

'That may be so, Rory, but the question is, will he wear her down this time? You saw it, Axon stands between their friendship, and Hades is a man used to getting his own way. Caitlin, he wants badly.' Woody rubbed his chin in thought.

'Over – my – dead – body!' Rory exploded.

Chapter Thirty-Four

Healing Dwarf Planet Pluto

A few days passed before Caitlin woke and felt better. Hungry yet comfortable, she found herself in front of a pleasant warm glow of a fire that burned bright.

'How come I'm here again? I remember the barn, getting a horse out…'

'There was an explosion. We thought you were dead,' said Jett.

'What do you mean?' Caitlin pulled the blankets down and saw some bruising on her arms. Pulling up the nightwear to the thigh, she saw more, but worst was peeking down her top to view a black and blue chest. 'Shytzer, what a mess. I can remember being thrown from a horse… but why haven't my team tried to heal me?'

He nodded. 'They light you up, but it isn't holding. There's something inside you deflecting it.'

'I've got no idea why. Has Axon come to visit? Maybe he knows what's going on.'

'He has come every afternoon, and I expect he will come again today sometime. We've both been worried sick. Welcome back to the land of the living, Glow.'

* * * *

After something to eat Caitlin drifted off to sleep, watching the fire crackle. A familiar voice woke her. Axon had come for a visit. Jett was full of enthusiasm as he made coffee. 'She actually ate breakfast herself today.'

She sat up to let Axon sit with her and as he did she cuddled into him. Just his nearness was enough to tear her up and send her emotions in turmoil.

'Are you here for a while, Axon? Looks like someone has missed you,' Jett said, putting their mugs in front of them on the coffee table.

'I should be able to stay a couple of hours. Kayden is holding down the fort for both teams while I'm here but sure he won't mind if I return the favour later.' He caught her sniff and wiped her eyes. 'Sorry honey.' He felt terrible not being able to stay when she looked so vulnerable. This was a sign of still how unwell she was, or she'd be pushing him out the door to spend more time with Jett and his family.

'It's okay, just need a cuddle.' She smiled and cheered up slightly.

There was a war going on out there that she was best not to know about as her fighting instincts would be to offer help. No way was that an option. He had seen first-hand how much Jett did to get her to this point and here he wanted her to stay until she could at least ride a horse again. It warmed him to see her; even though she was a bit miserable, he was over the moon she was on the mend. Between Orion and Cronus, he and Kayden were left with only short moments to visit with their girls. Axon glanced up at Jett with dark shadows under his eyes, showing a total lack of sleep. 'You've done wonders, Jett; when do you think she will be back on her feet?'

'Not for a few days at least. Whatever it was upsetting Glow, and not allowing her to heal has apparently lifted so let's just play it by ear. How's Cassie doing at her father's? Is she feeling better?'

'Why? What's happened to Cassie?' Caitlin sat up to listen.

'She was a bit poorly while you were. She was still okay to ride and help out, but Kayden wanted her safe. While Orion had them targeted, Kayden didn't trust him anywhere near her.'

'I could help.' Her eyes widened as she tried to look well.

'It's nothing we can't handle, and when you can get back on a horse, you are more than welcome to come lend a hand. So get better, okay!' Axon touched her nose affectionately and put his arm around her and went to move her closer.

She grimaced. 'Ouch.'

'Sorry, sweetheart, but see? You can barely move just yet. So don't even think about what's going on out there.' He stared at Jett. 'How come you can shift her, and she is fine?'

'I am a god.' He grinned. 'There is nothing a god cannot do.'

'Except heal her,' Axon teased, seeing his pompous pose.

'Well, anyone else… this little redhead just likes to mock me.' He grinned.

Caitlin gave him a warm glowing smile. 'How else would someone as important as you ever make time for little ol' me? I have to almost be blown to pieces to get any attention around here.'

'See what I put up with, Axon?' He shook his head in jest.

'Yes, I agree I have spoilt her just a tad, but you are the real culprit, Jett.' Axon had to laugh. The man did not stop fussing. Even now Jett had bent down and was making sure the covers were over her legs, so she kept warm.

He stood and put his nose in the air playfully. 'On that note, I'll give you two some privacy and will tend to some duties I have neglected of late.'

Caitlin slipped her small hand into his. 'I know you deserve a break after babysitting me for so long, but don't go for long, Jett. I need you too.'

'See, and your man wonders why I spoil you so.' Jett winked as he shimmered from sight.

After he was gone, Caitlin turned back to Axon. 'Now, back to Cassie and me. It's very noble of you both to try and prevent us girls coming to any harm, but just remember, it's also our jobs to protect, and we're very good at it. The charms of a woman can sometimes melt the meanest of hearts. If you're getting nowhere with Orion, then maybe one of us girls should be talking to him. We're both tougher than you think and can sometimes end a war just by being there with you.'

Axon grinned at her and shook his head. 'You can barely move, and you're trying to persuade me to let you come with me. You're unbelievable, girl. You're not going anywhere until Jett tells me you're all right, so don't even think about playing the hero for some time yet.'

'Well then, talk to Cassie; she'll agree with me and is most likely saying exactly the same thing.'

'You make me feel better just talking to you. I don't know why I even worry about you. You're a tough little one. I think you would take on the devil himself if he didn't give you what you wanted, and even in this poorly condition, you'd still win.'

Wearily, she leant back into his arms. 'Maybe, but not today; not the devil anyway.'

'You're still not well, honey, so save your energy. Let me give you that cuddle. I've missed you too.'

They talked until Jett returned; it was a nice visit, but Caitlin was drained and sat quiet, listening to the men chat. She was overjoyed that Axon and Jett spoke as friends.

'Glow is feeling better!' Jett said after a while.

Axon stared at her. 'Wish I could read your mind, honey.'

Jett grinned, pleased he had something of Glow that Axon never would. 'You don't have to, Axon, you can see how happy she is in her eyes.'

'Yes, they are intriguing and exquisite. But still.' Axon ran his hand over her head, feeling her silky hair.

Jett stared into the fire. 'Believe me, it's not a power you would want. I disconnected from reading minds and haven't used it for a very long time. That is, until I met Glow.' He turned to them. 'She overpowers my off switch and makes me hear her every thought.'

'In my line of work, it's a talent I'd appreciate. Why stop using it? It would help sort out the liars in your Underworld,' said Axon.

'It used to come in handy, but I've had it so many centuries now I just know when someone's having a lend of me.' He grinned. 'I was so surprised the first time I heard Glow Girl's voice. It was smooth like golden sweet syrup and as much as I tried to block it out, I couldn't, so

I just listened. I've been able to tune her out, but she's very powerful and when she wants me to do something for her, no tuning out in the world stops her coming through to me. It's the strangest thing.'

'At the house when I handed her to you, what was she thinking? You smiled as if she had spoken yet I knew she hadn't.' Axon raised his brow.

Jett laughed. 'You caught that, did you?' He sat back. 'She said, and I quote, "you must be crazy wanting to play nursemaid to a spoilt annoying redhead." It made me smile. She can be so funny sometimes.'

They both laughed, and Axon agreed. 'Sounds exactly like her, only being so unwell I would have thought her sense of humour gone.'

'Trust me, Axon, she's stronger than we give her credit for. She'd be out there now if she could defy me and get up on a horse.'

Axon nodded. 'Yes, I got that impression earlier when we spoke of Orion. But here, she is improving better than she could at home, so Cait goes nowhere until you say she's well enough to do so.'

'Thanks, Axon, your anxious Rider is far from ready.'

'Don't I get any say?' Caitlin asked.

Axon smiled at her. 'No!' He glanced at the time. 'And that's it for me.' He kissed her lips. 'Have to get back to it.' He stood, turned and shook Jett's hand and only for a split second did he reveal sadness to leave her.

The softie. Caitlin grinned. *He misses his girl... aw...*

CHAPTER THIRTY-FIVE
Chance Meeting

Upon waking a few mornings later, Caitlin stretched lazily and, with a smile, remembered Axon's visits. He missed her more each day; she could see it in those darkened eyes and sad smile. The more she improved, the more she missed him too. Jett was becoming busy from his sudden workload in the Underworld, and although Caitlin loved it here on Pluto, she didn't want to be a burden so had decided she would go home with Axon next time he visited. Her lip dropped. Jett was such a good friend, and she would miss him. *Can you clone a god?* She chuckled at the idea.

In the shower, she felt better when the water didn't sting her wounds any longer.

'Ahhh!' Caitlin welcomed the warm spray of water down her back as she wet her hair to give it a good wash. Having lathered and washed off the shampoo, she was pleased to actually shower now without help. Dried and with her hair brushed, she dashed naked to the fireplace in her room, and cheerfully did a victory jig by the warmth of the fire before getting dressed. *"I did it, yes I did it, by myself, by myself"* She hummed the tune again, smiling at her silliness, making an effort to ignore how tender she still felt. Being well enough to do things for herself put her on a high, but with a shiver from dancing around, she hurriedly put on her underwear. It was then that the door squeaked as it opened wide. Her instinct was to cover her privates with whatever was in her hands, and she squealed as she saw a man who stood with mouth gaping, just as stunned. His apology came fast as he put his hand over his eyes, swore and ducked out. The image burned into her mind and yet she had caught sight of him for only a couple of seconds. Still, it was enough. The mountain of a man filled the entire door frame. His lean masculine body bulged under the tight t-shirt he wore, and his hair was so unusual! Strands of rope-like hair were pulled back and tied in a knot. But it was his steel grey eyes that she still felt pierce her skin as, even in that split second, they took in every mark on her tiny frame.

'Excuse me,' he called out from the other side of the door. 'I was on my way to the gents and heard a noise.'

'As you can see I am no intruder.' *Christ what a giant of a man.* She hustled to dress.

'My apology ma'am,' he said, and she heard him stomp off like a baby elephant.

The intrusion on her privacy should have made Caitlin annoyed, but all she could think about was that hair. She wondered if he ever cut it as the rope-like strands of hair, even though tied up, reached the waist of his pants. It fascinated her and, immersed in thought, Caitlin tugged a warm jumper over her head, pulled on leggings and laced up the fur boots before realising this was also the first time she had dressed on her own as well. Chuffed and smiling at her image, a tap at the door had her spin around, hoped he was not back to try and apologise more. *No, he would have barged in.*

'Is that you, Jett?' Caitlin called out. She threw the towel in the hamper as the door opened.

'Well, don't you sound chipper?'

'Showered and dressed, all by myself, I might add.'

'Just came to get you for breakfast. I've had the dining room set as we have a guest.'

'We met already, well sort of. He heard a noise and thought I was a burglar.' Caitlin gave a shake of her head. 'He sprung me in the nude. I would almost bet he thinks we had a rip-roaring time last night with all my bruises.'

'The sneaky shit, coming up here to use the bathroom. Does this every time Melita is away. Has never believed in love and is most likely down there delighted he has finally caught me out being unfaithful.'

'So, he is a regular visitor here?'

'It's just one of my nephews. I only wish he had the decency to call first. It would have made things easier if I knew he was coming; at least I could have warned you. I'm sorry he gave you a fright, and although a blatzing fool, and arrogant, as you will find if you join us, he is a guest and won't hurt you. If he has embarrassed you, I can get breakfast sent up, so you don't have to feel uncomfortable facing him. He never stays long. I'll come and get you once he's gone, then maybe we can go to the cabin where it's warm and give you a change of scenery if you feel up to it.'

She tilted her head, interested in the insight he gave into his nephew's character. It sparked her curiosity. 'As you said, he won't be here long, and I'm more anxious to get out of this bedroom and have a change of scenery, than worried about what he thinks of me. Anyway, if I were that worried about being seen naked, I'd never be able to look you in the face.' She tossed her waist length curls over her shoulder, and her eyes sparkled with amusement. 'You men are like magnets when a girl gets naked. He must be related as that was perfect timing, as usual.'

A big smile spread across Jett's face. 'Okay, maybe we men are slightly tuned into the less clothed species of females, but we do it deliberately; you see your humiliation reinforces you are the weaker of the sexes.'

'Then, being of such a delicate species, it leaves me helpless to take care of myself and is my new excuse for being a terrible cook.'

'Ah, the visitor has been a worthy one then.'

'Yes.'

He smiled. 'You're feeling much better aren't you?'

'And hungry, so what's the plan?'

'I have told my help I am cooking for you today. Therefore, the plan, my lazy little kitchen witch, is to park your butt on the bench while I play chef and you torment me as you used to. I've missed your sarcastic wit.'

'You have company so if you give me grief I'll get your stickybeak visitor that owes me one, to sort you out, because I still can't.

'It would not surprise me you'd side with the new guy that I bet drooled over you, bruises and all.'

'Well, I doubt that. I'm almost positive he will never try to spring one of your floozies again. He took one look at me and practically ran out the door.' She giggled. 'I think I can officially say I turned the poor guy off.'

'Good. Stuff him. You're mine.' He laughed, transporting her down to the kitchen.

It was some time later they both carried the meals out into the dining room where Caitlin formally met the guest who sat, legs sprawled out at the end of the table, reading the paper.

'About time,' he scoffed sounding arrogant and quite rude. 'What, did you go make the damned breakfast yourself?'

Jett sucked in a breath and kept his calm. 'Well for your info, yes. Glow Girl here only likes my cooking.'

He eyed her, not even a little embarrassed he had barged in on her. He had the opinion Caitlin was a call girl while the wife was away and didn't even bother to introduce himself or inquire who she was.

Cait put his meal in front of him, feeling as if maybe she should drop it in the selfish pig's lap, but changed her mind when Jett gave her a sideways glance.

'Glow!' He smirked, reading her thoughts.

After a few bites, the guest spoke, his voice uninterested. 'So why Glow? What does that stand for, Glowworm? He smiled at his own humour.

'It's Glow Girl to you. Only Jett gets to shorten it.' She felt it time to wipe the sneer from his face. 'Strangers have to earn that privilege. And you, sir, have proved you are anything but a gentleman so far. Maybe in your circle, you are popular and funny, but I find you anything but.' She proceeded to season her food. She had said her piece and was content to ignore him for the rest of the visit.

The visitor's head jolted up, fork in mid-air. 'Jett?'

'I'm with her. While under an alias, for that short span of time we are able to put aside who we are. Glow isn't interested if you are a Ruler or that I am a god. When I'm introduced as Hades, a wide berth is given to the feared God of the Underworld. But you know what, I'm a man first, and I get no special favours from this one. No looks of heroism or terror at my touch. She also is of high standing herself and yet expects no pandering. You should be so lucky if you are given an alias and called her friend.'

Caitlin was unprepared for Jett's response or his.

The guest stared at her and put his fork down. He glanced at Jett. 'You might just have me there, Uncle.' Studying Caitlin again he relaxed his shoulders. 'Maybe I did get the wrong impression of who you were, young lady, but by the sounds of it, I never will know. So, as a social experiment because this idea intrigues me, can we start again? Although I am at a disadvantage as I have no alias.' He turned his attention to Jett. 'Did you tell her who I am?'

'Although I have said you are my nephew, Glow is not interested. To her, you are the guest.' Jett grinned at him, pleased he was coming around.

The guest turned back to Caitlin. 'I guess I've started off on the wrong foot so this should be interesting. If I promise to kerb my curiosity as to why you are here alone with my uncle when his wife is not here, what alias would you give to me? And be nice as I am giving you my word and that doesn't come easy.'

She already knew this about him just by observing him. He looked a hard nut to crack, and just a name was not going to make him a different person. But for the social experiment, she decided to give him the benefit of the doubt.

She had taken a long time to answer while summing him up and he started to get impatient. His foot began to tap. She grinned, and he stilled. He didn't understand why but suddenly this was important to him. He wanted to be a part of whatever it was going on here, and she was the key. Annoyed she weakened him with her grin but amazingly happy she was giving him what he wanted, his entire demeanour tensed and waited.

'I have summed you up without knowing a thing about you and have an alias if you don't mind my opinion of you so far.' She leant forward with hands clasped on the table in front of her, making the guest feel she spoke to him and him alone.

'When I saw you this morning, I thought you were a decent and polite gentleman, and that has not changed, as yet. Yes, your words have been abrupt, but I assume it is a way to hide your embarrassment and the awkwardness of seeing me naked. However, your eyes tell me more, and the images of how I got my bruises are where knives can cross, and enemies be formed. To move forward, I must clear this up. They were inflicted during a mission I was on and definitely not from a hot frolic with your uncle.' She saw his eyes dart and face redden. 'I do hope this has resolved any poor first impressions you had of me. That being said…' She smiled, and it was at that moment he saw how she got her name.

He tried to concentrate on what she was saying but her skin, in fact, her entire clothed body, started to shine. He found it remarkable. 'I see where you got the name Glow Girl. Pretty impressive.' He was in awe of her angelic features while doing… well, whatever it was she was doing. To say it didn't affect him would be lying. He was mesmerised and could barely breathe.

'Wow, my first compliment. Now it is my turn, to be frank with you. I find your most impressive quality visually is your swanky hairstyle. I have seen dreadlocks before but not as long and well-kept. Tied back they remind me of strands of rope, robust and stylish, which leads me to believe the wearer must have these qualities too. So, with your consent, of course, I would like to call you Aurek.'

'Hey, did she just swear at me?' He had been spellbound by her voice but hearing the name had snapped him out of it and made him unsure of what she just said.

Caitlin grinned. 'I said, Aurek. It means longhaired and as for me swearing, good Lord, not in the first hour at least.' She chuckled and sat back in the chair.

Jett pushed his empty plate away. 'Just wait until she does start. Because if you ever think up garbage like that about her again, Potty Mouth is what you'll nickname her.'

Aurek glanced up at his uncle, still getting the hang of what these names did. He felt no different. 'So you're Jett?'

'No guessing how I ended up with that name.' He ran his hair through his pitch-black head of hair. 'Zeus is Calyx, but this you knew. However, she did change Poseidon's to Razor because she says he needed one and the only other change was to Rhea and Cronus; she calls them, Honey and Ted Bear.'

'Well, I can guess why, the hairy sod.'

'Runs in the family.' Jett pulled some hair that stuck out from Aurek's shirt top and made him flinch.

'Ouch!' Aurek rubbed his chest vigorously and gave a slight grin. 'Well, I guess if everyone else is happy to be someone else around her, I certainly don't want to be left out. But was expecting bells and whistles to go off, it sounded so mysterious.'

'You will get it, give it time to sink in, and it might just save a friendship down the track.' Jett reached over and poured a second cup of coffee from the pot.

Aurek watched while in thought. 'So Glow Girl,' he said, and as he turned to her, his tone was less aggressive. 'Where do you come from?' He looked down and stuck his last forkful of food in his mouth.

'Everywhere, nowhere.'

His brows and lips pulled tight. 'So what do you suggest we talk about then if we can't ask questions?'

She shrugged. 'By asking me questions I can answer, like not where but how, not who but what and, not past but present.'

Jett explained and took over the conversation. Aurek had never seen his uncle so in tune with another person, ever. He didn't like feeling out of it, and that's exactly how he felt listening to them joke and laugh together. As if the one they referred to as Glow Girl felt his frustration, she suddenly included him. The atmosphere changed and for once, here on Pluto, he was actually enjoying the chat. Yes, dead souls and the Underworld came up as usual, but with jest; the stress of running such an operation he regularly heard in his uncle's voice was gone. At one stage the topic shifted back to Jett's immediate family. Aurek's curiosity was piqued, wanting to know how they handled Glow Girl.

Jett kept out the details of how she came to Pluto but kept it so entertaining his nephew didn't notice. 'Like the time she got away with hanging it on Ted Bear when he was going skiing. Told him she couldn't wait to see what a big old bear looked like on snow skis. Then proceeded to laugh as she gave descriptions of what the big old bear on his arse in the snow would look like. The little minx teased him all through the meal, gave him hell.'

'Seriously, if that had been one of us, we would have been disciplined right and proper.' Aurek got into stories of just that, the times he gave cheek and received a swipe from his grandfather's big sweeping paw. He enjoyed the time with them both so much he stayed for longer than anticipated.

A shiver from Caitlin had Jett on his feet and he moved the three of them into the den and closer to the open fire. While the men indulged in a drink and cigar, Caitlin chose to curl up in Jett's chair that claimed the best position in the chamber. The heat of the embers lulled her into a light sleep while she listened to the chatter beside her.

'What's with you and this one? Does Persephone know she's here?' Aurek spoke quietly as he watched her eyes close for the last time.

'It was a spur of the moment thing.' He glanced at Caitlin and for her benefit if still awake used Persephone's alias. 'Melita is with her mother so no, I didn't want to worry her unnecessarily. The main reason is that Glow and Melita have become good friends. If I had told her how injured Glow really was, that it was touch and go if she lived, she would have cut her time short. That would not have gone down well. You know how her mum looks forward to Melita's visits.'

'Why here though? Hasn't she got a family?'

'Wolf, her fiancé.'

'Whose name I guess is not really Wolf.'

'No, but for security reasons that is what he is otherwise known as.'

'Fair enough, continue.' Aurek knew any further digging would do him no good. Hades had always been a closed book, and this situation suited his personality. As for Aurek, he was getting a little impatient with the cloak and dagger dribble and shifted uncomfortably, yet for some reason he didn't want to leave. This was all too intriguing and not only did he want answers, but the heady scent of his uncle's guest had him addicted for lack of a better word, and he couldn't have left if he tried.

'Wolf fears for her life.'

'You mean, you fear for her life. You're in love with her too and use it as an excuse to have her here.'

'Yes I love her, but I'm not in love, exactly. Glow feels familiar, like family, yet much more. I can't explain it.' Jett shrugged.

Aurek watched her. 'If Glow Girl is to be a part of our family, she is certainly an attractive addition to it. Where does she come from, Earth or up here?' he asked.

'That again is a secret which I'm unable to share. As we expect our details to stay private, so does Glow and until ready to share her world with you, I recommend respecting the privacy issue.' He saw his nephew's face redden from getting the runaround and breathed out. 'What I am at liberty to say is she is loyal to a fault. Never question this about her and if she allows you more time with her, and I know she is ready to go home so you may only have moments, try to set aside your questioning of every damned thing you imagine is wrong and give her a chance.'

'It makes it hard when I come here and find what is possibly splitting you up from your family and the plan set in place for you, Uncle.'

'Before you say another word, it is not Glow who has made me drag my chain.'

Aurek stretched. 'So what's the problem if it's not her? You haven't been a part of the war for months, and now the family is cross with you. I want you to tell me what's going on, you know you are my favourite uncle, and I hate this… this sudden change in you.'

'Well, how about I ease your mind that the changes in me are for the best. Let's go and take a look at what has been keeping me busy.' He stood and leant over Caitlin. 'Glow, are you awake?' He shook her gently.

She sat up with a start. 'Sorry I must have dozed again. What time is it?'

'Time you got up and made us some dinner,' Aurek stirred.

'Sure!' She grinned at him. 'Ask Jett about me and my cooking. Seriously, I can guarantee he'd sooner eat barf than my cooking.'

'See what I have to put up with.' He smiled at her. 'Thought we might wander out and show Aurek our project.' Jett helped her up and made sure she was steady before letting her go.

'So again, I have to ask, why this need to spend time with her and not us? I mean the girl sounds as if she can't do anything. I can't cook, get blown up at work, hell she's a walking disaster.' Aurek stood, boiling that his uncle woke her to join them. It seemed to him Jett couldn't do anything alone anymore. In his book, this was bad, and his uncle needed saving from this woman. *Mmm but she sure smells good…* he followed them.

Jett slowed up and walked beside his nephew, leaving Glow to lead the way. 'Look,' he said quietly, 'Glow is unique in so many other ways. She is a straight shooter and has a way of making sense. She uses such simple solutions to problems solve and without her, none of what I'm about to show you would have happened. Her motivation and encouragement have not only made me strive to be a better person, but all this we have achieved together has made my wife and me so much happier. Come and I'll show you.'

'If this is the mystery that's kept you busy from the rest of us, it had better be a damned good one, or I'm calling Grandpa to talk sense into you. We haven't seen hide or hair of you for months.'

'It was for a good reason,' Jett said.

'Better be.'

'Coming?' Glow stopped and waited at the large, boldly-carved, reinforced doors. 'You just have to see this to believe it.' She slipped her arm through Aurek's, surprising him. Her enthusiasm was suddenly infectious.

'Hey!' Jett punched his arm. 'She's my guest and my friend. Go get your own.'

'She's got another arm, so use that one.' Aurek smirked.

'Come on guys, this is exciting, share.' Caitlin listened to them squabbling over her like members of her team did sometimes, and it made her miss them. With a quick intake of air, she was attentive to the people around her again. 'Wait until you see how talented an uncle you have.'

A tug on her arm left Caitlin confused when Aurek stopped suddenly and didn't move. 'Are you all right there?' She turned to him.

'Ah, yes and no. I mean – Wow!' He shook his head, his eyes like saucers. 'Did you just apply perfume? The fragrance has me riveted, and it's beautiful.'

Jett pushed at him to get him moving. 'Get used to it tiger, until she feels safe around you, her power will control you.'

'You're one cool witch.' He gave her a toothy kind of grin, then his attention was suddenly distracted as he viewed the overhead dome with its artificial lighting and heating that made the entire area look and feel as if it were a bright sunny day. The grand display of thriving plant life set around a waterfall that ran into a lap pool caught even Caitlin's breath.

'Oh my goodness Jett, this is so impressive now. You have done so much more since I was here last.' Caitlin spun on her heels and smiled at him.

'You got to be kidding me, Uncle Brainwave. This is unbelievable.' Aurek stood with a stunned mullet expression, his mouth open with admiration. His uncle's old fashioned incredibly cold and dull castle that he hated to come and visit had, outside, transformed into a beautiful paradise.

Caitlin felt pangs of pride as Aurek praised the entire setup. It took them about an hour to walk to the far end of the enclosure.

'What about the cabin? Have you done anything to it? I can remember we came up once for a ski after our last hunting trip. It was all so dark, cold and miserable that I thought we were better off where we were and never insisted on coming back here again,' Aurek commented.

'Hunting!' Caitlin picked up on the word. 'You two go hunting together? Can I come next time?'

Both turned and spoke to her at the same time. 'NO!'

Jett knew she wouldn't give up but decided to try and take her mind off it. Without a word, he put his arm around Aurek and Caitlin and transported them to what he had been transforming into a winter wonderland. In the cabin, he ignited the fire with just a snap of his fingers and smiled when Cait called him a show-off, before flicking a switch that lit up the mountain. While the men stood on the veranda in sub-zero temperatures, Caitlin kept warm by the fire and watched through the balcony doors. Still recovering, it weakened her powers to keep warm enough to join them.

The massively powered floodlights recently installed enabled Jett to show off not only the power generators but the ski lift he had installed before Caitlin's first visit. That told Caitlin it had been some time since Aurek's last visit or he would have known those changes at least. It left her to ponder why he had picked this day to visit, a time when Caitlin's unfortunate accident had her here too. A coincidence perhaps, as they happened a lot to her lately, and she hoped Aurek was not to become a pain in her side, sometime in their future.

Aurek was more than impressed, yet the cold had got to him. Inside he still shivered until Jett's tour ended in the next room, with the heated hot tub, another surprise addition that Aurek had only just discovered. 'Geez Uncle, no wonder no one has seen you.' He discarded heavy boots and clothes.

Caitlin turned to leave.

'Don't let my nakedness scare you off, sugar. I've seen yours; only fair you get to check me out.'

'No thanks, I prefer my men hairless.' She laughed out loud and left him to get into the tub alone.

'Join me, Uncle. Let the cute one wait on you for a change.' He called out to Caitlin, 'Uncle and I will have a couple of Moonjuices thanks, Glow Girl.'

'Like that's ever going to happen,' she called to him.

It was much later in the night that Aurek began talking of his most recent hunting trip that Jett had been invited to go on. 'At least I know why you didn't come last week, Uncle, you were stuck here babysitting.'

Caitlin ignored his dig, too interested in his hunting story, and after exhausted all reasons for him to take her on his next trip with Jett, gave up and lay quietly listening.

Jett refused to discuss it later when she brought it up again. To stop her nagging both of them, he said they could have a practice run. A sleepover out in the log cabin to see if she liked roughing it on the floor. He hoped her being uncomfortable would put an end to it. Instead, she wanted to stay awake until dawn, believing that this must happen on hunting trips with the boys. Luckily, the waiting eventually bored her, and with a little help from Jett's magic, she fell asleep early.

'Her fiancé would throw a fit if he found out I'd promised to take her hunting,' Jett told Aurek once she drifted off to sleep.

* * * *

It was just before dawn when Caitlin woke Jett and Aurek. She had fallen asleep on the floor with them while they chatted into the night. However, when they dozed off, they kept moving towards her and rather than get squashed by their pure size alone, Caitlin wiggled free and got up on the couch pulling a fur around her for warmth. It astounded her they didn't even stir particularly after all the grunting, growling and puffing she did while pushing them off her.

'Wake up sleepyheads.' Caitlin sat up, suddenly remembering where they were.

'Glow.' Jett checked the time, his voice hoarse from the Moonjuice and late night.

Aurek didn't murmur a word; his routine before anything was coffee. No servants were around, so he dragged himself off the floor and turned on the coffee machine. Coffee made for three, he handed them around, his drink already half gulped down.

'What's all the excitement?' he finally asked, watching Caitlin as she pulled back the curtain.

Jett chastised her as he ambled over to see what was so interesting to have her looking intently out through the window. 'What's got you so damn excited at this time of the morning? That hit you took has sent you loopy.'

'I just wanted to show you how spectacular your planet is at daybreak.'

Aurek loomed over her as he squinted to see out into the darkness. 'What are we looking at?'

'Wait.' She turned her head up and smiled at the huge man she had befriended. He wasn't such a bad boy as she thought. He was so not used to smiling, and his parted lips stretched awkwardly. The endearing efforts made her chuckle as she nudged him. 'Now! Impatient one.' She stood on tippy toes as the sun that only licked this planet brought it to life.

The light was faint, but at sunrise, the soft glow from the sun clashed with the two moons above which created a magical reaction as it hit the icy snow. The impact lit up the surface, making the ground shine as if diamond sprinkles covered it. These shining particles shot up into the sky, and as the sun and moons moved in unison, the laser show above them was quite magnificent. It only happened for a few minutes, and then it was gone, but it was one impressive sight and being an early riser, Caitlin had discovered another of Pluto's secrets and felt sure it had gone unnoticed until now.

'Worth it, Glow!' admitted Aurek.

'This place never ceases to amaze me. A phenomenon, right here on my own Home World and I never knew it.' Once again, Jett felt humbled by Caitlin's astuteness to discover a regular occurrence that neither he nor Persephone had ever noticed.

Your planet has so many wonders, Jett. How you're ever going to leave is beyond me, she thought to him, for his ears only.

He put his arm around her and whispered, 'Stay here with Melita and me. Don't ever go home.'

'Hello, I'm still here guys. Geez! Will you two stop with the secrets?'

Jett grinned. 'Go find your own friend to have fun with. Glow's mine and I told you, I'm not sharing.'

It had become a game with them both so before they could get into another argument on whose girl she was, Caitlin had a gripe.

'By the way, you both almost squashed me this morning. If you want to sleep together, you should have moved me out the way.' She poked at them. 'Had to crawl up on the couch to get away from you.'

'Don't go blaming us, girlfriend. You brought that totally on yourself.' Aurek put up his hands in a submissive gesture. 'You're the one that smells like cookies and cream. I just kept gravitating towards the delicious treat.' He nudged Jett. 'After last night I understand why you want her around all the time, lucky mongrel.'

Caitlin grinned. 'Well, I guess it's my fault after all.'

'Damn right it is.' Jett put an arm around her. He felt happy; not only for the friend she had become but for the way she made him view his planet. To show it off to his nephew tugged at a noble sentiment, an emotion he'd never felt before. He wasn't sure whether to hug her or toss her around, excitedly. Due to her injuries, he chose to loosely embrace her.

Caitlin realised she had hit a sensitive chord in Jett as he struggled with the ever increasing love for his life here on this newly created home. It was a planet shunned by many, and yet he felt proud of the Dwarf Planet he had named so long ago as Pluto.

With a skip of joy in her step, Caitlin knew just what he needed, so she leant over the bar, snatched up a half bottle of Starstarter and topped up their coffee with it.

She held up her cup to theirs. 'To Pluto and all its glory.'

They gulped theirs down.

'Glow Girl!' Aurek's stunned expression made her smile. 'A female that will toast with the treasured elixir of the stars and first thing in the morning! I think you have just become my new best friend.' He took the bottle from her and topped up his own drink. 'I guess we could make an exception next time we go camping after all. She's not so bad to hang out with, but no nagging us.' He had argued with Caitlin most the night. They debated his rule that women were never allowed on their boys' weekends away, specifically their hunting trips. For him to relent now, it meant she had finally won.

'For real!' Caitlin jumped about doing a winning jig.

Aurek had a frown and wished he could take it back. In frustration, he turned her around and moved her towards the kitchen. 'Quit it and get in that kitchen and cook me some breakfast. If you do a good job, I'll think about taking you – one day.'

She laughed so much she collapsed onto the chair. 'Jett. Tell your nephew he has Buckley's and none.'

'She can't cook – seriously.'

'I thought you were kidding me, not even some eggs and bacon? Are you for real?'

Caitlin put her hand up. 'Okay, Okay, it's been a while, so maybe things have changed.'

Jett had never seen her even try so sat back on the sofa to enjoy the show.

The pan came out the cupboard and, with a crash, landed on the floor as she clumsily placed it on the stove. 'Oops.' She held it up while she tried to light the burner and burnt her hand. The pan landed back on the floor. 'I got this, seriously.' She picked it up, not holding it correctly and dropped it on the stove with a crash. The flame went out, and they heard her swear under her breath. Both men were in hysterics by the time she got to the eggs that didn't get into the pan but instead dribbled down the side of the bench. Not seeing it, she slid along the floor, and Jett caught her before she hit it.

With a kiss on her forehead for effort, he dumped her on the stool near them. 'You are an utterly hopeless sweetie, sit before you kill yourself or we die laughing.'

It was a few hours later before Aurek got up to leave.

'We will have to do this again.' Caitlin hugged him.

'The gods would surely not put me through such torture.' He gave her his funny distorted grin that gave her the giggles.

'Then behave, or I will be sent to your door,' she warned.

An incline of his head and he was gone. He was a ruler, she now guessed, as they were the only ones permitted the luxury of instant transportation.

Jett took her home the next day. She felt safe here on Pluto and just for a minute had reservations.

'Is it safe to be back here? What if Axon and Kayden haven't formed a treaty with that ruler they have been having trouble with? The one that did this to me. I mean isn't that the reason Cassie was sent to her father's, because they feared for her safety? He sounds a lot to deal with, and if Cassie can't handle him, in my poor shape, I've got buckley and none of stopping a full-scale attack by him.'

'Oh, I don't think that's going to happen; in fact, I'm sure you'll always be safe from him from this day forward. Trust me.' He smiled.

Caitlin didn't really understand what he meant but trusted him implicitly that he had fixed it for her.

Chapter Thirty-Six

Orion's Surprise Visitor

Back home, Axon showered Caitlin with gifts, flowers and even took time off work for a couple of days to be with her. He had enjoyed every minute with her, but now it was time for him to go back to work. He knew she wanted to as well, but he wasn't ready to give her back to the universe just yet.

'I'm completely healed,' she pouted when he tried to evade her request.

'Soon.' He kissed a sulky Caitlin goodbye.

Jett rang her most days to check up on how she was and today was coming to see her. *Maybe this will cheer her up.* 'Anyway, your boyfriend is coming to visit today. He won't be happy if you stand him up.'

'Jett's coming?' She perked up immediately.

* * * *

Caitlin was thrilled to see Jett and, taking his hand, walked with him around the outer grounds of the estate so they could talk in private. The wolves followed from a distance, watching every move the visitor made. The guardian wolf, Russo, showed no trust in him, not one little bit. Caitlin was used to Russo looking out for her and ignored the fuss they were making because she walked with someone other than Axon.

'Come and sit with me Jett.' She saw him hesitate and worry for her when Russo moved close to the opposite side of her. 'They are just curious who you are and mean us no harm.'

He eyed Russo. 'Not so close, pal, she's my friend, not yours.'

Russo understood and moved a couple of steps from them and lay down, his eyes not leaving Jett. It made him laugh. 'Even the blatzing animals try to move in on you when they get a chance. The only time I get to talk to you alone is at my place. Want to change venues?' He gave her a wink as he sat on a boulder beside her overlooking a stream so clear they could see the bottom.

Russo got up again, and moved another body length away before dropping down on his belly sounding like he huffed.

Jett was amused but only for a minute. It was Cait he had come to visit and he wasn't interested in the over-protective leader of the pack. He had something to share but didn't want to make plans if she was still feeling poorly.

Suddenly, while beside the running water, her power took a shift, and he could feel it stronger than ever.

'You have your energy back. I can feel your magic spiking. Somehow you have recharged by coming outside.'

'I think it's the water. I felt it too.'

There must be a need for you out there again. When are you allowed to go back to work?'

'I hope it will be tomorrow. I'm so sick of this sitting around.' A kick sent her shoe flying, and she stretched out her leg, dipping her toe in the cold water and wiggling it around. 'Let's not talk about me anymore, what about you; is Melita back yet?'

'My wife comes home today.' He grinned.

'Where has she been? You were very secretive as to where she was so didn't push to find out but I've missed her.' Caitlin frowned.

I'm sorry I didn't want you to worry. Melita's mother took ill just after you came to stay with us and she went to care for her.' He shared.

'Is her mother alright?' Caitlin worried for her. Knew how much Melita cherished her.

'Yes she is well now and Melita is packing. I intend to go via her mum's house after I leave here and pick her up.' Jett tossed a flat rock, skimming it across the water, and watched it skip along the surface.

'And – I believe it's a marked occasion for your both. Happy anniversary. What have you got planned for her?' Caitlin asked.

He smiled. 'Actually, I intend to take a few days off. I was thinking about charming Melita by going on a second honeymoon.'

'Aw, that is so sweet.' She leant into him. 'Never picked you as a romantic man.'

'Stop it Glow. I can be just as loving as the next bloke.'

'Okay, then tell me, how many centuries would you say it's been since you took her somewhere special other than to family holidays with everyone around?'

'Point taken, but that's the thing, I want to romance her now. Since the changes to the Castle, she is different, since you, I'm different. We feel like a regular couple, as we don't let the Underworld define us anymore.'

'Then I think it's a fantastic idea and don't believe that you should keep her waiting another minute.'

'You're the best, Glow. You don't mind if I walk you back and take off? I would never have told you if you were still not well, but you sound like you again.' He grinned. 'And I know you'd rather be practising your craft getting ready for the next call out, rather than hanging out here all day with me.'

She chuckled. 'Seriously, you have been reading my mind again, haven't you?' she teased. 'Up until you mentioned Melita, I hadn't thought about anything but our conversation. But it does my heart good to hear you two love birds are going off for a few days' break. I just want to go and have some fun too, and you know how much I love a good training session, especially considering Woody is still here. That guy is a hoot. I may get to go a few rounds with a horse even… but don't share that with Axon.' She held her hand across her mouth. 'Oops.'

With a grin, he stood up. 'Friends don't dob. Your horse still not back from Pegasus?'

Caitlin shook her head and gripped his outstretched hand as he hoisted her up, and steadied her while she slipped on her shoe she sent flying earlier.

'Hope your mare comes home soon. You make a good team,' he said as they walked back arm in arm.

* * * *

While eating breakfast in the dining room, Axon told Caitlin how Orion had not given up his quest to hunt back on Taurus.

'Why would he do that?' She put her fork down to listen.

'Not once but twice now. Orion and his dogs were caught trespassing again last night.'

'What, after all that has happened? He dares defy the Cloud Riders and goes there without permission?' Caitlin was surprised at how brazen was this man.

'Aurus, the ruler of Taurus, is furious with the arrogance of the hunter and has approached Aldebaran for assistance. Aldebaran, as you can imagine, is livid about the broken treaty and threatened that if the Cloud Riders don't sort it out soon, he will.

'And that is why Kayden brought Cassie home last night. He was worried she would be seen as fraternising with the enemy and not get anywhere with Orion.'

'Well, maybe the damage is already done if he has found out she was staying on the Home World of Taurus, in the city of Aldebaran. I guess it will make a difference. We'll see, as the full team was sent out late last night to speak to Orion over the broken treaty. They should be back any minute.'

Axon had no sooner said that, when the Kayden and his team arrived. Axon stood up to find out how it went. Kayden had been hopeful before they left and had laid his bets on Cassie being able to turn it around.

'How did it go?' Axon asked as the team stomped past.

'He's a hard-headed son of a bitch.' Kayden was clearly annoyed.

'Did Cassie wear him down at all?'

Kayden shook his head. 'Wouldn't even talk to her, and we got nothing. I had to hold Woody back from giving him a good thump when he was so arrogant to the men.'

'It's your zone, Kayden. But remember I have a vested interest in this; he nearly killed one of my team. So if you want help, just say the word. Maybe a bit of extra muscle will help adjust the attitude of the self-indulgent dictator. '

'That is precisely what I hoped you'd say.' Kayden wiped the sweat from his brow. 'But I had my sights on just one of them.'

'Caitlin.'

'I'd like her to take a crack at it. That power she used to calm the gods might just work. Settle him down just enough to allow us some kind of exchange with him while she keeps the big guy quiet.'

'She'd jump at the chance to get out there again, but I'm not ready to send her.'

'Axon, if it were one of the men that wore the blast, would you be so protective? The girls are just as tough as the guys. Don't baby any of them; they have a job to do. If she says she's ready, she is. Get her out there and let her do what she's been given this gift to do. I bet Rory agrees with me.'

Axon's face reddened. They hadn't had words in a long time and doing so in his own home made it worse. 'I do not baby her, *ever*! And I take offence to you insinuating that I – *do!*'

Kayden stood with hands on his hips, unable to back down. He was a bit sour he even had to ask for Cait. He felt Cassie should have been gifted with the same skill or at least be able to access it, but as hard as she tried, there was a wall up. Some of Cait's gifts were hers to keep and hers alone. 'I need her.'

'I know. So does every other blatzing man in the solar system. One day!' Axon looked down, fuming.

Kayden slapped his shoulder. 'Let me shout a refreshment.'

'Might as well. Better make it a Starstarter, straight. You don't give up when you get your mind set on something and I know I'm not going to win, am I?'

'And a cigar.' Kayden grinned.

Axon gave up. 'I'm coming then.' His stubbornness was met with a laugh.

'Thought you'd say that.'

'Well, after I talk Rory into letting me be the one to go with her. He's so pig-headed.'

'Mmm love to be a fly on the wall with you two.' Kayden rolled his eyes with a smirk.

'No different to you and Woody.'

'Point taken – now, about that Starstarter.'

'And cigar,' Axon added, feeling a bit better knowing he was going too, regardless of what Rory had to say.

* * * *

Outside, Caitlin was given another horse to ride. 'Shargan is still recovering, Red.' Woody handed her the reins. 'That piece of shrapnel in her rump saved you from being decapitated and went in deep, but it's healing nicely. She'll be home soon.'

Caitlin took the reins of the new horse and patted its nose. 'I hear her bravery didn't go unnoticed and she is receiving VIP treatment back on the Pegasus constellation. Hope they don't spoil her too much. I want her back.' She huffed at having to ride a horse she didn't know. 'This horse better not put me in a stupid dress,' Caitlin complained while Axon lifted her up onto the horse. 'I liked the pants and boots that Shargan dresses me in.' She continued to sulk as the magic powered up and she waited for the glow to dissipate.

'Wow.' Axon stepped back and gave her a wolf whistle.

Caitlin looked down, excited for just a second at Axon's reaction until she saw what she wore. 'Oh – my – goodness, hell no.' Her hands went to her face, unimpressed. 'I knew it.'

The fleck in the sheer golden fabric glistened in the light. The material fell soft and loose down her back to reveal a tattoo of Shargan. The front fell softly across her chest in light folds that left little to the imagination and the gown that somehow gathered in the right places, sat elegantly on the horse. It was such a heavenly softness that even with the slightest of movement it lit up like fairy dust.

'Where's the halo?' Woody blinked.

'Bet it's dropped and ready to strangle you,' Rory teased as he arrived in time to see them off. His look alone let Caitlin know he was very pleased she was back on a horse.

'Smart-aleck!' She put her arms out to Axon, moving her fingers at him impatiently. 'New horse, this one's crackers.'

'You're staying put. We haven't time and anyway, I like it.' Axon grinned and jumped on his horse as they lifted so quickly off the ground she had no chance to make any further protests.

'You did that deliberately, Kayden,' she pouted.

'And if we are going to suck in the stubborn rogue ruler, I need a real angel on board to do it. Now quit the antics and enjoy the ride.'

'Hate you!'

'Love you!' Kayden turned and winked, as his comment made her smile.

'Okay, but if he laughs at me, I'm hopping on your horse, dressing like a man and whipping your hide.'

Axon and Kayden cracked up laughing. They both knew she wouldn't shut up now until they got there and they looked forward to the laugh along the way. Axon had fallen for her the very first trip. He met his match that day and gave in as they all had to befriend this mysterious beauty.

Kayden led and as they hit the clouds all chatter ceased, and his was the last word. *If she doesn't dazzle our boy in that outfit today I give up,* he communicated telepathically.

Axon glanced at Caitlin, aware she would hate this voiceless part of the journey where the chatter was silent due to the magic of the approaching portal.

* * * *

Coming into the airspace of Orion's Home World, Caitlin took her mind off the possible explosive situation ahead, and glanced around to see how the hunter lived. She expected overgrown meadows and bush, and to see livestock penned waiting to meet its fate. If they were invited for a meal she imagined the meat when cooked, to be still mooing and slapped on a paper plate to devour, she chuckled at the thought. Although she doubted a hunter would be so hospitable as to even offer a drink never mind a meal. Her thoughts wandered to what he might look like and she imagined a slightly ignorant man who spoke with a drawl. Possibly he'd be dressed like a farmer and would be in dire need of both a bath and a shave. She had never asked about him, and it was unusual for her to make an assumption until she met someone, but he had to be a real bad arse if the Riders had not yet broken him down.

Closer to the ground, she sucked in her breath. *How wrong was I.* The mountain range stretched out as far as the eye could see, rivers twisted within the gullies and tall blossoming trees lined the rivers. His house from the air looked like a tropical holiday resort and now as they landed out front, the enormity of the two-storey building filled her with a sense of helplessness. No wonder this guy wasn't interested in making a deal or amends; he had it all and what do you offer a man that has everything?

Suddenly an army of soldiers appeared. Caitlin hadn't noticed, too busy in her own thoughts. Guns weren't aimed, but were held at the ready as if they expected trouble. Caitlin turned quickly to Kayden. They looked trigger-happy, and there was an awful lot of rifle power.

Settle Cait, this is our usual welcome; Orion knows our power and is just flexing his muscles.

This was going to be a tough assignment, and Caitlin suddenly felt very unsure of her abilities. She tried to subdue the anger that kept raging for his vicious attack against her friends and for the pain he caused her personally.

Axon saw the frown, picked up her hand and held it. 'I see your emotions are all over the place, but you know how to control them, don't you?'

'I want to blow him up when I meet him. See how he likes it!'

'Caitlin!' Axon disciplined. 'Kayden has taught you how to deal with emotions on a job, or they can be your downfall. Use the technique to calm down, or we go home.'

She closed her eyes and did as she was trained. Using her inner power, she found the fiery anger and in her mind doused it with water. 'Flames out.' She took a deep breath as she opened her eyes and smiled. 'See how long it lasts this time.'

'If anyone can, I know you can do this.' He was glad she didn't look so stressed. 'Now go do your thing and if it goes nowhere, believe me, it's not from lack of magical sexiness.' He grinned. 'And if you do lose it, I won't be mad. We'll just have to find another way.'

'Can't promise anything at this point, just need to know you will support whatever I need to do.'

'I will.'

* * * *

They were shown into Orion's home, an enormous entrance similar to a grand six-star luxurious motel. Through double doors, the room acted as a grand sitting room that looked out over the immaculately designed outdoor area, complete with pool and meticulously manicured hedges and trees. This was surrounded by accommodation units, and from the view she'd had in the air, she knew each had its own jetty and motorised fishing boat.

She eyed the white furniture against blood red carpets. On the walls hung heads of beasts; the colours and décor were proof of his love to hunt. The splash of white gave her a hint that there wasn't only just darkness in his heart.

The twitter of birds caught her off guard. He had living creatures amongst the deadness of animal heads that hung heavily on the walls. The rug on the floor even sported a head. She wondered what sort of man would enjoy the hunt so much he'd take up arms, and start a war to have his own way. To judge him she felt the need to try this sport first.

Outside on the veranda, she was distracted and put her hand up. The colourful birds thrilled her when they perched on her palm, and even though distracted she kept her wits about her while listening for the villain of this elegant home to enter.

It was Kayden who spoke to Orion as he came into the room, but she heard no response. She lifted her hand for the birds to fly off so she could meet him, wondering about the greeting she would get from someone so arrogant that he wouldn't even speak to a guest that had talked to him. Possibly he gave a nod and that was it, *what a douche bag*. This had her more intrigued to see the person who owned all this magnificence, yet was so incredibly unsatisfied. She smiled at the birds, and at the same time turned. *Aurek! What's he doing here?*

Aurek already knew who was there; he could smell the delicious fragrance. *What is Glow Girl doing here, surely she's… no, she couldn't be a rider?* There had to be a reasonable explanation, he wanted to speak to her *and now!* He snapped his fingers at a servant. 'Fix the guests a beverage.' His superior tone surprised her.

He turned to Kayden. 'Is this one of your Riders?'

'A Rider but not directly one of mine. 'Her name is…'

Before Kayden could finish the introductions, Aurek hushed him with an upraised arm. 'I know who she is, she is Glow Girl, and it is she I have come to speak with. I was on my way out, and had no intentions of joining either of you today, until that fragrance…' His egotistical tone tapered off. 'Amuse yourselves. Get a drink, whatever.'

Orion had no intention to wait for permission; he had to have time alone with her. *Had Glow Girl tricked him? Did she know him?* To lose her friendship shook him to the core, in fact, Orion barely kept it together as he took her arm and led Caitlin quickly outside and into the garden.

It was at that moment when a stunned Axon and Kayden clicked that this was the friend she had met at Jett's. They could read how annoyed with her he was and were both ready to snatch her away if he flexed his muscles. They both knew Orion well. He was full of games; it was in his nature. Neither trusted him and what would happen next was anyone's guess.

'Did you know who I was? You did, didn't you? What game are you playing? I thought we were friends. This isn't good, Glow. You should have told me who you were.' He was angry, yet shattered at the same time.

Tears stung her eyes. She didn't understand his attack. 'I'm not here to see you, Aurek. I've come to talk to Orion. He's the son of a bitch that nearly blew me up. I have no beef with you.'

His tone grew almost high-pitched. 'That was *you*!' His hand ran roughly over his matted hair. The dreadlocks today were clean and a little frizzy at the roots from a vigorous lather. She could see his mind tick over. 'All the bruises! I did that to you? Are you serious?' The bench seat creaked as the force of his body weight sat heavily on it.

'You're *Orion*! No! You couldn't be that arrogant, hot-tempered, selfish man.' She collapsed beside him, bewildered. 'You're lying to me, you're my friend. We drank together, laughed and even shared dark secrets together. Please don't say you're him.'

'I'm so sorry, Glow. I'm the monster you hate. Hell, I feel sick that I did that to you.' Orion got up and spat in the bushes.

Had he just been sick, did he care he hurt me that much?

He turned and stared at her. Glow Girl had her head down and to lose her respect and friendship at this point, upset him more than he understood. Why he felt this way towards her, he had no clue but knew if it wasn't sorted out somehow, it was he that would be the loser here. He bent down in front of her. 'Your bruises…' He shook his head and looked to the ground. 'I wanted to kill the bastard that did that to you, and now I find it was me.' Orion glared at her. 'Why are you still sitting here? How can you stand to be anywhere near me and not run?'

They locked eyes while time paused, as if she saw deep in his soul. He knew that was impossible or was it? *I will miss you Glow.* His eyes betrayed his thought. She squeezed her hands tightly in her lap, not taking her eyes from him, her next words so quiet he strained to hear. 'You're just Aurek to me, and you're my friend. Before, when you did the unthinkable to me, you were Orion. Aurek could never do that, not to me, I am sure.'

She patted the seat beside her and as if under a spell, he moved at her request. As she stood up and left him sitting the effect was angelic. Her gown looked saintly and floated with each movement.

She turned her back on him, and he eyed the flawless complexion of a woman he'd most likely never see again. The thought stabbed at him.

He dropped his eyes and felt the softest touch lift his chin.

'I stood to show you, look, the marks of the tragedy are all gone. Not even a scar. Feel.' She shifted side on so his hand could feel her back and at the same time gave him the most adorable smile that moved him.

He rolled his eyes as she watched him intently. 'Yes it's better now.' His hand dropped down and held hers with the same care he had on Pluto.

'Orion is evil, and it was immorally wicked of him to have attacked the Cloud Riders. As a result, from trying to protect all our precious horses, not only I but my own horse Shargan was hurt badly, and we both ended up in much pain. Truthfully, I should have you flogged for such an act. That being said, as my friend, Aurek, you have never harmed me, and even now you feel sick to think you did so. How about we start again?' She extended her hand, and he took it.

'Hi, my name is Caitlin Warner, and I am a Cosmic Rider, attached to Axon's team, not Kayden's, and don't ask why I am here helping out. I guess I just wanted to meet the swine, Orion. Kick him in the shins, pinch his ears, and maybe bitch slap him a few times.'

Although he found her sweet and was pleased she was trying to make him feel better, his unhappiness at the pain he'd caused her wouldn't subside. The only thing that would cheer him up is knowing she felt safe with him again, as she had while on Pluto together. He couldn't raise a laugh as he was feeling so horrid.

'Caitlin, you are Glow Girl to me, and so you never have to think of me so poorly. I would like to keep the name you gave me when you knew me as your friend.'

She smiled, let his hand go and sat beside him. 'Aurek.'

'Yes, Glow.'

'Does that mean we can put aside our true selves and as friends, talk?'

'I would like that if you can put what happened aside for a bit.'

'I can do better than that.' She raised her hand and placed it over her heart. 'Caitlin, the Rider, in your company does not exist. We are the two we were when we met at Jett's. Teasing, fun-loving buddies.'

'I would appreciate that more than you know.'

'Me too.'

'So what now?' He gave her a sideways look.

'Cheer up, get off your butt and show me around this oasis. I couldn't believe what I saw when we flew in. You're one hell-of-a-catch! Want to marry me too?'

'In your dreams, Glow Girl. No woman is getting a ring out of this man.'

'You're gay, then. I'm crushed, and hundreds of woman all over the galaxy are shattered.'

'Give you gay. Spread that rumour and you'll see Orion flex his wicked ways again.'

'Orion will get his just desserts if he ever crosses my path again.'

He eyed her, forgetting for a second how she liked to stir him. 'Can you seriously put it aside?'

'Look, tosser, I'm not scared of your tough, bad-boy side, so don't even go there.' She straightened with dignity.

He thought her adorable. The copper hair toned by cool, bright-green eyes provoked him with gusto. 'Call me a tosser!' He snatched up the temptress and threw her over his shoulder.

Caitlin's reactive squeal had Kayden and Axon at the ready.

'It's okay boys, don't get your jocks in a twist, just taking cheeky here on a tour.' He put her down when he saw the daggers from the men watching. He didn't want them to leave and take her just yet.

Caitlin ran her hands down her thighs and straightened her dress before she slipped her arm through his and smiled. 'Well, I'm waiting.'

His weird but welcomed grin was the first since their arrival, and to her, that said it all; they were friends again. Axon and Kayden were speechless. His smile was a phenomenon neither had seen before.

* * * *

After the grand tour, Aurek stopped for a moment, his brows pulled in tight. 'Please don't let work spoil what we have. This here, with us two, it won't change my mind. I'm still not prepared to give in.'

'Aurek, my dearest new friend. I have forgiven that side of you which is untamed, and that is as far as I go. You will face the music, but not by my hands.'

'So whether or not I give in, it's of no consequence to you; we remain as we are right now.' Aurek's eyes were wide in anticipation of the answer.

'You have my promise.' Caitlin shook on it.

* * * *

Axon eyed the two as they walked in, Caitlin all smiles and full of life on the arm of Orion. He looked almost charming until Orion spotted them. His demeanour changed and the arrogance of the man met earlier, was back. Axon wondered if the expression was a glint of gloating. *I am in a win-win here. It doesn't matter if I agree of not, she will stay loyal to me.*

Caitlin spotted the uncertain, almost hateful stare of the men in front of her. 'Come.' She dragged Orion over to them. Axon glanced at Kayden who wiggled a shoulder, a habit when he was over the antics and in two minds to settle this one way or another.

'This is Aurek, the new friend I told you about.' They both froze as Caitlin worked her magic, not allowing either of them to move until she was ready. Axon knew she could control the ones she worked on, but this was the first time she had used it on them. The release of pent-up frustration dissipated as she continued to introduce Axon to the hunter.

'All your family know my fiancé as Wolf, and if you don't mind, I prefer this name to be used while off world and off duty.'

'Off-duty! Like hell' Kayden shook out of her controlled force long enough to respond.

'We are going to spend some time together, Kayden. I have assured Aurek we will all enjoy this sanctioned visit that he has been kind enough to host.' Caitlin stared at him.

Kayden was instantly calmed by the essence of mutual friendship released into the atmosphere. *Cait Why?* He telepathically sent her a message before he was subdued by fragrance like no other. It lifted and left Kayden and Axon calmer. *Had it not affected Aurek?* Kayden was surprised, as Aurek had kept talking the entire time and was actually being polite.

'Wolf, so glad to put a face to the name. Glow never shuts up about you. And Kayden, if we must stay pleasant to please Glow here, then so be it. I'm happy to call a truce while she is in my home. She has convinced me I can trust you and even though I have my doubts, I do trust her.'

Kayden folded his arms. He had shaken off most of the agreeable magic. 'And I am yet to trust you!'

'Touché.'

'Okay, that's enough shop talk.' Caitlin grabbed hold of Aurek's arm again.

His devotion to her was noticeable as he turned to show them into the games room. Here they played billiards, darts and before long, the afternoon quickly turned into late evening. It was when Kayden got the hang of saying Aurek and not Orion, that they all started to relax. It was easy for Axon as it was normal to use aliases with his planet Rulers. Kayden found out first hand why Caitlin used other names. It had confused him when he heard she did this but he realised it was sure easier to get to know Orion when he was normal and not acting like a spoilt overbearing Ruler.

'Stay for dinner,' Aurek was quick to invite them, when he saw Kayden make a time-out signal to Axon.

'Sure, we'd love to stay for dinner,' Axon agreed and saw Kayden suck back. Axon put an arm around him. 'Tell me you're not under the thumb and have to get home to Cassie, you're kidding right?'

Kayden ended up agreeing to stay.

Axon knew how important this was to Cait during the early stages of talks and man, was she negotiating up a storm. He would be seeing how this played out but not for too long. He only had so much patience when it came to sharing his girl.

They ate dinner together and continued the competitive banter until they slurred, making no sense. It was then that Caitlin struggled with them to the guest rooms where they were to crash for the night. She told Kayden he was in no shape to sit on his horse, never mind control the trip home, so he followed the servant who unlocked the cabins by the pool.

Caitlin laughed at Axon as he told his last joke and dropped heavily on one of the beds.

Aurek had stopped to help Kayden who banged into a wall and, laughing, almost slid down it where he was happy to stay the night.

'No you don't.' Aurek slipped an arm around him and yanked him up. 'Come on big guy, I might not like you yet, but I'm sure not going to let you sleep there all night.'

'Ah, you like me then,' Kayden kidded.

'Don't go spreading that shit around. I like no man.' He laughed aloud and started Kayden off again. His foghorn outburst had the boys in fits all night.

Caitlin turned to see Kayden and Aurek arm in arm and wasn't sure which one carried whom, but they both fell together, face down on the larger of the beds. Both chuckled like schoolboys while sliding pillows under their heads and grunted and groaned as they kept their massive bodies from rolling onto the floor. Finally, they were asleep, and she curled up with Axon and dozed, her mind still trying to work out a plan to turn this war around.

Next morning, Caitlin woke up feeling bright, but the men suffered. She wondered if she had hit them with a bit too much magic as she had never seen Axon so drunk or wake with even a slight hangover. Aurek rolled from the bed and pressing a button, ordered breakfast to be served out on the patio. It wasn't far for them to go and, nursing sore heads, they sat around afterwards with coffee.

Feeling half human, Kayden put his cup down. 'Best we head back.' He frowned as he checked his messages on the NAVpager.

'What, you're not coming hunting with me today?' Aurek

blinked. 'I thought last night you said you were in.'

Axon shrugged. 'I vaguely remember talking about it.' He saw Caitlin wasn't ready to leave. She hadn't got what she came for but left it up to Kayden. They were in his zone and so they waited for the commander to decide.

'I suppose if a couple of girls like yourselves can't handle your booze, you definitely won't deal with blood and guts the next day hunting,' Aurek stirred.

'Girls, us!' Kayden threw his head back and laughed heartily with Axon.

'I have got a couple of NAVwheelers out there you can granny drive if you think you can keep up.'

'Stirring bastard! We'll see who can't keep up and comes home empty handed.' Kayden stuffed the NAVpager in his pocket. 'What do you want to do, Axon?'

'Don't have to ask me twice. Shoot, I can wangle a bit more time off if it's to kill something. Rory can handle things while I'm gone.'

Caitlin had her hold on the men, and they weren't going anywhere until this mess was sorted. She put her hand up. 'Me too, I'm in.'

'I don't think so, Glow. Told you before, men only.' Aurek tried to sound bossy. The truth was, he didn't want her anywhere near a possible hunting accident. His land was unforgiving at times, and mishaps occurred. It was rugged and just how he liked it.

'I'm a guest and should be treated equally!' she huffed and crossed her arms.

'Come on guys, help me out here,' grumbled Aurek.

Axon loved that she was using her stubbornness on someone else for a change and didn't intervene. *Give him stick, beautiful.*

Kayden shrugged. 'Doesn't worry me. She may be Glow to you and Red to us, but to a predator, she's trouble,' Kayden put in, unsure if Aurek was aware of her powers and in case he wasn't, left it at that.

The dry, hot morning turned to a sizzler by afternoon and to alleviate the heat, the men guzzled down Moonjuice while lugging guns and supplies. It gave Caitlin time to wander about, enjoying nature in its raw state.

On their return and after handing their catch to the servants, the loud, rowdy hunters dived into the swimming pool, and there they stayed; only getting out grabbing more bottles of Moonjuice as they ran out. With them sunburnt and acting the larrikins, it gave Caitlin time to wind down. Not having to use so much power to control them, she sun-baked and enjoyed their banter, sometimes entering into it but mostly allowing them time to bond alone. She hadn't realised how much alike Kayden and Axon were. They hit it off, but when they clashed, as both were so stubborn, she or Aurek had to mediate. Many times it was Aurek that stirred them up, and it was his underhanded cunning that amused her the most. *He is one funny guy,* she'd grin to herself. Finally, Kayden crashed on one of the pool lounges while Caitlin struggled and dumped Axon on a bed. His weight clumsily thumped on the mattress, and the crack of something left the bed at a funny angle. Out cold, she left him and went to find Aurek who had found relief on a tree and laughed at her poised shake of her head and hands on hips.

'Bed, now!' Her disciplinary tone made him laugh, but surprising her, he did as she asked and put an arm around her to allow Caitlin to struggle with his large uncoordinated body.

He noticed her deep sigh as he flopped onto the bed opposite Axon. 'See Glow, that's why I didn't want you to come. We men can be real tossers. Hunting triggers the testosterone,' he slurred.

She chuckled. 'It was an experience I'm pleased I got to experience. My sigh was a good one, relieved the three of you are unharmed and in bed.'

'You're a good mate, Glow Girl, and the prettiest friend I ever had.' His inebriated smile made her grin. 'Glow?' His voice trailed off.

'Yes.'

'Am I your best pal too?' He blinked, as if waiting for a blow.

'You're my newest best mate. I have Jett too, remember?'

'Ah! That's right, but only because that mongrel got to have you all to himself for days. Not fair Glow.'

Before Caitlin could think what she was saying, or think he would take her seriously the kidding words that came out next were a surprise to both. 'Well if you stop trying to blow up the Cloud Riders, Wolf might let me spend a few days with you as well.'

'Really!' He sat up straight and slurred, 'You better ask him Glow Girl, I like that deal.' And he fell down and went straight to sleep.

Axon had woken in time to hear her words. 'He'll blatzing well hold you to that,' he growled as Caitlin slipped into his arms for a cuddle.

'I was just messing about; he won't remember a thing tomorrow.' She pushed aside his concerns and fell asleep.

* * * *

Axon woke Caitlin with a kiss, and when she moved to get up, he pulled her back to bed. Caitlin squirmed out of the romantic arms. He moaned, wanting a few more minutes.

'We have company,' she whispered.

He put his head up and looked around. 'Ah, I remember now, we didn't get home again last night, did we?'

'I'll go rustle us up coffee.' She shifted from him and planted her feet on the ground before he could snatch her back to him again. She glanced over towards Aurek's bed. His eyes were wide as he watched her, and a slight smirk curled the corners of his mouth.

'I suppose I'd better get up and help or we all know what sort of a nasty-tasting coffee we'll end up with.' He shifted from the bed and stood lazily waiting for her to put on her shoes.

He led her into a large commercial-style kitchen. 'See this button here?' He pointed to a blue covered switch. 'When you're finished cooking and loading the dishwasher, you flick this blue baby and the whole room vacuum seals and is a massive big washing machine that cleans the walls, floors and benches.' One of my inventions to keep the help to a minimum. Over the years the trust has diminished with the continued war between Aldebaran and my Home World.'

'I saw some guards as we flew in, but they weren't great in numbers and I have seen only minimal domestic help. It must be concerning to you when you're on your own. You aren't one of the most favoured owners, and to top it off, you take so many risks.'

'Don't you worry your pretty little head about security, my sweet.' He almost gritted his teeth. With little confidence in the newfound relationship, he felt she pried into his affairs a bit too much at times, torn between their two worlds that were miles apart.

'Sorry, didn't mean to poke my nose into your business. Honestly, it doesn't interest me about how you protect yourself, I just wish to know that my best best new buddy has smarts enough to keep from harm. It would break my heart if anything were to happen to you.' She looked up affectionately.

Aurek saw this was genuine concern and cursed himself under his breath for the arrogant snipe. 'I have more than enough security and my army is strong and close. You just can't see them, but believe it when I say that even now, they are all around us.'

She touched his face affectionately. 'I need you to stay safe. You are important to me. Thank you for making me feel better.'

He looked down at the charming woman that with just in a blink of an eye had changed everything he knew to be true. For the first time ever, he knew exactly what she meant, for he too would do anything to keep her safe. It was then his heart clenched. *She will go today.* He needed more time, but why? He wasn't in love with her and yet there was something that encased him as he stared into her glistening emerald eyes, so enchanting, so divine.

The low vibration of need in his voice made her shudder as he said, 'I remember what you said last night. This is where we draw a line in the sand, where I find out if what you say I will always trust. I want you to stay a while longer – without them. Do you trust me or only while you are guarded? I want more from you, Glow, and need it if we are to go any further into this friendship.'

'Aurek, pl–ease.' She rolled her eyes. 'I've only just come home. Axon will have a fit if I do this to him right now. You know in your heart you can trust me.'

'Glow, it has to be now! You know I will honour your engagement plans to Axon. If you leave me like this, now, it will devastate me. He will have you for the rest of his lifetime. I ask for only three days of your time.'

'Why three?'

'I want to take you somewhere special. Somewhere you do nothing but nag of me to take you.'

She breathed in deeply and calmly exhaled. 'Oh, I see.' She gave him a grin. 'How much Moonjuice do you have here?'

'Plenty– why?'

'You better bring it out, 'cause we're going to need more than Axon drank last night for him to agree to this demand. You know he will want something in return.'

Aurek knew that but could promise her nothing; her words left him speechless.

Caitlin shrugged at the helpless silence. 'Don't worry. I'll see what I can do, anyway.'

Aurek turned with a heavy heart, worried he'd pushed something so new, so fragile. Still, he had to have her, and if it came down to it, Aurek would fight for her.

Axon and Kayden sat on the lounges around the pool while they waited for them to return. Aurek noted the fun was over as he handed Axon his coffee. They had showered, and their appearance was all business. It sent a clear message; this was the end of the visit and definitely, their last day.

Caitlin lowered herself quietly into one of the chairs and sipped her coffee while she eyed the three of them. Aurek had thrown her with his request, and she'd lost focus. Gone was the hold she had on the other two, and she sat powerless as Aurek's appearance altered also. His face was a mask of non-expression as it had been on their arrival. Ready for it or not, it looked as if it was time to stop the games and do what they came here to do.

Kayden leant forward, full of no-nonsense intent. 'What do we have to do to wrap up this meeting that will satisfy you enough to end the bitterness towards Taurus and us?'

Caitlin observed the strong Ruler. He was again, Orion. He's face was impassive; his strong square jaw set stubbornly, showing he was sticking to his fixed point of view. *This man has no intentions of backing down.*

To him, his terms were simple. 'I want a permit to hunt on Taurus. They have more than enough bulls, and I know you agree, Taurean steaks are like no other.'

Both men nodded in agreement and yet they all knew this could never be. Orion had to see sense, and the debate went on for a couple of hours until Caitlin thought her head would explode. The talks were going nowhere. Orion's frustration was evident, and she needed to come up with something, fast.

She stood up and poured two shots of Starstarter. Ignoring Axon and Kayden, she sat on a low stool in front of Orion and handed one to him and kept the other for herself. 'Cheers!' She lifted hers and swallowed the immortal elixir that was well known for its calming effects. However, by drinking it straight, the immortal male could become light-headed and agreeable or the opposite, moody and unpredictable. She wished for the light-headedness that would have him more pleasant.

Orion copied her with an eyebrow cocked, unsure what she was doing. She had her back to Axon and Kayden, deliberately cutting them off. This was between her and him now. She had regained her power and given them enough time.

'Aurek, tell me something. How long do the steaks last in your freezer? I'm referring to the expiry of the taste.'

'Six months, give or take.' Aurek had let go of the argumentative tone he held. Not knowing where she was going with it, he smiled within. First and foremost he was aware that he could trust her; figured Glow was taking over because she had come up with a plan. Finally, she was coming through for him, and it cemented all the reasons why he felt as he did about her. *She does have my best interests at heart.* He concentrated hard on her next question, wanting to give her every bit of information she required to make an informed decision. He would have loved to know what she was thinking. Jett told him she was a lateral thinker, so he waited in anticipation.

'And to fill this freezer of yours, how many days hunting would it take?'

'At least a couple of days.' An excited buzz stirred within him. Where was she going with this? He didn't care, he wanted it all, including her, and couldn't breathe for fear he might not end up with it.

'So it seems simple to me, and maybe Aldebaran will trade. You love to hunt, and Cassie tells me her father loves to fish. Maybe once every six months, you could spend one weekend on Taurus killing only what will fill your freezers. In the meantime, Aldebaran and his friend Conom can come here on that weekend, have a holiday on Orion's Belt and fish until they too, fill their freezers.'

There was silence for a minute before Kayden rubbed his chin thoughtfully. 'You know Aldebaran may just go for it. You're right. He and Conom enjoy fishing when they come and stay with us.'

She waited for Aurek to answer. Would he go for it?

'Glow!' said an irritable Orion.

Caitlin knew what he was getting at and lowered her head to think. He was no frills, do as I say, kind of guy. He had asked her kindly for three days of her time. If her commitment to stay would change his mood and have him consider the deal, it was worth throwing it in for good measures. *He had better be planning a hunting trip!* Suddenly she smiled, and her eyes sparkled as she thought of a way of them all getting what they want. *Me too!* Even with her head down, she could feel Orion and Axon's eyes burning into her. Orion's; with a need to have his last request met. Axon, aware of Caitlin's outburst the night before, knew this was why she had paused and would be daring her to consider it. At this point, she knew his reply was going to be a definite, No! Yet her need to end this peacefully overpowered the dedication to her fiancé.

She sent an apology to Kayden telepathically to pass on to Axon later. *Tell Axon I had no choice, Orion would not have given in without me. I have had to control him with too much power and with you leaving so soon, he is not yet ready to settle any other way. A couple of days and he'll be okay. I trust him and so should you.*

Don't be a fool. I will find another way, Kayden communicated back.

This is it, and you know it. You have tried everything, and you asked me to help. This is me helping. Not your way but the way the universe is asking me to handle it.

Closed to Kayden's further silent communication, she turned back to Aurek. His eyes fixed on her as he waited. His chin jutted out with obstinacy, his brows pressed together firmly. He wanted her too and wasn't going to let it go. She touched his cheek as she stood up and waved a hand in the air. 'Before Aurek agrees, I have a request of him.' She smiled at him as she tapped her chin in thought. 'He has asked for time with me, or there will be no deal.'

Orion nodded and eyed Kayden and Axon, daring them to interfere. Axon was about to open his mouth but clamped it shut. Caitlin knew Kayden had just spoken to him telepathically and their silence gave her the go-ahead to continue. The entire time she knew that if Axon disagreed he'd snatch her up and transport her out within seconds. She had to appeal to his honour.

'As a child, I had dreams. Books gave me hope there was more to life than the dungeon I called home. One of those dreams was to go hunting and experience the thrill of the chase, and I believe that dream almost ended when you, Orion (she could never lay the blame on Aurek), planted that bomb. I demand retribution so that the punishment fits the crime. You caused me much pain, and now I will become a pain in your side while you fulfil my wish to go on a professionally organised hunting trip.'

Aurek sat up straight. He didn't know what she meant about her childhood, but the others did, and it was working. Axon's eyes filled as her words stung. He had promised to take her and never got around to it. Aurek could see the guilt of a promise forgotten by a man very much in love. He felt for the guy, but his own needs overpowered his sentiment for Axon. His eyes rested back on the woman that was taking away the anger built up over time, melting it away with her cunning, but compassionate, nature.

She didn't miss Axon's hurt; another reason Orion cared for her. With an outstretched hand, she leant towards Axon and cupped her hand over his. 'I know you promised me, sweetheart, but circumstances have had us pulled in different directions. An opportunity has now presented itself for me to go with a fully experienced guide.'

'Only if Jett will vouch for Aurek. And only then,' Axon warned. He was not totally rolling over to the swine who was making her say this and who had now made him feel like a crap partner.

'So be it.' Caitlin glanced over at Orion who had calmed down. 'Surely this is the best solution to resolve it once and for all? Aurek gets his fully-negotiated demands, I get to go camping and hunting. Time off, Yay!' She rolled her eyes at Axon and made him grin. 'And – you and Kayden are back to DEFCON 5. We all get what we want.'

'Did Aurek say he would take you hunting?' Axon angled his head

'Nope, that was my idea.' She wiggled her head and flicked her hair back confidently.

Axon turned to Orion. 'This deal goes ahead only if my demands are now met. I want papers signed immediately to include no further harassment towards any Riders now or in the future. And this thing here, with you and her– Man have we got the better deal,' he ended with teasing jest. No use showing the grudge. He, like Kayden, wanted it over.

Caitlin slapped his arm. 'You'll keep!'

He pulled away. 'Ouch, that hurt!' He chuckled and glanced at Orion. He had a smirk, one that gloated, *say goodbye buddy, she's mine, I won.* Axon considered if he should wipe the sneer off his face, but Caitlin interrupted his plan. She spotted it too, and with hands on her hips, she huffed. Her green eyes flashed like a dagger to the heart and copper hair seemed to light up, confronting his arrogance.

'There is a condition attached to my time with you. You must promise me, Aurek takes me, Orion stays at home!' Her words cut into him although he had no idea why. *How did she do that?*

Axon smiled as the mean look disappeared quickly at her flare up. His girl snatched the malice from him as if her words came with a whip, the sensation of her temper stung, and he knew the feel of it well.

Axon had endured it once or twice himself, and even though Orion deserved it, he felt for the guy. With his dignity in tatters, Axon wasn't surprised when he almost bowed at her feet to get the forgiveness that would take away the wound to his very soul. Axon hid a grin and knew she was well and truly able to handle him and suddenly felt okay about letting her go. In a way, Orion was doing him a favour. He hated her being in the thick of danger as a Rider and for a few more days he could breathe lightly for she would be safe, away from it all. He doubted by the way Orion was with her, that anyone, even Zeus the god of all gods, would be able to take her from him.

Caitlin accepted his humble apology and, once sure it would be Aurek that took her hunting, an aura lit up around her that encased them both, and as it died down Aurek's features were soft, caring and Orion, for now, had gone.

With a clap of her hands, she released him from her magic. He was fine and what she had put in place was up to them to talk through and fix. She glanced at the pool. 'Well then, with that sorted I'll leave you men to discuss the finer details.' Her smile was infectious. 'I see a spa that calls for me.' She tossed her hair and, with hips swaying, wandered off.

'You'll need a costume,' Aurek called out.

Caitlin waved her arm. 'All good,' she said, and as she walked closer to the water, her gown disappeared, leaving a skimpy two-piece swimsuit in the same material as the dress. Axon gave her a whistle, and with a chuckle, Caitlin dived into the pool, swimming the rest of the way to the bubbling warmth of the spa.

'What the hell!' Her change of clothing took Aurek by surprise.

Kayden liked her style. She was one cool negotiator. She'd put a plan in motion and left him to finalise the deal, giving him back the control and his balls he thought he had lost. He wondered if he strangled her would anyone notice, and the idea made him chuckle to himself. 'Our Red is full of surprises; sure you still want to take her hunting? She's a handful.'

'No luggage to lug around. Hell yes!'

'She won't have her horse, so sorry mate; you'll need to provide a wardrobe for a princess.' Axon slapped his back as he stood and shaded his eyes to see where Caitlin had gone. She appeared at the end of the pool, and he relaxed when he spotted armed guards surround her while she was out of his reach and sat back down to chat.

'Sure, no probs, whatever she needs.' Aurek kept a shield up to protect how he felt until the talks were over, but Axon could see how happy he was to spend time with her, his eyes saying it all.

The spa was warm. Caitlin lay back, enjoying her time alone, only to look up occasionally to see either Kayden or Axon talking on their mini NAVcom's, away from the meeting, apparently discussing it with Zoren.

The last conversation Caitlin overheard was Kayden's speaking to the wizard, Aldebaran. He invited him and Conom for talks, and it sounded as if the two notorious warlords had accepted and were on their way. Smiling at how quickly these guys moved from one Home World to the next, she figured they would be transporting in at any minute.

Aldebaran and Conom arrived, and the men huddled in a circle, the volume on the heated conversation becoming louder by the minute. It was for this reason only that she decided to join them and intervene. Out of the spa, she allowed the magic of her horse to ready her and dressed to impress. A clear of her throat caught their attention long enough for them to look up at her.

Kayden stood up. 'Ah, here's Caitlin now,' he introduced her to the men who had been quite boisterous.

She nodded and shook the first outstretched hand. 'Aldebaran, your daughter talks highly of her father. It's an honour to meet someone so wise.' She shook Conom's hand. 'Cassie tells me you are her hero, who saved her from certain death, and more than once. She tells me you are the Ruler of the fertile lands of Monoceros, Home World of the Unicorn.' She smiled, and added, 'and you're every bit as handsome as she describes you.'

'She actually said that?' He grinned, his face lit up and pumped out his chest at Kayden.

'Piss me off, and we will be the ones with the problem,' Kayden warned him and sat back ignoring Conom who laughed heartily.

Conom was the loudest and most irritated of the group, so she worked on him first. 'That means you live next door to Orion?' she said to Conom.

'Yes, Orion and I go way back. I have been here many times in the past.'

'Then if you know your way around, maybe you could escort me while I stretch my legs. It's that or have a guard stomp beside me like a herd of baby rhinoceroses.' Her magic was so strong not one of them could look away. Conom stood, and she slipped her arm through his. 'Aldebaran, are you coming?' She gazed at him with stunning green eyes that charmed him.

'One of yours, no doubt?' Aldebaran glanced at Axon.

He grinned. 'Yep, and she's mine, so keep your minds on the deal.'

Amused, Aldebaran stood, taking up her offer. His eyes not leaving Kayden, he said, 'this is my first visit, so maybe a short stroll will allow me to discuss this deal in private with Conom. That's if Caitlin is as good at keeping secrets as my Cassie.'

'She is a Rider, Ald, stop worrying,' Conom answered.

Caitlin smiled. 'Now we have that sorted,' she said as she eyed both men, 'I believe we can walk and at the same time maybe the two of you will get to see what's on offer here?'

Conom, amused by her ability to make him warm to her so suddenly, patted her hand. 'Not sure it will do any good but guess it can't hurt.'

Once she had their attention, her magic eased, and both men breathed out a sigh. Now they had calmed she relaxed too, and the walk became less tense.

'I'm going hunting myself you know, not on Taurus, but my first adventure in the wild. Orion has a debt to pay to me,' she casually mentioned and chuckled. 'The poor man has no idea what he's in for.' Caitlin continued to entertain them, mostly with stories of her time with Cassie whom she knew they loved to hear about. They wandered around the chalets to the back of them. Here, Caitlin stood quiet, allowing them to reflect upon the view and hoping it was of interest to them.

'It's changed since last I was here. Hell, Orion's built chalets and each one has a private jetty that includes a boat; the dude's gone all civilised.' Conom scratched his chin in thought. 'This could work, Ald.'

'Isn't that the River Eridanus?' Aldebaran pointed.

'Runs for miles. Darn good waters for breeding giant perch. Wouldn't mind taking a few of them beauties home.' Conom licked his lips.

It was then Caitlin couldn't help but give them a hard time about their capabilities as fishermen. It was after a few laughs the conversation became serious.

'It's a deal then?' Conom turned to Aldebaran.

'It looks that way,' Aldebaran replied. 'And that's only due to Caitlin. If it were not for her showing us the benefits of this deal, we'd still be at the table arguing.'

Conom eyed her. 'And I take it, this swapping of venues to hunt and fish was your idea.'

'Only if you like it?' Caitlin raised her brow and grinned.

'Not just like.' Aldebaran's gaze swept the river and boats. 'Can't wait.'

'Is this deal only for us or can we bring a guest?' Conom asked, and Caitlin realised he meant Cassie.

They both stared at her. 'Look, take it to the table. I'm sure Cassie will be more than welcome.'

'You think you know me that well, that Cassie is who I meant.' Conom was suddenly irritable.

'Conom, seriously. I know you're one of Cassie's guardians and I mention her name and your face lights up.' She smiled. 'But let that just be mine and Aldebaran's secret. I promise we are the only ones who can see it.'

He spun his head to Aldebaran. 'You see it too.'

Aldebaran slapped his back. 'Mate, this Rider is different. You saw it the minute she stood in front of us. Of course, she sees right through us both. Even knew when to stop using her power on us. She is one talented cookie. As for me… are you kidding me you're not in love with my goddamned daughter? Blatzing shithead.'

Conom stared at Caitlin, and within seconds his shoulders had relaxed. He was one scary individual when angry, but to her credit, she stood up to him as Cassie had done and he liked it. 'Don't like redheads.'

Caitlin grinned. 'Good, Axon will be thrilled. I don't like men with tattoos.'

He laughed and was back to the calm man she had stood with earlier. She was amazed it took no power that time to control him, just guts.

'Ready to go back and tell the guys your decision?' Caitlin was pleased it was moving along nicely, but these powerful men could change their minds in a split second. She wanted them talking sooner rather than later.

Aldebaran folded his arms, and looked at her thoughtfully. 'You have admitted this was your plan from the start. If this is to go down, it does so with your stamp. I think I talk for both Conom and me when I say we have confidence in you, and you alone. Last time there was a loophole, and it left us exposed. This time I want this ironclad, as I don't know, nor will I ever, trust Orion.'

'You're damned right there, Ald,' Conom agreed.

'Then trust me!' Caitlin spoke to them both of how she saw it and they agreed with a handshake. The deal was done, and the decision was made. As they walked back to the others, she hoped they were strong enough characters not to go back on their word. Only she didn't figure on Aldebaran's intuition.

'By the way, this entire thing was ingenious of you, Caitlin.' He viewed her slyly as they walked.

She flicked her hair and lifted up her face in a cheeky self-assured way. She had let Aldebaran believe he was the stronger by easing off on her magic but she wondered if she should take control of him until papers were signed. Instead, she decided to hear him out. Cassie said he was a stirrer.

'You can't con a conner young lady,' he continued.

'Why Aldebaran,' she said with poise and with an upper-class tone. 'I have no idea what you mean.' His next move surprised her, and she squealed when he picked her up over his shoulder and carried her back, dumping her in the pool. She had not expected this playful side, although she should have known that, being Cassie's father, he would be spontaneous. She came to the surface, gulped for air and at the same time lifted up her hand and flicked her powers lightly towards him. This put Aldebaran off balance, and he too tumbled in. Caitlin laughed so much she nearly choked as they pulled themselves up on the edge of the pool to dry off.

Aldebaran's expensive shoes were now ruined.

'Sorry about the Berlutis.'

'I did ask for it. You and Cassie have far too much in common. But I like you, Red, and she likes you too.'

'Cassie told you about me, then?'

'I know your powers, and know she likes you.'

'So I wasted them on you?'

'It was fun, but don't muck with me again or else, deal?'

'Deal.'

He stood up and pulled her up, using his own powers to transform them back into dry clothes.

'Wow, good job.'

'Yes, I can do that too.' Aldebaran grinned. 'Where do you think Cassie got it from? Certainly not her wretch of a mother.'

Caitlin was suddenly taken by the hand and moved by Orion. He now stood between her and Aldebaran. 'Leave her the hell alone, or you deal with me personally.' His nostrils flared as he turned to Axon. 'And you're just going to sit there and do nothing while this evil little man treats her so appallingly.'

'I'm okay.' Caitlin was surprised he had worried.

Aldebaran kept calm as he spoke, which surprised them all. 'Axon has trust in all his Riders, even the females in his team. They are well equipped with the power to handle even, as you so rudely stated, an evil little man such as me.'

Conom intervened. 'I would watch what you say next, Orion. Caitlin is the only reason we have agreed to this sneaky goddamned treaty. And after you have apologised to Ald, you would do well to trust in her as we do.'

'What, so it's a deal.' Orion's mood instantly changed and he grinned in his strange blokey way and made them smile too.

'Deal!' Aldebaran shook his head. 'How the hell I still agree to it after this just went down between us is beyond me, but it's done.'

Conom stood with his arms crossed, the muscles flexing. 'Caitlin has our backs, she promised us she will handle the treaty so if it isn't the way the redhead just made us see it, we know you didn't listen, and we're coming back for revenge.'

With nose in the air, Caitlin huffed at them and tossed her hair to the side. 'That will not be necessary and to prove how true to my word I can be, I have organised a little replacement for me while I go and arrange for the contract to be drawn up and pack a bag for my hunting trip. Someone I am sure you will all enjoy the evening with.' She put out her hand. 'Axon can you take me home?'

I guess I'm leaving.' Axon stood up.

'Hey, that's not playing fair. We were expecting at least a few drinks to seal the deal. Maybe a few laughs.' Conom eyed her, his frown noticeable.

'Oh, I think you'll still enjoy yourselves pretty much.'

Caitlin pointed to the sky, where a horse appeared through the overhead clouds. 'This party is only just about to start. Have fun boys.'

'Cassie!' Kayden, Aldebaran and Conom said at once, grins from ear to ear.

'She's good!' Aldebaran squinted his eyes at the glare, a suspicious smile at Caitlin.

'Hell, she's better than good.' Kayden kissed her head as he raced past her to meet his woman.

Aurek, shocked by her sudden departure plans, looked confused.

'You can pick me up tomorrow.' She blew him a kiss as Axon transported her out, not waiting for a second longer to have time alone with her before she left him again.

Axon's last line of sight was Aurek, well Orion. The pet name had begun to stick. The man had the biggest smile on his mug, and his damned woman had put it there. 'Mongrel for taking my woman hunting,' he mouthed, and Aurek broke up laughing. What he replied, Axon didn't care. She was his for the next eighteen hours.

* * * *

On Ara and while Caitlin packed, Axon spoke to Jett.

'That sneaky flaming nephew of mine is going to take her where?'

'Hunting at some private location; he won't tell me where, that's the only thing.'

'It's okay, I can track her if I think she's in any trouble.'

'That eases my mind. With you keeping an eye on her too, she should be right then.'

'Can't talk her out of it?'

'Nope! She tells me I'm not her husband yet so I can't order her around.'

'Sounds like Glow. Oh well, if her mind is made up, all we can do is keep tabs on them. If he is as good with her as he was here, there shouldn't be any issues. If not, I'll personally wring my nephew's damned neck.'

Axon was pleased he could rely on a god such as Hades. Caitlin had done a remarkable job with him, but he also knew with all these men she had falling at her feet, he was going to have to step up and be more to her than them. It was him that wanted to be waiting at the end of the aisle when she said, I do. He had already started to understand the way the universe pushed her in different directions and each time, so far, it was for an outcome he could never have achieved so simply. He hung up, feeling much better. His intention would be to discuss the wedding when she returned, and he didn't want any more excuses from her. *Now, to find my woman and make her forget every other man alive.* He was on his own mission now.

Chapter Thirty-Seven

Hunting in the Wild

Hesitant on how to dress for something like a camping trip, Caitlin decided to put on shorts and thinly strapped singlet over a pair of bathers. Not having her magical beast to clothe her, she had to be prepared. All Aurek would give away was that the days were sometimes windy but humid and warm, nights cool. This had her try many hairstyles. In the end, braided sides were secured and clipped up with the rest of her hair. With sunnies tucked on her head for later, she had only just bent down to tie up her hiking boots when she heard voices.

Aurek had arrived, and Caitlin moved from her room and leant over the top floor landing. 'Hi there, shorts and hikers okay?'

'Perfect.' Aurek sounded bright and grinned as he watched her run down the steps. She was glad they were alone, except for Nigel who fussed as she reached the bottom of the stairs, slipping on her backpack.

'Is Axon here to see you off?' Aurek glanced around.

'Nope, he's gone. Axon and the team had a call out early, so it's just us. Whenever you're ready, we can leave.' She thanked Nigel, and he stood away from them.

Aurek didn't have to be told twice. He was impatient to get an early start. With an arm around her shoulders, he transported them from her Home World, Ara.

Goddess of Peace

* * * *

Caitlin blinked with the bright sunlight and slid her sunglasses over her eyes. A log cabin came into view, and by the thinness of the air, she knew they were up high on a mountain. The valley below was a long way down, and even the river that ran between the mountains seemed so far away.

'It's so green – peaceful – silent – not even the whistle of a bird and I get the strongest scent of pine and lavender.'

'I'm glad it pleases you.' He bent and picked up some pre-chopped wood from a pile beside the cabin and motioned for her to do the same. 'The appeal of a good hunting trip is to cook what you catch.'

Caitlin struggled to pick up even one of the thick logs. 'Guess we're going to starve then.' She shrugged, dusted her hands, straightened and followed him inside, empty-handed.

Once he dumped the wood by the fireplace, he turned and shook his head at her. 'Sit down while I get another armful.'

You don't have to tell me twice. The backpack was shrugged off her shoulders, and with a grin, she flopped onto the sofa and stretched out, arms under her head. 'Well, come on! Quickly now!'

'Up, lady muck!' He helped her back to her feet. 'Not letting you get away with that behaviour. One in, all in.' He bullied her until he saw her hands and the ripped skin from the attempt to help. 'Really, are your hands that delicate?' He looked upset. 'I know they felt soft, but geez Glow, you poor little pumpkin. And here you are acting all tough as if you didn't hurt yourself.'

'I'm sorry. I should have warned you how much work I am.'

He lifted her onto the bench and from a first aid kit in the drawer, dabbed her grazed skin with lotion and laid a plaster across each hand. 'Please tell me in future to stuff off if I go flinging orders. I'm just not used to having someone so fragile.' He kissed her hand, and the kindness made her smiled so brightly she glowed, literally. It took him by surprise, and he stepped back as the glow highlighted her hands before disappearing.

Caitlin chuckled at his reaction while she removed the plasters, and the afterglow took away the redness it left. 'See, not so fragile after all. It's better now.'

'I know to be one of the Riders you are powerful, but to heal yourself, that's beyond cool.' He was flabbergasted. 'The name Glow. That's how you got it isn't it?'

'Yes, but sadly I didn't do this.' She held up healed hands. 'My team mustn't be too far away from us, and it's their magic I must have just tapped into. No – unfortunately I can't just do it myself.'

'That's right, you mentioned they had left when I got there this morning. Hope I have you to myself.'

He saw her listen for something and smile. 'Yes, all yours.'

'Bet they were ticked off.'

'That isn't the word for it. The boys would have loved this, but even so, Rory would never intrude. No– they are up there somewhere working their tails off while I partake in this little adventure all on my own.'

'With me!'

'The two of us.'

'Well, I'm happy today you were able to fix what I caused. You are off kitchen duties, soldier.' He held her hand and searched for marks, but there was none. 'Sorry, Glow.'

'Accepted.' Caitlin jumped off the bench. 'Now I'm better, can we go?' The warmth of light in her eyes flickered with excitement, and with it, Aurek felt a sudden adrenalin rush. In fast motion, almost quicker than the eye could follow, he had gone out, got another load of wood, placed it by the hearth and stood back in front of her.

'Now we can go.' He laughed as she slipped her arm through his, ready for transportation.

'This time, lazy one – we walk.' He picked up his backpack, tossed it over one shoulder, a gun over the other and left Caitlin to follow as they trudged along a narrow dirt track that took them farther up the mountain.

Yellow flowers brushed soft against her legs, and she couldn't resist the urge to stop and touch them, which caused her to lag behind. Aurek saw her interest and thought her unusual that even the slightest things gave her such pleasure, so he picked one and put it in her hair. 'A keepsake.'

He liked her smile and wondered if this trip was about hunting for either one of them. A ladybird that crawled on a branch now fascinated her. The intense expression as it now crawled on her hand was like a child's and yet he knew her strengths; she fascinated him.

Higher up the hill, the air was thinner, and he heard her puffing and stumble at times after him. He stirred about her unfit state when she plonked down on a rock and drank a full bottle of water. 'Too much lying around with that uncle of mine, he's spoilt you, made you lazy.'

Instead of the usual teasing reply, her hand went up to stop him. 'What's that sound?' she whispered.

There was dense bush not far from them and dropping down his backpack, gun in hand, he crept slowly towards it. 'What do you want to catch for dinner? It may be a rabitto.' He had them on their bellies waiting for it to come out.

'Fish!' she whispered and chuckled at his stunned look. 'Just mucking with your head.'

He ignored her fooling around, rested the gun in her arms and held it steady for her. Knowing now how fragile his new friend was, he held it tight, so the force of it going off didn't leave a bruise on her shoulder. Once aimed, he got her to squeeze the trigger. The sound made her jump.

'That shut you up didn't it? I bet life became real without the magic of your horse protecting you from sounds.'

'Hell yes. Now I know I've been spoilt. That was loud.' She slapped him playfully, 'What happened to health and safety? Where are my blatzing earmuffs and goddamned safety glasses, rotten shytzter?' It amused her to continue giving him a hard time until her ears stopped ringing. 'Anyway…' Her attention was back on the rabitto. 'Did we get it? I'm not doing that again.'

'Direct hit. You got it, babe.' He put the gun on lock and swung it over his shoulder.

Suddenly her mood lifted. 'Wahoo! She jumped up and high-fived his outstretched hand.

They retrieved their kill, but all the bantering and laughing had scared the rest of the creatures off. The one they did get they took over to a little stream nearby. Here, Aurek cleaned, gutted and washing it in the fresh water before securing it tightly in a sack. As he worked, her fascination with all that surrounded them spiked curiosity. 'Where are we? You can tell me now, I can't blab where we are going to be followed.' She chuckled at his half grin. 'I mean, the Ruler from here must be so proud. This land is so plentiful and alive.'

'This is the Home World of Mensa, named after the Ruler, Lord Mensa. This is one of my favourite constellations to frequent. The two of us have shared many hunting trips and go way back.' He gestured towards the hills. 'These are the Table Mountains of Mensa. When we get over the next rise, you should get a good view of his homeland if the mist has lifted by then.'

At the top, Aurek stood holding Caitlin on a cliff edge so she could see the village below. 'It's old English culture, only this one's not in ruins.' A few loose rocks fell as she strained to peer further over the steep overhang.

'I gotcha,' Aurek calmed her when she became nervous.

The castle below had been built into a mountain, and the architecture was quite exquisite. The roofs of the cottages towered up like witches' hats, and a massive stone wall appeared to run around the full length of the township. She couldn't help but get a warm feeling about the people; living so close to each other they would surely have to be a friendly community.

'It's so charming and check out the gardens. How meticulous are they!'

He was pleased she liked it and enjoyed her company as she chatted happily about what their lives must be like, while he steered them in search of some quail he knew rested not far away.

The journey back to the lake was educational, and Caitlin enjoyed every second of it. Aurek amused her when he snaked along the ground, aiming the gun up and to the left of him towards some quail. He was a big man and how he thought he was camouflaged was beyond her, but he did get his prey.

As they sat by the waters' edge, Aurek showed how to pluck the birds while they were still warm. The feathers easily came out. A quick wash and they were in the bag with the rabitto.

She slapped her hands together to remove the fluffy residue before removing her shorts and a tank top and diving into the coolness. She was glad she had decided to wear a bikini underneath. The swim down proved to be further than she thought although she delighted at the clarity of the water, the bottom so visible she could see every brightly coloured stone. After a gasp for air and diving back down she went to retrieve one of the odd pebbles that caught her eye. Lifting out of the water and resting on a ledge, she washed the sand from it and admired the tones in the green stone.

Aurek joined her to see what she had discovered. He wasn't surprised she had found something else to amuse her. It seemed, no matter where he took her, he too felt her joy of seeing this Home World for the first time. He wanted to study nature at its finest through her eyes.

'What have you found this time?' He sat beside her.

'Not sure, thought it might be a gem.' She held her hand out flat so he could see.

'Ah – that is Torpez stones. This is the only world you will ever find them.' He picked it up and held it to her neck. 'Matches your eyes, and it would make a most impressive pendant.' He handed it back. 'Take it back with you.'

Her giggle muffled as she dived back down and positioned it where she found it. When she came up empty handed, Aurek looked confused.

'I'd never take something so precious that doesn't belong to me unless the owner wanted me to have one. It belongs here for others to find and admire.'

He shook his head. 'You are one good young lady. I need to teach you to be a bad girl or those gods will eat you alive when you go back to work.'

'I can be bad.' She pulled a school teacher face that he laughed at.

'Sure you can. How about we go and explore a little before that goody two shoe thing you have going on rubs off.' He took her outstretched hand and pulled her out of the water. 'I saw something go in behind the waterfall. Maybe there's a cavity where we can catch something other than a stone.'

Both climbed the embankment and followed a slippery path behind the waterfall and into a cave. Caitlin ducked around Aurek and straight in ahead of him. He followed quickly, ready to snatch her up if there was something dangerous in it.

'You've got no fear,' he scolded. 'What if you're confronted by a begrizzo or who knows what else lives here?'

'Then you can take out your big gun and shoot it.'

'That's of course if I had it on me,' he retorted, unamused she was taking this so calmly. He had to take good care of her, and if she got even a scratch, he felt sure Axon would wring his neck.

She slipped her hand in his. 'Come on, don't wimp out on me now.' She pulled at him to keep walking.

They got to an underground chamber, which gave them three options. As Aurek debated what tunnel to take first, she lunged at him from behind, making him think it was something coming at him. He jumped, and her squeal of delight cracked them both up as it echoed so loudly. A flutter from birds she'd scared had their eyes flick up to the roof where glow-worms rested, and their brightness lit up the cave. 'Keep that up Glow, and I'll throw you over my shoulder and take you home,' he threatened.

She grinned. 'Okay, I promise to behave.' She kept her fingers crossed behind her back. *Sure! Call me a goody two shoes!* She chuckled silently.

The first corridor led nowhere. The second led into a cave of bats that hung upside down. The things were so big they were the size of a small human. It got her thinking. 'Maybe vampires live here, and this is their incubator. Bet they're in the next cave hanging by their human-like feet. If they chase us, I'll protect you.'

'Glow, you're worse than taking a kid hunting, you've got such a vivid imagination,' said Aurek, as they entered the next tunnel. 'Anyway,' he humoured her, 'even if they did exist they could not exist in this hot sunny climate.'

Caitlin held his arm tightly, not giving in to his factual statement. 'But I didn't believe immortals existed until I became one,' she whispered and ran off from him into the next cave.

There were no vampires; in fact nothing much of interest, but even before Caitlin got to the entrance he had snatched her up and was looking around to make sure it was safe. Her giggle got him going, and he laughed with her. 'I just wanted to show you I can be a bad girl.' Yet in his arms she became serious. 'My saviour! You'll never let me come to any harm now, will you?'

'No – I won't, but no more testing or being bad from now on, well not until you go home. Then give that boyfriend of your hell for me. The blatzing sly dog gets to laugh like this all the time.'

He teased, but did he? She saw a serious side as he put her down. *Maybe I should come clean and show him I can look after myself...* Yet for some reason she enjoyed seeing him so attentive. She guessed by his reactions this was the first time he had actually cared about anyone.

'You really know how to rattle a guy, Glow.'

'Girl!' She hadn't finished having fun with him and ran out of the cave and at the bank, kept going and did a racing dive in the water. Aurek followed, and they swam freestyle back to the opposite side. The laughter echoed as they clumsily scampered up the bank and out the water, running and shoving each other until they reached their towels where they dried off.

'Give you girl – you're the bad girl. For that, you carry the catch all the way home.'

'My pleasure. At least you can't say I didn't help and make me starve.'

They had walked only a few paces when he took the catch off his struggling hunting buddy. She was quiet, and he hated it.

* * * *

When they got back, Caitlin poked around the fire after he lit it and kept it from going out while Aurek got the vegetables from the pantry. Once he began preparing the food, she walked over to talk. 'Where did all these fresh ingredients come from?' She leant over the bench, munching on a piece of raw carrot.

'Lord Mensa had his chef stock the pantry for us.' He saw a look of concern. 'Don't worry, we have this cabin to ourselves. I told Lord Mensa there was to be a female guest, so doubt we'll see anyone in this area. He won't be expecting me to do much hunting either – if you know what I mean.' He raised an eyebrow. 'Only way I could get him to leave us alone.'

Her smile told him all he needed to know. She was happy just to be with him too. He didn't think he would enjoy this as much with a woman, but so far she had been nothing but a pleasure to spend time with. 'Here, want to help?'

She pulled a face and blinked. 'You're game. Sure, I'll give it a go.' She took the peeler from him and started to take the skin off the potatoes and carrots. While they worked, they shared a bottle of Moonjuice and chatted, with the peeler becoming the butt of most the jokes as she wrestled with it. 'Stupid thing, I give up.' She picked up the empty goblets. 'I'll pour us another drink.'

Aurek shook his head. 'For someone that's a part of the strongest crack team in the galaxy, girl, you're hopeless in the kitchen.'

'Hey – if you want me to blow the damned skin off, just ask. Peel it, forget that. My brain doesn't work that slowly.'

He shook his head, giving up.

They ate and, once tucked up in their sleeping bags, Aurek told her hunting stories until they fell asleep in front of the fire.

* * * *

In the morning, she stirred in his arms and her annoyed shove woke him. 'Are you right there, Romeo?'

'Cookies and cream?' This was his apology as he rolled over and pulled himself up. 'It got so intense I couldn't resist you any longer, and when I cuddled into you, it must have been what you needed, because the sweet scent just evaporated into thin air. I experimented and moved away from you, and it happened again. You have some built-in security system. It draws those around you in to protect you – very canny.'

'Oh that! I thought you were coming on to me.'

'Not likely. Not scared of Axon, but scared to death of my Uncle Jett.' He raised an amused eyebrow.

'I have no idea why it kicked in last night and no clue how to control it yet. Guess you made me feel safe so thank you for that, but I think we will keep it from Jett. I agree, with the two of us alone and sleeping together, you might end up in the Underworld.' She grinned while putting her socks on.

'Would have been worth it if the redhead was a bit more mischievous but seems I got none, so not worth mentioning.'

'Sod off!' She pushed at him. 'The only thing you will feel from me is my wrath, buddy.'

He lay on his back. 'Here you go, make me want to hug you and love you to bits. Then in the morning, you just dump me like a discarded old security blanket. Push me away and leave me with hurt feelings that I'm not good enough for you.' He sounded dejected.

'Aurek, you're so full of it. As if any woman would ever hurt your feelings. You've got enough egos to last ten lifetimes. As for being my security blanket, I promise not to discard you until we leave here. Then I'll dump your fine arse for someone else, as I always do.' She rolled around the bedding in hysterics. He tickled her, making her laugh more.

'Little witch. I won't let you forget me, and you won't be dumping me for anyone. You're my girlfriend now, and Jett can buzz off.'

Aurek checked his watch and stopped fooling about. He pulled her to her feet. 'Quick– or we won't make it.'

He tossed her some warm clothes and a thick jacket and made a flask of coffee while she dressed. Trudging back up the hill Caitlin kept up but wondered why he was so keen to be somewhere this early in the morning. At the top, breathless but glad of the exercise,

Caitlin flopped down beside him and took the coffee he handed her.

'I think you'll like this.' He pointed to the darkened space before them. Her eyes followed his view.

Dawn broke and the sunrise shot across the sky. Vibrant colours burst above them. Where the horizon met water; the mirror image threw out a mirage that took on the appearance of a big ball of fire in 3D that soared across the air above. It was as if the sun was right in front of them, but she knew that wasn't possible. It was a fantastic illusion, and she leant against Aurek, glad he'd dragged her out of bed to share it with her.

* * * *

After a long chat, they made their way back down the hill and between the mountains, came to a valley of massive rocks.

'Hey there, come and join me,' a voice called to them.

Aurek waved and gave Caitlin an apologetic frown as they headed towards the person who had suddenly disappeared into a cave.

'Who's your friend?'

'It's just Lord Mensa. No doubt he has his sights on something. He gets so self-absorbed, it's a wonder he even noticed us. Guess I can't be rude. Let's go say a quick hello and be on our way.'

At the entrance, the darkness made it hard to see, so Aurek took her hand to lead her inside. Deep inside the cavern, they found Lord Mensa digging around for bugs in the rocks. He glanced for only a second at them before filling up his bag with the bugs he'd collected. As an immortal, he may have been hundreds of years old, but Caitlin thought he looked in his early forties, as intense steel grey eyes peered out from an unruly hairy face. The solid build suggested he kept his physique in tip-top shape and somehow, now facing them, he gave off a vibe that left her feeling at ease around him.

'I am Lord Mensa; and you are?' He put his hand out to her in a friendly greeting manner.

'Caitlin Warner.' She stepped towards him and shook his hand, not sure why she used her real name.

'She prefers to be called Glow Girl,' Aurek added.

'Well, I can certainly see why – for you are just glowing.'

'The fresh air and warm weather are just what I needed.'

'Glad you are enjoying my Home World.'

She smiled at the kindly gentleman. 'Yes, I'm having the best time. Aurek's has needed a lot of patience teaching me to hunt.'

'And knowing my boy, no doubt there were plenty of entertaining stories.'

He eyed Aurek. 'You call him Aurek; remarkable. Good nickname for the lug. I kept telling him to cut those locks off so he can get himself a real woman, but he won't listen to me. Maybe you can convince him, Glow.'

'First impressions always count, so please excuse me when I disagree. I think the locks make him look hot.'

Aurek stretched and tilted his nose up. 'The girl's got good taste.'

Lord Mensa scoffed and laughed. 'Honesty is refreshing and very rare these days but a little misplaced on him.' He threw the hunting bag over his shoulder and picked up a rifle.

'Where are you heading?' Aurek asked.

'I'm going down the valley to the South Mountain. I want to see if I can track that big begrizzo we went after the last visit. He's been harassing the townsfolk, killing the stock.'

Caitlin didn't miss the show of disappointment in Aurek. 'I take it you mean a grizzly bear?'

'Yes, and I can tell you're not from these parts. Earth roots?' Lord Mensa questioned.

'She spent some years there studying.' Aurek told him a little white lie to cover up she was actually from there, although Caitlin wasn't sure why. He was a good friend. Secrets weren't usually kept from mates.

Caitlin agreed, and nothing more was said. But she could feel the adrenaline rush coming from Aurek once he heard what Lord Mensa was going after. To hunt something so dangerous and significant, he would be in his element. Caitlin slipped her arm through his. 'We'd like company if you don't mind ours. I'm sure you wouldn't knock back the offer of a couple of extra hands to help trap that old bear.' She felt Aurek squeeze into her, excitedly, showing he could think of nothing better than to join in the hunt.

'Sure!' Lord Mensa's optimistic look was no surprise to, Caitlin. She had guessed he was about to invite them anyway. She eyed him. There was something astute about him, maybe he had even planned to be here to catch up with Aurek and get his help. *He would surely know Aurek would take me to see the sunrise this morning to begin our second day.*

'If we leave now, we can be in big rock canyon by mid-morning.' Lord Mensa took the lead up a path leading away from the rocky terrain. Here they passed a cobblestone path that took them to an old brick cottage.

Caitlin had always loved the character of buildings, and this charming little café had it all. It was surrounded by delicate leafy trees, vivid floral natives, and positioned within this setting were animal-shaped chairs and tables with claw legs. A kindly elderly woman, complete with a frilled apron and hat, waited on patrons and waved as they passed.

'I always thought when men talked about camping it meant roughing it in the bush. You know – with bugs and spiders crawling all over you, freezing at night and eating maggots from a tree when you all got so drunk you couldn't shoot straight enough to catch anything. Yet here I am, sleeping in a log cabin with a fire and passing cafés in the middle of nowhere, an endorsement of how many hunters go home with full bellies but empty-handed.'

Aurek gulped and stumbled over words as he tried to give her an answer.

She put her hand up. 'It's time to admit it's all make-believe, a con of adversity to keep us women at home.' She laughed at their shocked expressions. 'I'm right aren't I?'

Aurek composed himself. 'Look here, young lady, you ever tell anyone our secret, and you're in big trouble.' His tone serious.

'Bully!' She grinned. 'You are so going down when I find you a girlfriend.'

'You are my girlfriend.'

'Tell Wolf that to his face.'

'He's just your fiancé, not going to argue with the man, just stealing you from Jett.'

Lord Mensa slowed to talk. 'Okay! This is getting hard to follow. I thought you two were an item. Who are these other two?'

'Don't even try to work it out, buddy; she has a string of us bowing at her feet. I'm just evening out the playing field and telling her how it is. I figure I have a couple more days to brainwash her before I take her back, and that should just about do it.' Aurek eyed her devotedly.

'In your dreams, sugar!'

'See what I go through? She has me jumping through hoops for her, and all I get is attitude.'

'You sound like an old married couple.' Lord Mensa walked to his left to miss fresh cow dung.

'No fun Lord,' she said and nudged Aurek.

'Do you two ever shut up?' He picked up the pace and ignored them. Both turned on him instead of each other.

A little way up a muddy path he stopped for a second and turned to them. 'I wish I had never tried to break you two up. Please, feel free to go back to rubbishing each other again.'

'No way, you make us laugh more.' Caitlin ruffled his hair as they scooted past him.

'You won't beat her, buddy, so you know what they say,' Aurek said.

'Can't beat 'em, join 'em.' Lord Mensa finished the cliché.

'Yep! And if we don't hurry up and get in the lead, she's going to go in the wrong direction, and there will be another half hour of bantering with her before we move on.'

Lord Mensa held Aurek back for a second. 'I like your friend – a lot.'

'Me too,' Aurek agreed but thought it strange of him to say so soon after meeting her, and she didn't even have her cookie fragrance turned up. He moved quickly into the lead to get them to the canyon where they thought the bear hid. The less time she spent with his friend, the better. Didn't want him tagging along once they left him to go back to the cabin. It was his time with Caitlin; there was not going to be any competition hanging about if he had his way. But much to his displeasure, Lord Mensa hung back with Caitlin and chatted to her the rest of the way. Mad as hell, he stomped ahead.

Her wit and yet innocence to pause and touch everything along the path had Lord Mensa intrigued. Caitlin had stopped again to admire boulders and massive trees which lined the edges of a riverbank. Here, water as clear as glass ran over the rocks and her fascination was with the small, rainbow-coloured fish, which fought the current as they swam upstream. While he watched her shoo away some wildlife that were poised and ready to eat them, he heard a sound and realised they were where he wanted them to be.

'This is it,' he called out to Aurek who had missed the mark. He was way ahead of them. 'You with us still, sport?' *That boy's not concentrating at all.* He shook his head. *Never does when there's a girl around.*

Once Aurek had joined them, Lord Mensa pulled out the little bag of bugs he'd picked up from the cave and held them up. 'Bait, a bear's delicacy. They're like an oyster is to us.'

'Yuk, if they taste like oysters it'll make the begrizzo run a mile.' She shuddered.

'Glow, I can't believe you don't like oysters. Have you tried them Kilpatrick?' Aurek asked.

'I've never attempted to eat them any which way. I reckon they'd taste like salty slime.' She blinked and pulled a child-like face as if served a lemon.

Lord Mensa held back hysteria and winked at Aurek. 'To be a good hunter you have to go through an initiation and eat at least half a dozen oysters, or you are never taken again, isn't that right, sport.'

Aurek nodded. 'My oath, that's the rule.'

'You're both having a lend of me. No way, that's disgusting. I couldn't imagine anything worse... Yuk!' Her tongue poked out and nose screwed up.

They both laughed at her reaction.

'How about you guys eat the slimy shelled crustaceans since you like them so much and as my initiation, I'll catch your furry menace for you?'

'That, I would like to see,' said Lord Mensa.

'I wouldn't encourage her if I were you. She's gutsier than that begrizzo,' Aurek remarked.

Lord Mensa scoffed and put his arm around her. 'What – this little soft soul. Take down such a beast, you sure?'

Aurek shrugged. 'Don't say I didn't warn you.'

They picked up the trail and upon finding the beast, energy levels spiked when they thought they had it cornered, but each time it managed to find a hiding spot by the time the guns were cocked, and they'd miss. Caitlin decided you needed a lot of patience for a sport such as hunting and hers was slowly running out.

It was late afternoon and the light had faded before they cornered the begrizzo again. Without warning the beast lunged at the three of them, knocked Lord Mensa over and headed for Aurek. He fired a shot into the animal, but unfortunately, the bullet didn't hit its target, and the snorting hefty lug of fur continued on its path.

With no other thought but to save her friend, Caitlin shot her hand up and let out a stream of power. The beam zapped the beast and stunned it. The bear wobbled before falling to the ground. Aurek fired another shot, and by then Lord Mensa had fired into the begrizzo as well, and both their shots finished him off.

Aurek and Lord Mensa slapped hands and jogged towards the bear, excited they had brought it down.

'Come with me and help butcher this beast.' Lord Mensa pulled out a big knife and made sure it was dead before he transported the animal from their sight.

She stood thinking of how excited Rory and the boys would have been if they were here.

Aurek was full of beans. 'Did you hear him? He just invited us back to the castle to help break up the carcass and stay the night. I know the butchering is not something you would enjoy, but after that, you would get to have a decent meal and sleep in a real bed tonight. But if you prefer not to go it's okay, I'm happy either way.' He did want Caitlin all to himself but this was a big deal, bringing down a begrizzo. The bragging rights and slicing it up was a hunters' ritual but he would leave it up to her. She was his first priority.

Caitlin could hardly spoil the light that now radiated from him. Had she made this happen or was it the adrenalin rush from the kill? Either way, she was watching the hard-core brute she first met disappear before her eyes. Left was how a man should see life, feel life. He looked a man now, a real man, sexy, alluring, sweet and caring. He would not go if her answer was no. Her work here with him was almost done, and yet she wanted to stay. Why?

'As if we're going to let him take all the credit for bringing down the town's terror! I believe it to be your shot that took him out. '

'You're the best, Glow.' He put his arm around her and transported her into the barn where Lord Mensa and two dark tanned islanders were standing over the begrizzo, admiring the coat. Caitlin sat on a bale of hay and watched with interest until they started to remove the fur. Uninterested in the glory they shared in the bloody butchery, she jumped down and strolled around the stable. She stopped at one of the stalls. The door was open, and a colt stood shaken and frightened with the noise the men were making. Its mane was black and curled around its face, which, in a kooky way, reminded her of Jett. She knelt beside it and patted the colt. Eventually, it lay down, and she sat beside it – startled when a hand touched her.

'Sorry, I must have dozed off.' She reached up to let Aurek help her up, pulling a face. 'Phew, I hate to tell you this, but you pong.'

'And you stink like a horse.'

She touched a wet patch on his shirt. 'Eww… is that blood? Yukko!'

They smiled at each other. The truth was so much more fun with Aurek.

'Shower,' he suggested.

She nodded. 'Yes please!'

He transported her into a big bedroom with an ensuite where an old fashioned four- poster bed dominated the room. Unable to stop herself, she sat and sank into the luxurious bedding, admiring the embroidery around the edge of the sheer gold material that fell like delicate fairy wings from the canopy above. Too lazy to bend down she kicked off her shoes and loved the feel of the royal blue carpet that was surely too soft to be Earth-made. Relishing in luxury, her eyes wandered to a mural that took up most of the visible walls. Curious, she walked over for a closer look. A youngster, sweet in her puffy silk skirt and angel wings was depicted in her early life. Next came someone looking like her, not a mother, but the same child grown. The story showed a torturous life's journey, but in the end, she stood with poise and position inside her temple in the sky.

Exquisite, Caitlin thought as she ran her hand over the tapestry. Strange emotions ran through her when she realised the young girl had identical green eyes to her own. Blinking with surprise, her mind elsewhere, she slowly turned towards the shower Aurek came from. 'Wow, you look hot Aurek. Talk about fancy duds, your appearance is that of a true Lord in those clothes. The ladies are going to take one look at you, catch a whiff of that masculine aftershave and I doubt I'll see you for the rest of the night.' She smiled. 'But if that was the plan, it will work.'

'I can spruce up as good as the next man.' He liked the fact that she noticed as it was for her. He wanted to show her she didn't need to be embarrassed to have him around her upstart Rider mates who looked like bloody gods every time they sat on a horse. *How can any man compete with that image?* He breathed out, glad for once she saw him as more than just the hunter. 'There are clothes in the wardrobe and lingerie in the draws. Lord Mensa said to help yourself.'

'Like what?'

'Evening attire; there will be dignitaries sitting at the table, so dress to impress. Would you like me to wait for you?'

'I'll find my way downstairs when I'm ready. Just keep them entertained, so they don't start dinner without me, I'm starving.' She eyed the closet.

'Will do,' he said, but his gaze was not on her but rather on the portrait beside her. It surprised Aurek how like she was to the woman in the picture. *Those eyes.* He pushed the thought away, bowed politely, as one would expect to do when dressed as a Lord and received a smile. It left him feeling chuffed.

On her own and freshly showered, Caitlin stood wrapped in a towel and was in a quandary as to what to wear. She had dragged out dress after dress from the wardrobe. Finally, hiding at the back of the wardrobe, found a dress in her size. Unsure, she screwed up her nose. It was not exactly what she looked for but would have to do. Next, dug through the nickers and luck had her find a stretchy lace sets of lingerie. *Sort of my size,* she was glad they were stretchy and then pondered why the wardrobe and drawer were full of clothes. *For visitors like me,* was her best guess. Pleased enough with her selection she dressed quickly and, closing the door on the mess she had made, hurried down the stairs to find Aurek.

On the bottom floor, a crowd stood gathered, chatting while holding long-stemmed wine glasses. Men in red and gold uniforms held open the solid door of carved wood as more people arrived. Caitlin had paused at the bottom of the staircase, suddenly out of her depth with such royalty surrounding her. It was as though time had stood still. Men wore tails and top hats, and the women on their arms had big hair, big hats and even bigger dresses. Hoops and layers of petticoats on thin-waist lines pulled in no doubt by the old-fashioned bone corsets.

The waiters stood behind each chair and helped seat the guests at the longest, most elegantly decorated dining table she had ever seen. From the fine bone china and polished silverware to the candelabrum where soft candlelight highlighted the luxurious setting, it was sublime.

She had thought the bottle-green gown suited her, and was maybe a bit over the top, with the gold weave in the fabric that made it glisten as she moved. Yet amongst all this, she felt very plain Jane.

Lord Mensa was unexpectedly at her side. 'You look the belle of the ball, dear. Come, allow me to introduce you.' His kindly features calmed her nerves as he took control of who she met and where she sat… *next to him, of course.*

During dinner, Caitlin became light headed with the Ambrosia and unusual taste of the food she ate and later that night tried to explain to Aurek. 'Getting used to the different food and wines on each Home World is difficult for me. Maybe there's a magic potion available to change the way my taste buds react,' she slurred, 'and explain why it is again, that I have to go to bed.'

'It was a wonderful evening, Glow. You were the life of the party but if you don't sleep this off, our day tomorrow will be ruined,' Aurek said as he pulled back the covers before helping her from the bathroom, where she had changed, and onto the bed.

'Lord Mensa is a cool dude, hey!' Caitlin flopped back on the pillow, and he covered her up.

'He seemed a little too attentive towards you. Be careful, sweetie. Emotions in men such as him can get confused.'

'But he's kind of father-like, you know – old! He knows that, right?'

'Old-worldly, but not old by any means.' Aurek smiled at her frown, noting Caitlin had no idea she had been the centre of attention. Also, she was oblivious that her entire persona had attracted nearly every man in the room when she lit up. He decided to play it down. 'We have an early start tomorrow so forget about it. We'll be gone in the morning, and that will be the end of it.' After she fell asleep, he sighed, grabbed a pillow and made himself comfortable in a chair. No way was he leaving her alone to maybe attract a midnight suitor, especially after the sweet bouquet she was giving off. Aware since meeting her that this was to calm others around her, tonight he believed the fragrance had fear mixed with it, and this alone kept him alert and ready.

Unable to sleep, Aurek gave up; his mind on Glow. She was funny, innocent, sweet, irritating, moody, but most of all, the friend he had always wished for, kind, considerate and full of character when she spoke of him. She had put him on a pedestal to all who listened, and no matter how Mensa rubbished him, she saw nothing but the best in him. Aurek couldn't remember a time he had laughed so hard as when she scrambled up on her chair surprising them all and threatened to take them all on if they kept rubbishing him. It was then he decided it was time to take his hot-headed, inebriated friend to bed.

On their way out the next morning, Aurek asked who had scared her last night. She shrugged. 'I don't know.' Then she stopped. 'Hang on, there was a man last night that kept catching my attention. Long hair, blond I think, with deep blue eyes.'

'The one with the funny laugh, like a donkey; you had him in stitches.'

'He was the only man there apart from Lord Mensa that I really remember.' She smiled. 'Apart from you of course.'

'To be sure of your security, I'd better keep you close until we get out of here.' He took her hand and led her down the stairs. 'I have our flasks from yesterday. Let's stop by the kitchen and fill them before we head off. If we don't get to Shyanne Heights by noon, we'll miss the angaroos.'

'What are they?'

'On Earth, you would call them kangaroos, only here, they're completely untameable and very dangerous,' he said as they arrived in the kitchen.

'Ah, thought you two might try and sneak off.' Lord Mensa had just brewed fresh coffee, took two more mugs from the cupboard and poured them some.

Caught out, they sat to chat for a few minutes before heading off. 'Sorry, we didn't mean to be rude, just wanted an early start and I was a little hesitant about security here. If anything happens to Glow, I'm in deep trouble. I prefer to be out there on our own, if you can understand my concerns.'

'What spooked you?'

'One of your dinner guests, long blond hair, laughs like a donkey.'

'Ah him, yes, I saw the look Glow Girl kept giving him, and had the man watched. Her intuition is superb. We caught him trying to sneak into Glow's room last night. No weapons, turns out, just infatuated.'

He sat back, slits for eyes, as he watched Glow. 'It was as if blondie was under a spell. Snapped out of it early this morning and swears he doesn't know what he was thinking.'

Aurek squeezed Glow's hand to quieten her. He was aware that she was about to confide in her powers to hold others to her. For some reason, he didn't trust Lord Mensa with that information and couldn't give a reason why even if asked. They left with a final wave as they were let out the main gates of the castle.

Caitlin strode beside him trying to keep pace, but Aurek was not slowing down to chat. 'That's the second time you have kept something about me secret from him. Why?'

'I'm not sure, it's the way he stares at you as if he sees someone else, it's unnerving.'

'Seriously, I didn't notice.'

'Don't worry, we're on our way, and free from his clutches. If he was going to do anything it would have been just now; he wouldn't have let us leave so that makes me feel better. And as for your abilities, he didn't see you stun the bear, so let's just keep that our little secret.'

'You caught that, did you?'

'Glow, the begrizzo was right on top of me. No way, an animal that size could have missed me if you hadn't pushed him back. As for "Blondie" that dude you attracted last night, that's a whole other story. Got any ideas?'

She shrugged, unsure. 'Mystery to me.'

Her comment that she had no clue worried him further. Caitlin stopped when he did and turned to him. His mind was churning. 'Look, I don't trust any of this. Do you mind if we go somewhere else? I have many places I can take you. We'll go back to the cabin, pack our gear and get out of here.'

'I like that plan too. I just want to go hunting, not be hunted.' She smiled, and he relaxed.

'Good!' He gave her a nod and although there was not much further to go, he decided not to chance them walking along the overgrown path they were on. He transported them both back to the cabin to collect their belongings.

Chapter Thirty-Eight

Kidnapping Foiled

At the cabin, Aurek rushed to pack his gear.

'Quick, Glow, I have trust issues with more than the one you spoke of with the donkey laugh. Lord Mensa had a weird look in his eyes. I'm getting us out of here now!'

'Are you sure about your friend? I mean, he just seemed a little hung over to me.' She rolled up her towel and shoved it roughly into her backpack. She was annoyed the hunting trip here was being cut short because of trust issues. 'You do know I can take care of myself.'

He glanced up at her tiny frame, and his eyes were unconvinced. 'Glow! Hurry!'

A noise outside had her stop and listen. 'What was that?'

One set of footsteps thumped heavily up the wooden stairs, and the door flung open taking them off guard. Both wondered who would dare invade their privacy without knocking. Aurek was at Caitlin's side in a flash, his stance threatening, his eyes glowing angrily.

Blondie who laughed like a donkey stood there, his breathing heavy, his long hair matted from a bad night's sleep.

'What's going on?' Caitlin's voice was pitchy as he slammed the door shut behind him, fumbling for a catch to lock it.

'Quick! Get out of here! They're coming!' He pointed to the open window he wished them to flee through. 'Go, there is a brush-covered path and a cave to hide in. I'll hold them back.'

'Who's coming?' Aurek's angry tone chilled the air. 'What are you babbling about, man?'

'Lord Mensa. I heard him tell the guards your woman has powers he needs to complete his kingdom and he wants her. They are coming to get her. He is with them, and I know him well, he will kill to get what he wants.'

Caitlin put her hand up at Aurek whose temper had him torn between turning into Orion or to staying her kind friend. Lord Mensa had been in his life a long time, and the disbelief this was possible had left him speechless and stunned. 'Let me speak to him.' She stopped him from pouncing on the man who sounded a little insane and yet they both knew something was wrong or they wouldn't be packed, ready to leave.

'What are your powers; tell me quickly,' Caitlin said, and kept calm, as her inner-self read that he was telling the truth.

'I can block magic; why?' he replied, puffing from the hillside jog up to the cabin.

'Don't even think about it. I'm getting you out of here now!' Aurek was firm. 'Axon and Jett would have a fit if I were to allow this confrontation to go ahead with a Ruler, even one meant to be a mate.'

With the firepower his hunting buddy might turn up with, Aurek could see no way of her handling this amicably. *Glow Girl might think she's good but I know Lord Mensa, and she is no match for his powers.* He made a grab for her, but Caitlin moved from him, slipping from his grip.

'Glow, don't fight me on this! It's not something your man will want you involved with.'

She shrugged his hand away for a second time. 'Talk to him?' Caitlin said with strong persuasion. Her sudden flare out of red hair and glowing green eyes astonished him. Was this his Glow Girl? 'He's your friend, Aurek. This is stupid. What if it's nothing and you blow your friendship because of me and because we ran?'

Aurek's clenched jaw released. 'You must listen to me Glow. This is no game here. I don't hang out with nice guys. This guy is the real deal and dangerous. Time to go!' he insisted.

'Look! Blondie here can stop Lord Mensa from taking my

powers. It's okay, trust me, I can protect you if he gets rough.' She stood with hands on her hips, hair brazen, and manner tough and uncompromising. 'It's time you trusted me–*fully.*' Her stern tone and the magic she shot from her mind made him stop and listen to her.

She didn't wait for his answer, but instead snatched his hand up in hers and the intruder's in her other one.

Aurek tried to transport her out, but somehow, she had rendered him incapable of anything but holding her hand and listening to what she said. She had him in a trance and the only thing he could do at the minute was to obey her.

'Stay beside me – both of you.' She gritted her teeth at Aurek and shook his hand. 'I don't need you fighting me. Quit it and let me concentrate.'

Aurek stopped the use of his powers. He had never seen Glow Girl in action like this and suddenly understood why she was such an intricate member of the elite team of Riders. Up until now, she had been so fragile he thought he might break her and yet now he felt sorry for Lord Mensa. The guy had no idea what he was walking into, and he almost wanted to warn him, as he was still unsure if Donkey Laugh was telling the truth.

She eyed the stranger. 'Blondie!' She snapped him out of his dazed state. 'Lord Mensa will take my powers.' Blondie's eyes were wide. 'Yes, this has happened to me before,' she confided. 'I will feel him do it and when he does, I'll squeeze your hand, and it is then, you must block him but do it discreetly. He mustn't know he hasn't overpowered me.'

She turned to Aurek. 'If this goes pear-shaped, I will allow you the power to transport us out, but only when I say, not one second before or I will freeze you to this spot permanently.' Her smile gave him a shiver down his spine.

Had she just threatened him? 'Bitch,' Orion mouthed, now standing beside her. Aurek was gone, and his pessimistic unstable side was ready for a fight. He would run from no man and would discuss her threat later, *with luck before she turns me back into wimp-boy, Aurek,* he secretly sneered.

She smiled at Orion who had suddenly found his voice.

'You read thoughts, hey!'

'Maybe.' She shrugged. 'Or, maybe I know you well enough to just know what you were thinking.'

He melted a little at her, even as Orion she had won him over. 'I should fight you on this and get us the hell out of here now. Jett's going to be fuming when he hears I caved.'

'Settle.' The pitched brassy words cut.

He flared, temper sliced back at her. 'Suit yourself, your funeral... Did you just chuckle?' He couldn't believe she had no fear of him.

'Look, Orion, I know your manhood is feeling bruised, but this is what I do. I'm a peacekeeper and do not intend to hide. If I run from this, he will follow, seek me out, and that can get messy for all those around me. We're in a prime location where no civilian can be hurt. Trust me – work with me – please. Just find out why he feels this is necessary so I can work out a solution.' She smiled reassuringly. 'I didn't do that bad of a job during my negotiations with you– did I?'

He smirked. 'You railroaded me and had me in a spin. I would have given you my whole flipping empire in the end if you had asked for it.'

Caitlin's eyes lit up happily. 'Orion, I do believe you're funnier than Aurek, so you can stay f o r now.' The lightness ended abruptly as Lord Mensa transported into the room, a guard each side of him. They were the darkly tanned muscle men she'd met in the barn, the previous night. The guards were so tall they bent over slightly to see her. She jumped at the sound of the shotgun being loaded and cocked, now pointed towards her and Orion. She felt the weakening of her powers immediately on their entry and squeezed Blondie's hand, feeling better when they returned. She rebooted the power needed and readied her energy for whatever lay ahead.

She could feel Orion's rage go through her, fuming that he had a gun shoved in his face. As it grew, she could feel the dark side of his nature come out fully, and Orion now stood beside her, angry and almost out of control.

'Are you frigging kidding me? Are you seriously thinking about killing me over a female?' Orion yelled at him.

'Logic is not one of my finer points.' Lord Mensa was shaken but kept calm.

'Bullshit! We're mates. What are you thinking man? Get those guns out of our faces, or I swear I'll wipe the blatzing floor with you and your goons… *Lay them down now!*' His temper exploded; the sound of his tone was venomous and ear piercing.

It was so loud and the vibration so painful, Caitlin put both hands up to her ears.

'You can yell all you want, but Caitlin stays!' Lord Mensa spoke with vicious intent.

'Then be prepared to fight.' Orion's growl lowered yet was just as intense. He shook with rage, and Caitlin knew if she didn't defuse this situation soon, he would pounce, and she would be unable to hold such a force.

It aggravated Lord Mensa even more; his face reddened, the vein in his neck pulsing rapidly. 'Move away from her pal… I'm not joking... I-will-shoot-you! I'm giving you one chance and one chance only to walk away. Leave the female, and I will ignore that outburst and our agreement for hunting will continue to stand. Fight me on this, and you'll be the loser. I have you surrounded. 'Outside…' Lord Mensa yelled and pointed, 'are my army who hold infra-red automatic weapons, and these are pointed at you, Orion! My order is to shoot if you move a muscle towards me, and that goes for you too, donkey man.'

Caitlin was calm as she viewed Lord Mensa. 'So the huntress becomes the hunted.' She could feel Orion's stress for getting her into this mess. Lord Mensa's eyes burned into her, the threatening glare of a dominant conqueror.

Caitlin stood firm.

Lord Mensa intended to win without confrontation. He had thought of every scenario, but not this and it infuriated him she was acting as if having a gun pointed at her was normal. *Who is this person?*

Caitlin could read his expressive eyes. 'You have no idea who I am, do you?'

'I don't care who you are as from this day forward, I will title you with a new name, and you will live here on Mensa for evermore. As for prior family and friends, yes they will grieve your loss, it's only natural, but I'm sure not for long. You don't seem very handy to have around, other than your gifts.' His voice was deadly and threatening while making every effort to break her cockiness and scare her.

'If your intent is to have me all to yourself, I at least deserve to know why.' The reasoning quality of her tone amazed Orion as he almost swayed to the sugar sweet pitch.

It riled up Lord Mensa further and what was even more frustrating to him was that he hadn't yet ruffled her feathers. He scowled. 'I've searched the galaxy for a powerful goddess such as you. My aim always has been to take over Taurus. That delicious beef will be mine and you, young lady, are going to help me get it. That power of yours I can feel. You are beyond all I have met. I am about to have my biggest wish granted.'

His confession stunned her but not her new and loyal comrade next to her. 'Over my dead body will you put one filthy paw on her!' Orion yelled at him, but Caitlin held him firm with her power so he couldn't lunge.

'That, my old friend, is your choice. This was once your dream as well, but I can already see whose side you have chosen. Kill you I will if that is your wish. She has every quality I've ever dreamed of and more. She will be mine, Orion. Oh, and before I kill you, I must thank you for bringing her to me, fancy that, putting her right into my hands. You could have run, but you stayed, that was your first mistake. The second will be if you move.'

'She is a Cosmic Rider, you idiot. You'll never get away with it,' Orion snapped. 'They'll wipe your blatzing Home World off the map when we don't return, you cynical old fool.'

'You know hunting accidents can be so terrible.' He tut-tutted. 'I'm sure if I placed your clothing from yesterday with the blood all over them, nice touch, by the way, scattered about it will convince them it was that big black begrizzo I caught that was the demise of you both.'

Caitlin squeezed Orion's hand to let him know she had this and to calm him down. She felt him slightly relax and now controlled again, continued in her own defence.

'I was never lucky enough to have a father, but last night, I loved you as one. You made me feel happy as I sat beside you, having you so proud of me I felt blessed. The way you honoured me in front of your friends and family made me want you in my life for many years to come. How sad for me that you were only thinking about turning me into one of your slaves that would jump at your command. And if I remember correctly, you were even referring to us as your kids.'

'Stop it! You're twisting it. Last night I was drunk and having fun with you both. It was this morning in the kitchen that your powers became apparent to me. I am smarter than you think and surprise, surprise, I noticed you had the hum of goddess-like powers. Now I find I can't have you leave. Although heaven knows why... you sound a right royal pain.' He folded his arms, satisfied he had this in the bag, and it was going to be an easy win.

'Oh really?' Her eyebrows went up.

'Oh yes, my dear girl. You might have those standing beside you conned, but I see right through you. The gods have sent you to me to give me what I crave. Taurus is all I have ever wanted.'

'No! You have wanted something more, be honest,' Caitlin snapped.

He stretched his neck from side to side. Real emotion kept him quiet.

As soon as Caitlin said the words it sent a dagger to his heart. 'What about your daughter, the one you never saw grow up? The one that maybe should be my age now, but who never survived? Is she who you see, when you look at me? The reason you're not thinking straight right now?'

'You're guessing and clutching at straws. You don't know anything about me!' he snarled. His brows were squeezed so tight, his eyes were slits.

'Then tell me about you. Because from where I'm standing, for someone of your calibre to even think of hurting your best friend and destroying my life, man, you have got to be in a world of hurt.'

Rage shook his body with her insolence. He would make her pay for this later. There had been enough talk and he was sick of hearing her twist the outcome to benefit them. His arms went up, 'Take her! Kill the other two!' he ordered.

Caitlin closed her eyes, and could sense the fingers on the triggers that hesitated before doing as commanded. They weren't bulletproof; neither could she shield the two men that flanked her. These were the ones now targeted, and her heart pumped as she worried she had made a huge error in judgement. It was too late to release Orion so he could transport them out. The fingers had started to squeeze the triggers, but Caitlin was optimistic she could put a stop to this onslaught and end it peacefully. *Calm yourself,* she recalled Kayden's teachings. *The answer is controlling the situation first. If it can't be, remove and destroy. Take no chances or prisoners.* Her focus was now on every firearm that surrounded them, aware the triggers were being pulled. It was too late to stop the powerful emissions that threatened to cut her two friends to pieces. Drawing extra power from the hands she held, Caitlin snatched the guns from all who held them and faced the offending weaponry to the sky. The fire power now well above them hit a central position above the cabin, and on impact, the explosion was massive and thankfully the strong roof protected them from the sparks and flames of the aftermath. The army, however, had no cover and were blown metres back. With a glance out the window and listening for heartbeats, Caitlin saw they were mostly unconscious but alive.

Her mind now went to the two guards inside. They too met the full force of her power and were flung backwards, slamming hard against the wall. Stripped of their weaponry the blow had knocked them unconscious. She took the entire army of guns collected up in the air with the power of her internal sorcery. Way above and now at what she hoped was a harmless distance, Caitlin sent up a flash and blew the weaponry to pieces. The power of the explosion was not only deafening, but the force of it shook the cabin; trees cracked and fell over, and even part of the veranda wall crumbled. She could have taken them up higher, but wanted some theatrics. Maybe not so much as this though; she hoped no one was hurt. Her friends and the tyrant in front of Caitlin, she held fast, not allowing harm to Lord Mensa, *yet*.

'Wholly blatzing shytzer!' Blondie's eyes were wide.

She didn't know who looked shocked the most, Orion or Lord Mensa. 'Now!' she said calmly. 'Do you want me to let Orion here go, and you can sort it out between yourselves, or are you ready to discuss this like an adult?'

Lord Mensa was motionless, shaken. He had not expected what she was capable of. His frame weakened to let her know he was giving up. He sat worriedly in the chair at the table, lost in turmoil.

Aurek stood calmly beside her. Orion was gone, and it was only now she trusted him to help out. 'Okay Aurek, you're up. Go talk to him. I need to know he won't come after me.' She spoke quietly to him, but upon releasing him, she saw he had tricked her. It was Orion who jerked away from her. His fists shot out as he laid a punch into Lord Mensa's jaw, knocking him and the chair over. He pulled him up roughly and slammed him into the wall. It cracked with the forceful shove, and blood oozed from the corner of Lord Mensa's mouth and nose as he was punched more. On the fourth blow, Orion slammed his fist into the wall. The hole almost punched through to the other side.

'You're just lucky Glow's here with me, and I don't want her to see me so wildly out of control. If she hadn't held me back, you'd be the one taking a little visit to the Underworld, mate. I can't believe after all these years you would turn out to be such a selfish prick!' he roared. 'I should kill you right here, right now, for what you've just attempted.' With a swift toss, he threw the older man back into one of the other chairs near. 'Rot in hell, I don't care what she does to you.' He stomped back to Caitlin, his rage controlled so as not to frighten her, wishing he hadn't even gone that far. She'd asked him to talk, but for now, he just wanted to hit Lord Mensa instead. It would be best if he calmed down first, *for her*.

Caitlin went over to the table and sat with the crumpled figure. He straightened, put an elbow on the table and leant his head on his fist, defeated. She pulled up her legs and wrapped her arms around them, her gaze glued to him as she waited for him to speak. He had a lot of explaining to do. She certainly wasn't about to let him go until they sorted this out.

He felt her eyes burn into his, and his head inclined, embarrassed. At that moment his guards came to and, helping each other up, stared at Lord Mensa.

'My Lord, what happened to you?' They waited for what they should do next, but without weapons, it was all about fists and with them clenched they looked more than ready.

Lord Mensa waved his hand. 'Get out of here, go back to the castle and take your useless royal army with you.' He was done, had lost the fight, and with Glow Girl's powers he knew he had no hope of winning this battle, ever. He turned to Glow Girl. 'How did you know? I mean about my daughter?' he asked so quietly she could hardly hear him.

'From the mural in the room we stayed in. The little girl had green eyes exactly the same as mine and yet when we went for dinner, she was nowhere to be seen, even as the depicted teenager. A guest that had known you for years didn't know who I spoke of either. Someone so adored would be by your side or known to your friend. I guess I just put two and two together. There was no magic needed to work that out.'

'You were right. I lost my daughter in the early years, just after that first image. I instructed the artist to give me a likeness of what she might look like years later in the hopes I would recognise her when I found her. I've grieved for her for so many years and yesterday when I looked into your eyes, I saw her again. Then when you left this morning, it ripped my heart out all over again, as if I just lost her for a second time.' His grief was real; she didn't have to look at him to feel his misery.

'Why didn't you come and talk to me and tell me how you felt? Maybe if you knew how I felt about you too, it might have made it easier somehow. We could have worked through it together without all this unnecessary fuss about Taurus.'

'I just couldn't let you leave. I actually figured that it must have been more than just you, it had to be something you could give me. I was confused and didn't understand my emotions. I nearly crumbled into a big mess when you spoke of my daughter. I had not thought of that at all. I realised it might have been the reason but I had gone crazy, and it was too late, I had got into a mess and didn't know how to dig my way out.'

'You could have said, "Sorry, I mucked up!"'

'I freaked out that you would leave here angry, that I'd never see you again so thought, hell, I'm in this deep, take the girl and run. I just wanted my look-alike daughter back and wanted my pain to stop.'

'I would have hated you.'

'Anything was better than just letting you go. I miss my daughter so.' Lord Mensa's face was wet with hatred for using such severe actions to win and yet his strained features were frustrated and hurt with the blow of losing *her*.

Caitlin pulled out a lace hanky and dabbed the blood that dribbled down his chin. 'Growing up I was told my mother died at birth and my father was on the run. I've grieved all my life for a father I never had, and you, for a daughter you never got to see grow up. Fate throws us together, and it's destroyed, gone, in mere minutes. It sounds such a waste.'

She stood up and put out her hand to him. He looked up and taking it, got up.

'You're leaving.' He looked even more miserable.

She smiled. 'Not yet. Let's just see first if fate is going to give us a second chance.' She put out her hand again.

'Hi, I'm Caitlin Warner, and you are?' She grinned.

His mouth quirked at the sides. 'My title is Lord Alfred Mensa. I had a beautiful daughter, who would have looked exactly like you if she had reached your age. Today I would have been so proud of her if she had grown up half the woman you are Caitlin and was able to forgive an old fool like me so easily.'

'I'm sure she would have been very much like me. She also would have been proud of her father for seeing the wrong and also trying to correct it cordially.' She then looked around at the intruder. 'Thanks for your help, kind stranger, but we can take it from here. You have been very honourable, and I'm sure the Lord here will make sure you are well looked after from now on. You have a power he will want to keep close to him in the future.'

Blondie smiled, bowed and left.

Her attention was then on Orion who wasn't buying any of it and paced furiously. Somehow, she had to bring them both back to a happy place. This wasn't his argument, it had been hers, and she was damned if she would let their bond break because destiny had him bring her here.

She moved over and slipped her hand into Orion's, and his mood changed the minute she touched him. He slumped his wide shoulders and rolled his head to relieve the pressure he had been under. 'You okay, sugar?'

She smiled.

He grinned, and she saw that Orion had gone, Aurek was back. Not in a great mood but in control again.

'Nice you could join us again Aurek,' she teased him.

She turned back to Lord Mensa. 'We were leaving, but I have decided to stay. I'm afraid I've destroyed all your guns.' She gestured with her hands. 'Oops.' She shrugged. 'But Aurek still has one so if you two would like to join me, I'm going hunting.' She stuck her nose in the air and walked out on both of them, trudging up the hill, optimistic they would follow.

Sure enough, the door slammed shut, and she heard two sets of footsteps, no talking, but she was not alone and knew that here, with these two, she never would be again.

It had been a long walk to the top, and none of them spoke. When Caitlin was just about to give in and start a conversation, large hands grabbed her. 'Okay, okay, you win. If you're going to keep ignoring me until I give in, then I give in already. I'm wasting my day with you being mad.' Aurek turned and put out his hand to Lord Mensa.

'Mates again, to please the girl neither of us can do without.' And they shook hands, smiling at what he said.

Lord Mensa cupped his other hand over his friend's. 'I was foolish, insane; thank goodness she's smarter than both of us. I hate to think now how that could have turned out. Sorry, old friend.' The remorse in his voice supported the depth of his apology.

Caitlin moved towards them. 'Now that's over, can we please go hunting? I was promised angaroos for dinner if I remember correctly.' She pulled at them both with eagerness to continue the day with less stress. Now that they had at least shaken hands, she skipped ahead of them, entertaining her still moody, but happier, companions. The memory of the hunt the previous day came to mind, and it was a perfect topic to engage them both.

'Did you see the look on the begrizzo when he went down and knew he was done for?' She turned to them, walking backwards. 'Now that was a look.' She giggled and turned back around, and a smile spread across her face when she heard them reminisce.

By the time they reached the angaroos, the tension was out of their voices completely, the casual banter of two blokes back on a hunting trip overpowered what had just gone down, *with just a little help from my magic.* Caitlin walked with a swagger of the knowledge that she had learned more than hunting on this trip… could you imagine the look when the guns went off? She couldn't wait to tell her Rider friends…*now that was the look!*

Secret Uncovered

Late that afternoon they came across a swimming hole. Caitlin moved away from the two hunters who had reddened the water around them while washing the blood from their bodies and clothing. 'Yuk, you guys. That's disgusting.' She swam over by the waterfall.

When they were finally clean, Caitlin joined them and stirred them up, until Aurek pushed her under the water playfully. When surfacing, she saw him grimace at the idea he might have hurt her. Aurek wasn't used to games with girls, which made her want to be more annoying than usual. 'You're so cute when you do that.' She liked that look of uncertainty, grinned and dived away from him.

He chased her, his big hands finding her within seconds. 'When I do what?'

'When you put that look on your face; like *how come she likes me*?'

'Well, how come?' he wanted to know.

'Because you accepted my friendship before you knew who I was. You liked me for me, and I for you. It's that simple.'

He grinned. 'Yes, I guess it is.'

She splashed water at him and looked around for Lord Mensa.

'Look at Mr High and Mighty over there not wanting to have any fun. Is he always this boring? Let's go stir up the old dude. Can he swim?' she whispered, and Aurek nodded. 'Let's drag him in the water, being a Lord has turned him into a snob. We need to fix that!'

She giggled, and getting a wink from Aurek, raced him back. Aurek was just as keen to have some fun and this time had an ally to help stir the pot. He was surprised when Caitlin pulled at his leg when he got in front of her. It gave him such a shock he stopped, and she sped past him. *Little wretch!* He bit his tongue until reaching her.

She jumped up on the bank. 'I won, I won!'

'You cheated; it doesn't count when you don't play fair.' He restrained himself from picking her up and dumping her back in the water.

She winked and pointed, his attention now back to why they were there. They grabbed a hand each and dragged Lord Mensa in the water. He struggled, but finally gave in and pulled them in with him. They mucked about, stirring him up until he finally caught hold of Caitlin.

'Your skin; you feel like a child.' His voice softened. 'I'm terribly sorry I nearly hurt you.'

She smiled and ran her hand over his wrinkled frown. 'I know. I forgive you.' Her tone too was caring. 'You would have made a good father. I'm glad we ended up friends.'

He coughed. 'If you would let an old fool into your life, I would love to get to know you better.'

'I already have. But no more games. My friendship at this point with you is fragile, so tread carefully.'

His voice shook. 'I'm so sorry and promise from now on to never hurt you again.'

Aurek got out. The abruptness of his departure surprised Caitlin. Had she upset him by giving in so quickly to a man that almost kidnapped her?

'Give us a minute.' She turned back to Lord Mensa, who nodded. Out of the water, she eased herself quietly next to Aurek. He seemed almost spaced out.

'You okay? I'm sorry if that upset you. I don't understand what my attachment to Lord Mensa is either. It's like I've known him all my life. Don't be mad.'

'Forgive me if I'm wrong, but the way you both were with each other just then, it has brought me back to reality.' He took hold of her hands and held her attention. 'Call it an epiphany or madness, but I think he *is* your father,' Aurek said and shook with the disclosure.

Lord Mensa overheard and planted to the spot, rendered speechless.

'What! That's insane! What makes you think that?' She sat up, aghast.

He let her hands go and decided to disclose a secret he had long kept. 'I've had many talks with Lord Mensa about his earlier years before I met him. I know he wasn't lying because after telling me his deep dark secret some years back, he was terribly shaken. In an emotional turmoil, he talked of a daughter that he had to hide from certain gods who were hellbent on killing her. It was pre-destined that his daughter would only need to look evil in the face to turn them from their wicked ways. Her presence would save many from being killed, and prevent others from following this destructive behaviour.

Knowing his daughter was to be this prodigy child, he tried to keep his little girl, safe, but in the end, it was he who endangered her. Mensa had no choice but to give her up to save her. Devastated it had come to this, he paid a good sum of money weekly to a couple of trusted allies. They promised to keep her hidden, healthy and alive, somewhere safe so that the gods she was to change wouldn't find her and kill her before she blossomed.'

She pulled a towel around her, shivering from the story, *or is it?* 'It is hard for me to believe one person alone could be feared by those as mighty as a god.'

'Some may say they are mighty because they create fear in those around them that dare to oppose them. Over time, some of the gods have become an unstoppable force, terrorising those that dare stand against them. The courageous immortals that have been game enough to take them on in the past have failed miserably. They paid with not only their kingdoms but their lives. Mensa told me that once his daughter came of age and went through immortality, her powers would be beyond imagining and the prophecy was that a new style of ruling would evolve and their godly tyrant ways would never to be tolerated again.'

Lord Mensa found his voice and sat beside them. 'Aurek, this was a secret shared only with you. What if she…'

Aurek put up his hand. 'Let me finish… the other night, Glow, you also confided you had spent many years, until your late teens, locked underground, that you never saw the light of day. After you had told me your innermost secret, I was so shocked and emotional that you two might be father and daughter that I couldn't speak. I couldn't tell you then; you would have called me a liar and been angry, and maybe even demanded to go home. I needed you too, and so, kept quiet.'

'What made you tell me now?' Caitlin's cheeks were wet with tears, and Lord Mensa was no different. Aurek was sure now.

'I still wasn't sure, I mean with all that has happened, I started to wonder if Lord Mensa could be your father from the way he acted. He was nothing like you at all and to tell you the truth I didn't want him to be anywhere near you, certainly not as a parent. But that little scene in the water was such a father and daughter thing. It made me see you both clearly, and I can't do this to you Glow, I dare not take away the chance to have a parent even if it is only to yell at him for your devastating childhood.' He turned to face Caitlin again. 'Even those green eyes in that mural, they look like yours. It all fits.'

She stared at Lord Mensa. 'You're my father?' she said with a shocked expression. 'You lied; you told me your daughter died, she didn't… did she?'

He coughed to regain some composure. This confession from Aurek had left him with mixed emotions, he felt awkward, embarrassed and yet full of hope for a future he had wished to come true. All he could do was tell Caitlin the truth, the rest was up to her, as he knew he certainly didn't deserve her love. 'You're right, Caitlin. It was easier to say you were no longer alive than to admit what I had done. Your name was Shardarna Louise Mensa, and although I never knew where to find you, I hoped with all my heart that you were alive and happy.'

'Why didn't you come for me once I became immortal?'

'When it was time, I came to collect you and not only found you missing but discovered how those lying crooks had mistreated you. I went into a fit of rage and killed them on the spot. I went crazy trying to find you and searched everywhere. It wasn't until much later that I realised they must have changed your name. Unfortunately, there was nothing legally filed, so I had to come home emptyhanded. What you don't know is I still pay a detective who continues to search for you, and we follow up every lead. But lo and behold, fate has stepped in, and in only hours of meeting you I have destroyed any real relationship we might have had, haven't I?' His voice cracked, and his lips quivered.

'You have made both our lives hell, and I should hate you. Surely there was another way?' She moaned, feeling the hurt of him leaving her, something that still stung when she remembered.

He shook his head. 'After your mother passed away, you were my light. I couldn't bear to give you up so for the first few years, I travelled the world with you. You were a human child, so I couldn't hide you up on the Home Worlds here; the atmosphere is all wrong for Earth dwellers. But on Earth, we were only in one place for a few weeks, and one of the gods would find us. I knew they were tracking me and my powers which continued to exposing our whereabouts. Never thought those filthy dogs would hide you underground. With no magic yet, you would have been safe being brought up as a normal child. You could have attended school without me around, and they knew this. I gave you up to keep you safe, and it gave me comfort to know that without me you would make it through to immortality. I could never have come to you, I've never been left alone and been hounded with raids and continually infiltrated with spies. I'm sorry, love, I tried to keep you with me, but there was no other way. I wasn't able to protect you.'

He reached over, patted her hand and pulled away knowing she wasn't ready for a father's affection. Instead, he sat calmly and answered question after question and then Caitlin finally shared with a father she thought she had hated all her life, how frightening her childhood was without him. They sat on the bank for a long time and talked freely. Both were miserable about the past and yet sharing it somehow began the healed process that they knew would take time. Some of the wounds Caitlin felt, had already been kissed away as he hugged her while she cried much of it out. 'You actually killed them?' She looked up at one stage.

He nodded. 'Made them live the fate they dealt you, beaten and locked underground, but for them, there were no visits to feed them. Sorry if that upsets you, Caitlin, but you have seen my temper.'

Caitlin wiped her tear-stained face and stiffened. 'You know I'm a Rider and cannot condone what you have done or are about to do with the Taurus takeover. Know this… father or not, if you continue on your current path, I will fight you on it.'

'If you choose to accept me now as your real father, I would never need more. I have fretted for you, my beautiful daughter, for all your life, and if you would let me stay in yours now, my promise will never be broken.'

The sun had gone down, and Caitlin shivered. 'I need…'

'You need to warm up, Glow.' Aurek stood and pulled her up. 'Give her time to process what has just happened here, Lord Mensa. Don't force an answer right now or you'll not hear what you have been waited for. You've been honest and done all you can, so now let her come to you.' He smiled at Caitlin who looked grateful. He could see she looked washed out and needed a minute. 'How about we move this conversation to a warmer place? Would you like your father to come or do you need a break? He will understand either way. I'm happy if you wish to finish this back at the cabin.' Aurek put an arm around her. 'But you're frozen, and a fire and some food are what is sure to make you feel better.'

She looked at him, and back at Lord Mensa. 'Can we invite him for dinner?' She eyed Aurek.

He nodded. 'I'm sure he would like that very much.'

* * * *

Dressed, warm and sitting in front of the fire, Caitlin took the seat on the sofa next to Lord Mensa. Aurek passed them each a goblet of Moonjuice and sat the other side of Caitlin. The three stared into the fire and drank in silence.

In turmoil, knowing they had to leave tomorrow, Caitlin took a big swig. Much played on her mind as the fire crackled and spat out embers. There was an overwhelming need to be with this man, her father and get to know him better. As a daughter, she wanted to hug him and give in, allow him time to fill in the gaps of her lost life. Yet she hesitated, taking the time to weigh up her options. Could she walk away… her heart said *No!*

Yet her focus was also on Aurek. Her time with him was part of a deal to end the war with Taurus, and so far, she had miserably failed in her side of the agreement. They had barely had a moment alone since meeting Lord Mensa, and now with all this going on, Caitlin was unsure how she could honour her side of the treaty before leaving the next day. How could she make this right for all parties? She sighed. A real friend would help her through this, *and Aurek is doing me proud.* As for Lord Mensa, maybe she should allow him to be the parent and quit worrying. *That's his job!* She consoled herself, feeling better.

She leant in and nudged Aurek, who looked rattled. 'You did the right thing. I am glad you helped me find my father.'

'You're okay then?' He searched her face.

'More than okay. I'm right where I want to be at this moment.' She felt proud of the level of friendship that had developed. What the situation between her and him alone had put him through was enough, never mind dealing with all the father-daughter stuff. She held up her goblet first to him. 'To my new best friend Aurek.' She tapped cups with him, and they took a sip. After that, she turned to Lord Mensa. 'And here's a cheer for discovering that you are my father.' She smiled when she raised her goblet to him. 'Never did I think I would be catching a parent on this hunting trip, but here we are. So future friends or foe, this has been one hell of a ride.'

Lord Mensa touched cups with her and took a sip before he raised his goblet back to her. 'To my long-lost and much-loved daughter. May she forgive a cantankerous old chump who promises from now to always be dependable and… truthful.' Lord Mensa toasted his daughter. Leaning forward, he raised his goblet to Aurek. 'And to my oldest friend who brought us back together, I am eternally grateful and forever in your debt… and I deeply apologise for my melodramatic behaviour.'

Aurek twisted his lips in an effort to grin. 'Guess if Glow can forgive you, I can. After all, I've always known you were a belligerent pain in the arse and an egotistical prick, though not to me directly. So make this your first and last time. All that said, I am no angel either, so what happens on a hunting trip stays on a hunting trip!' He held up his own goblet. 'To a healthier blood sport next trip; let's try to make it animals only.'

Caitlin noticed he eyed Lord Mensa with Orion-like eyes, but it was over, and everyone's moods improved. With the new-found peace, Caitlin was able to ease up on the magic, enabling her to listen to the men tell of spectacular events of old, giving them all a good laugh. Caitlin was even able to tease them again as she had when they went hunting for the begrizzo. She relished calling them out when the stories were almost impossible to believe. 'Bull twang!' she chuckled at one stage. 'I intend to frequent these hunting trips to lay to rest some of these imaginary yarns.'

'Really! That ain't going to happen again. You're trouble, girl.' Aurek tickled her playfully and made her giggle.

Lord Mensa shook his head. 'All joking aside, as far as I'm concerned, guns, blood and guts is not a place for my only daughter. When you visit here Caitlin, it is within the castle walls so I can satisfy my urge to spoil you and thus make up for the lost years.'

'What! You think you can refine me… Ha!' She laughed at his serious expression. 'Wait until I tell Axon how you wish me to act in your presence… fine dining and dressing up like a rich, posh lady.' She shook her head.

As far as Lord Mensa was concerned just as long as it was an adventure they could experience together he knew it would be amazing. But he could not predict how her current family would handle all this once they found out what he had done. If she did visit, he was almost sure Axon would insist on being with her, and they would stay in the castle protected. For this reason, he thought it best to steer her from the whole idea of hunting. 'Ah, the fiancé, I hadn't thought that far ahead. But while we're on that subject of Axon, I doubt he will even let you come back here after he hears what happened. Never mind me worrying about how to say, No!… you are not coming hunting.'

'Don't concern yourself with what Axon will or won't do. He knows me and still wants to marry me. I'd say that speaks for itself.' She shared. 'He also knows, as you have found out, I can look after myself and, between you and me, he and the boys were probably hoping Aurek was the one to muck up. That's something they would get great pleasure in hearing about.' She turned to speak to Lord Mensa. 'As for you, well this story is going to blow their minds. That's if Jett hasn't already eavesdropped and dobbed.'

No sooner had she spoken the words, when Jett and Axon shimmered in from a vortex. With brows pulled in, neither looked in a good mood.

'What the hell's been going on?' Axon's face reddened, and his forehead wrinkled as he viewed his fiancé in between the two men. Aurek he knew, but the other fool he wanted to punch, no questions asked.

Lord Mensa stood up quickly, feeling the heated exchange and if it did come to knuckles he didn't want his daughter hurt. If one of them could read the situation, all her tears might be misunderstood. He extended his arm to shake his hand, eager to defuse the tension. 'Axon, I assume. I am Lord Mensa, ruler of this terrestrial, and after what seems to have unfolded here, father of your fiancée, Caitlin.'

'What!' Axon's head snapped around to see the truth in Caitlin's eyes. 'How? You should have let me know, we were worried sick, Cait. You've been sending some kind of weird vibes through to Jett. He's been on tenterhooks all afternoon waiting for me to knock off.'

'Then if you knew, why not pop in then? Teach you for putting work before me.'

'I was giving Rory a hand as the team were short one a feisty redhead. And anyway, if you wanted us here sooner you know you only have to call Jett for help?' He eyed her, his moodiness apparent.

She rubbed at her forehead, worried how to tell him without him going off half-cocked and taking her home. 'Well I had to kick my father's arse first.' She gave her dad a grin. 'Then stop Orion from killing him.' She tried to make Axon smile, but with no luck, she continued. 'So it was a little intense to think of anyone else at the time. And to tell you the truth, I didn't need anyone's help, just time to sort it out.' Her fiancé was always irritable when he first knocked off and today was no different. 'Let's leave this lot to chat while we take a walk.' She slipped her arm through his and turned her head up delicately. 'Miss me… did you babe?' She smiled lovingly.

He rolled his eyes. 'Yes, but that does not let you off the hook. You are so grounded when you get home.' He gave her a slight grin.

Outside, Axon stopped a little way down the path. 'So you really kicked your father's butt and went up against Orion.' He started laughing when they were away from everyone. 'Geez, Cait quit picking up men, I don't care if they are your father. Give me a break.' He was now in a better mood and teased her.

She grinned when she saw how happy that news had made him. 'You bet I did. Blew up every gun in his goddamned palace but I won.'

'So you have all made up.'

'Just about. Aurek king hit my father, so I've used a bit of power getting them through the boy crush break up, but they are just about there. Hardly using any magic at all now.'

'So you okay, beautiful?' He smiled at his talented fiancée. 'You really did have us worried. It wasn't a, "come and get me now vibe", so we decided to make it a late call to give you time to sort it out.'

'We had our moments.' She shook her head. 'Unbelievable how it unfolded.'

'Sweetheart, you would be the only girl I know who went hunting and caught a parent. Couldn't you find any angaroos?'

She laughed at Axon's quirky humour. 'Sure, but since when have I ever done normal?'

'Any doubt he is your father?'

'At first, but not after spending this much time with him.' Her eyes lit up. 'He even laughs like me. Stay for dinner and judge for yourself. I guarantee Jett's already in there giving him the once over for me.'

Axon agreed. 'Jett knows him, I can tell. He has been unusually reserved about coming here.'

'But why? It was Jett's suggestion for Aurek to bring me here. Did he know?'

'Cait, there is a lot Jett keeps to himself. You have broken through some of his barriers but the layers to an ancient Ruler such as he runs deep.'

'I know. Aurek is a test at times too, although he has turned a corner, a big one, and become a real friend. Even so, I feel there is more to this meeting Jett has orchestrated.'

'Figured as much or you would be asking for me to take you home since Orion's temper has been extinguished.'

'I think it's best to play this out fully to see where it leads. Mensa talks about superior beings that mean me harm, threaten death, evil men that still search for me. The same ones who have apparently hunted for me all my life and are why my father had to give me up. They continue to raid his Home World looking for me and keep him under constant surveillance. If I'm to stop this lunacy, I have to learn more.'

'Just be careful, honey. I know you feel safe here with these men, but never underestimate the powers of evil.'

'Are you worried about your fragile little girl?' She grinned.

He threw his head back and laughed. 'My god no! I'm worried about them!'

'Rotten sod.' She slapped his arm. The movement had Axon excited, and he snatched her up in his arms, his mouth finding hers with luscious desire. When he let her go, his eyes were glazed and loving. 'Come home soon, honey, okay.'

'Stay for dinner?' She leant into him. Her heart tingled with love for this gorgeous man that trusted her completely.

His voice was sexy, alluring. 'Are you on the menu?'

She moved away and slipped her hand in his. 'Soon,' she whispered to him as they walked back toward the cabin. It was their time for only a moment, but times like this, they cherished.

'What is it that smells so good?' Axon took the lid off the large pot and took a whiff as they strolled back inside.

'Angaroos with baked veg.' Aurek took that moment to baste the meat while he held the cover up.

Jett looked over their shoulders. 'Want to stay for dinner, Axon? Aurek always over cooks.'

'Just invite yourself, Uncle.'

'Tosser.' Jett ruffled his hair. 'Dish up, we're starving.'

While having dinner, Aurek filled in the gaps for Axon and Jett. Both had a laugh about the begrizzo, thinking that was funny until they heard how Caitlin had stood up to Lord Mensa and his entire army, holding back the furious hunter and destroying their weapons.

Axon already knew, but it was even funnier the second time around as Aurek did exaggerate a little.

Jett grinned a lot but kept his wits about him. Lord Mensa hadn't recognised him yet, and he waited for him to connect the dots. Yet it didn't seem he was alert. Too interested in his daughter.

It was time for them to leave. Jett stood to wait and listened to his nephew brag for the last time about his day with Caitlin. *Girlfriend stealer!*

Aurek shook his head, while expressing the sight of her. 'Honestly Axon, the speed she snatched the guns, it even knocked out two of his biggest and most trusted guards he kept at his side. You should have seen their faces when they woke and found she was still standing. Hands on her hips, red hair flamed out around her and a cute little pout that he had hurt her feelings.' He eyed her affectionately. 'You got some gal there, Axon. You're a lucky man.'

'Yes, I know, and I'm taking her home with me,' Axon stirred him and at the same time got up from the table. 'Come on Jett, time to make a move.'

Aurek stood so quickly his chair flung backwards. 'You're not taking her anywhere, even if you are her damned fiancé. Firstly I've had to put up with her father intruding in on my trip for two days. Next things, you two, her goddamned bodyguards, arrive, invite yourselves for dinner and now almost my entire time with Glow has been imposed upon. This is bullshit!' He glanced at her and back at Axon, indignant and flustered. 'You owe me more time with her, or you can kiss your treaty goodbye.' He breathed out with frustration. 'So you better think again, you-blatzing-lot-of-unsociable-manipulators-of-my-time!' Orion had arisen and flexed his muscles.

'You are acting like a selfish shit now, Glow has a life!' Jett poked him with a finger.

Aurek stepped back from Jett, annoyed. 'I'm not in the mood, Uncle. This is so unreasonable. I want– No, I demand… another three days.' He saw Caitlin's expression and knelt beside her. His entire temperament changed. 'I haven't even had time to show you the mountain ranges yet. That's where the real hunting begins.'

Caitlin had spoken to Axon and knew he was checking where the resistance would come from if she left. Neither expected the reaction would be so strong from Aurek. Being in the situation with Lord Mensa and losing his cool as he had done, damaged the work she had put into him. Orion had begun to appear, his mood ready to flare at any moment at the thought of her departure.

Axon was quick to observe. He winked at her, letting her know he now trusted her call. It was not the time for her to come home. 'Cait are you happy to stay with Aurek another few days?'

'Love to, if you can spare me.'

Axon cracked his knuckles, thinking. 'Well, guess you can't blame a man for trying. Okay, new deal! Three days it is then. But any more nonsense like today, Aurek, and Cait comes home straight away. Do I make myself clear?' Axon wasn't going to leave it without a stern warning.

'Deal!' Aurek strode into the kitchen and started to clean up the mess to give Caitlin a moment to say goodbye. A slight grin of smugness now etched the corners of his mouth.

Lord Mensa had been pleasantly funny while Aurek told the story of what an arse the Lord had been. To have someone similar to what your daughter may have looked like walk into your life and feel such a strong family connection, would not have been easy. Yes, he handled it all wrong, but he was just lucky it was his Cait, someone smart enough to see through the tyrant's behaviour. Although they had found each other, it was now up to Caitlin, not him. If he worked hard, he knew she'd forgive as she had done with him. Axon, shook his extended hand when offered. 'Good luck winning Cait back. But don't disappoint her, ever, and us two will get along fine.'

Lord Mensa looked grateful. 'I only want a chance to be the father I have always wanted to be… if she lets me.'

'She stayed, it's a start.' Axon grinned and turned to his girl. Jett had his arm around her, chatting privately… *of course, he was*. 'Time to go, Jett,' he said, and gave Caitlin a final squeeze. 'Have fun, precious one; I'll see you in a few days.' He kissed her sweetly before giving her up.

'Aurek.' Axon eyed him. 'Please do something wrong, so she busts your cheeks.'

Aurek laughed heartily. 'Not likely but you can dream.'

Axon laughed too as he and Jett faded from sight.

Lord Mensa picked up his gear. 'That's some man you've got there, Glow. I can see he makes you very happy. As for me, I'm exhausted. It's been a long day. I hope you kids don't mind, but I'm going to make a move. You're quite welcome to come and stay in the castle tonight if you wish.'

'We're good,' Aurek called out. 'But have something to discuss with you. How about you meet us in the morning for breakfast at the café on the hill?'

'Sounds perfect. I'll see you both in the morning then?'

Aurek moved around the bench to shake his hand goodbye, wanting to let him know there were no bad feelings. After he had left, Aurek threw an arm around Caitlin. 'You don't mind us meeting up in the morning for a bit?'

'Surprised, and pleased.'

'Thanks for staying, Glow. I wasn't ready to be back in the real world yet.' He kissed her head and went over to the fire. He picked up the empty basket, and filled it with logs from the front porch.

Caitlin chatted as he worked. 'Bet you feel like you've been on a roller coaster.'

'We have, but it's over, thank goodness.' He put the basket beside the hearth and tossed a few logs from it onto the fire.

'I'm happy to hear that, and more than delighted to have the bonus of an extra few days. I wasn't ready to go back to work either; I feel as though I haven't left.' She looked spent.

'Yes, well, how about you let me try to rectify that, starting now.' He cranked up some music while he made them a hot drink.

'Now that's what I'm talking about.' Caitlin took her cocoa and clunked mugs. The night was theirs at last. Aurek put down their drinks and pulled her into his arms to dance.

He was excellent at rock and roll and had them up dancing for quite some time before they flopped down on the cushions in front of the fireplace and talked until dawn. They had only just drifted off when Lord Mensa arrived with breakfast.

'Thought I'd save you the walk and give you breakfast in bed… well so to speak.' He smiled brightly, and his smile turned more brilliant when Caitlin gave him a big hug for being so thoughtful.

'This was a nice gesture, old man,' Aurek remarked as he swallowed down three pancakes with syrup, all in one go.

The servants he brought fussed around them, giving them five-star service, and it was an extra thrill to see Caitlin eating for a change. He had gone to great lengths to ensure it would be food she was used to eating. Since his daughter had been there, all she had done was pick like a bird and push his Home World delicacies around her plate.

During the meal, Lord Mensa did most of the talking, as he could see they had barely slept. However, all immortals revitalise once they have eaten, so after breakfast was over, and Caitlin looked refreshed, he asked a lot of questions about Axon. The main one had her stuck for words.

'I was wondered why you two aren't married yet. He obviously adores you. He was so sweet with you last night, it did my heart good to see someone so very deeply committed to you. The guy would hand you the universe on a platter if you asked for it.'

'He is pretty off the charts adorable.' She smiled dreamily, and then pondered the first part of his question. Her usual response was to say her life had been too busy to get married, but to say that to her father sounded empty.

'I have wondered that too, old man,' Aurek added.

'So what has been the hold-up sweetheart?' Lord Mensa said.

'Maybe I've been waiting to find my father so he can give me away.' She nudged him affectionately.

'Well, I'm here, and been waiting for this day for long enough,' said Lord Mensa.

'That was why I wanted to talk to you this morning. How about we help Glow organise the wedding right now, while she has time off?'

'What? Don't you know what a big deal it is? I mean it's not something we can throw together in an instant. It will take months of planning, and I haven't got a venue or anything, never mind the time it would take to dedicate to such a massive project.'

Lord Mensa sat thinking. 'You are making this far too big a deal, Caitlin. Aurek has apparently kept you here for a very noble reason. I thought he was acting a selfish twit as usual, but lo and behold, the guy actually wants to do something lovely for you. So let's break it down and see how we go... now try to think, there must be somewhere you've been that screamed, *wedding*.' He cocked his head to the side with a cheeky expression as he pushed her to give an answer. To see his only daughter find the happiness he always hoped she would find was more than a dream. Between him and his buddy, they could move mountains right now, today, to make it happen. 'Oh, and it's on me of course, the entire wedding. Money is no object.'

'You both honestly want to spend the next three days planning a wedding with me and not go hunting... at all?' She eyed them.

'We can go hunting any time of the year, but you only get married once. Between us, let's make it an amazing wedding, so the union sticks and lasts an eternity.'

Mensa's hand slapped the high five Aurek held up to him. 'There's only one man I've ever heard of and now met that is anywhere near good enough for my little girl, and he was here last night.' He smiled at Caitlin. 'And I'm not letting you lose him.'

Caitlin's expression was thoughtful, hopeful, as her coy smile warmed Aurek. 'Where? I can tell you have somewhere in mind.'

'Actually, it wasn't until we arrived on your Home World within Orion's Belt that I imagined how simply divine it would be to have a wedding there.'

'My home?' Aurek was taken back.

'From the air, I spotted the resort style grounds, modern chalets and the daydream to have such opulence around me on my special day, triggered the fantasy. A beautiful walk through picturesque gardens, lighting, soft music and delicate blooms that lined the way to my man.' She blinked and smiled.

'Are you kidding?' He slapped his leg. Aurek wore one of his amusingly abnormal grins Caitlin found endearing. 'You really want it at my house?' He sounded chuffed.

She nodded. 'I know, it's a crazy idea, but seriously, I just loved it. I can remember thinking, wow what could anyone offer this guy to stop him being naughty? He has everything anyone could dream to have.'

'I'm honoured, even if you did think of me as bad.'

Caitlin smiled. 'Well, you proved me wrong. That day I met my friend Aurek there, not the man I expected. You took me for a walk in the grounds where a magical garden bloomed, and life and its sounds filled the air. You made me love it even more.' She grinned. 'Honestly, you wouldn't mind, then?'

'Mind? I must insist.' He looked across at Lord Mensa and back at Caitlin. 'By the time we two are through spoiling you, this will be the biggest event ever.'

'Steady guys, I just want something simple.' Her eyes darted as she was feeling as if ready to make a run for it.

'Jett's going to be so blatzing jealous!' Aurek puffed out his chest.

Caitlin held her hand up. 'Hold on, maybe we're getting a little ahead of ourselves here, big is scary, and there will be no ruffling the feathers of my other bestie!'

He could see the sudden panic that filled her eyes and even though he hated to give in to his uncle, for Glow he had to start to compromise or risk hurting her. 'How about this,' he proposed. 'We give and take with the festivities. You ladies can have your hen's night on Orion and us men can duck over to Pluto for the buck's night. I'm sure the lads would enjoy a night ski. Nothing makes a man want to warm up next to his woman more than after a night on that ice world. He will be begging to be with you.'

Excited, Lord Mensa slapped the side of his leg. 'That's it then, wedding is on.'

'Yep, looks that way.' Caitlin grinned.

Lord Mensa punched the air and let out his joy, picked her up and swung her around happily. Suddenly he stopped dead. 'Pluto! Hades! Tell me Aurek didn't say that planet.'

Caitlin was stunned with his sudden mood swing. His face was so red, it looked ready to explode. 'Yes, Pluto, why? Hades was here last night. I don't see the issue here. What's going on?'

'Hades! Here!' He was even more exasperated.

'Yes– Jett. You met him last night. One and the same; Jett is how I refer to him to keep his identity secret to outsiders, but you're hardly a stranger so you might as well know.'

His tone was so low she strained to hear him as if something was so secret he was afraid to share with her. 'Caitlin, it is he and Zeus that have hounded me for years. Hell! I've never met him personally, just their army and the roughneck goons they send to watch me. After last night he now knows you are my daughter and he and his brother will be together right now planning your demise. Honestly, Caitlin, you should have told me who he was; we could have kept it a secret about me being your father.'

'Dad, please don't do this. You have feared for my life since I was born and I want you to stop hiding me. I'm all grown up now and can take care of myself. I only surround myself with the most caring of people, and they love me as I love them. Jett is one of my dearest friends, and even if my time was up and I had to die by anyone's hands, I would choose a friend to kill me. I feel safe with Jett, so protected in fact, that if I had a brother, I would wish it to be him. We have a bond so strong the devil himself would have a hard time breaking it. Ask Aurek, he's seen him with me and knows what we share.'

Aurek agreed. 'He's absolutely smitten by her and would never let anyone harm her. Why do you think he came last night? They share something, and he feels her; even now he will know she has got upset and will be worried.'

She held her father's hand. 'Jett already knows who I am. When I first met him, I told him about my life, and he disappeared for a week. He went and checked out my story and would have guessed who I really was, but still chose to love me anyway. Things have changed for Jett. He's content and is the last person in the universe that would ever frighten me. Actually, I believe he planned this meeting between us. Didn't he Aurek?' She eyed him.

'What, he knew you were bringing her here?' Lord Mensa turned nastily toward Aurek.

Aurek nodded. 'He suggested it. I didn't understand why at the time, but I had no plans to cross him. He was very strict about how to care for Caitlin and grilled me for hours before allowing me to take her anywhere. There were so many other beautiful places I could have gone to, but it all makes sense now.'

Caitlin was desperate to end the tension. 'The war between you two is over. This was his way of letting you know. Don't look at him like Hades the enemy, but Jett, one of my dearest friends, one who will spend forever trying to make it up to me. Give yourself a chance to heal by making the first step. The only way to do that is to leave the past in the past like yesterday when I forgave you.'

'Yes, you did forgive me! But Caitlin, I'm family! It's easier to forgive blood.'

Aurek shook his head. 'You don't know your daughter. To fill you in might help you see the person we have all grown to love. Jett kidnapped her and yet she forgave him and chose to stay with him for months. I tried to blow her team up twice. She was so close to death Zeus summoned my cousin Apollo to come down and bring her back to life. When I realised she was one of the Cosmic Riders and it was her I almost killed, I literally threw up. I was beside myself with grief, but Glow forgave me and chose to spend time with just me, so I too could heal. You have taken up some of the time she promised me, and I can confidently say that she won't go home now until she has honoured our agreement. You saw her with W o l f last night; they are so deeply in love that any other woman would have gone home eagerly to be with her man. Not Glow, she still has room in her heart for us and chose to stay. No thought for her own needs. That is how forgiving your beautiful daughter is to us. Tell me she didn't inherit a little of that from you, my old friend.' He smiled.

Lord Mensa shook his head. 'Wolf? I heard you call him that last night.'

Caitlin grinned. 'That is Axon's alias as I will give you one before you meet Jett's family, to keep you safe until you're confident in their presence.'

'Let's hope Zeus never finds out then. If Hades has caved, I guarantee his brother will not have or ever will. He stands to lose the most as he will not be beholden to any man… or woman. This I am sure of.' Lord Mensa looked miles away before moving his head and breathing deeply. He had lost the battle but never again was any man going to stop him from being with his daughter. If an alias had protected his daughter thus far, it would protect him, and he was all for it. 'So when the time comes to introduce me to these gods, what will you call me?' He raised a brow cheering up some.

Caitlin had already given this a lot of thought and realised he had too. Her family would always be a target due to the position she held with the Cosmics. The name was an obvious choice, and she smiled as she spoke. 'Torpez, after your exquisite precious stones.'

With a toss of his head, he belly-laughed. 'I like it.'

Aurek slapped a hand on his back. 'So you are in, old boy? Are you happy to go to Pluto for the buck's night?'

'Well, put it this way, I don't think I can forgive Hades for the hell he put me through, but for Caitlin, for now, I will look upon him as Jett and put our differences aside, at least until after the wedding. But mark my words, I have a score to settle with Hades and man to man, it will happen.'

Caitlin covered her ears. 'La la … don't want to know about it. But if either of you gets hurt, I will step in.'

Aurek snatched her up in his arms, laughing. 'You will stay out of it Glow. Men's business, bruises heal and unless your father has retribution, he will not.'

He put her down. 'Now, about the dress.' Aurek spoke to her father.

'Already on it. Saw to it this morning before I left. I have known you long enough, my boy, to know exactly what you wanted to talk about today. My dressmaker is on her way here now to measure Glow. A gown of French lace is already being designed,' said Lord Mensa.

Caitlin shook her head, and red curls fell loosely about her. 'Aurek, when did you come up with this plan? Is this the reason for the tantrum to get me to stay a few extra days?'

'Guilty!' He winced, his mouth holding back a smile. 'When I saw how cute as a button you were with Axon, I thought hell… if I can't have her, Jett's not getting her either. I want you an old married woman, so he leaves you alone. You're my girl!' He crossed his arms stubbornly, then seeing her look, he quickly backtracked. 'Not funny… okay truth, I want to do something nice for you like you have done for me. That's all.'

Caitlin stood up and hugged him. 'Thought so, and it's lovely of you, both of you,' she added as she also hugged her father. 'But can we slow down you two?' She chuckled, sitting back down. 'Geez! For a start, we live in a magical world. My horse will dress me in any style I so desire. So save your money, please.'

Mensa leant forward. 'Even so, Caitlin, I would still like to have a dress made up for you, a real one to keep. I've waited for this day since your birth. Let me spoil you a little, please?'

Caitlin patted his hand. 'It would be sweet of you to do so, but dresses take forever to be made. I think Axon is planning to elope with me if we are not married soon.'

'There's nothing that can't be done when you are Lord over all who dwell here. I promise it will be ready when you are.' As he spoke a horse-drawn carriage pulled up, and swayed heavily to one side as a rather large woman stepped out. With pink hair and pins stuck in her apron, she dragged the tape measure from around her neck and without writing down a thing, measured Caitlin and was back in the carriage within seconds.

'Mustn't dilly-dally,' she said as she waved out the window with a hanky. 'I have a gown of much importance to make.'

'Are you all for real?' Caitlin chuckled. 'I feel like Alice in Wonderland, already late for the tea party.'

Lord Mensa took both her hands. 'Allow me this pleasure, I beg you.'

How could she say no to either of them? Both waited for her to give them the go ahead.

'How long will your team take to make the dress?'

'I'll work them around the clock, so two days max.'

'How long will it take you, Aurek, to organise the event? And I only want a small private affair.'

'I have three days left with you. If we have any hope of surprising that man of yours, we obviously need to work fast. Between a few helpers and us we should get most of it organised before you have to go home.' Aurek waited for her reaction.

Her eyes were bright and alight with excitement. 'Then it's home and what's the plan to prevent Axon from whisking me off to elope?'

Aurek made patterns on an NAVtablet he pulled from his pocket. This he used to compile time frames they had already discussed. 'Three days to organise the event, another day for the hen's and the buck's night, and the following day… is the wedding. That's five days in total. So on the fourth day when you go home, Axon can be told it is his buck's night and no ifs, buts or sneaking off will get him out of having a wedding with all us attending. Uncle Jett will track you, Cait, and bring you back. He will have no option but to follow our plan.'

'Maybe I should contact him now and tell him, save all the worry. I don't think he likes surprises anyway.'

'Maybe we should gag you!' Aurek laughed. 'Axon's going to be so happy you're finally committed solely to him, he'll not care, trust me.' Aurek rubbed his chin, his mind now elsewhere. 'First things first.' He turned back to Caitlin. 'Who's the best person to organise your friends to come?'

'Someone who is going to love all this cloak and dagger stuff. Rory will be thrilled to know a secret Axon doesn't know.' Caitlin's eyes shone brightly, knowing Rory could at least be involved.

'While you speak to him, I will contact Uncle Jett to organise our side of the family,' Aurek said. 'And while I'm at it I will arrange a hunting party. The food on the menu at the reception has to include meat of the best quality.'

'Did you need help? I know Rory would be in that as well. You're talking about Taurus right? He'll be stoked.'

'Good, that's two of us.'

'I'm in.' Lord Mensa was eager.

'That makes three and is all we need.' Aurek looked pleased.

'Hey! What about me?' Caitlin asked.

'Not to Taurus.' Aurek was firm. 'It's too dangerous. Aldebaran may have given us the okay, but he knows as well as I do that this deal is for men hunters only. Aurus, who is the current overall Ruler, is not trustworthy when there is a lady present. He is a fool and a dangerous one at that and will go to war rather than give up a woman he has decided is his. Jett would never allow it and if Axon knew he would take you home immediately!'

'Surely the guy is no worse than you two. You know I can handle myself. You're taking Rory. That's not fair,' Caitlin grumbled.

'His laws prevent females having any say. It is the Home World of the bull and all that it represents. Sorry, but your welfare and virtue are at risk and we will not budge, Glow, no way.'

She grinned. 'Then the bull love-lust thing runs rampant among the menfolk too?'

He touched her nose. 'You are too sweet and innocent to even know what I am talking about. Now, stop nagging.' He shook his head.

Lord Mensa agreed and put his arm around his daughter. 'Come on feisty one, let Aurek leave. He still has to call in and speak to Jett about the buck's night.'

'Yes! Can't forget the most important event, the boys' night!' Aurek gave a wonky grin, teasing Caitlin.

She screwed up her nose and put her finger up.

'Did you just give me the birdy? That's it. When I get back, young lady, you have some serious crawling to do.' Aurek spoke to Lord Mensa. 'It will be easier if we leave now and coordinate this from my house. Don't want a certain god coming here and guessing who Caitlin's father really is… do we now?'

In an instant, they were transported to Aurek's Home World on Orion's Belt.

Aurek spoke to a couple of guards before going over to talk with Caitlin and Lord Mensa. Both strolled in the garden that was his pride and joy. Little did anyone know but he had a passion for gardening and was chuffed Caitlin wanted her wedding to be within the flowering beds of his hard labour. They stopped when he approached. 'I have to leave if I want to achieve anything today. Glow, I have instructed the guards to take you to the NAVcom. Please get Rory's coordinates and send them through to me on this device.' He handed her a small disc with some buttons. 'I can call in on him to keep it private after seeing Jett. '

'Would you like me to organise everything with Rory rather than you going out of your way?' she offered.

He shook his head with a slight grin. 'You have to allow me some manhood. Let me call the shots for a bit and care for you like I promised I could. While we are hunting tomorrow, you can do whatever you wish.' He eyed her, amused, and added, 'except go home to Axon and blab.'

'You know me better than you should.' She grinned. 'I guess

I can find something to do while you both go on an exciting hunt looking for Taurus prime with your big guns.'

'That's my girl, and I promise you'll not be bored while I'm gone. I have a plan.'

Chapter Forty
Encounter with the
King of Gods

It was day two of Caitlin's stay on Orion's Belt. Before heading out on his hunting trip for the day, Aurek had stopped at Caitlin's door and knocked.

'I'm decent,' she called out. 'You can come in.' She was dressed and sat with the French doors open, admiring the garden while drinking tea the butler had fetched for her.

'Lord Mensa and Rory will be here any minute. You okay?'

'Sure, I might have this and go for a swim.'

'Might want to get showered and dressed. Jett will be here in an hour to pick you up.'

She dumped her cup lopsidedly on the saucer and stood up. 'Far out, you little sneak. That is so cool.'

'I told you I had something planned.'

'Next time, I will believe you. Where's he taking me? What will I wear?'

'As it's my uncle, I would say somewhere hot and relaxing, so dress sun smart.'

The butler interrupted them. 'Your hunting party has arrived, Squire.'

'Got to go, have fun!' He tipped his hat to her.

'Will now. You too,' she called after him and shut the door before doing a joyous jig behind it. She giggled when she overheard Aurek grumble, 'bet she's doing a happy dance because Uncle Shithead is on his way.'

The butler answered, 'Would you like me to detain him, sir?'

Then came Aurek's answer, 'better not, he might turn you into a toad again.'

To this, Caitlin fell on the bed pulling the pillow over her face to laugh. *This is such fun.*

Not wishing to waste the day dawdling, Caitlin scrambled off the bed and, once in the bathroom, closed the door behind her. She wanted to sing at the top of her voice, and not be overheard. In the shower, her giggles increased as the tune gurgled unrecognisably each time her head went under the water. Caitlin's mind was also on her fiancé. She couldn't wait to discuss her pending wedding with Jett. The tune changed to a marriage ditty and she called out in a musical tone, "Three more sleeps." Her voice was pitchy, but she didn't care. "Then I become Mrs Axon Stanton." While singing, her left hand lifted so she could admire the ring Axon had put on her finger. The diamond sparkled under the water and gave her tingles of happiness. Even while dressing, she hummed more wedding tunes and spun in circles like a little girl. Her high-spirited frame of mind made her cheeks flush, and the glow of her skin radiated her mood.

'Your visitor is here, Miss Glow,' the butler called to her through the door.

'I'm ready,' she called back and, smiling at her reflexion, she left the bathroom.

Footsteps on the floorboards outside her room made her swing around as Jett peered around the corner.

'He said you were decent.'

She squealed his name, excited he had arrived.

His big arms folded her up in a nice warm hug. 'Missed you, Glow.' He looked pleased to see her too.

'Were you worried about me the other day?' she stirred after he let her go.

'As a matter of fact, I was, well that was until I found out what you did to your father. God help him if he had of been a stranger.'

She grabbed her bag. 'I would have let Aurek off his leash. He had turned back into Orion and was one big dude to handle when cranky.'

Jett grinned, 'It's been a big few days for you. How about we go somewhere relaxing?'

'Was hoping you'd say that.' She tossed her handbag on the side table, grabbed her bathers off the bed, and stuffed them into a beach bag she had packed with a towel, sunscreen and sunnies. 'I'm ready then,' she said, and slid sunglasses on her head.

'Well, don't you look refreshed and happy? I hope you told that brat of a nephew of mine to nick off, that you're my girlfriend again?'

She slapped a hand over her mouth to muffle a laugh before speaking. 'You two are so much alike. Now play nice.'

'Not until you tell me I'm your favourite.'

She chuckled. 'You're both my favourites; now stop it.'

'I have you for a whole day, and I will use my power if I have to, but I will get my way.'

'Planning this wedding has put him right up there,' she teased him.

'That crawling snake. I knew I'd have my work cut out for me today. But by sundown you will be mine again, I swear he will not steal my girl.'

She leant into him laughing, he was such a funny man and had missed his skylarking.

He smiled, his dark caring eyes gave her comfort, always had and no man could give what he gave. It was a friendship that would last the ages, this she was sure of, and he didn't ever have to prove it. He winked, knowing exactly what she was thinking. He loved making her laugh. In that moment of quiet confidence and comfort with each other, he transported them to Dolphin Island within Delphinus.

Caitlin squealed and splashed him when he accidentally landed them in the water instead of on the beach. He had missed the fun they enjoyed together and even now it mystified him how he could be so in love and yet still hold this strong feeling for his Glow. The smallest of gifts gave her pleasure, and he shivered with the power of the vibe she set off inside him. Glow's magic was getting stronger, and he pondered for a moment if it was due to the joining of her with her father.

'Let's get changed. We're wet anyway.' She started trudging up the sandy bank.

'Yes, I'm coming.' He almost ran after her as she headed for land. Like a magnet, she drew him to her and for today, with just Caitlin was exactly where he wanted to be.

The resort staff gave them towels, and after drying off, they lay on them chatting. Never had Jett confided in anyone as he did in Caitlin; she had such an innocent mind, and a word here and there settled trepidations like no others could. 'You know I love you Glow.' He met her compassionate eyes.

'And your Melita and I love you too, but differently, as you do me.'

He liked that she got it, that his deep affection was as a friend, sibling and the deity he believed her now to be, his goddess, best friend and confidant.

* * * *

'Hades, what are you doing here?' Startled by a familiar voice, they shaded their eyes to see his brother, Zeus standing over them.

He nodded towards Caitlin. 'Glow Girl, what a surprise!'

'Calyx!' Caitlin was quick to stand and giggled shyly when he wrapped her in his massive, golden-haired arms for a hug. 'Is Zuri with you?' She peered around him to see if she was near.

'No, this is a business trip. I'm entertaining a business associate.' He moved to look over her head and gave Jett a wink.

A gentle movement had her at arms' length. 'You've recovered and look well.' He smiled, 'and your perfume is delightful. Do they make a water resistant fragrance now?' He noted her look and picked up a ringlet of her red locks. 'I only say that because your hair is still wet from a swim.'

Jett had noticed how strong her "fear bouquet" had become but figured it was because they were alone and once she settled it would ease up, which it did. Yet he had noticed it got strong again seconds before his brother arrived. He was showing up as her inner fear, and it surprised him as they had met a few times now. However, this scent was different and made him wary, so much so he decided to hide the truth, not wishing his brother to know of Caitlin's secret weapon, her calming agent against the most notorious of tyrants.

'I bought that perfume for her a while ago; the magical scent lingers on her skin for days and is enhanced by heat.' He put his hand up, gesturing to the hot day.

'Thanks,' she mouthed as she dropped beside Jett. He had her back as always, and she relaxed beside him while Calyx made small talk. Jett finally stood up and pulled Caitlin up with him. 'Well we're off to have some lunch, so I guess we'll catch up later.'

'What, I don't get an invite?'

'Course, join us.' Jett's face, however, said the opposite. He had hoped his brother would be on his way as always. The last thing he wanted was to share Caitlin when this would be their last time together before she married Axon. The thought worried him. He questioned if Axon would be so willing to share her once they were man and wife. He contemplated how to get around the new treaty he signed. It stated in the contract to "never again" kidnap her, and he had smiled at the wording. He knew Axon had drawn it up. He couldn't imagine any existence without her anymore so would definitely be going back to re-visit that agreement if Axon stopped her visits to Pluto.

Calyx grinned and ignored the obvious, "nick off will you" look his brother gave him. 'Thanks, bro, we'd love to join you both. My business associate is good at her job, but the conversation is proving to be a real tooth puller.' He winked again at Jett as if he understood the double meaning.

Caitlin was no fool and as she eyed Calyx, she felt sorry for his wife, Hera. He was here with another woman, flirting with his eyes, and she knew now the stories of Zeus being a lady-killer were true. Caitlin had befriended Zuri, this being the alias of the goddess Hera. She wished now for her sake that the newly improved god she knew as Calyx would see the light and stop his cheating ways. The sadness in Zuri's eyes… she now knew the reason. *His wife knows.*

At the restaurant, Calyx overpowered the room with his entrance. All heads turned as his striking good looks caught their attention. The leggy tall blonde with far too much makeup and a tight red dress, who hung off his arm was barely noticeable due to his vibrant personality.

As he held the chair for her, the perfume almost gagged Caitlin. Her only option was to sip on water until her senses adjusted. The blonde woman started to talk when seated and didn't stop until her meal arrived. Peace, at last, Caitlin thought, and Jett nodded, agreeing with her. She kept forgetting he could read her every thought and grinned. *And did you get a load of those boobs, what a fake!* Jett spat his drink and gagged.

Calyx gave him a hard pat on the back. 'You right there?' He looked concerned as both men eyed each other. Calyx suddenly understood by Jett's impatient sigh, that he wasn't enjoying the company of his brother's friend.

Caitlin picked it up too and was glad she wasn't alone.

'Calyx, we are brothers, so you will understand when I say, four is a crowd. I want time alone with Glow, to talk to her, not listen to that waffle. I can barely make out what Glow is thinking with the ramblings of your friend. If you want to stay, she goes!' He glanced towards the woman who still waffled to Caitlin, not taking a breath. She wouldn't have heard a word he said.

Calyx's head swung towards his lady friend. He had not noticed her since they arrived at the table. His mind was elsewhere, but with Jett mentioning it, her voice unexpectedly irritated him too. His nostrils flared. 'Enough, I can't hear myself think, woman. Go find someone else to bug or I will turn you into one!' he seethed with teeth closed in a growl.

The woman almost ran from him. The tone even shook Caitlin, but if she was to be with superior beings, she had to get used to how they spoke sometimes. To settle down, she decided to let the two brothers bond and with a smile, got up. 'My shout!'

'What with?' Jett was amused. Caitlin never carried money with her.

'Hey, who needs money when I have a table to book it to?' She chuckled and, giving them no choice, she left them to have some brother bonding time.

When she came back, their differences had been sorted and whatever was said had cleared the air.

'Here we go.' Caitlin had a waiter beside her holding a tray. She sat while he placed the drinks in front of them.

'What's this?' Calyx sniffed the aroma. 'Ah, you are mixing our drinks. She wants us in a better mood, brother.'

'Then let's not disappoint her.' Jett clinked goblets with them both and drank his down. Licking his lips, he looked up at the waiter. 'Another round of whatever that was.'

'Moonjuice, Starstarter and your friend's secret ingredient coming up.' He left.

Both tried desperately to find out what it was, and even tried tickling her, but she didn't give it up. It did work. The elixir loosened their tongues, the conversation becoming vocal, competitive and what she hoped for, lots of fun.

* * * *

A sobering dump in Aurek's pool as they miss-landed had them in stitches as they scrambled for the sides and pulled themselves out. 'How did we end up back here?'

Calyx had scratched his head before he swam to catch up. Once out of the water, the three of them headed for the deck chairs, opting to have an afternoon siesta. Calyx pulled his lounge next to Caitlin's.

'Can't get enough of that scent you wear. Now, don't move while I sleep or I'll have to use my magic to keep you here.' He flopped onto the deck chair beside her, his eyelids dropped on impact, and a slight snore escaped him that made Caitlin chuckle.

'Shh, sleep sweetie.' Jett ran a hand over her head before he too collapsed.

* * * *

'What's going on, Cait?' She woke to Rory, his arms folded and his eyes alight with seething fury.

'They're wasted,' Torpez said.

'You think!' Rory stared back at Caitlin.

Aurek shook Zeus awake. 'What are you doing here, Uncle?' But the god closed his eyes again, ignoring him.

Caitlin was between them and put her hands out and slapped them both on their arms. 'Wake up you two! I'm not taking all the blame by myself.'

Both men sat up, rubbing their eyes.

'It's Glow's fault.' Jett was quick to blame. 'She was in charge of drinks only she tricked us by mixing them.'

She made a defensive sound. 'You didn't have to drink them.'

Calyx's hands went up. 'No way am I going to take the blame either. I'm with Jett. It was all her fault.' He was enjoying the blame game just as much.

Caitlin chuckled. 'Whatever, it worked. You both had a good time and don't tell me you didn't.' She slapped them both again.

They laughed with her. Both woke happy from an enjoyable day and ignored the hands on hips and huffy looks they were receiving.

'Who's your new friend?' Rory asked in the tone of, *hell no, not another one.*

'Rory, meet Calyx, Jett's brother.' Caitlin introduced Rory, although his expression didn't change as he shook his hand.

Rory still hadn't been able to let go of the protectiveness he felt towards her. He was especially ticked off Axon was getting so lax with her security. If this was how she was acting around these gods, especially someone as powerful as Zeus, this was stopping right now.

'Calyx,' he said and gave a polite nod before he folded his arms again and stood back assessing the situation. He didn't like this at all. Something didn't feel right, and as soon as the introductions were over, he intended on speaking to Caitlin not only about her behaviour as a Rider but about whatever was going on here. His instinct had his hackles up.

Caitlin pointed to her father. 'And this is Torpez from the camping trip I told you about.'

'Refresh me.'

'The begrizzo, remember?'

'Ah, that's right.' Calyx shook her father's hand for the first time ever. 'Pleased to put a name to the story. Where are you from, Torpez?' Calyx had an uncertain look in his eyes. 'I'm sure I know the face.'

Caitlin's father had grown a full faced beard and had mentioned how much weight he had put on of late, so luckily for him, Calyx shrugged. 'You look like someone… but…' He tilted his head and looked him up and down. 'Nope must be too much of that elixir Glow Girl had me drinking.' He brushed away his thoughts with a sweep of his hand. 'Where did you say you were from again?'

Jett was almost sure Calyx would not recognise the man he hounded. Even he'd had a hard time identifying Lord Mensa when meeting him the night before. It had been many years since Calyx met with Lord Mensa and afterwards, it was his squadron leader who was instigating and carrying out the many raids on behalf of Calyx. Yet he was still astute enough to question. Jett was just about to intervene when Caitlin rested a hand on Calyx's arm.

'Like you, he prefers to keep his Home World private, but what I can tell you is that his land is picturesque and,' she smiled, 'is now short of one big old bear.'

'A begrizzo you say, they are mammoth and hard to catch.' Calyx was intrigued. 'Was it a big mongrel?' His interest was genuine.

'Sure was. The killer beast was as tall as a two-storey building and one wide. We had quite a battle bringing the oversized furburger down.'

Caitlin chuckled…'He gets bigger every time this story is told.'

Calyx patted her hand that was still on his arm. He liked it and smiled at her. 'It's a man's bragging rights, Glow.'

With him not needing any further calming, Caitlin took her arm away from him. 'Then I will leave you two thrill seekers to your tale that I have now heard many times over. Rory has asked to speak to me, so call me if you want the real story.' She waved her hand in a gesture, blowing them off, and stuck her nose in the air. This action made them laugh, and although she had moved from easy earshot, she kept a watchful eye on both while listening to Rory. She was pleased when Calyx placed an arm around her father and directed him to the bar, where they sat and chatted. 'I love a good hunting story, continue,' she heard Calyx say and during the possibly over-exaggerated tale, heard them laugh on and off as it unfolded. She stood half listening to make sure all was well while Rory drilled her about her drinking.

'Caitlin, relax, they're fine, now start talking.' Rory walked her away from the others. He could see she wasn't listening to him and was getting more frustrated than he had been when first arriving. 'I want to know who gave you permission to go out getting drunk with the planet Rulers while on the job. It sure wasn't me!'

'I only had a couple to get them in a better mood with each other. So what – you never drink with any of the Rulers?' She threw it back at him.

'That's different, Cait, I'm a man, and your behaviour is unbecoming of you. And by sleeping between them, you're acting like a tart instead of a Rider.'

'You know why m e n do that. I can't control the scent I give off. Get over it, Rory,' she yelled at him.

'Caitlin! Quit this crybaby boohoo, shit. It's me you are talking to here, and I will not pander to you. I'm ordering you to try and regulate that power for all our sakes. These deities have no idea how innocent you are or what you have been through. Need I remind you these are ancient men who are used to getting their own way? So stop throwing yourself at them to get your way. It won't always work, but you don't understand this yet, and that is the innocent in you. I am and always have been your teacher and voice of reason and deserve more respect.'

She hung her head. She wasn't sure at all what she was doing and he was right, she would always need him, her saviour. 'Rory, all I know is something overpowers me. It sets me on a course I cannot deviate from. Then it's gone and leaves me to deal with the situation I have been put into. At the minute I'm me, here, talking to you. But at any moment I can be steered into a new mission. I don't mean to hurt or scare you, but this thing is big, and I have no control when it takes me over, dumps me in a situation and leaves me to sort it out.'

'What! Really? Does Axon know?'

She nodded. 'He thinks the universe is fuelling me. He trusts that I will learn to control it as we all do when given a new gift. Zoren thinks I channel an ancient goddess. That she teaches me to be the one I was put here to become.'

'Cait, you should have told me. I can adjust the team's powers to give you more will to control it. I hold things back too, but we should never do it from each other. I don't think even Axon knows how much stronger our team has become since taking on the Cloud Riders' powers. We were extraordinary anyway. Now it's intense.'

She poked at his chest. 'You're no better than me, your abilities are still growing too, aren't they Rory?'

'Shush.' He quickly looked around to make sure no one was near listening.

She motioned for him to bend closer so she could whisper and put her hand to his ear. 'I know what you are capable of and that we've both continued to evolve, but I'd never tell a soul if that's why you are worried about me drinking with the gods. I lock everything I love up inside so no one can find that information. I store you all in my secret garden, you know, where I used to hide from the pain before I met you.'

He held her face between his hands. 'I know my secret is safe with you. You are my dearest friend, Cait, and always will be. I just don't want them finding out about your capabilities. One day, you may just need that talent of yours to save not only you but all of us.'

His sweetness brought tears to her eyes. 'From now on, that's locked deep in my secret garden too.' She patted her chest area. He pulled her in for a hug. 'Just don't shut me out, please trust me, okay.'

Her wet eyes stared up at him. 'She does.' A voice unlike hers, but coming from Caitlin's mouth, spoke to Rory, and his eyes widened, her grip not letting him move. 'For saving her life her bond with you is forever, but you must trust in the measures put in place to prevent this war that is imminent. Hades will fight beside Zeus to claim Mercury. Her work is not complete.'

Caitlin collapsed against Rory, and he scooped her up and laid her on the lounge. 'Caitlin, you okay?' he whispered close to her ear, not wanting to attract any of the others to them. He had been given a message but needed to talk to her privately. She fluttered her eyelashes as she came around. 'Rory, what happened?'

'You don't remember what you just said?'

'I said…' She frowned. 'I keep it locked deep in here.'

He smiled. 'Yes Cait, that's all you said.' He knew now that she would be off on another mission soon and this news had him panic. He wanted her home until it went down.

'Time I took you home, Cait.'

'Agreed,' she said, unsure why she passed out. She figured he was right, she needed to rest after all that had transpired over the last few days. She was sure Aurek wouldn't mind so long as she was back for the hen's night. After all, he had said how busy he was going to be. Best go home and let the team help her get into top form for the big day.

Rory smiled. 'Three days will go fast, and then you'll be back here on Orion's Home World for the pre-wedding party the girls are organising for you.'

'I guess Aurek's happy now; he should be okay with it when he finds out I just passed out.'

'You did well with him. He's a changed man.'

'He is rather adorable. You know he has organised everything.' She shrugged. 'So what's left?'

'Exactly… now go say your goodbyes while I get the horses ready.'

When she hugged Jett, he agreed with Rory. 'You need some time to rest before the big day. Have some girl time with the other members of your team.'

Aurek agreed with them too. He didn't like what he saw in Calyx's eyes when his uncle looked at her. He wanted her as far away from Calyx as he could get her. He might have been family, but Aurek knew that look only too well.

'You must be sick to death of us demanding menfolk.' Her father smiled, but she could see the underlying meaning. He was worried for her to be around, not Calyx, but Zeus, her biggest threat. 'I'll call you,' he whispered, winked and gave her a gentle squeeze.

Calyx sat watching her with intensity and stood with a strange look on his face as she approached him. He had moved away from the others. Coming closer to him, she wondered if he'd picked up the connection between father and daughter. Even though it was only a short reunion between them, the family bond was strong. Her hands shook so she hid them behind her back as she approached him. 'Rory thinks it best that I go home and have some time with him and the team before the wedding.'

Calyx sucked in his breath when she put out her hand to him, shuddered and pulled her into an embrace. Her only thought was why had her perfume become so active it would affect him in that way.

With a sigh, he let her go but continued to hold her hand. It was a definite grip of authority, with no intentions of dismissing her yet. 'You fascinate me Glow Girl. Why couldn't you have been a bad girl and single? I would have followed you to the end of time to claim your heart.'

'Yes, but at least knowing I'm not your kind of woman makes me more fun to be with.' Her teasing words had his eyes gleam with golden lights, as powers ignited within in them that willed her to stay with him.

'You still have two more days before you have to go home. Let's blow this boring location off and go let our hair down. Live a little before your big day. You know you have always wanted to just go and do something outrageous and fun. All those years of nothing, and now stuck with a team that still wants to lock you away and keep you safe. Come with me, Caitlin, and you will have the best two days of your life. You have the rest of your days to be dull and uninteresting.'

Jett yelled at him, 'Stop it Calyx. Cait, he's using his power over you, fight it, tell him no.'

Caitlin looked at Jett with glazed eyes and back at Calyx. Rory tried to grab for her, but Calyx was quick and put up his free hand. The bolt of light he projected tossed Rory backwards. The force had him hurtle towards Aurek, and Lord Mensa and the three of them slammed into a huge statue that shattered on impact. Jett was immediately on the attack, and his eyes glowed red, fire flamed towards Calyx, but it stopped a NAVmeter before it hit him. There was a shield around them, and the flame just bounced off.

Caitlin didn't register the attack. Instead, her eyes swung back to Calyx, captivated by his adoring smile. 'Come with me Cait, I won't hurt you and promise to bring you back here in two days.' His words sounded sincere.

Jett called to her and begged her to fight him, not to go, but her mind belonged to Calyx and accepted his offer.

'You, my evil friend, are going to get me into so much trouble. My family will ground me for the rest of my life for doing this.'

'Then I will make sure every day you are grounded, you will look back and say it was all worth it.'

In her mind, she knew this was reckless behaviour, but in her heart, she so wanted to see the world through the eyes of the most powerful god in the universe. He was enchanting and empowered her with his charm, his charisma too hard to refuse.

He looked across at Jett irritably and using telepathy he spoke his intentions.

I will forgive you, brother, for hiding the one in the prophecy, for she has poisoned your mind with her magic. I am stronger than this female and will find a way to destroy this toxic ancient one that threatens us gods. If she survives, it will be by the will of me, the real god of the heavens. I will not bow down to anyone, let alone a female. This is not a request, but a warning, brother— do not speak of what I have told you or search for us, or you know what I will do. I have waited a long time for this moment, and you will not spoil it for me.'

And with that Zeus transported Caitlin away. Jett had thought his brother had changed and that things would be different. *The god's arrogance lives on.*

CHAPTER FORTY-ONE

Up in Arms

Zeus transported his prey to his own Home World on Jupiter. He had every intention of ending this prophesy and here, he could do whatever he wished. The battle began and despite his feeling for this immortal female he held, Zeus intended to kill the Rider Caitlin, but every attempt failed, and not one mark did he leave on her. He pulled his hands from her throat. The will to live was strong in her.

Frustrated, Zeus threw up his arm at the heavens and cursed the day they had instigated this change that would destroy all he held sacred.

'Why!' he called out, and his thunderous voice created a tremor on his Home World that caused a landslide. He wanted to kill her on home soil to show the heavens that he was still the mightiest of all. He had chosen the rocky canyon far from any townships, low enough to block out the sounds of a fight to the death. Caitlin Warner, known as Glow Girl, stood against his ridicule and onslaught of hatred, her auburn hair turned fiery red where sparks lashed at him if he came too close. Her glistening green eyes glowed with vicious intent as the two began a battle that Zeus believed he would win. Casting an eye out wide, he glanced across the landscape where the mountainous terrain and gullies had been chopped up and flattened, crushed by hours of battle. Nearly losing his footing, he transported himself and Caitlin to safer ground. In his arms, she looked childlike, no threat to anyone. He had fought with the goddess within her and won. She had been banished, yet the body that held the goddess still lived on. Her thick lashes fluttered, and eyes the colour of a perfect emerald stared up at him with adoration, her smile captivating and alluring. *How is this possible?*

He had got rid of the goddess and yet the control those eyes had over him were even stronger than before. He thought Glow Girl to be the most beautiful woman he had ever met and yet still wondered if she was the enemy. He could hear the hum of a deity and this surprised him as he saw the entity hiding within Glow Girl, leave this body. Her visual ghostly departure hissed as it dissipated into nothingness. No, surely there was not two. *Was Glow Girl in training and in fact a goddess as well?* Was the other a guide to teach, make the gods bow to her and then leave the one he knew as Glow Girl to continue on. Well that plan was foiled and now she was gone he smiled with cunning. Knew he had banished the evil one she was now gone…*Or was she?*

'Calyx,' Glow Girl spoke in the tone of an angel. 'Where are we? Have we arrived on Earth yet? I must have fallen asleep.'

Amazed she had no recollection of the fire-breathing combat they had been locked in, he smiled back, for some reason unable to hurt this side of her; Glow Girl, the special woman he had laughed with, danced with. He had left after the holiday at Dolphin Island so happy he could have burst. That was before he knew who she really was, who Glow Girl protected inside, the goddess and mother of all created. She had come to destroy him, have him bow down before her. He hated this person that had brought love and happiness to his family, and even though enchanted, this was a fight to the death. He knew already that if he were unable to kill what remained of her, he would turn this woman evil. But to do this, he had to unlock her secret door, find her weakness. He would win! He'd win for him, Hades and the rest of his family that she had corrupted. War was inevitable, and her death was too, one way or the other. When this was done, it would send out a message to the universe never to dare oppose him, the mighty god Zeus, ever again.

'Are you okay, Calyx?' She leant on her elbows. 'You look upset. Did I do something wrong?'

As she spoke, a thought came to him. To find her weakness was to give her complete happiness and he had two days left to do it. 'Sorry Glow, I was worried for you, that's all. Had to make a stop on my Home World, but ready to go now.'

Her eyes lit up. 'We're on Jupiter. Can I see?' She attempted to sit up.

Calyx laughed and swept her into his arms. 'Another time, beautiful. You asked to see some of Earth's finest, and that is precisely where I intend to take you. We can visit here anytime.' He transported her away, glad she had not woken to the mess of the landscape he and the goddess had made. He wore a smile. One down and one to go!

Chapter Forty-Two

Friend or Foe

As Caitlin sat and gazed across at the Grand Canyon in the Arizona state, sipping coffee from a flask, she took in the breathtaking view and wondered where the last two days had gone.

Calyx had dined her in Paris at the Eiffel Tower. They swam together in the warm waters of the Great Barrier Reef, the largest coral range in Australia. They drank champagne while overlooking Angel Falls in Venezuela, the biggest waterfall and nineteen times taller than North America's Niagara Falls. He had transported her then to Africa where they went on a safari to Lake Nakuru National Park. Here she saw real life lions, leopards and buffalo, with Calyx pulling her out the way of an enraged charging rhino. They enjoyed a picnic lunch up on the top of Mt Everest in Nepal. They even spent a night in Alaska at a ski resort. It was here that Calyx allowed them to take a cable car for once, instead of the usual instantaneous travel, a joy she stirred him over. 'I can't believe we are taking transport,' she kidded him. At the top, they viewed the snow-capped mountains, hanging glaciers and the famous northern lights. Then with a lot of laughter, and errors on her part, he helped her ski back down the mountain where they huddled by the open fire.

Today they were sitting on a mountain top admiring the view below. Caitlin's thoughts drifted as Calyx topped up her martini. She never refused one thing he offered. He was right; this was a whirlwind experience that was both exhilarating and romantic, a time she would never forget. He ticked all the boxes for a perfect travel companion, and she leant into him, attracted to all he offered. At the same time, the sun peeked over the rugged range before them, its brilliance reflecting in the sky above.

'It's breathtaking.' Her body relaxed into him further, awestruck by all she could see and feel.

Calyx pointed to the Colorado River below. 'It's taken the last six million years for the water to carve out that massive gorge. It's 446 km long, and at that point,' he gestured a hand movement, 'it's 29km wide and 1.83km deep.'

He watched her hand come up and brush the curl of blond hair he had tried to flick away from his eyes. Her touch sent a shiver down his spine. He didn't want to feel this way about her and he stood, pulling her to her feet.

'Ready to go?' he asked more harshly than he meant it to sound.

'Sure, I've worn you out.' She suddenly became alarmed.

'Sorry, that came out wrong. Even with my transporting abilities saving us hours of travel, the time has still gone too quickly. There is so much more I would like you to see, that's all.'

'So where now?' Her eyes lit up, and the frown was replaced with a quirky grin.

'Las Vegas.' He eyed her. 'I booked us into the casino.'

'Wahoo!' She jumped about; the blanket fell to the ground. 'Rory said it wasn't wise for us to go there when we lived on Earth. He was always worried for our safety. He's going to be so ticked off and jealous I got to go.' She continued to jig around while an amused Calyx picked up their gear and transported them to the lobby where they were quickly bustled up to the penthouse on the top floor.

In the room, they showered and, still a little grumpy, he ordered her to get some sleep. She heard him on the phone organising after-five designer clothing to be brought up to the room for later, and once the phone went down, she argued. 'I'm not tired, we can sleep tonight.'

He put his hand up. 'No more, woman, I have barely slept,

and neither have you. If I don't get a couple of hours, I'm going to be like this for the rest of the day. We've pulled another all-nighter, and I'm bushed.'

'And cranky!' she mumbled as she scrambled onto the king-sized bed beside him, sulking.

'Our clothes will be here in a few hours. Until then I need peace.' After a few minutes, he sighed and rolled towards her. He wanted her last day to be all glitz and glamour but if they didn't rest neither of them would give a damn by early evening.

She fought him and her own exhaustion. 'I don't want to go to sleep,' she whined, 'I don't want to miss anything.'

'Shush, please close your eyes.' He traced his fingers gently across her forehead and around her eyes until they dropped shut.

When she woke, they lay together, his arms wrapped loosely around her. He felt her watch him and opened his eyes. 'Sorry about before.' He pulled from her and, standing up, stretched.

Caitlin slid off the bed and went into the bathroom where she turned on the taps. The water took no time at all to fill the oversized tub. 'Mmm, what to choose?' Her hand ran over the many perfumed bath salts before picking one. Finally enjoying some private time, she undressed without worry and slipped into the warm aromatic suds, every muscle seeming to scream out its thanks.

A tap at the door stirred her from the daze that had her almost drift off again. *What's wrong with me?* She didn't generally need so much sleep.

Calyx walked in. 'Hope you're decent.' He still sounded a little surly, yet it didn't bother her this time. She was just as tired. They had been overdoing it, but hell, this was once in a lifetime. Like her, he looked for something to wake him up and chose a hot shower. She much preferred the bath.

Tossing aside his clothes with no shame that she was there, Calyx clunked the shower door shut. Water splashed on the floor when he stepped out quickly to retrieve his razor. Caitlin did her best to avert her eyes, but he was one good-looking man, and she had to duck under the water to muffle embarrassed giggles.

When he emerged this time, he threw a towel around his hips, his mood much better. Apparently feeling playful, he turned his head seductively towards her. 'If you'd like a sample of a real man just let me know. I'm happy to oblige.'

'Stop it.' The sponge in her hand was hurled at him. 'I have a hot man already.'

'There are hot men baby, and then there is a man that knows how to satisfy his woman.' He dropped his towel, giving her a full frontal.

Caitlin's face flushed crimson as she ducked back under the water. Coming up for air she heard him still laughing at her naivety as he moved into the other room.

'Glad I amuse you so much.' She wiped soap from her eyes.

He heard her sullen tone and called out, 'don't stay in there all day. I have a limo arriving soon. I want to show you the sights before we eat.' He figured luxury would get her in a better mood.

Once wrapped in a towel she checked where he was and found him unzipping the dress and suit bags, choosing appropriate clothes for them to wear. 'Our meal, is it the liquid variety or are we actually eating this time?' She interrupted his thoughts.

'Both.'

'Sounds good.' She padded barefoot over to the double vanity, plugged in the hair dryer and hummed while drying her hair.

Without warning, her towel was removed, and she stood naked looking into the mirror at Calyx. She turned and used the hair dryer and hands to cover her privates while trying to snatch the towel back.

He held it up out of her reach. 'Don't know why on earth you would ever want to cover up such perfection. You know you're very beautiful, Cait. My offer still stands if you want to have a real man make love to you.' He was surprised with her flushed red cheeks and eyes that flashed with embarrassment. *She's a virgin, you're kidding me.* His amazement was learning Axon had not yet taken her as his. It made her fair game in his book.

'How do you know you have picked the right one if you don't experiment?' He stood so close to her with his nakedness that she started to shake. He reached out and held her against him. When her eyes closed, he knew she was close to giving in. 'You feel adorable, let me show you how wonderful lovemaking can be, little innocent one.'

As soon as the words escaped his lip, she stiffened. He had guessed her secret, and it astounded her.

He sighed. 'Don't worry, your virginity is safe with me, I would never force you, Caitlin. If I were ever to win a woman like you, I would want to do it fair and square.' He let her go. 'If you want me, I must let you come to me.' He tied the towel back around her exposed body. She stood unmoving, stunned. 'I didn't mean to scare you, but you can't blame a guy for trying.' His voice was seductive, alluring. Not having her respond, he strode out of the room, leaving her shaken and unsure of what just happened.

Had she wanted him too? Unsure about anything at the minute Caitlin sucked back the desire to crouch down and cry. With strength that came from within, she envisaged calm as taught by Rory and with composure finished drying her hair while working out how to face him. *He walks on the side of evil, of course he would fight a little dirty to get me to make love with him.* Even though she felt no influence of the inner voice that usually spoke to her, she had learned much from her; all but how to control the essence that exuded from her when around evil. This she felt was the reason for him wanting her. She cursed the male-attracting gift. As Woody had warned, the sweetness might drive a powerful individual to want, even demand sex. She felt a pang of guilt for Calyx acting this way.

Her nerves in control and now dressed in the undergarments and bathrobe, her courage returned and she came out to retrieve the evening dress and shoes. The tilted head, not looking directly at her, and the flatness in his eyes, showed she had battered his ego which made her decide to give him time-out. Carrying her dress, Caitlin went back into the bathroom to finish getting ready. The outfit was a perfect fit. *He has good taste.*

Her mood improved and, now willing to tackle Calyx head on, she came out to face him. 'I'm sorry...' He didn't look up so she sat on the end of the bed and continued. 'I don't fully understand the male desire or this inner fragrance of mine. I guess being around it too much, must drive a man to strange lengths if you thought me sexy.' She gave a shy grin. 'So, I have a proposal I think might cheer you up.'

He eyed her now with amusement.

'What about if I go and entertain myself downstairs on the tables while you organise a woman to come up here and visit you for a while?' Her offer was sincere and her tone painfully kind.

He shook his head. *Did she not have a breaking point?* 'Even after I try to force myself on you and scare the life out of you, and honestly, you should be slapping my face about now, you apologise as if it's your fault and try to give me a solution to my selfish behaviour. Are you sure you're not a saint, Caitlin Warner?'

She frowned. 'You have been so perfect. I don't ever want to be the one to make you look sad. Yet I have, this is my doing, and you know it. My stupid smell is spoiling everything.'

He breathed out a sigh, got up, walked over to the bed and slumped down beside her. 'You're not spoiling anything.' His tone was calm as he wiped the small tear shed for not being able to make him as happy as he made her. 'Thank you for the offer to relieve my anguish, but no other woman is of any interest to me while I have you. To be perfectly honest, you're right, you are driving me insane with your love potion, but I can control myself and promise to leave you alone if you also promise never to go off on your own. It would be more of an insult if you preferred to be somewhere else other than with me.'

Her hand slipped shyly into his. 'There's nowhere, or no person, I would sooner be with right now than with you either. I was just trying to give you an out for a while if you needed a break.' Her words were sincere and just what he needed to hear.

'You're not like anyone I have ever met, Cait. Come on, let's get the hell out of here and have some fun.' He stood up, and smiled warmly as he put out his hand and she wrapped her delicate fingers around his.

Caitlin's smile at that moment he would never forget. She was back in high spirits, and it was he who had made that happen. By taking his hand, she trusted him again, and it was him she chose, to take her on their next adventure.

* * * *

In the limo, Calyx pointed out the different landmarks of interest as they drove toward a grand hotel that resembled a castle. The modern-day kingdom transported her into a forgotten land; it was very charming, as was the man on her arm. He showered her with lovely compliments about the way she looked, held her hand through most of the meal and laughed with her during the live show. Late that afternoon, they stepped onto the *Desert Princess* paddle steamer and took a tour of the picturesque Lake Mead. It was here, in the fresh air with her cheeks flushed, that he held her and had to use all his might not to kiss those incredibly pink lips.

Back at the casino, he could tell she was tired but could see only disaster if he took her to the room the way he was feeling. His plan was for her to be so tired that she would give herself freely. He wanted this woman badly, and by night's end, he would have his way. Once his, the plan was to turn her evil… *or kill her.* He hadn't yet decided.

'Feel up to a flutter with me?' He pointed to the tables.

'Poker, it's one of my favourites. Do you play?' she asked.

'I can hold my own.'

It was late in the evening before they returned to their room for a bit of downtime. Nervous about the money she carried, Caitlin handed it to Calyx to mind.

'Well, aren't you the lucky one. What are you going to do with your winnings?' Calyx asked her as they lay on the bed laughing as he held the hundred dollar bills up high and let them fall. The cash floated around her.

'Give it to you, of course, to pay you back for such a wonderful holiday.' She turned to look at him as he rolled towards her. 'That's if it's enough?'

'You'll do no such thing.' He touched her nose and smiled. 'I should pay you for being the perfect companion.'

'Then I'll ask them to give it to their favourite charity. I have no use for money.'

'Isn't there anything you think you would like? Car, jewellery, clothes, shoes?'

She shook her head. 'Axon has dressmakers come in and fit me out in designer clothes when I'm at home, and I have no use for jewellery up there as the magic of my ride removes it.' She put her hand up and admired her ring. 'This gets taken off before I ride as I'm scared I'll lose it.' Her expression was serious. 'My friends and family are my precious treasures now… and I don't need to buy them.'

He moved some hair from her face, his eyes a little glazed. 'How can I corrupt you if you won't even take the money you have won fairly?' He touched his hand on her eyes and put her to sleep. This was his time, and he needed to think. She clouded his mind, and he had no intentions of stopping out of polite courtesy this time. Once asleep, he pulled her in close to him and not realising how tired he was, he dozed too.

When Caitlin woke, she heard the water running into the bath. 'Come on little lady.' He helped her into the bathroom, her tired body leaning up against him, her legs barely moving in time with his long strides.

'I'm so tired.' Her hand covered the yawn.

'If you prefer you can shower with me. I'll hold you up.' He grinned roguishly at her.

'I'm all right.' Her hands fluttered and shooed him out to give her privacy while getting into the bath.

Not giving up on his campaign to seduce her, he gave her a goblet of bubbly before he took a shower. The sound of her giggles when the bubbles tickled her nose stopped him, and he turned back around and sat on the side of the tub. 'Well, if I can't enjoy your love, at least let me enjoy your body. Let me wash your back.' He moved her forward and ran the soapy sponge across her shoulders. Not one protest did he hear from her lips as he ran the soapy sponge gently down her back.

It felt nice. Caitlin's skin was so sensitive to anything at the moment and enjoying it so much she sighed and relaxed as he moved the soapy softness along each arm and down her back again.

'You are starting to weaken to my charms.' It struck him that the more tired she became, the weaker her powers. 'I'm breaking through aren't I?' he was murmuring, and she listened and could hear him, but his voice was sending her into another world, and as he said, she was weakening against his charms. Her mind had no other thought but pleasure, and even as he slipped into the bath behind her she had no other fears or thoughts but of him. Arms wrapped around her and she melted back into him, his seductive voice overpowering her body and soul.

Calyx couldn't believe it was finally happening. *I have won.* He continued to run the sponge over the woman in his arms while whispering sweetly close to her ear, nibbling the lobe and shuddered with joyous nervousness now he had caught his prey at last. This powerful woman was his, and he could barely breathe for fear of her snapping out of it and using her gift to pull from him.

Caitlin could feel his naked body press against hers, and it felt so intense and inviting she had nothing left to resist the raw lust that built between them.

Calyx turned her and laying her on top of him, in his arms, he finally did what he'd longed to do since they first met. He kissed those lips, he hungered for. The delicate and sweet response made his head spin, and his world turn upside down. Tears ran down his cheeks for the love he felt at that moment. What was he doing? He pulled back from her and got out the tub. Leaning in, he picked her delicate frame up in his arms and with lips on lips, carried Caitlin over to the bed. Reaching out, he snatched up the towel from the warming rack and holding it under her, laid the woman he had finally conquered, on the bed. *Mine.* He smiled as his hardness tightened. He had her on fire and watched her legs relax as she waited. He could see her needs were now just as great. He lowered his body on top of her, only moments away from feeling her moist loveliness, yet turmoil struck him like a brick to the head. He paused, holding his manhood from entering where it longed to be.

'You're an angel, and I fear if I take you now, I'll never be able to let you go,' he whispered hoarsely, as the need for her almost overpowered his strength to put a stop to it. The predicament he had them in used all his will to control.

'My love,' she whispered, and quivered delicately, wanting him desperately.

'I can't do it to you, Cait, it would destroy us both. My magic has fooled you into a lustful state, and once you come out from this trance, you'll be devastated at what we did here. That's because it's not me that you love or think you are giving yourself to.'

'I don't understand.'

Yes, he had tricked her, wanted to win, but it was she who in the end had won. Surprised by so much passion, it melted his very core, had every molecule alive and dreamily wishing he had won this kiss fair and square. But he hadn't, knowing it was a stolen moment, not of her true giving. He slumped in desperation of love he knew would never be his as it belonged to another. He threw a rug around her.

'Sleep Cait, and when you wake, you will think it was all just a dream, a vision of you with your handsome fiancé.' Still heavily under his command, she closed her eyes.

Chapter Forty-Three

Merciful Me

Calyx held Caitlin in his arms, wishing desperately it was him she'd chosen. He was aware he didn't deserve even her friendship for his treacherous attempt on her life just days before. He drove off the ancient goddess, believing it was her that was the temptress he had to destroy or be destroyed. Instead, it was Caitlin herself that was the one to bring him to his knees. The prophecy had forgotten to mention that to steal even one kiss would be his downfall. It threw his emotions into a state of despair, a deep lustrous magical moment they would never share again. If only he hadn't caught that look; the one a father gives a daughter as he said goodbye. He'd reacted spitefully. He knew exactly who she was and he set in motion a plan to destroy the woman and the myth that surrounded her.

Over the past two days, he'd used trickery against her protective magic to unlock her forbidden secret. For he had learned over their time together that to destroy her innocence would dampen her powers and help him destroy the powerful deity she had become. That, or be the one in command and have her devoted to him always. He had almost given up when he found the key, the weakness that he assumed to be a lack of sleep, or possibly love. *Only a fool would think she loved me.* He was sure the first reason to be more believable as he'd filled her so full of adventure and fun and had exhausted her. *That had to be it!* Yet the knowledge of how to beat the most powerful woman in the world came too late, for he was now so madly and deeply in love with her, his heart sang just to be near her. In the end, she defeated him. The battle was over. *And I'm giving up.*

He quivered as he remembered holding her naked in his arms and kissing her. With no idea he was devious, she surrendered completely to him. Her kiss was so powerful it sent shockwaves right through his body. If he hadn't had her under his spell, he would never have known the full extent of how much love she really carried. It gave him insight as to why Axon was so smitten and could see no other.

If fate had only let me find her first, it might have been me she'd give her sweet self to. This was his punishment for putting the fear of god into her father, forcing him to lock her away for so many years. The tale continued of her as a little girl locked underground until Rory found her in her late teens. He knew now this was true. His eyes had filled as the story revealed her being an uneducated, frightened teenager. He found it hard to believe as it unfolded she'd had no schooling, no family, no life until Rory. Over the last couple of days, he had joked with her, laughed at her memory as if she had made up a tale for his enjoyment alone. Sadly, it was no tale. Fed scraps, left to fend alone, she only had enough light to see during the day. How cruel had he been, had they all been, his entire family who feared her. They made her existence hell while they searched to destroy her.

A tear ran down his cheek. He knew she would come when they could not find her and did everything to prevent this one woman entering the universe. Now as he contemplated it all, an entire lifetime of magic didn't stop what had been written, and he thanked the universe that was so. He thought of how he trembled carrying her to bed. He wanted her so badly he could barely breathe, but it was all wrong, he was wrong. He was petrified that even the little he had done so far may have spoilt this beautiful flower he nearly de-bloomed, and now he wrapped her up. Being unable to feel her softness would help him keep her innocence intact.

He shook off his fear of what may have happened, thankful she was still Glow Girl, a princess amongst gods, and rolled away from her and reluctantly left her to sleep.

In the chair, he viewed her behind the book he struggled to focus on, reading the first paragraph repeatedly without making sense of it. His heart was still over on that bed, his concentration on what his next move would be. If he could not have her for his own, he would instead, stand beside her and make sure only one man ever touched her. He would protect her until the end of time, and she never needed to know what a monster he almost was.

When Caitlin woke, a blanket bound her arms and wiggling freed them. She felt energised, refreshed, although maybe a little fuzzy on how she got naked. She still trusted Calyx implicitly. He had proved to her over the past few days to be maybe a little flirty and overzealous at times, but a good man and she had grown to love him as she did Jett. They were of the same father, so felt it was natural for her to care deeply for them both.

'Hi, sleepyhead.' Calyx looked comfortable in the armchair, a book in his hand. His amusement showed as he watched her twist and squirm to get free of the blanket he'd secured her in. 'I got you up for a bath, and you fell asleep in it, so I brought you back to bed.'

Caitlin shook her head. 'Really, I can't remember having a bath. My memory is a little fuzzy although I can recall thinking Axon was here. I must have been dreaming.' She gulped. 'Um, the rest is private.'

It pleased him her memory was vague. 'Well, I guess if you're missing him that much and he is that real in your mind, I'd better take you back. I've kept you from him for far too long, and it's definitely time we both went home.'

Caitlin sat up, eyes wide, her alertness back now the magic he had used to keep her by his side had been removed. The last thing he really wanted to do was give her up, but the longer he drew it out, the harder it would be. *It's time I let her go.*

Caitlin reached for the t-shirt he left on the bed and, pulling it over her head, gasped, 'I'm getting married in two days. Hells bells, I've not even tried on my wedding dress.' Her hand slapped against her forehead, all the thoughts of pre-wedding jitters hitting at once. 'Oh my god, I'm getting married.' She scrambled to her feet and started jumping up and down on the bed with a mix of joy, fear and elation. Her little squeals of delight had Calyx on his feet feeling ever-emotional and wanting, now, only the best for her. The t-shirt was so big on her she tripped over the bottom of it and ended up in his arms. 'And you have given me the best time ever. I so love you for that.' Caitlin hugged him.

He wasn't expecting that reaction and put her on her feet. 'Get in the shower and let's get you home before you fall for the both of us.'

'Silly.' Caitlin looked back with a grin. 'You can love more than one person, but you can only be in love with one.' She put her hands in the air and spun around before skipping off happily.

* * * *

While he waited for her to ready herself for the trip home, he pondered what lay ahead, where to go from here. Neither Jett nor he could ever hurt her now. He was also helplessly committed to her. The war between their planets to bring Pluto back in line was still such a big need for his family. To have his brother back with them had been their only conscious thought for such a long time.

He heard the shower turn off and Caitlin squeal. It was a joyous sound, not at all threatening, so he waited for her to come out, a towel wrapped around her middle and one around her head, face flushed and her eyes dancing with a thought she had.

'I've got it!' she exclaimed, but he had no idea what the excitement was about. His issues were huge so he didn't think it to be anything that would cheer him up; still, with patience, he pulled himself out of his doom and gloom to listen.

'You are the King of all the Gods, right.'

Where was this going? 'Well yeah? That is stating the obvious,' he teased.

'Therefore you can change the law and make anything happen, is this correct?'

'The Congress of the Heavens makes the final decision, but yes, that is basically correct,' he answered, and watched as her delightful green eyes took on an emerald glow. It then dawned on him that with Caitlin's purity of heart and the kind way she looked at life, maybe she had something worth listening to, although he doubted it. If he, the King of all Gods, could not clearly see any way out of this but to fight, then he couldn't expect her to either. However, at this point, he would give any crazy idea consideration.

She flopped on the end of the bed, brushing out her vibrant red curls. 'When I was at Jett's, in the cabin, I studied the planets on the wall. You know, the mural painted on the tiles in his hot tub room?' When he nodded, she knew he was listening.

'You have my attention Cait. Continue.'

'Well!' The brush stuck on a knot that had her pull furiously and smile when it released. 'I know Jett's happy now, but something is missing.'

'And what would that be, please pray tell?' He was amused by the way she dragged it out. Almost as a child would do to get your full attention.

'Promote him. Make him the King of the Dwarf Planets.'

'Hold on there.' His hand went up to stop her.

Caitlin knew he wouldn't listen but was prepared; ignoring him, pointed the brush at him and carried on with conviction and faith in her words. 'Hades is a supreme Ruler and Ceres, Haumea, Makemake and Eris will benefit from the strong leadership only he can offer. They too will want to advance their worlds once they find out what he has accomplished. To have such comfort and technology, those and many dwarf planets to come, would look to him for help to create the same warmth and inviting environment on their worlds as he has.'

A pause gave him a moment to think. This time he didn't interrupt, as getting his head around such a thought was overwhelming. *Could it work?*

She twirled strands of hair around her finger, creating ringlets that bounced, making him smile. 'Your brother is so brilliant, but you know that don't you?'

Calyx nodded but needed more from her.

'Then you also know how he will work relentlessly to develop his group of Dwarf Planets. I also have no doubt his work ethic will drive him to bring them in line with the rest of your more advanced Home Worlds. We both know him well enough to know this empire he builds will stand alone. In time, he'll be so proud of his accomplishments that you would have to remove him screaming and kicking,' she gave a chuckle at the thought, 'if you wanted him to ever change back to one of the core planets you and your family continue to reign over.'

He had never heard her refer to Jett as Hades before, nor with such passion. His real title stunned him and was glad he had not cut her off by saying what he intended, that it sounded ridiculous. Her passionate outburst showed how much faith she carried for his brother. He pulled at his chin. 'You may just have something.'

'I have so much belief in Hades.' She grinned. 'Jett… I will even go so far as to say that if he takes such a path, he will be hailed by many, and maybe become one of the greatest Rulers in history.'

He breathed out deeply and leant back in the chair, folding his hands in front of him in thought.

'I need to give this proposal some consideration, Cait. Please don't discuss this with anyone until I run it past my family, but who knows.' He shrugged. 'Could it really be this simple to solve?' he muttered as he got up, and tossed his clothes aside while walking to the shower.

'Men, they are so messy.' She bent and scooped up his things while listening to him hum for the first time while taking his shower.

When he came out in a towel, Caitlin smiled at his near nakedness that didn't daunt her anymore. Today, she was viewing him so differently after their time together, enabling her to see past the tyrant, the god and the man he was when they first arrived here on Earth. She was not sure how, but felt he had become a loyal friend and that there was no need ever to fear any part of him again.

He chatted as he dressed and smiled at her listening with her back politely turned. He was pleased she was still the girl he brought here and was glad he hadn't changed her, not one bit.

'I can't say it'll work, but it has got merit, and I'm definitely happy to put it forward to the Congress of the Heavens for a vote if my family agrees.'

'It warms me so, to think you are prepared to make an attempt to put an end to this war.'

The kindness of her words and the sweet melodious tone to her voice set off a quiver in his body. He figured from his reaction it was going to take some time to dampen his deep feelings for her and fought the urge to hug her.

'If I could do anything for you, my sweet, it would be to end the feud and keep you as far from the dangers it represents.' He kissed her forehead as he passed her to sit down and put on his shoes.

Zeus felt so happy now for doing the right thing. He couldn't wait to return Caitlin to Jett to show he had kept his promise. Jett need never know how close he came to not keeping it. *He knows me better than anyone in the universe and wouldn't have trusted me one little bit.* Maybe now though, Jett would regain the confidence once held for him and together they might find a way to end this war. He'd arrived on Earth two days ago with an evil plan to destroy the woman at his side, and today he would leave as a changed man and the woman who now stood by his side he knew would always be there for him, *and I for her.*

CHAPTER FORTY-FOUR

Orion's Belt
(Clandestine)

Aurek sat in one of the chairs on the patio by the pool. 'You have to try and calm down. Glow is a smart girl; she can take care of herself. You don't see Axon freaking out, do you? He told us last night that Rory would know if she were dead or ill and she is neither.' Aurek sought to appease his Uncle Jett who had just arrived.

'If I can't feel her, how can Rory? That's ridiculous. He's just hopeful and trying to stop me from driving him crazy with my concerns.' Jett blew off the conversation with a flick of his hand. Sitting opposite his nephew, he took the cigar offered and after lighting it, leant back to think. Concerned not to have felt anything from Cait since his brother took her, he had paced and worried, and driven Axon mad with communiqués.

'What?' Aurek saw Jett freeze. His hand was up, demanding quiet.

'My brother has released her; she's alive.' He punched the air and whistled through tense gritted teeth.

Aurek high-fived him. 'Is he bringing her here?'

'Yes! Let Axon know.' Jett was joyful, listening. He could hear her now; as they got closer, her thoughts ran through him like liquid honey.

Aurek's call was short to Axon. He was in a meeting and left the urgent message to be passed on. Quickly he tapped out from the conversation, not wanting to miss what was going on as Jett continued telling him what he could hear.

Jett stood, too wound up to keep sitting. 'He knows I'm here and is coming to see me before he takes her home.'

'Is Glow all right? He hasn't turned Glow into the witch he always threatened, has he?' Aurek wanted more details. He may have tried to keep his uncle calm, but inside he was just as stressed. Uncle Zeus was one seriously angry dude when he was threatened and like Jett he had seen the look as well between father and daughter, then Zeus's reaction which landed Rory and Lord Mensa on top of him. Was he game enough to confront him over it? *Maybe not.*

'She's still *her, and okay,*' Jett communicated to Aurek, so relieved his brother had not killed her. 'Calyx knew when he took her who she really was, and I felt for sure it was the last time we would ever see our Glow Girl.'

'She still might be touched by dark magic, she might not be the same girl.'

Jett tried to calm himself, sure she was still innocent by the calming thoughts he could hear. 'I don't think so, she seems just fine.' How wrong he had been about his brother, and even though mad and insanely jealous Zeus spent all that time with her, he was overwhelmed with brotherly goodwill for how, in the end, Zeus had dealt with it. 'He has let her be and, let her live.'

'The reason why, we may never learn, Uncle, but it is going to make an interesting story over time and in all corners of the universe.'

* * * *

'Look, Uncle, they've arrived.'

'He won't let her go just yet, but when he does, she is mine. You stay away until I make sure she is all right and this is not trickery.' Jett stood with hands on his hips, waiting.

Jett surprised Aurek with the onslaught of anger that bubbled out.

Calyx glanced at Jett once in focus. He paced, and knew he couldn't get to Caitlin yet. *He can wait!* Zeus kept his force field around them both while he checked Caitlin was okay. He comforted her while he double checked he had done nothing to harm her delicate persona. 'Don't worry; I won't let them give you a hard time for coming with me. I'll stay and take the blame. It's my punishment for taking you from them.' He ran a finger gently down her face, touching her soft skin, and his heart broke knowing how much he was going to miss her. Satisfied she was all right, he released her from the magic he used to keep her contained while they spoke.

She blinked, turned and saw Jett. Her feet barely moved towards him before he snatched her up and transported her to the other side of the pool away from Calyx. When his brother stayed where he was, he looked for any signs of her being ill-treated. 'Did he touch you? You can tell me, and I'll darn well knock him into the next universe.'

Calyx heard his threat and didn't blame him. He would have said the same if someone had stolen Caitlin from him.

She smiled and, knowing Jett could read her mind, gestured for him to sit with her and thought the answers to him, keeping it private for just him. The respect she gave him by doing it this way gave him the power of knowing that her words were for his ears only. His frown smoothed out, his worry eased.

Calyx watched them and knew she had eased his brother's fears. He was jealous he had the power of telepathy. *How I would love to be able to read her mind.* His features saddened for that would never be either. Axon had her heart; Jett had her thoughts, *and me, I'm left with what I deserve.* He sat heavily and took the Starstarter and Moonjuice m i x e r Aurek offered.

Aurek saw his uncle's face drop watching Glow with Jett. He put his hand on his shoulder and squeezed. 'I know how it feels; I have lost her too. They have her everything, and we have been left with an open wound.'

'Bleeding.' Calyx sighed, and gulped the elixir down in one go, putting his goblet out for another.

As if she heard, and yet he knew she was too far away, her head snapped around towards them, as sadness broke her happiness. Saying something more to Jett, she got up, his hand gripping hers as she calmed him to trust her. Moving towards them like an elusive angel, she put out a hand each to them to hold, which they did without speaking. The blissful feeling of her energy encased them and the glow surrounding the three of them was so bright, Calyx and Aurek wanted to close their eyes to listen as she granted them their wish. They could feel her love float through them, all sadness dissolved, and only what she gave remained. The light dulled and they opened their eyes, both smiled so brightly, they too shimmered in the elusive illumination for just a while. She wasn't moving her mouth and yet they heard every word spoken.

To my gallant knights of the universe; I would never leave you bleeding, as you would from this day forward, never leave me in that condition. We have a bond that time or threats will never break. You may not hear my words as Jett can, you may not have my heart as Axon has, but you will carry my happiness within you always. However, with this comes a price. You will carry my pain if I'm hurt. Do you accept this gift that the Goddess of Peace shares with you?'

Aurek nodded. 'I do.' He spoke eagerly.

Calyx could barely speak. He was now positive he hadn't destroyed the goddess surrounding the prophesy. This person before him was a powerful deity in every sense of the word and more. She was his Caitlin. He knew her now, and she was calling the shots, using her given powers to forgive and reward their future loyalty. He was now in-love with her and couldn't care less, was overwhelmed with such a precious gift.

'With all my heart and all I have to give, it is yours always.' Tears of joy stung his eyes as his sincerity was accepted.

So be it and don't say I didn't warn you. The last of her magic spun around them, almost lifting them off their feet.

As quickly as it began, it was over but not the bliss they felt as she released them. That feeling intensified at her squeals of joy as Axon shimmered in. The jolt of happiness had them both high five one another and flop back down in their seats. They were at last content to just be, not an ounce of hurt left inside, but this floating happy feeling that kept a smile on their faces. Neither had any interest in changing that.

Axon stood with Caitlin, arms around her, and his frame melted as he listened to how much she had missed him. Rory stood beside them, arms folded and as usual, surprisingly calm.

Calyx had to give both of them credit; they trusted her abilities completely. He remembered back to the look Rory gave him the day he knocked him off his feet when he took her. Jett was beside himself and yet Rory brushed himself off and stood as he did now. The only difference today was that he had lost the darkness in his eyes; every other expression was the same. He knew then that darkness was a warning, *bring her back or you are dead*. That look burned into Calyx's mind. A man that speaks only with his eyes he had never encountered before. He was an incredibly capable guardian of the Planets and between just the two of them, they were a powerful force alone, never mind the other team members he had not yet met. This group of Riders they had scoffed at, laughed about, yet at this moment held his respect. *To cross swords with this lot, well not today anyway.* His smirk gave away he still believed he was the superior one. But today he was a contented man and was on a new mission. *For her!*

'*Jett, we have to talk.*' He sent his brother a message and both men disappeared.

CHAPTER FORTY-FIVE

Sneaky Men Friends

Once Jett had his brother alone, he grilled Calyx hard and eventually under the god's oath never to repeat it, Calyx told his him the sordid details. Jett listened and was shocked when Calyx confided he had fallen in love with Caitlin. Although not happy learning of his deceit and love for his Glow Girl, Jett was relieved this now secured her future. No fool would dare hurt her under the King of Gods' protection.

They arrived in time to hear Aurek and Rory telling Axon of the pending wedding that had been planned behind his back. That he was only being told now as they were throwing him a buck's party and he was to be there.

'You sneaky, rotten sods.' He looked down at Caitlin. 'You would have been coerced so not blaming you honey.'

'Oh, she didn't need any arm-twisting,' her father said, and laughed.

'Yep, my father was in on it too.' Caitlin beamed.

It was a happy man that now hugged his soon-to-be-a bride. 'So we have a buck's party tomorrow night, and it's on Pluto.' He turned to Rory, still soaking it in. 'A night on the slopes with the boys, drunk. Can I just watch?' This made them all laugh.

He took one arm from Caitlin and still holding her with the other, punched Rory in the arm. 'Still, can't believe you kept it a secret – traitor.'

'You betcha! You missed the hunting trip too. I'll fill you in on that blast when we get home.' Rory was happy to rub it in.

'Unbelievable!' Axon glanced at each of them. 'You're all secretive rotten sods, but so glad you sorted my little woman out for me. I had started to plan a trip to Vegas and do that drive through registry to get our marriage licence.' He shook his head.

'Not long now, babe. I'm going to make an honest man out of you finally.' Caitlin leant into him lovingly.

Aurek took her by the arm and pulled her next to him; an action that had Axon scowl and he looked ready to take him on.

'She isn't yours yet! Don't even think we're giving you a chance to sneak into her room until the big night. She stays here with me until you are both married, and that's written into the wedding planner contract.'

'Cait!' Axon had thought he was taking her home. She shrugged and grinned. 'They made me sign it. I don't think they trust you, honey!' She chuckled.

Axon let off some choice language, but the boys stood firm, Rory standing up to him. 'Majority rules big guy.' He threw a comforting arm around him. 'Come on, let's blow this star and go get a beer.'

'Are you in on leaving her here too?'

'My idea! I know exactly what you'd be doing if you took her home tonight and it wouldn't be putting her to bed in her own room.'

A few more flavoursome words had come from Axon before Rory dragged him out. 'I guess I'm going… see you at the altar, gorgeous.' He blew her a kiss. 'And there better be one!' he grumbled as they faded from sight.

Chapter Forty-Six

Time Forgotten

Caitlin woke and pulled the curtains back to show a pleasant spring morning. The glass felt warm from the morning sun so she unlatched and opened the window. Seeing the men, she called out, 'What are you guys doing up and about so early?'

Calyx and Jett were walking towards the house. They had stayed in the chalet on the far side of the grounds and were quite rowdy until well into the night. Caitlin hardly slept due to her impending wedding and was glad when they switched the NAVbeams off and went to bed. It was only then when it became pitch black and quiet that she enjoyed some uninterrupted slumber.

'We want to steal Aurek for the day to set up the buck's night with us.'

'Really.' She frowned, stretching out and looking below her at Aurek who was waiting to discuss it with them.

'Hang on, I'm coming down.' She closed the window and left her room. Sitting on the staircase bannister, she slid down. Jett had come to meet her and only just made it in time to catch her at the bottom.

'I told her not to do that,' Aurek scolded, arriving seconds after.

'Phewie!' Her nose went up in the air, as she still rested in Jett's arms. 'Knew one of you would get here in time. And that person now gets a wish for saving me.'

'Thanks Glow. I can take your ex–boyfriend then.' He put her on her feet.

'Sure! If that's your wish?' The light in her eyes gave away how happy she was.

'It is.' He grinned. 'Will you be okay?'

'I have Bree and Lisha coming. Actually, they will be here any minute. We intend to have a spa morning.'

Aurek folded his arms. 'I know when I'm not wanted.'

'Sorry, but this is girls only.' She chuckled at his look, turned and darted back up the steps. At the top of the stairs, she had a thought and leant over the balcony at the men who were about to leave. In a cheeky voice, she called to them, 'By the way, if you have to have strippers, please make them fat and ugly.' Their laughter cut short as Jett transported them out.

* * * *

Once Caitlin had the place to herself she put on bathers and went out by the pool. With guards all around her, she threw a towel out on the ground and sat beside the water's edge to work on a suntan. *A medium tan would be nice.* Her hands worked sunscreen over her skin while enjoying the warmth on her back. Lathered up, she lay back on the towel and closed her eyes.

A shadow disturbed her light. She put a hand up to shade the sun from her eyes. 'Woody!' She hadn't been expecting him to come for a visit.

'Hi Red.' Woody stood in the middle of Bree and Lisha. Bree knelt down beside her and gave Caitlin a hug.

'You have no idea how much we've missed you, Cait. Jett's family have been at war against Mercury, and it's been so tough out there without you.'

Lisha ruffled Caitlin's hair. 'I even missed your annoying chatter. I just wish I had your talent as I would have blown them all up weeks ago.'

Bree huffed at Lisha. 'Thank goodness you don't. There'd be no planets left for us to look after.'

Caitlin chuckled. 'So you two still haven't changed.'

'Well, we sort of have.' Bree smiled. 'I actually like her now. She even listens to my opinions instead of blowing me off.'

Caitlin eyed Lisha. 'Really.' It had taken Lisha time to adjust to her brother's relationship with Bree. They had been inseparable, and when his attention suddenly switched to his new girlfriend, it left Lisha feeling on the outer. Bree had worn the anger she should have directed at Rory.

'Bree's okay– I guess. But hurry up and come home, will you. I only have so much girliness in me, and then I'm like, far out, where are the boys, give me a beer and let's watch some footy.'

Caitlin and Bree cracked up laughing. Lisha hadn't changed at all.

Caitlin stood. 'So, Woody, what have I done to warrant this visit? I feel fine, power's all good and I'm more than ready to start back at work once the wedding's over.'

'How about you ladies go settle in and give Caitlin and me some alone time to talk?'

'Of course.' Lisha snatched up Bree's hand, snapping her fingers at the hired help to direct them to their room.

'Let us know when you're finished, Woodsta,' Bree called out. 'I want her too you know.'

Woody put up his hand in a gesture for her to leave them. 'Go! Baby Bree.' He turned back to Caitlin. 'She is such a sook when you're not about.'

'Been around them a bit?'

'Had to; it's been crazy up there over the past few months while you've been tied up. Caitlin, you have no idea what it's been like out there. It's a wonder Axon has held it together. Has needed your help and blew us all away with how patient he has been with all the nonsense surrounding these spoilt gods and Rulers and their demands of your time. He missed you a lot you know.'

'And I him, but honest, this is the first I've heard anything about the war with Mercury. I guess I've been a bit busy.'

'Not sure what's happened but right now it's gone quiet. This the reason I was able to come here too. There hasn't even been chatter over the NAVnet. Axon thinks it has something to do with what went down between you and Calyx.'

'This is the reason for your visit?'

'Yes. Axon has asked me to have a chat with you and see if you might share it with me considering you know I can be trusted. Maybe I can help you through any hardships you may have faced and not wanted to discuss with anyone else just yet.'

Woody used a large amount of magic to loosen Caitlin enough to share her experience. Finally, Caitlin gave in. She knew Woody could be trusted, and didn't need his magic, but maybe without that she might have not told him about the kiss. With legs crossed and back straight, she opened up about the good and bad of her time with Calyx. How they battled, and she had won. With his magic it opened the door to the kiss they shared and how he manipulated the event to make her think she had dreamt it. That the kiss was actually shared with Axon not him.

Woody shook his head at her confession. 'Calyx thought his magic was strong enough to hide what he did, but the goddess side of you exposed it. I wonder why?'

Caitlin couldn't answer him. She was only able to tell him she felt the kiss was a small price to pay for the memories of the world he had shown her, and, for the freedom of life he now gave unselfishly. 'All I know is from this day forward, I never need hide or feel the wrath of the gods again. It's over and what remains is a strong friendship that I believe will last for all time.

After talking for a while, Woody brought up the subject of the hidden gift she had been given for her alone.

'Do you recall the conversation?' He jogged her memory.

'You said I had a one-off power to erase a link to a moment in time. The only problem is that you warned it might erase my entire memory that surrounds it.'

'Cait, this might be why it was given to you. What Calyx did to you was wrong on so many levels. He forced you to go with him using magic and attempted to kill you. Only it failed and all he achieved was to chase off the goddess who was teaching you. In the end, strength learned in your youth made you the stronger deity. But even then he persisted in trying to win you over and after wooing you, he stole a kiss.'

He took a breath and continued. Hoped she took his warning serious. 'What's done in the line of duty is nobody else's business unless you want it to be. What is our business is when you spend time with someone as powerful as Zeus. Then it is our duty to warn you of something neither of you may be aware of. In the event of even an innocent kiss, someone as powerful as Zeus might have left something inside you. It could eventually eat away and diminish your magic, or he may have the power to lock in on you, control you if need be.'

'You're kidding, right.'

'Sorry, but I have to give it to you straight up. I never joke when it comes to these matters.'

Her eyes were wide. 'Calyx would never do that. I only see devotion and love for me in his eyes now. I swear I would pick up deceit if it were there.' She didn't like what she was hearing but had to seriously consider this to be true of Calyx. He was the god of all gods and what if he had played to win and hadn't given up? She didn't blame Woody for now wanting to interfere, this was major, and she couldn't just dismiss something that could affect her future as a Rider.

Woody knew this was hard for her to hear but felt it was important to give her some much-needed advice. 'Either way, it is risky to do nothing when you have the power to do something about it. Break the link you both share. You are pure, and he has an evil that could fester and take control of your innocence.'

'I will lose everything.'

'To do nothing, you risk the purity of your powers and maybe your position as a peacekeeper. If nothing happened then you would be okay, but if it did and he takes control of you on a mission, can the team ever trust you again?'

She heard a voice. 'What's this about trust?' Axon gazed at her.

Woody was angry that Calyx had put her in this position. 'The rotten swine kissed her,' he growled while staring at Axon.

'Yes, I know, he came and told me a little while ago. That's why I'm here,' Axon replied with sadness.

'I'm so sorry Axon!' Tears sprang to her eyes.

'We have no idea what that might do, Axon. She has the power to erase it, and I believe she should use it,' Woody insisted.

'But it was only a silly kiss!' she cried out. 'My trip, it was so enjoyable, so memorable.'

Axon sat the other side of her and using his thumbs, gently wiped away her tears. 'Let me replace the memories, Cait. Let me be the man to fill your life with happiness, and when we kiss, it will be real and never will you need to feel ashamed – pick me, Caitlin.'

'I do, Axon. I swear it's you I'm in love with. I'm yours, always have been… if you still want me?'

'Until death do us part! Cait, honey.' He already knew the swine used magic and she would not have kissed him freely otherwise. But deal with him later he would. For this moment was about the woman he was in love with and to hear she still wanted him made him the happiest man ever. *She chose me over a god.* He thanked the heavens.

Tears ran down her cheeks. 'Let me try to access this gift, but you both better stand back in case it gets crazy.' She closed her eyes and built up her power. Carefully she went in search and found the firm link between her and Calyx and snapped it. With a terrifying scream of anguish she watched. Floating from her were memories of their few days together; spinning and entwined they began to rise. For her eyes only, picturesque scenery, laughter and fun turned around in front of her. She wanted them back and put out a hand to hold them dear to her, but a hole appeared, taking away the swirl of whispers, laughter, places and the kiss that intermingled into nothingness, and with a sharp clap, the portal snapped shut, a n d her eyes blinked with the glare. She slumped, her mind exhausted from the magic. The man who held her became the centre of her thoughts, his hands, and his muscles that flexed in worry as he wrapped her in his arms. This was where she now wanted to be, not just today, but always. Her eyes opened to Axon, his smile loving and grateful she had done this for him.

Woody's voice broke her trance.

Did I faint?

'Do you remember where you have been the last few days?'

She suddenly felt tired, emotional. *What has worn me out? I don't want to talk, just wish everyone would leave me and Axon alone.* 'Here with Aurek. Why?' she snapped, her eyebrows furrowed with the strange question.

'I need you to answer very carefully. When was the last time you saw Calyx?' Woody persisted. He figured it would have been a powerful spell and she'd been exhausted for the next twenty-four hours. But it had to be done, and he needed to find out if it worked before leaving.

'That's a strange question, but okay, I'll play along. On the beach at Dolphin Island, when I was with Jett. He was a woman, but the rest is fuzzy, why?'

'Now apart from right now, when was the last time you saw Axon?' he asked.

'Last night at dinner,' she said, confused. 'He was there with Jett, Rory and Aurek.'

'Think carefully, was there anyone else at the table?' he pressed.

She looked at Axon. 'I don't understand, it was only us, or I would remember.'

Axon smiled. 'You did the right thing honey, you're quite correct, it was just us. He was just testing your memory.'

She jerked upright with renewed vigour. 'I feel great!'

'Careful, Cait, you may need a minute,' Woody warned.

'A minute? I can't wait one more minute.' She wrapped her arms around Axon. 'Marry me tonight! Let's take off now and go find a little oasis somewhere to tie the knot. I don't want to wait until tomorrow. I need you now, and for always.' She sobbed into his arms. 'I don't want to be away from you ever again.'

He rocked her and calmed her down. 'I would love that too, honey. But if we elope, our friends will be so disappointed. They have put such a significant effort into planning a beautiful wedding for us. Are you sure you want to let them down?'

She wiped her face with the back of her hand and sniffed. 'Suppose not.'

'I think you might have what they call wedding jitters.' He smiled. 'Look, I've still got a few hours before I have to leave for the buck's night, so how about I spend it with you here, relaxing?' He saw her puffy eyes and worried for how sad and confused she seemed.

'Will you come back here after the buck's party then?'

Woody intervened, seeing that Axon was close to folding and giving the whole night a miss for her. 'You shouldn't see the bride the night before the wedding.'

His tone snapped Axon out of the decision he was just about to make. He glanced up at Woody with a shrug and helpless twinge in his eyes. 'You sure we can't make an exception?'

'Trust me, Axon, you don't want to promise her something us boys will not allow.' Woody confirmed his thoughts on how it would go down if he cancelled the traditional buck's night.

Axon's shoulders slumped as he held his bride-to-be, her tears like a heavy weight on his mind. 'Please don't cry, honey, I'll try to work something out.'

Caitlin clung to him until he was ready to go and cried in his arms before he left. Then she clung to Bree, fretting terribly for the man she loved. With calm now in the universe, it allowed her time for herself, and it hit her hard how much in love she was. Her head swam with their time together, before the madness, when just a touch from Axon filled her body with an almost uncontrollable passion. She had hidden it in the back of her mind while working, but now, today, it rushed at her like a freight train, her emotions unable to prevent the tears of joy he was going to be hers for always, and at the same time sadness that she couldn't have him now. Her impatience for waiting to give herself to the man she loved overwhelmed her.

'I don't want to be anywhere else but in his arms and in his life.' Her heartache was real as she spoke to her friends while using the last of the second box of tissues. The hen's night was not going well while she sat so distraught.

Her ache for Axon and the hurt carried across the miles to Jett, and her unhappiness was so disturbing he gave in and made the call to combine the two parties. A godly entrance had them all aghast as he lifted Caitlin into his arms and encircled every lady there in his bright light, transporting them all to Pluto.

Tense at first, the party kicked off when Caitlin finally smiled, now comforted by her man.

Axon held her possessively, lovingly, and sent out a special request into the universe; his wish was to have her want him this way always. That forever more she was happy and content to stay by his side.

Now united, both watched their friends enjoy the night from the warmth of the cabin, encircled in each other's arms.

Only once did Axon leave her side, happy to sit up at the table when a carrier arrived with important papers to sign. It was here on the eve of his wedding when all his dreams were now realised that he witnessed Jett and Calyx sign a treaty declaring war on the offending planets was over. His girl had not only put herself out there to prevent a catastrophic event but had come back to his arms. She had picked him; preferred him to gods, and his heart couldn't have swelled with more pride.

'Caitlin, can you join us?' Calyx asked.

Keeping the fur wrapped around her for warmth, she sat with them.

Calyx got up and made sure she was comfortable before sitting opposite. 'Caitlin gave me this idea, so I want her to be a part of this when I announce it publicly.'

'Did I?' She gave Calyx a look of uncertainty but kept quiet. Axon being near was all she could think of as she breathed in his expensive fragrant aftershave that she loved and had missed. Her ears pricked up, and Caitlin jumped up and hugged Jett when Calyx informed them that the Congress of the Heavens had approved his motion to make Hades the King of the Dwarf Planets. Although she couldn't remember saying so to Calyx, she shrugged at her confusion. She might have said it, just couldn't remember. In fact, she didn't care, it was a brilliant idea, and that was all that mattered.

Axon pulled Caitlin on his lap, not allowing her time with any other man tonight. She was his, and he wanted to make it perfectly clear to the two men with him that he had won. Or had he? He pondered, still ticked off they were so determined to have Caitlin still in their lives, that they insisted that she be a portion of the terms of the treaty. Now sworn in, their part played in Axon's ever growing team were guardians to Caitlin. If she were out and about, one or the other, or both, were to be at her side whenever he or Rory couldn't. He knew how important she was to the universe and understood Zoren approving this, but he didn't have to like it. He eyed the two men who looked adoringly at his woman. Zoren had got it right. Who better to protect his jewel but two so powerful? Zeus, King of the Gods and, Hades, with his new title, King of the Dwarf Planets. She trusted them both with her life, even though she didn't remember that connection with Calyx. Yet looking at his determined set jaw to keep her in his life, Axon figured it wouldn't take him long to gain back that trust.

He smiled at Caitlin and held her hand. 'By the way, I have another little surprise for you. After the wedding, we will be on our own again.'

'Just us?' Her eyes lit up.

'Both ranches have been re-built. Everyone is going home.'

'I should be sad, but I'm not!' She chuckled happily.

'See, nothing wrong with her now. I should take the little imposter back so we can man-up and enjoy the buck's night the way it was intended,' Jett scoffed.

Caitlin's head turned towards him and had their eyes locked. Just that quick glance had Jett's face softened, and he smiled. Axon breathed out. Caitlin still controlled the show and he doubted she'd not have one ounce of empathy if either of them crossed her. He suddenly felt sorry for them, for the phenomenon was true; they would be loyal to her always.

'Or not!' Jett got up and ruffled her hair in a friendly gesture.

Calyx stood too. 'Time to join the party. Looks like Axon's got this.' He stared at Caitlin for a moment, smiled and left with his brother.

'Have fun you two,' Jett said to them as he waited for Calyx to go through. He slapped Calyx on the back. 'Your shout brother.' They went off happily.

Axon shook his head and grinned at his woman. *How and what did she say or do to them to get them to leave?* He could tell she had said something to Calyx when he stood as he hesitated and listened. And they both seemed almost too pleased to be leaving her. He thought they would at least stay for a drink. It didn't make sense. She was evolving faster than he could keep up. Would he ever really understand how gods and goddesses communicated? Most likely not; all he did know was he had won the love of his life, and she had better not start sending him off once they were married *or look out*. He grinned, thinking it. 'You ever do that to me, and I'll smack your backside,' he teased.

'Don't know what you mean.' The smile she gave was both cunning yet sweet.

He picked her up and settled with her by the fire. His suspicion was confirmed. There was his delicate Caitlin who needed him desperately, and then there was *her*, the one he had no name for, a capable unwavering protector of all things good. Right now, she was his Caitlin, and he was going to love his woman until the universe took her from him again. And tonight, he was optimistic that her work was done. Well the goddess side of her anyway. Amazed how she had learned at her tender age how to separate herself from the deity she had become and could still be the girl he had fallen in love with. He was so happy he now saw the difference.

He smiled and wrapped them both up in furs where they talked and dozed during the night, holding each other until she was taken away from him to get ready next morning. She promised not to cry anymore, but she did as soon as she left his arms.

Orion's Belt
(Home World)

Back on Orion, Aurek had organised a team of beauticians who buffed, pampered and dressed Caitlin. It wasn't until in front of a mirror that she finally cheered up. Her glittering golden gown fitted to the hips and had a delicate sheer overlay that shimmered with each movement and flared out with a one-metre train that easily moved with her. Delicate gems sewn into the bodice gave it elegance, unlike anything she had ever seen. The time spent on her hair she thought worth it. The long red curls now fell in glossy dainty ringlets. On her head sat a stylish tiara that held fast a sheer, gold-woven veil.

'This is it.' She smiled at the image. 'I'm going to marry the sweetest man in the universe.' Her heart jumped as it always did when she thought of him. Feeling peace within the planet sector, there would never again be a reason for them to be apart. Caitlin was so ready to be Axon's wife, 'and with a bit of luck,' she said and blew a wish-kiss to the image, 'perhaps a mother.'

Her mind floated with happy thoughts as she gingerly made her way down the staircase to her father. Arm in arm he guided her through the impeccably decorated gardens and the sight so unbelievably enchanted she had to tell herself to breathe.

The skies were full of chariots from the Home World of *Auriga,* and mystic winged horses from *Pegasus* lined up and led a path to her husband-to-be. She figured all the Universal Home Worlds had been invited, as so many stood out in their glory. The ones that couldn't fit in the gardens watched from the chariots and horses above.

Before her, and lining a path to the pergola and her awaiting wedding party, were magnificent birds from the Home World of *Phoenix*. Their blue-purple-crests and tails feathered elegantly out, and with their golden wings open, the display was an impressive and most welcoming sight.

The *Lyra* Home World had sent down musicians who played the lyre, an ancient musical instrument that Caitlin already knew was Jett's favourite. She smiled, knowing he would have organised the soft melody to calm her, a tune she was much familiar with after living with him for so long.

Suddenly the notes changed as she entered the rose petal path, setting off a puff of glittering fairy dust that fell from the many chariots above, the music now so sweet it made her feel as if she was walking on a white cloud.

As she neared Axon, he had tears in his eyes and trembled at her touch. 'You look like an angel, so angelic and beautiful. I'm scared to touch you.' He tried to smile.

She thought he looked the most handsome man she had ever seen. He very rarely wore a suit and today she felt his sexiness was off the radar. The gold shirt and tie matched her gown and yet served another purpose. It also picked up the golden glow that his eyes had taken on from the happiness he must have been feeling. She reached up and touched his handsome face, and he quivered. 'Your touch is what I crave, only this time when you hold me you must promise me you'll never let me go.'

He lifted her hand and kissed it. Knew she meant off world. They had talked about it and her wish was to only go day trips to the planets from this day forward. 'I promise.' He grinned blissfully.

After they had taken their vows, the *Columba* Home World supplied hundreds of pure white doves that at that moment were released. The birds flew elegantly through the air, surrounding them for a while before moving away, the enchanting couple receiving applause from all as it was announced they were now man and wife and Axon could kiss the bride. Two birds remained and lifted up her veil as her new husband laid her back in his arms. The love and tenderness of a very first kiss as a married couple was in his eyes as his lips met hers with warmth and a loving tingle lingered for them both. The crowd erupted again with the joy of their passionate commitment, and moments later, you could have heard a pin drop as they signed the register. At the top of the stairs, Axon paused beside his wife for the first time, allowing all that knew them to join him in his happiness.

'Glow Girl,' someone called out and pointed to the sky. A chant broke out as the words appeared across the sky. Caitlin's eyes followed theirs to the writing.

Glow Girl, our Goddess of Peace.

She jumped slightly at the sound of crackling and banging in the sky as fireworks framed around the golden letters, the fireworks became background hiss against the loud chanting. The full dedication to her overwhelmed and amazed her as she watched. The sight was so lovely and the accolade so sweet, tears ran down her face.

'That's what you are being hailed as, honey. You've worked hard and given your heart and soul. You belong up here with us now Glow Girl.' He smiled back in awe of his wife and holding her hand, guided her through the sea of well-wishers.

She squeezed in close to him, and he groaned, a sudden need to make her his immediately. 'Honey?'

She grinned sympathetically. 'Soon.'

'Now!' He transported them away from the grabbing hands and hugs to their honeymoon suite.

'I am the Lord of Planets and Supreme Ruler over gods and now you. Therefore, my dutiful wife, you will love me whenever I say.'

She couldn't believe his arrogance and began to laugh. 'You're kidding me, right.'

Not able to keep a straight face, he grinned. It had been a while, and Caitlin had forgotten how funny he was and loved that he had made time to flex his muscles in an attempt to make her laugh.

Next thing, to Caitlin's surprise and amazement, they were back in the grips of the wedding mob. She glanced around, sure it was Jett, the only one that had access to her thoughts, and in hysterics as Axon scanned the crowd for the culprit. He knew the only one with a device to become invisible was Jett and found him up on the step next to Calyx removing his magical helmet. Axon saw the look they shared and started to laugh. Jett and Calyx, stood with arms folded, grinned and strode off, leaving Axon to ponder how to sneak her off next.

'They think they're funny.' He laughed with Caitlin, as both saw the funny side of it.

'Lucky he knows you as well as I do. Otherwise, he'd have dumped you in the pool after your Supreme Ruler power trip.' She chuckled.

He let out another whole-hearted laugh. 'I was just testing the waters. Rotten sod protectors.'

'What do you mean?'

'Remember I told you Zoren wants you protected 24/7.'

'Um yes.' Her face flushed that Zoren felt it necessary, but would argue the point after their honeymoon.

'Well, meet your new bodyguards.' He screwed up his lips.

'Those two!' Caitlin was amused. 'Oh my, I can see you three are going to be quite a handful.'

With no time to consider what the future held and yet excited Jett would continue to be in it, her moment alone with her own thoughts was gone as Rory picked her up and spun her off the ground. The rest of the team pushed through to join in and congratulate them. She glanced at Axon, loving her husband, the man she just married.

Axon saw the emotions that had choked her up after the tribute to her goddess status. Acting the clown, he knew exactly how to make her laugh and was why he attempted to run with her. He was aware that Jett would never allow his antics until after the reception. She was so proud to be Mrs Axon Stanton and knew this was exactly where she was happiest. Up here in the floating universe, loving, and living with all her dear friends, but more importantly with her husband and partner, for the rest of time.

Personal Message
(From the author)

Thank you for purchasing my book.

If you enjoyed it, please take a moment to leave me a review at your favorite book retailer?

To discover more about the

Magical Comos Collection and my other books
visit:

www·debbiebehan·com

A new adventure starts with:

Catlin II
Masquerade Magic

Cheers!

Debbie Behan